W9-BNW-107

JAN -- 2013

DON'T
SAY A
WORD

Center Point
Large Print

Also by Beverly Barton and available from Center Point Large Print:

Dead By Midnight
Don't Cry
Dead By Morning
Dead By Nightfall

**This Large Print Book carries the
Seal of Approval of N.A.V.H.**

DON'T
SAY A
WORD

BEVERLY BARTON

CENTER POINT LARGE PRINT
THORNDIKE, MAINE

This Center Point Large Print edition is published
in the year 2013 by arrangement with
Kensington Publishing Corp.

The text of this Large Print edition is unabridged.
In other aspects, this book may
vary from the original edition.
Printed in the United States of America
on permanent paper.
Set in 16-point Times New Roman type.

ISBN: 978-1-61173-616-8

Library of Congress Cataloging-in-Publication Data

Barton, Beverly.
  Don't say a word / Beverly Barton. — Center Point Large Print ed.
  p. cm.
  ISBN 978-1-61173-616-8 (lib. bdg. : alk. paper)
  1. Large type books. I. Title. II. Title: Do not say a word.
PS3552.A76777D68 2013
813′.54—dc23
                                                            2012036763

Prologue

Despite the sultry summer heat baking all of Chattanooga, the deep limestone cave was pitch-black and extremely cold. The man with the high-beam flashlight slowly made his way down through the connecting tunnel, turning on the electric lanterns hung at intervals along the way. He wasn't a killer yet, but he soon would be. He was tired of waiting, tired of the years of pain and heartbreak and the suppressed fury locked inside his head. He stopped and rubbed his temples with his fingertips, feeling the onset of another violent headache.

The lanterns cast a strange white light that sent elongated shadows onto the craggy rock walls. It was damp so deep in the earth, and rife with the smell of mold and rot and sulfur. Once he reached his secret room, he pulled on a heavy military-green parka. He kept it hidden there for times such as this, for days when he wanted only to retreat from the real world and everybody in it. For times when he hurt so bad inside that he couldn't stand it a minute longer, couldn't stand to go about and pretend to have a normal life or be a decent human being. He wasn't normal, not

5

anymore. He might even be going insane. Maybe he was already. Maybe he always had been. He didn't really feel insane, not all the time. The actions he was contemplating now were completely crazy. He knew that. Still, he craved them. Savored the gruesome details of his murderous fantasies. Thought of little else but finally, after all these years, exacting his righteous revenge.

Moving across the big cavern, he sat down in an old brown rocking chair at the crude table he'd made out of planks and sawhorses. He gazed down at the objects he'd placed on the table, caressing each one. Everything was ready now. He'd purchased all the supplies he needed for his first kill. He'd been careful, had planned for years how he would carry out the darkest of his fantasies. He had driven all the way to Atlanta to buy the yellow ski rope. He'd selected a small sporting goods shop in Powder Springs, one without a surveillance camera, run by a teenage clerk that didn't have a clue. The twelve-inch fillet knife was purchased in Knoxville at a seedy fishing and hunting discount store in a strip mall. Some of the other things he had made himself, to suit his specific needs. Yes, it was all coming together nicely—all the errands run, the knife sharpened to a razor edge, the coins polished and counted out in distinct piles.

The large Murder Book was also on the table. He had spent years collecting and pasting photographs and newspaper articles on its pages. There were a dozen people who had to die; maybe more, depending on what his victims told him before they took their last breath. The book's pages were separated with numbered tabs. He had placed each person in the book in the order they would die. He pulled the book onto his lap and opened the unadorned black cover. There, on page one, staring arrogantly at the camera, hiding all his wicked vileness behind a smiling facade, was victim One, the worst of the rotten, lying lot he was going to enjoy killing.

A white Bible lay beside the Murder Book. He opened it to the page marked with a narrow, red satin ribbon. The book of Proverbs. He found the right page and placed his finger on the verse that gave him permission to do the deeds he contemplated. The familiar peacefulness flooded down over him like a soothing balm, and he grew strangely calm and determined. The time had come. He would start tonight. He would take someone's life for the very first time. He had it planned down to every detail, every exigency, and every possible eventuality. He would kill and mutilate and wreak God's vengeance on the guilty and wicked.

But could he do it? Could he go against every principle he had believed in for his entire life? Could he get his revenge? Kill in cold blood? Murder with pleasure? Did he have the stomach for the gruesome, bloody acts he had dreamed about doing for so long?

Oh yes, he thought, staring down at the smiling photograph of One in his Murder Book. Yes, he could. And he would. Soon.

Chapter 1

Will Brannock awoke to some very warm lips nibbling on his bare shoulder. He turned over, more than willing to spend another hour or two in bed with Pam Ford. She was scheduled to fly out again to New York and then on to Rome, and Will meant to enjoy her until her plane took to the air. A flight attendant, Pam rarely got assignments in Chattanooga—every two or three months—but when she did, they always spent time together. She was an old friend, a real beauty, who made it crystal clear up front that she wanted no strings attached, just a good time together when she came to town. All of which suited Will just fine. The last thing he wanted was a committed relationship. It was out of the question. But Pam didn't care. She was always hot and eager and highly imaginative in bed. Will couldn't argue with that.

"Wish I could stay a few more days," Pam whispered in her husky voice, her tongue licking at his earlobe. "It's been so long this time. I've missed you."

"Me too." That was only partially true. He liked her, she was as desirable as any woman he'd been with, and they always had fun together. But spending more than a day or two in a hotel room with her was too much of a good thing. The occasional tryst suited him just fine. And if it never happened again, that was fine, too.

"We've still got some time," she said, rubbing her soft naked body against his bare chest. Pam turned him on, no doubt about it, with all that curly, dark red hair and those clear grass-green eyes. A dedicated runner like he was, Pam was built, toned and tanned and always ready. He'd met her through his sister, Colleen, who worked for the same airline, and they'd enjoyed these short romantic interludes ever since. No ties, no promises, no cohabitation, but a hell of a lot of fireworks between the sheets.

Will rolled on top of her and tangled his fingers in her hair. She laughed, but she was more than ready and so was he. He brought his mouth down on the hollow of her collarbone and heard the familiar weak moan. Pinning her hands over her head, he felt the growing need inside himself. So when his cell phone dinged on the bedside table, he muttered a low curse and pulled away.

"No, let it ring," Pam said, her pouty voice full of erotic promises.

"Can't do that. Hang on. Don't move."

Will let go of her and sat up on the edge of the bed. He grabbed his cell phone on the second ring. The screen identified the caller as J.D. Cass, one of Will's fellow special agents at the Tennessee Bureau of Investigation. He hit the button.

"Yeah, J.D. What's up?"

"Hey, you busy?"

"You could say that." Will glanced over his shoulder at the way Pam was moving her body around provocatively. She held out her arms for him.

"Too busy to do me a huge favor?" J.D. was saying.

J.D. wasn't one to ask favors, huge or otherwise. The guy was always on the job, always working a case, completely dedicated to his career. Will liked and admired him, although they'd only been in the Chattanooga field office together for about a year and a half. Last year, J.D. had solved one of the biggest cases the city had ever seen. The Rocking Chair Murders had been horrific for everybody concerned. Four women had died at the hands of a serial killer before J.D. and Will managed to take him down in the basement of an old church. They barely got there in time to save the last victim. J.D. was still involved in wrapping up that trial.

"I'm down at the criminal courts," J.D. continued. "The damn trial's gone into recess again.

Now they're discussing the admissibility of defense witnesses. Tam and I have both been waiting for hours to be called."

Tam Lovelady was the detective with the Chattanooga Police Department who had worked that serial killer case alongside J.D. Both were subpoenaed to testify and had been cooling their heels while the trial motions went on and on. "Bummer. Okay, J.D., sure. What'd you need?"

Will felt Pam's mouth on his back, her tongue tracing patterns, and he shut his eyes as she slowly kissed her way up to the side of his neck.

"My kid sister's coming in today out at the airport. I'm supposed to pick her up, but there's no way I can get away. I know you took a few days off, and I hate to ask, but is there any chance you can break loose and go get her for me and drop her off out at my house? I'd owe you big, Will."

Why not? J.D. was in a jam. Will was taking Pam out to the airport in a couple of hours, anyway. "Sure. When's she due in?"

"Any minute now. Her name's Julia. You've heard me mention her, right?"

"Yeah, the Julia with the marksmanship medals. Okay, no problem. What's her flight number?"

"Flight eight twenty-four out of Miami. US Airways."

"Is she expecting me?"

"I can't get through. She must've turned off her

cell on the plane. Or forgot to charge it. She has a tendency to do that."

"What's she look like?"

"Long, dark hair. Five foot seven. Pretty. Actually, she looks a lot like Zoe. You'll like her. She's a real sweetheart. She just signed up with the Chattanooga PD homicide division. Man, it's going to be great to see her. Even better that she's going to live here in town."

"Right. I'll get out there as soon as I can." Will watched Pam purse her lips in disappointment, get up, and move off toward the bathroom. She looked as good from behind as she did from the front.

"I appreciate it, Will."

"No problem. Don't worry about it."

"Tell her to turn on the damn phone and give me a call."

Will punched off and stood up, stretching as he walked toward the bathroom. Julia Cass could wait a little longer. He probably wouldn't see Pam again for months, and he intended to give her a proper good-bye.

Julia Cass was mightily ticked off but trying her best not to show it. God knew, she wasn't the most patient sort in the world, and J.D. should've been here to pick her up nearly an hour ago. Not that she was surprised. How many times had he left her sitting at school or the library or the mall, when they both still lived at home? Back then, either his job kept him overtime, or one of the floozy types he liked to date in his younger days. She glanced at her white wristwatch again. Everybody from her flight had cleared out, and the next round of passengers was beginning to check in.

Her cell phone battery was low, so she couldn't call him, and the nearest pay phone was out of order, so she spent her time watching the travelers rushing around and willing herself to be patient. She loved her older brother dearly, she truly did. He had practically raised her since their mother had left the family when Julia was too young to remember. Her father died when she was fourteen, and after that, J.D. was father, mother, and brother to her. He had worked nights to support them, until he graduated from college and then the police academy. The only thing she hadn't liked back then was his choice of women. They were all sexy and alluring and trashy. Certainly not the kind of women J.D. wanted her to hang around with. But he had always been there for her, and he was the major influence that brought her into a law enforcement career.

"J.D., I am absolutely going to kill you if you don't get here soon," she muttered under her breath.

Watching the people on the concourse, she searched yet again for her brother's tall figure.

She didn't see hide nor hair of him, but she did notice a tall, good-looking guy walking past her with a striking redhead hanging all over him. *J.D.'s type of gal before he met Audrey Sherrod,* she thought. Bored, she watched the couple move away toward the gate across from Julia. He was a hot guy, all right, but she had a feeling he knew it, too, and all too well. The red-haired girl was dressed in a tight-fitting Delta flight attendant's uniform and pulled a black, wheeled suitcase. The guy was wearing a black University of Alabama T-shirt, dark jeans, and black running shoes. He was obviously seeing his ladylove off to work, and was he ever.

Julia watched the pair step behind a pillar and succumb to a blatant and totally inappropriate make-out session, which Julia could still see all too well in the window reflection. The lengthy embrace was mostly brought on by the woman, who, yes, was all over him. The kiss that followed wasn't exactly G-rated, either. In other words, they liked each other *mucho* much and didn't mind showing it.

Not particularly into PDAs or voyeurism, Julia glanced away and watched the other passengers rushing hither and thither to catch flights. She'd give J.D. ten more minutes, and then she was catching a cab out of there. Her bloodhound, Jasper, was waiting somewhere down in baggage claim, and he didn't like being caged up anymore than she did. She wasn't a teenager anymore, and she didn't have to wait on her big brother's whims. He would be mad, but so what. So was she.

Glancing back at Mr. Romeo in the black T-shirt, she watched him give Red one last, lingering kiss. It looked to Julia like he was now itching to end the perpetual and steamy I-really-really-mean-it farewell, and she would bet a dollar he was relieved when the flight attendant finally extricated herself from his clutches, rolled her suitcase to the desk, and with one last wave and blown kiss, disappeared down the tunnel en route to her plane. Her handsome Lothario sauntered away and leaned back against the pillar, looking around as if searching for somebody to take her place.

My God, was he really on point for a new squeeze? she thought. Fascinated by him, largely because she had nothing better to do, Julia watched a blond flight attendant hurry past and then head straight for the same guy. Dapper Dan grinned and hugged her, then kissed her on both cheeks. Good grief. *Two-timing jerk,* she thought, glancing away in disgust.

Ten minutes passed. Julia spent most of that time watching I'm-So-Hot-And-Know-It waving and smiling at one flight attendant after another. Oh yeah, this guy had found a good hunting ground for guileless female prey. All he needed was a quiver and two dozen Cupid arrows. Jeez, some guys were just so full of themselves. He looked good, that was for damn sure; she couldn't deny that. He looked to be about six four or five, maybe even six foot six—really tall, probably even taller than J.D. His hair was dark blond and short, gelled a little on top, and he had one of those chiseled *GQ* model faces. High cheek-bones, square jaw, lean muscular body like a pro athlete—a basketball player, maybe. If not, she bet he was a marathon runner or a long-distance swimmer, and she had a feeling he was a man who enjoyed himself more than anyone else possibly could. Unfortunately, he reminded her of J.D., back when he was young and stupid and slept around with anything that wore a skirt.

As the next flight departing from her gate was announced over the intercom, Julia stood up. Okay, she'd waited long enough. Time to think for herself. Jasper, poor baby, was going to be mad as hell at her. She picked up her purse, glanced once more at the guy, and found him staring hard at her. He gave her THE FATAL GRIN, and let that be one written in all caps. She resisted fainting dead away, not that she was a woman who ever would. She watched him amble over her way, all easy charm and appreciative smile. Julia stared at him. Surely he wasn't going to try his luck with her, too. She almost laughed. *Fat chance of that,* she thought.

He stopped in front of her, that deadly grin

16

back in place and meant to melt her into a deeper puddle than the Wicked Witch of the West. In fact, she bet he had to wear boots, he left so many puddles in his wake.

"Hi there," he said to her in a deep, Josh Turner kind of voice. "Are you sitting here waiting for somebody to pick you up?"

"Not you, if that's what you're trying to do."

The guy laughed, genuinely it seemed, and then he seemed to realize that she really did think that's what he was up to. After that, he did have the decency to look sheepish. Up close and personal now, Julia saw that he had big brown eyes that were looking her over pretty good. He also had a killer dimple in his chin. Oh yes, God had been good to him, abundantly so.

"I didn't mean it that way, trust me. If your name is Julia Cass, though, I'm your ride."

Oh great. J.D. sent a practiced womanizer, out on the hunt, to pick her up. Julia was not thrilled, but it beat sitting there waiting forever. "J.D. sent you, I presume?"

"Yeah. He's tied up at the trial."

Julia knew about the ongoing trial for the Rocking Chair Murders. J.D. had told her it was just getting started and would probably last for a month or more. Well, at least J.D. had a good excuse for not showing up. She picked up her leather handbag and black carry-on, ready to get out of the crowded airport.

17

"Well, what d'you know. Will Brannock himself, in the flesh, and lookin' fine. How're you doin', sweetie?"

Julia looked at the petite and busty little flight attendant with the Deep South accent, who headed straight over, rose onto her tiptoes, and gave Will Brannock a quick peck on his cheek. Just one cheek—guess she didn't measure up to two-cheek status yet. The auburn-haired girl and Will Brannock chatted for a couple of minutes about the nice day and how long it'd been since they'd seen each other. She promised to call him soon before she hurried off and joined several other flight attendants who were just disembarking from a plane out of Charlotte, North Carolina. Julia waited until the girl was out of earshot.

"You got those flight attendants taking numbers, or what?"

Will Brannock laughed again. He found her funny, it seemed. "It's not what you think. Most of them are friends of my sister."

"So your sister's a flight attendant, too?"

"Nope. She's a pilot. Delta."

Well, that wasn't the answer Julia had expected.

"My name's Will Brannock, by the way. I work with your brother."

"*You're* a TBI special agent?" She couldn't help the skeptical tone. He didn't seem like a cop. She'd expected him to be the aforementioned *GQ* model.

Will placed his hand over his heart, assuming a feigned hurt expression. "That's right, Ms. Cass. No need to be so shocked. I'm old enough to shoot a gun and everything."

"I figured you were twenty-one, at least. Well, let's go. I've got a mad dog to pick up."

Julia headed off down the concourse, Will Brannock striding along beside her. Although she thought he was a man on the prowl, somehow she found him a rather amusing man on the prowl, which usually didn't happen. Nevertheless, J.D. was really going to get an earful for sending a flirt out to get her.

Trailing Julia Cass down the concourse, Will Brannock decided J.D. Cass's sister was a bit prickly but not bad-looking. In fact, she was pretty much spot-on gorgeous with all that thick, straight, black hair and those big brown eyes. She reminded him of that film actress, Catherine Zeta-Jones. Too bad she was the little sister of his best friend. Hooking up with her wouldn't do, not at all, and especially since Julia Cass was going into law enforcement right there in Chattanooga. Nope, that would not be a good idea. He never dated a woman who lived in the same town. That way nobody ever got too close to him, and more importantly, never found out anything about his past.

Too bad, though. Julia Cass was indeed a looker, even in her loose black T-shirt and faded jeans.

She was fairly tall—five seven, J.D. had said—and had a strong, lean body, at least from what he could tell. He liked tall, lithe women. He had never dated a policewoman, but Julia Cass just might be worth it, if she wasn't J.D.'s sister. Since she was, though, and J.D. was his partner, he needed to make an effort to be friendly. Small talk was definitely in order.

"You have a nice flight, Julia?"

"Yes, it was fine. We landed about an hour ago, I'd say. It's a good thing these airport chairs are so damn comfortable."

"I'm sorry I'm late." He was, but couldn't say he regretted the extra time with Pam, either.

Julia Cass glanced up at him. "Look, I'm sure you have a good reason for being late. And I do appreciate your coming out here to get me. I'm sorry if I'm coming off rude. I'm just tired. It's been a long week."

"You're not coming off rude," he lied. On the other hand, he rather liked her. Why, he did not know. There was just something about her that made him want to smile. Something that he'd better shake off ASAP. *She's a no-no,* he thought. *Yep, a definite no-no.* But that didn't mean he couldn't lust after her like all the other guys he saw turning around and taking second looks as they passed by.

"I've got my bloodhound over there in a travel crate. How about helping me sign him out?"

20

"Does he bite?"

"I'll let you find that out for yourself." But she smiled a bit, so he knew she probably wouldn't sic the dog on him. Maybe.

Following her around to the back of the carousel, he saw a guy in a blue-and-white airport personnel uniform standing beside a big, black rolling suitcase and a large dog carrier. Will stood back and watched a tan bloodhound exit the cage, stretch lazily, and shake all over until his black ears flapped and his tags jingled. Julia Cass knelt down and gave her dog a hug that any red-blooded man would covet. She adored her dog, no question about it.

"So you're a K-9, I take it," he said to Julia, who was attaching a long purple leash to the dog's halter.

Julia turned her face up to him. She had undoubtedly the prettiest brown eyes, a very light brown that shone almost gold in the overhead lights, surrounded by long and thick black eyelashes. He bet she had a nice smile, too, not that he'd ever get to see it; not with the Bigfoot-size wrong foot they'd gotten off on.

"I do hope you're not calling me a dog. But to answer your question, this is Jasper," Julia told him, and with downright civility at that. He could see the pride and love on her face. The woman loved her bloodhound. Jasper was a lucky dog indeed.

"That's an interesting name. No Spot or Rover or Buddy or Sam?"

"Jasper was the name of Max de Winter's dog."

"Daphne du Maurier. I remember that book. Max de Winter's the guy with the crazy house-keeper named Danvers, who burned down the house at the end."

"You've read *Rebecca*?"

"Yeah, I thought the guy in the movie was a little chauvinistic. Treated Joan Fontaine like a pet instead of a wife. The Germans used that book as a code source in World War Two. Did you know that?"

"You've read *Rebecca*?" she repeated.

"I went to college. English lit. *Pride and Prejudice*. *Emma*. Stuff like that."

"No, you're not telling me that you've read Jane Austen, too?"

"No, actually I'm kidding, but I've seen the movie where Keira Knightley plays Elizabeth. I try to see all her pictures." Actually, his mother was the fan of those kinds of movies. So was his sister, Colleen. He usually dozed off in the middle of them. All that formal bowing, and those stiff collars made his neck itch.

"To answer your question, Special Agent Brannock, Jasper was my K-9 partner until I made detective. I trained him from a pup. I still make him available if a law enforcement agency requests my help."

"Does that mean you'll use him at the Chattanooga PD, too?"

"Of course," she said as if he were somebody with no dog smarts at all. "Chief Mullins asked me if I'd be willing to work him at the department. I'll work detective in the criminal division. But I'll be on call to deploy him whenever and wherever he's needed. Jasper's cross-trained to work search, cadaver, and explosive tasks."

Will went down on his haunches and rubbed the dog's ears. The bloodhounds and other service dogs were valuable assets to law enforcement. They performed a dangerous service and had saved the lives of many an officer and soldier in the field. Truth was, he loved dogs, too, mutts and otherwise. Actually, he had three of his own waiting at home right now.

"Hi ya, Jasper, boy," he muttered, roughing up the dog's long ears and patting his back in the boisterous way his own dogs liked. At least, two of them did. "I bet you put all those other police dogs to shame, don't you, boy?"

Jasper leaned up against his leg, looking up at Will with some big, liquid brown eyes, already liking Will a lot better than his owner did. When Will smiled up at Julia, she was gazing down at them with approval. Aha. Will now knew the way to Detective Julia Cass's heart. Not that he was interested in her heart. Nope, not a bit. But if he were, that certainly would be the way to go.

"It's a good thing I brought my truck. He can ride in the back."

"I don't think so."

"On the other hand, I've got a big front seat."

Julia did smile this time. For an instant, Will could see her resemblance to J.D. He wondered if she had J.D.'s gut laugh, too. But, holy cow, shock and awe, the lady was warming up toward him. That was a good sign. No fisticuffs or cursing matches on the way to J.D.'s house.

"So which way, Special Agent Brannock?"

"I'm parked out front. Call me Will. Please."

Suitcases and dog in tow, they made their way out of the terminal to the busy access street. As they left the coolness inside the terminal, the August heat hit them like a bomb blast. Will headed for his truck, remembering that J.D. had called her a "real sweetheart." Will hadn't seen a lot of that thus far. In fact, Jasper was a hell of a lot friendlier than Julia Cass, at least in the licking department. And Jasper wagged his tail when Will pooch-talked to him. But he wasn't giving up. The luscious detective was a challenge. Nobody loved challenges as much as he did. She was going to be his friend, come hell or high water.

"Here we are," he said, gesturing proudly at his black-and-chrome honey of a truck.

"Oh my God, that's yours? You've got an H2 SUT Hummer?"

Julia Cass looked first at the Hummer, then at

24

him, awe evident in her eyes. She was practically drooling over his truck. He did so love a woman who knew her trucks. "Yeah, I just got her two weeks ago."

"I figured you for a red Corvette."

Will frowned, somehow sensing that was some kind of indirect insult. "Why's that?"

"So you could pick up lots of flight attendants. Why'd you think?"

"You injure me, Cass. I guess you're saying women won't be impressed by my Hummer?"

"Probably not. Except for me. I love it. In fact, I almost got one myself."

"Almost? What did you get?"

"Nothing yet. I drove a Mustang in Nashville, but I sold it cheap to my neighbor's son, Josh. He's getting his driver's license next month. Now I want a truck or SUV. I was looking at Hummers like this one on the Internet a couple of months ago, but they're a little too pricey for me."

Absurdly pleased that she liked his truck, he said, "Well, consider this a test drive. Maybe you can get a good deal here in Chattanooga."

The traffic was wild and woolly around the airport, especially around the noon hour, but he took Airport Connector Road to 153 and they were on their way. Will glanced over at Julia again and liked the way she wasn't getting all freaked out that the sunroof was blowing her shiny black hair all over the place. Out in the sun, he could see some red glints in it. In fact, she acted like she loved the feel of the wind whipping through her hair. Man, she was so damn good-looking. He wondered what kind of cop she was. If she took after her brother, she'd know her stuff inside and out. Something told him she was not just good but very good at her job, and at lots of other things, too.

J.D. lived over on Signal Mountain, which would take a good fifteen or twenty minutes, so Will decided to make nice. Maybe they could get to know each other. Be friendly. "So, how do you think you're going to like living here?"

Julia glanced at him. *Man, those eyes,* he thought. Just like his mother's heirloom topaz earrings.

"I'm going to like being closer to J.D. I haven't seen much of him for the last few years. Not as much as I'd like, anyway."

"So you didn't get together much, huh?"

"He usually made it to my house for Christmas, but that's about it."

Will knew he was making a mistake with his next question but couldn't help himself. He had to know. "You married? Engaged or anything?"

"No."

"Boyfriend?"

"No." Julia paused, looking a trifle uncomfortable with the conversation swinging toward personal, and Will braced himself for a sharp retort. Instead, she merely said, "What about you?"

"No one special."

"That redhead looked pretty special. Could've fooled me. Guess it was all that making out and groping each other that you did in public."

"We go out when she's in town. Doesn't happen very often. It's not serious. Just good friends."

Julia didn't comment. He wondered what she was thinking and decided it was better if he didn't know. He liked Pam, respected her, but he wasn't in love with her.

"Mind if I call you Jules?"

"Yes."

"J.D. calls you that sometimes."

"He's my big brother. He's got special privileges because I like him a lot."

"So tell me, Jules, that's quite a hound you've got. Slobbery but sweet."

That brought a small, reluctant chuckle. Wow, he'd cracked the ice—a minute little hairline crack, true, but a thaw might be possible, given ten years or so.

"As I said, I raised him from a puppy. He's part of the family. And he's a decorated law enforcement officer. So treat him with respect, or you'll deal with me. And he doesn't slobber. Much."

Will glanced down at Jasper where he lay on the front seat between them. His ears were blowing in the wind, too, and he was enjoying the fresh air coming in from the sunroof. Huge, soulful brown eyes gazed up at him. He was slobbering, but just a little. "He's well behaved. You must be a good dog trainer."

"Thank you. That's where I've been, actually. Conducting a law enforcement K-9 training seminar in Boca Raton."

"So that's where you got that dark tan."

"I did get to the beach a time or two."

"A beach sounds good to me. I like to surf." Julia didn't answer, so he said, "K-9 work takes a lot of patience."

"And a lot of brains. More brains than all you special agents need. Just ask J.D." She looked straight ahead but the corners of her mouth were turned up. She was teasing him, that was clear, but her words were provocative. He put on his turn signal and passed an old lady in a poky green Ford Taurus clogging the inside lane.

"My brains are so massive, so impressive that they'd leave yours in the dust, Detective Cass."

"That sounds highly unpleasant."

"Okay, Jules. If you're so brilliant, what's the capital of Montana?"

"Helena."

"What's the capital of Wisconsin?"

"Madison."

"North Dakota?"

"Bismarck."

"Norway?"

"Oslo."

"Thailand?"

"Bangkok."

Will frowned. What was this girl, a geography major? "What's the capital of Marakistan?"

"Batke."

"Gotcha, Jules. I made that up."

"So? I made mine up, too."

They laughed together. Julia said, "Okay, your turn to answer some questions, Brannock. You look like you might be a real whiz at chemistry."

"If it's between a man and a woman, I know it well. I feel it now."

Julia presented him with a quick and deprecating look. "Oh my, the charm of you. I don't think I can stand it."

"You can't stand it in a bad way, or you're so taken with me you can't stand the excitement?"

She changed the subject. "What kind of weapon do you carry?"

"Glock Seventeen."

"You're kidding. I do, too. Seventeen-round magazine. Four-and-a-half-inch barrel."

"Laser target indicator. Leather hip holster."

"Exactly."

"Okay, I guess we're just two peas in a pod."

Julia laughed. "I bet I can shoot better than you."

"I bet you can, too. J.D. brags to us now and then about all your sharpshooting medals."

"Chicken."

"I do happen to know how to shoot down anybody that gives me trouble," Will told her.

"Are you including me in that remark?"

"Sure. Watch out. I've shot up plenty of defenseless women in my life."

"I'm not defenseless, believe me."

"No, and I haven't shot that many women, either."

"I have an idea. Why don't you concentrate on your driving before you kill us both? I'm warning you, don't even think about having a wreck with Jasper in the car. He's dear to me."

"Yes, ma'am, Detective Jules."

That got another chuckle out of her, one she cut off almost at once. Will was more than pleased. Good grief, she might even like him a little. He actually made her forget to be prickly—for a few seconds, true, but, hey, that was a start. Crossing to the passing lane, Will increased his speed. It was a beautiful day, not a cloud in the sky. He was eager to get Julia Cass home and then take his boat out on the lake. The crappie would be biting just before dark, and he meant to be there to catch a mess of them.

"You like fishing?" she suddenly asked him.

Well, the two of them were on the same wavelength, all right. "I was just thinking about fishing. Are you a psychic, or what?"

"You've got a Bass Pro Shops catalog on your floorboard. And fishing gear in the back.

30

That's the extent of my psychic abilities."

"I do love to fish. Why?"

"Just wondered."

If this woman loved Crimson Tide football, he was a goner. "You root for Alabama, I take it," he said.

"You take it wrong. I hate Alabama. Tennessee's my team, orange and white all the way, forever, and I have plenty of UT sweatshirts to prove it."

"I hate Tennessee. Guess we can't get married after all."

"Boohoo," Julia said.

"C'mon, Jules, you're breaking my heart here."

"Like I said, boohoo."

Yep, he liked her. A lot. When his cell phone dinged, he pulled it off his belt and looked at the screen. It was his boss. "Yeah, this is Will Brannock."

"You should pull over when you talk on your cell," Julia advised him from the passenger seat.

The minute Will heard the somber tone of Phil Hayes's gravelly voice, however, he kissed his fishing trip a fond see-you-later-maybe. One thing the special agent in charge of the Chattanooga field office did not do was call up to partake in some inane chitchat. "Where are you, Will?"

"On Twenty-Seven South, heading downtown. What's going on?"

"We got a murder today, very high-profile. You familiar with the name Lucien Lockhart?"

"The judge?"

"Yeah, they found him dead today at his home in Woodstone Circle."

"Wow, that's an old-money neighborhood. Not what you want to hear."

"That's right. This is going to be big."

"And we've got jurisdiction? I thought Lockhart sat on the state supreme court."

"He did. Until he got appointed to the federal bench about a month ago. That drops this case into our lap. I want you to go lead on it. I'm at the scene now with Willie Mullins and some of his investigators. CPD secured it for us."

Will glanced over at Julia, who was scratching Jasper's ears and pretending not to listen to Will's end of the conversation. "I've got Julia Cass with me. Willie hired her on in homicide. Should I bring her along? Let Willie advise her?"

"That's J.D.'s sister, right? Yeah, Willie mentioned her to me. See if she wants to come along. Didn't he tell me she was coming in today?"

"That's right. I just picked her up at the airport."

"What? Tell me," Julia demanded, alert and all ears from the second her name was bandied about. "Bring me along where? What's going on?"

Will finished his conversation with Phil, punched off, and explained the situation as concisely as he could.

"You bet I want to come along. Maybe Jasper can show off his stuff."

"It's a state investigation. TBI is in charge."

"I gathered that. If Chief Mullins is there, he can fill me in on what he wants me to do. I'm sure the Chattanooga PD will be helping you out. We collaborated on cases in Nashville."

Julia Cass seemed as eager as he was. She was certainly ready to get to work. Yet something else he liked about her. He took the next off-ramp and headed for the Woodstone Circle neighborhood. Looked like he might get a firsthand look at Julia Cass's law enforcement skills, after all.

Chapter 2

Julia wasn't quite sure what to think of Will Brannock. He was amusing enough, she'd give him that. She usually went in for funny guys. On the other hand, she kept seeing images in her head of that less-than-subtle romantic scene at the airport, with him pressing the buxom and eager flight attendant against the column. He wasn't the kind of man she'd want to go out with, not if he holed up with every flight attendant that set down on a Chattanooga runway. But he was a friend of her brother's and a law enforcement colleague, so they'd have to get along. He had been witty and pleasant enough taking her home, but now it was crunch time. It would be more than interesting to see how he would handle this investigation. He seemed as anxious as she to get to the scene and find out exactly what had happened to the judge. It wouldn't take them long, either, not the way Will Brannock drove. He apparently had the ultracool Hummer souped up, had a heavy foot, and probably fantasized about driving at Talladega. All the joking from him was over, though. Now that he'd gotten the official summons, he was as serious as Sunday church.

As it turned out, Judge Lockhart had enjoyed quite a nice lifestyle. Woodstone Circle was in one of the most desirable areas of Chattanooga. Will told her the subdivision was built on a gated circle drive lined with mansions owned by some of the city's elite. When they reached the entrance, Will pulled up and stopped at the massive gate. While he flashed his badge to the CPD officer controlling traffic, she looked at the wide oak-lined street and bet it took some serious bucks to buy a home in the private haven on the other side of this wall. As Will drove into the subdivision, she admired the homes, most of which were big and stately and hidden behind brick or stone walls and lush green vegetation.

Julia was new in town, but she recognized money and privilege when she saw it. And she saw it in the Lockhart mansion. It was bigger and more impressive than the other residences and located near a private neighborhood park that sported lots of old magnolia and pecan trees and lush green grass. Yessiree, these wide and shady avenues oozed *we've got lots of money and don't mind showing it*. At the moment, the Lockhart enclave was not hard to find. Four CPD cruisers were parked around its private gated driveway, and uniformed police officers were still stretching out the yellow crime scene tape. Several unmarked cars were also there, no doubt belonging to Will's TBI cohorts, but no sign of a medical examiner's van.

Will flashed his badge and was motioned through the intricate wrought-iron gate and up the concrete driveway to where the house sat, surrounded by giant oaks and maples. A white brick wall encircled the grounds: emerald-green lawn and well-tended flower beds of blue hydrangeas and lots of snowball bushes. They pulled up beside a splashing, three-tier marble fountain with the Greek goddess Diana in the center, holding an urn overflowing with water. The house itself was *Gone with the Wind*-ish and built in the pillared, Greek Revival style. It had long galleries both upstairs and down, white brick chimneys, and a porte cochere on the east side. White spindle rockers and lacy wrought-iron tables sat on the galleries, and red geraniums, marigolds, and purple alyssum spilled out of big clay pots everywhere. Huge spidery green ferns hung in white pots at intervals along the upper gallery.

Will Brannock killed the engine and turned to her. "I need to talk to Phil. That's him over there with Chief Mullins."

Julia followed his pointing finger and saw two men standing together under one of the twin silver-leaf maple trees shading the front porch. "Let me get Jasper secured away from the scene, and I'll go talk to the chief."

Opening the passenger door and stepping down from the Hummer, she stood back and let Jasper leap to the ground, then led him by the leash deeper into the side yard. There was a small cluster of tulip poplars, replete with a white lattice arbor and bench, that would give him shade from the glaring sun. Luckily, an ornamental goldfish pond was nearby, in case Jasper got thirsty. The day was very hot. Now, just after midday, it was probably already nearing ninety degrees, and she knew from experience that it might take the forensic techs a long time to sweep the scene.

The victim was an important man, well-known, well connected, and a federal judge, to boot. Law enforcement would have to pull out all the stops in this investigation. She wondered if the news media of Chattanooga were the same kind of barracudas she'd had to deal with at the Nashville Police Department. If so, the very second the networks got wind of this sensational crime, they'd be all over the place with their satellite trucks and TV vans, and would cause the investigators a ton of grief and complications.

Stooping to stroke Jasper's back for a moment, she watched the bloodhound lie down, his brown eyes questioning her, wanting to go to work. He was no stranger to crime scenes. He was ready to sniff out the villain. He loved his job as much as she loved hers. She stood, looked around, and watched Will Brannock approach the man he'd identified as Phil Hayes, who was dressed in a white dress shirt, yellow tie, and tan suit. Brannock had pulled on a black TBI cap. He towered over his boss, who had immediately started an animated conversation with Will.

Farther down the yard, at the end of the back porch, she could see Chief Mullins with some of his uniformed officers. She took a brush from her bag, brushed off her clothes thoroughly to rid herself of any trace of Jasper's hair, and then headed at a swift clip toward her new chief. Excitement was burgeoning inside her. It had been awhile since she'd been on a homicide case like this one, and she hoped the Chattanooga PD would get to play an integral role in the investigation.

When Chief Mullins saw her approaching, he walked over to meet her. He was a handsome older gentleman with ebony skin and white hair, an all-around super-nice guy. J.D. had told her he

37

was easygoing and even-tempered, with a keen intelligence that saw through any kind of deceit. She had liked him immediately when she'd come over from Nashville for the initial interview. He also happened to be the father of her new partner, Tamara Lovelady, which might or might not end up being a sticky situation. She had met Tam briefly, and had gotten good vibes from her, too. Petite and curvaceous, Tam was a lovely lady with caramel skin and coffee-colored brown eyes and a ready, friendly smile. J.D. had assured Julia that even though Tam was pretty much a rookie detective, she had proved herself very good at the job. If J.D. vouched for her, liked her, and trusted her, Julia knew that she and Tam would get along just fine.

"Glad you happened to be with Special Agent Brannock, Detective," Chief Mullins said the moment she reached his side. "Looks like you're gonna get a baptism by fire. I know you aren't slated to start until next Monday, but now that you're here, I'm gonna make use of your experience. I'm shorthanded in homicide with Tam out for the trial. J.D.'s caught up in that, too, right?"

"Yes, sir. I'm ready to go. I've been off duty way too long. Just tell me what you need."

"TBI has full jurisdiction here, but Phil asked me to give him a liaison officer to help Will Brannock handle this investigation. You'll be working hand in hand with him. You got any problem with that?"

Julia wasn't at all sure about the *hand in hand* part, but she wasn't about to say she didn't want to work with Brannock. She wasn't about to give up the opportunity to get involved in the case, either. "That's fine with me. Let me make sure I understand the jurisdictions. He'll be in complete charge. I'm here to help and assist. Right?"

"Right, but I think y'all will get along just fine. He's an exceptional investigator, and from what I've heard, so are you."

"Thank you, sir. I'll do my best, I promise you that. Do I need to check in at headquarters before I start working with Brannock?"

"No. You got your badge and all the paperwork lined out last time you were here. You're on your own from here on out. But be apprised, I want to be notified every step of the way, so I expect weekly written reports—more if you can find the time. E-mails are fine, if you're out of the office, and you will be. Because of the notoriety of this murder, Phil might want a task force set up down at the TBI offices. If you need more help from our department or run into jurisdictional sticking points, just say the word and I'll take care of it. I'll support you one hundred percent."

"I appreciate that, sir. I don't anticipate anything like that happening."

"C'mon then, let me show you what's gone

down here. The crime scene's around back, and damn gruesome, too."

Julia followed him down a flagstone path that rounded the south end of the house. A large, rectangular aquamarine pool sparkled in the sunlight in the middle of the flagstone patio behind the house. Rosebushes in neatly tended beds lined paths that meandered through a myriad of shade and fruit trees. Julia could almost visualize the lady of the house wandering along through the garden and snipping fragrant red roses to display in a crystal vase on her glossy dining room table.

"This house has been in the Lockhart family for years," Chief Mullins was telling her. "The family made its money in the lumber business, and most of the patriarchs for the last five decades have been attorneys or judges. They also have been known to associate with criminal elements from time to time, so I can't say I'm especially surprised Lucien ended up dead by violence."

"Did you know him personally, Chief Mullins?"

"Yes, I did. He was a charming old gentleman, but you trusted him at your own peril, if you know what I mean. Hate to speak unkindly of the departed, but the truth's the truth. I call it the way I see it."

As they moved along the sun-dappled path, Julia caught her first sight of the victim. Lucien Lockhart's body was on the back porch, hanging by the neck from a yellow ski rope tied to a thick wood rafter. Will Brannock was already there, standing on the lawn directing the CPD officers and police technicians to stay off the porch. She glanced at Willie Mullins, wondering if he resented the TBI taking charge of the scene and ordering his people around.

Chief Mullins seemed to sense her question. "We work well with the TBI here in Chattanooga. They helped us bring down the Rocking Chair killer. Your brother was lead on that one and did a hell of a good job. So did Will Brannock. It hit a little too close to home for a lot of us. Audrey Sherrod, especially."

"I'm sorry to hear that."

Audrey Sherrod was J.D.'s new girlfriend. Julia had met her several times and had been rather impressed. She was quite a nice lady, not the kind of woman Julia was used to seeing her brother date, but Audrey was a good influence on him. One thing for sure, she had made him happier than Julia had ever seen him, and that was all Julia cared about.

When they reached Will Brannock, the chief addressed him directly. "I've assigned Detective Cass as the CPD detective to help you on this case. Phil asked for our assistance, and we're glad to oblige."

Will looked down at Julia, and she wasn't exactly sure that he was pleased that they'd be working together. All the previous levity on his part had flown the coop; he was dead serious and his next words proved it. "Okay, just so you know, Detective. I'm in charge. You follow my orders, understand?"

Not exactly thrilled by that little speech or his condescending attitude, Julia nodded politely and prayed he wasn't hopelessly clueless about investigatory procedures. She had no idea what kind of experience he'd had with the TBI. J.D. had never mentioned Will's background to her. Come to think of it, he'd never mentioned much about Will that wasn't job-related.

"Phil called in our crime scene vehicle out of Knoxville when he got the call early this morning, Chief. They should make it here any time now," Will said to Chief Mullins. "He thought it best under the circumstances."

Mullins nodded. "That's fine with me. We've got two other murder cases that we picked up yesterday. I need my investigators to work those scenes, as soon as we can get them there."

As Chief Mullins moved away to speak with Phil Hayes, Will said, "Well, looks like we're working together right off the bat, Detective."

"Sure does." Julia pulled Jasper's grooming brush out of her back pocket. "You might want to get rid of any dog hair on your clothes before we get started. Wouldn't want to contaminate the scene."

"Right. Thanks."

While Will moved a few yards away to brush himself down, Julia walked down the sidewalk to where Judge Lucien Lockhart's body was hanging. She stood there for a moment by herself, observing the scene while it was still basically undisturbed, realizing at once that this murder wasn't some random act of violence. The victim had definitely been staged. He was naked except for a pair of white swim trunks, and blood had streaked its way from his mouth, down his chin, and over his chest and legs. Below his dangling feet, the killer had placed a small set of metal scales with a crossed-swords finial. What did that mean? The scales of justice? Some kind of equality statement?

"Here, put these on," Brannock told her, handing her plastic gloves and paper booties. She snapped on the gloves and stretched the paper booties over her white Nikes. Brannock already had on his protective gear.

"Is that what I think it is on the left side of that scale?" she asked him.

"We think it's part of the judge's tongue. It looks to me like the perp pulled his tongue out and sliced it off about three inches back. He left it here for us to find and took the tip of the tongue with him. A souvenir, I guess."

Despite being a veteran homicide detective, Julia was somewhat shocked that such a mutilation murder could happen in an exclusive and gated area of Chattanooga, Tennessee, and involve such a well-known and distinguished citizen. Julia stared at the small amount of blood pooling in the left tray of the scales under the piece of Lockhart's tongue. She stooped down and examined it, then looked at the coins stacked neatly in the right-hand tray. "That's a bunch of dimes. A tongue balancing out with money."

"Yeah."

"He's sending us a specific message here. We figure out what it is, we can get him."

Will gave her an appraising look. She held his stare. He said, "The perp had this all planned out, all right. Down to every gory detail."

"And he had plenty of time to play around with the vic." Julia shook off her aversion to the horrific cruelty of the murder and tried to assess the scene without any emotion. It wasn't exactly easy, not in a case like this one, but she had trained herself to do it. She turned and faced Will again.

"He wrote *ONE* on the floor in blood. I think that means he's just getting started."

"That's exactly what he means."

"Who found the body?"

"Lockhart's housemaid. Name's Maria Bota. She called nine-one-one, completely hysterical. Said she found him when he didn't come inside for breakfast. She noticed some drops of blood

44

and followed the trail from the swimming pool to where the body was suspended on the back gallery. The CPD officer first on the scene says the maid lives out back in a converted carriage house. He took her out there to calm her down and told her to sit tight until somebody came out and interviewed her."

"Anybody else at home when the murder occurred?"

Will shook his head. "Not unless they took off. We can't do much out here until the medical examiner shows up and releases the body. How about we go find out exactly what that maid knows?"

"Let's do it."

Will walked alongside Julia Cass, already fairly certain that she knew precisely what she was doing, would do it well, and by the book. He was curious to see how it would be working with her. She was thirty-four, if he remembered right from J.D.'s account, and young, beautiful—hell, she looked more like a model or an actress than a cop. He just hoped she was as good as her first impression made her out to be. He had a gut feeling that this was going to be a bad one. He was going to need all the input he could get. From Julia Cass and everybody else involved in the investigation.

"Have you handled many homicide cases?" Will asked Julia.

"I worked homicide in Nashville for ten years. I've seen a lot of terrible things."

"This terrible?"

"No. Not a severed tongue. That tells me this guy is sick, seriously disturbed, or somebody with a tongue fetish."

"Probably all three." Will hesitated. "I've had some training in profiling at Quantico. Serial killers, mainly."

"If you're thinking this is the work of a serial, I agree. I hope we're both wrong."

"It could be simply a grudge thing. Lockhart was a judge. Judges tend to irritate people."

"From what I've heard, the victim hasn't always played by the rules."

"Yeah? Who told you that?"

"Chief Mullins. And J.D., too. I remember him being ticked off by a case he was involved in. Said the judge was entirely pro-defense and didn't make any bones about it. Pretty much ignored the facts and let the guy go."

"We'll have to check out his cases. See if we can find any threats against him. Hopefully the maid will be able to tell us if he's gotten any intimidating calls or disturbances here at the house. Maids usually know everything going on in a household."

"You that familiar with maids?"

"No, but I know people who are, and treat them like members of the family. She'll know

46

a lot about this family; trust me on that."

Walking along the curving flagstone path, they turned around when they heard the TBI forensic technicians out of Knoxville round the far end of the gallery. There were three men and two women, all dressed in white jumpsuits. Will knew most of them by name and waved them toward the porch where the body was, but he kept walking, wanting to interview the maid sooner rather than later. The CPD officers indicated that she had been hysterical from the moment they arrived on the scene, and they hadn't been able to get much out of her. From his experience, that was probably for the better. He and Julia were experienced interrogators. And this would give Will an opportunity to check out Julia's skills right off the bat. He hoped for the best, but he was still in charge. Julia was used to being lead investigator herself, but she was backing off and letting him give the orders, at least so far. He appreciated that.

The maid's quarters were located at the far end of the swimming pool enclosure. It looked very nice, like a small English cottage with fragrant yellow roses growing up a trellis beside the front door. Everything was neat and clean, the walk swept, and lots of pots of purple and white petunias. One large Boston fern hung on a lantern hook beside the front door. The door stood wide, and Will could see through the screen that the maid was sitting in a blue recliner in the living room. She was clutching a little boy who appeared to be around three or four years old. The woman looked as though she'd never let go of the child again.

"Hello," Julia said to her through the screen door. "May we come in, Ms. Bota?"

The maid didn't say anything but she nodded. Julia opened the screen door and went inside. Will followed. If Julia wanted to take the lead in questioning, that was fine by him. If he had to jump in, he would. It would give him time to watch Maria Bota's body language and see if she was telling the truth.

"She looks scared, Brannock, real shaky," Julia said, lowering her voice. "How about letting me talk to her, woman to woman?"

Will nodded, and they both approached the frightened mother and child.

"You are Ms. Bota, right?" Julia asked the girl. Her voice was calm and soothing. "My name is Julia Cass. I'm a detective with the Chattanooga Police Department. This is my colleague, Special Agent Will Brannock with the Tennessee Bureau of Investigation. We're here to find out who killed your employer. We're going to need to talk to you about what you saw."

Maria Bota was an attractive girl. Will estimated her age to be about nineteen or twenty, twenty-one tops. She had very black eyes, now red and puffy and swollen with tears. Her hair was even darker, tied back in a long, straight ponytail. She looked terrified. He waited while Julia knelt in front of the trembling young woman.

"We just want to ask you a few questions. Please understand, there's nothing for you to be afraid of. We're only here to help you. Okay?"

Maria nodded but held herself as stiff as a board. The child had his head on her shoulder, but he peeked out at Julia from under his cupped hand.

"What a beautiful little boy," Julia said in that same low, comforting voice. "What's his name?"

Maria's shoulders relaxed a little bit and she spoke in heavily accented English. "Julio. He's three."

Julia smiled at him, lightly touching his back with her fingers. "*Hola*, Julio. My name's Julia."

"*Hola*," he mumbled into his mama's shoulder.

"May we sit down, Ms. Bota?"

Maria Bota nodded. Will sat down in an old, light green velour Queen Anne chair, and Julia took a place on a white slipcovered couch near the woman and child.

Will said, "I know this has been a hard time for you, Ms. Bota. Thank you for talking with us."

The maid nodded again. Julia looked at Will, waiting for his lead. He gave it, nodding for her to take over.

"The officer outside told us that you found Judge Lockhart's body. Is that right?"

Maria began to shake, enough for them to notice and for the baby to raise his head and look at his mama's face. He puckered up. Julia laid her palm over the distraught woman's hand. "It's okay. But we really need for you to tell us what you saw this morning. It's very important that you tell us everything."

Maria looked down and hugged her child closer. "I fix his breakfast, like I do every day. He leave his order on the kitchen counter for me every night. He get up real early. Five o'clock, some-times even before sun come up. He take swim, then he dress and go to work."

"Was he up early this morning? Did you see him?"

Will watched Julia, garnering more respect for her ability. She was leaning forward, interested and calm, but completely nonthreatening. She was asking the right questions. Maria was responding to her. Julia Cass was going to turn out to be a big help to him.

"Yes, ma'am. I think so. I hear his voice before I got out of bed."

Will said, "Could you tell where it was coming from?"

"I think from the pool. My bedroom window was open." She stopped, looking down at her feet.

"Was something wrong, Maria?" Julia asked her. "Did you hear something out of the ordinary?"

50

There was something wrong, and both he and Julia could sense it. What? What wouldn't the girl tell them?

Maria kept shaking her head. "No no. He always swim, very early, sometime still in dark. I did not think he was going to be . . . going to be . . ."

When Maria looked up, her dark eyes wide and horrified, Will knew she was probably remembering the way the mutilated corpse looked hanging by the neck, pale and bloody.

"It's okay. Are you sure it was his voice, not somebody else's?"

"I think so, but I was sleepy. I fall back to sleep for a little."

"What time did you get up?"

"I set alarm for five."

"Okay."

Will took over for Julia. "Can you tell us exactly what happened after you got up? Just take it slow and try to remember everything you can."

Maria looked at Julia for reassurance. Julia nodded and smiled encouragingly.

"I got up and took shower. I let Julio sleep till I go to big house."

"Does the judge allow your son to stay with you when you work?"

"Yes. The judge very good to Julio. His wife, she not like me much."

Will glanced at Julia. They hadn't heard about the wife yet. "Mrs. Lockhart was here last night?"

"No, sir. She in New Orleans to visit her *madre*. She go there many times."

Will didn't know if the wife had been notified yet. He doubted it, but she would have to be, and then checked out. The family always came first on the list of suspects. Especially the spouse. Clear them, and then start in on other family and friends. He already had agents canvassing the neighborhood.

"So after you and Julio got up, did you see the judge then?"

Maria answered Julia's question. "No, I take Julio to the big house and make breakfast. Lucien like coffee strong and eggs in special way. How do you say, Benedict?"

"Eggs Benedict," Will said, but the fact that she called the judge by his first name didn't escape his notice. That indicated their relationship could be more personal than just maid and employer. When he looked at Julia, their eyes met. She had noted it, too.

"Please, go on."

"We set table and I clean up kitchen while we wait for him to come down."

"And did he?"

"No." Maria's voice dropped to a whisper. "That when I went to see if he was all right. He always on time for breakfast. When he not in house, I walk out by pool." She swallowed hard, looked down, and twisted her fingers together. "That when"—her voice got lower—"I saw the blood."

"And you followed it?"

"Yes, sir." Her gaze met Will's, and he could see the anguish in her eyes. "I have never see nothing so awful." She began to cry, and Will could see that her tears were real.

Julia patted her back and murmured a few reassuring words, but she gazed at Will. There had to be more that the maid could give them. She was asking his permission to continue. He gave it.

"Maria, please," Julia said softly. "You've got to understand how important it is for you to tell us everything. Any little thing that seemed out of place to you, anything he said or did, you have to remember and tell us. We want to get whoever did this. We need your help."

The maid wiped at her tears and let the squirming toddler get down off her lap. Julio immediately went to Will and stood at his knee, looking up at him with big dark eyes. Will smiled at him, but the boy just stared at him with that clear, unblinking innocence. He was a cute kid, and Will hoped to God he hadn't witnessed the murder scene. He refocused his attention on Maria when she began to speak. Again, her words were breath-less, barely discernible.

"There was woman here last night."

Both Will and Julia perked up at that. Okay, now they were getting somewhere.

"What woman would that be?" Julia asked.

"It is woman who come when Mrs. Lockhart go away."

"He's having an affair?" Will asked.

"She is one he pays for."

"A call girl?"

Maria shrugged. "I not know. She came after dinner but was gone when I got up."

"You don't know when she left?"

"No, sir. But cameras in driveway. They tell you."

Will was surprised. He had looked for surveillance cameras when they arrived but hadn't seen any.

"We didn't see any cameras," Julia said quickly to Maria. "Where are they?"

"Hidden. The judge afraid sometimes. He get threats."

"What threats?"

"I not know."

It was something to check out. Maybe Mrs. Lockhart could clue them in. "Where are these cameras?"

"They hide them in flower pots and on house. Some up high, in trees."

"Is there a camera on the swimming pool?"

Maria shrugged. "I do not think so."

"Is there anything else, Maria? Anything at all? Did you hear the woman's voice when you heard the judge before dawn?"

"No, only him. He laughing, I think."

54

"Do you know the woman's name?"

Maria looked uncomfortable, and Will wondered if she'd been warned not to mention Judge Lockhart's midnight guests. "It Ginger, I think. But I never saw her up close or talk to her. He tell me stay here and keep Julio inside when he see her."

"Thank you, Maria. Would it be okay if we came back and talked to you again if we need to?"

That was Julia. Maria nodded.

Will said, "If you think of anything else, you'll give us a call, won't you? Here's my card."

Outside, under the cool shade of a pecan tree, they looked at each other.

"We just might have a video of the killer," Julia said, her eyes alight with excitement.

"Let's go find those tapes."

Chapter 3

The killer sat at his makeshift table, a single candle flickering in invisible air currents. He stared down at the white paper plate holding about an inch of Judge Lucien Lockhart's tongue. The cave was very cold tonight, and he could hear the slow drip of water somewhere down the long, dark passage. Fingers entwined and resting on the table, his shoulders relaxed, he felt totally tranquil, almost serene. He had done it. Single-handedly he had sent Lockhart to hell, where he belonged. No one saw him enter or leave Woodstone Circle or the Lockhart grounds. He had been stealthy and controlled, and that was the key. The execution of the murder had been absolutely perfect.

Now, he was safely back in his hidden lair, untouched, unsuspected. At that thought, he almost laughed to himself. Lair? Him, have a lair? Who would've ever thought he would creep down to such a dark, spooky place as this, of all things? He never would've dreamed it possible. But it was a place to hide, to plan, and he couldn't have chosen better. No one knew about this cavern; no one would ever guess where he was when he disappeared for a time. He'd finally worked up the courage to turn his fantasy into a lethal reality.

When he'd seen Lucien Lockhart helpless, terrified, and most of all, humbled, he had loved it. Loved the twisted horror on Lucien's face when he'd gotten hold of his tongue with the pliers. Loved the power he'd felt. The explosion of fiery satisfaction had sent shivery sensations skittering down his back. He had never felt such triumph, never in his entire life. Now, he was surprised at how much he craved another such act of depravity. He already knew the disgusting animal he would choose next. Victim Two. A man who deserved to die just as much as Lucien had.

But first things first. He opened his Murder Book and gazed at Lucien's photograph, and then he squeezed out a dab of Elmer's glue on the page just below his image. He picked up the tip of Lockhart's tongue and pressed it into the glue. He would let it dry, and then he would turn the page. As he wiped the blood residue off his fingers, he saw that his hands were shaking. He was new at this game of murder, raw and inexperienced. A little reaction was under-standable. Despite his age, Lockhart had been strong and athletic. But so was he, more so than other people might think, and he'd had the element of sheer surprise. God, that man had been arrogant. Lucien had ordered him off his property as if he were some kind of railroad bum. Judges were used to ordering people around and enjoyed exerting their power and authority. Lucien Lockhart wouldn't be ordering anybody around now. No, sir. Lucien Lockhart was done for.

He stared down at the severed tongue glued in the book. The blood had congealed; looked black now. But how many words had come off that tongue that had caused families such unbelievable grief and anguish? How many fraudulent orders had been spewed out, to disappoint and infuriate innocent families? The judge had deserved to die, no doubt about it. The world would now be a better place. *The fraudulent tongue shall be cut out,* he thought with righteous vindication.

One down, he thought, his pleasure rising higher and higher until it verged on carnal ecstasy, *and number Two, here I come.*

In a large closet off Lucien Lockhart's oak-paneled and book-lined library, they found a long and technically top-notch bank of video camera monitors. Julia stood back and observed while Will Brannock sat down in a tufted, maroon leather swivel chair in front of the eight screens and expertly rewound the videotape from the camera that overlooked the front driveway. As if he knew what to do and had done it plenty of times. She wondered about that. Was he specially trained in surveillance at Quantico? He certainly worked with an unfailing confidence with this electronic equipment. She looked back at the other screens. One at the front door, one at the back door, and another at the double doors at the side of the house under the porte cochere. The one at the entrance gate showed that the uniformed officer who'd waved them inside was still fending off the first swarm of pushy reporters and curious gawkers. The camera at the back door caught a glimpse of Will's forensic team, working on the corpse, all performing their tasks as thoroughly as Will was performing his.

Hating to admit it, she acknowledged her

admiration for the way the TBI handled things, with expertise and organization, and every resource they needed. She had seen J.D. at work a couple of times, and he was the same way. In fact, she had toyed with the idea of joining the TBI, maybe in their behavioral science unit, but had put it on the back burner for now. She felt she did her job well, had received commendations, and would probably be a good candidate to transfer to another agency. If she paid attention to Will and the other state investigators, maybe this case would be a good tryout, just to see how she'd fit in. So far, none of them had acted overbearing and condescending, at least not much, but that might be because she was J.D.'s sister. There were more cameras focused on the sweep of the backyard in the grassy space below the pool and garden, others in the trees pointed down at various sections of the brick wall protecting the Lockhart property. She saw Jasper in one, sleeping in a flower bed and smashing the pansies. Uh-oh. Unfortunately, there were no cameras trained directly on the swimming pool. Too bad. Her guess was the judge liked to cavort and skinny-dip there with his paid sleazy companion and didn't want the missus to enjoy the video of their shenanigans. If they got lucky, one of the cameras had caught the movements of the killer.

"These cameras are all motion-activated and set to run together. For our review, I'm going to set them to stop and wait if any one camera picks up movement," Will told her, fully concentrating on the controls. "I'm going to set the start time to six o'clock a.m. yesterday."

Julia leaned down close behind Will and watched over his shoulder as the videos fast-forwarded, stopping periodically at brief appearances of the judge and Maria going in and out of the house. No one else showed up until around eleven thirty p.m. when a vehicle turned in at the front gate.

"That's a Lincoln, right?"

"Brand-new model," Will replied, brows knit, not looking at Julia. "Silver-gray. Single passenger. Enter Ginger."

My my, but Will Brannock was quite the professional when on a case. Didn't waste words, didn't even speak in complete sentences. Just short and pertinent phrases. A verbal slam-bam-thank-you-ma'am. Gone was the joking, smiley guy facetiously asking her to name state capitals. The Serious Detective was now on the clock. Truth was, that was a good thing; this was somber business. Will was a professional. She admired the way he was leading the investigation.

Refocusing her attention on the monitors, from one camera she saw the car stop at the front gate. Then another picked up their purported Ginger rolling down her window and smiling lasciviously up into the camera lens. She was a female, all right, and yes, about as female as you can get: very pretty young girl, long, coppery hair flowing in loose curls sprayed to look soft, and a low-cut gold dress that would win an Academy Award for Best Obscene Gown and which showed a lot more of Ginger's goodies than most people wanted to see, especially Julia. Will might have a different response to that stimulus, but he wasn't drooling on the keyboard, so she guessed he wasn't overly interested in Ginger's impressive six-inch cleavage. Will was on point, all right.

Julia watched the mystery woman punch the buttons on the security box. She kept smiling sexily up at the camera, certainly knowing exactly where it was. Her full lips were painted scarlet, of course, and her eyes were all smoky with black eye shadow and mascara. She said something into the microphone, which they couldn't hear, but it was highly provocative; count on it. Last but not least, Busty Belle blew a kiss to whoever had answered the call up at the house. Julia hoped she didn't pull down her top and show her boobs, just to spread some icing on her sexy little cake.

"Looks like the judge liked to order out for dessert," she said to Will.

"Yeah. It appears Ginger knows her way around this place pretty damn well. She's a regular, all right. We need to get her in for questioning."

Julia watched as the girl waited for the gate to open, and then drove on through. "Hey, Will, zoom in on the license plate. That would simplify finding her."

Will punched some buttons, stopping the image of the vehicle just before it left the frame, and hit another button. The Tennessee license plate appeared on the monitor. Turning to look back at Julia, he said, "This surveillance panel is something else. I know this security company. It's out of Atlanta. They monitor these systems from their home base and call in the authorities if any alarms are set off."

Julia picked up the phone on the desk and pressed the phone-log button. She punched through the list of calls. "No call came in to ask if the judge was okay, but we need to interview the security company and find out if there have been any security alerts in the last couple of months. As clean as this scene looks, the perp might have been casing the place for weeks."

"Right." Will was jotting the license number down on a notepad. Pulling out his cell phone, he said, "I'll get Quantico to check out this plate and then I'll put a call in to the security company. Go ahead, run the tapes. Yell if anything else comes up."

Julia watched him walk out into the library, already punching numbers on his cell phone. She could hear him talking as the monitors stopped again and the woman got out of the Lincoln underneath the side porte cochere. Her skirt was very short, twelve inches at the most, and her red heels were almost that high. She was an obliging call girl, out to do her duty, by hook or by crook. The woman climbed the steps on those ridiculous spike heels. How, Julia couldn't imagine. It must be like walking on two reinforced ballpoint pens.

Ginger looked directly into the camera at the side door and made some very suggestive movements with her mouth. She obviously thought that her judicial client was working the monitors. She looked extremely relaxed and comfortable, even eager to get her particular brand of show on the road. Oh yes, she'd been out to visit Lockhart before, probably plenty of times, and probably every time Mrs. Lockhart was enjoying her mama's balmy weather way down yonder in N'Orleans.

"The number traced out to the Elite Escort Service. The address is downtown, near the river, I think."

"Well, surprise, surprise. Maybe we ought to pay them a quick visit. See how many pretty women we can run in tonight."

That got a grin out of Serious Will. "The security company got no alerts or calls last night, only a couple in the last six months—once when squirrels got into the cameras. Another time, Mrs. Lockhart's dogs messed with a camera wire. They're concerned over the lapse in this system."

"Well, duh. I'd say they've got a major breach of security here."

Will returned his gaze to the monitors. "Okay, let's sit down and watch the surveillance all the way through. Odds are we'll get a glimpse of the killer. I hope to hell we will."

Julia sat down in the other swivel chair. No one else appeared on the films, not even a dark-cloaked figure lurking around in the shadows, which was probably exactly what the killer did. "It looks like the call girl's the only lead we've got."

Will nodded and pulled out his cell. "Right. Let's give them a call. Get her full name."

"Give me the number."

Will stood back, handed her his phone, and watched her dial the number. She hit speaker phone so he could listen in. Two rings and then a husky come-hither-sucker female voice came on the line. "Elite Escort Service. How may we help you?"

"This is Detective Julia Cass at the Chattanooga Police Department." Her own title sounded strange rolling off her tongue; she'd said Nashville PD for so long. But it was the first day she'd used it out loud, so there you go. "I need to speak to whoever is in charge."

Loaded silence. "May I tell her what this is all about?"

"It's about a joint TBI and CPD murder investigation. I'm sorry, that's all I can tell you at this time."

"Oh shit. I mean, one moment, please."

Several minutes later, a different female voice answered. Billy Goat Gruff, as if she had smoked three packs a day since she was two. "This is Donatella Casey. I'm the owner of Elite. How may I help you?"

"You can help me by telling me which one of your girls serviced Judge Lucien Lockhart last night."

"I'm not sure I know what you mean."

"Ms. Casey, please don't play games with me. You either cooperate or we'll have to come down there and take you downtown for questioning."

Donatella was suddenly eager-beaver agreeable. "Her name is Ginger. She won't be available until tomorrow morning."

"Ginger who?"

"Ginger Jones."

"Where is she now?"

"She's in Charlotte for a party. She'll be there overnight."

Surprise, surprise, Julia thought. "We need to see her first thing in the morning."

"All right. I'll arrange it. Is she in trouble, Detective?"

"We'll need to talk to you, too, Ms. Casey."

"I'll be here."

"Tell Ginger it wouldn't be wise to try to skip out on us."

"Oh, she won't. I'll see to it."

"We'll be there at eight o'clock sharp."

Julia hung up the phone and smiled at Will. "Okay, Brannock, we can talk to her tomorrow morning. Hope eight's not too early to drag yourself out of bed." She started to make a crack about his redheaded "friend" but decided against it. He wasn't in such a jovial mood anymore. But neither was she.

"Good, that'll give us time to go over the videos for the last two weeks. I'll take half and you can take half. Do you have the equipment to play these kinds of DVDs?"

"I have a laptop." Julia grimaced as he handed her a handful of DVDs. "Great, I do love the movies."

Will smiled. "Then you're in luck. Have fun tonight."

"Same to you, Special Agent."

J.D. Cass didn't make it home to his rental house on Signal Mountain until almost six o'clock. If Julia was already there, he hoped he wasn't in the doghouse with her for not picking her up himself. God knows, he'd made her wait often enough when she was a young kid and he was responsible for her upbringing. He regretted that sometimes, now that he was older and had a teenage daughter to raise. Zoe was a handful, a lot more headstrong than Julia had ever been. But now, now that he had Audrey Sherrod in his

66

life, everything was better than he ever could have dreamed. Even his daughter was behaving herself, following Audrey's very ladylike example.

Smiling, he realized that he was ultra-eager to see Julia. Until he'd met up with her when she was in town to interview for the CPD detective position, he hadn't realized how much he'd missed his sister. In the last couple of years, they'd had just a time or two together. It had been way too long. They called on birthdays and holidays, of course, but no long talks, no quality time together. He'd been shocked when Julia told him of her decision to relocate to Chattanooga, but he couldn't have been more pleased. He wanted her around. He wanted her to be part of his new life. Now that he'd met Audrey, he hungered for a close-knit family, for a normal life for him and Zoe and Julia. He entered the kitchen from the garage and dropped his keys on the counter.

"Well, it's about time you got here, J.D.," complained Zoe, from where she was sprawled out with her iPod on the living room couch. "Where's Aunt Julia? I thought she'd be here by now. I made a Roman-style pizza with all fresh ingredients. It's Audrey's recipe, so it ought to be really, really awesome!"

"Good idea. And I don't know where she is."

"You said you were going to pick her up. What, did you stand her up? Like you used to do me?"

Zoe had not yet forgotten that J.D. often put

his work before her. He was a cop; it was going to happen from time to time. But now, Audrey was usually there to fill in for him, which had ended a lot of the animosity between him and Zoe. She loved being with Audrey, anyway. But not as much as he enjoyed it. He looked forward to getting her back in bed as soon as he had the opportunity.

"Will picked her up for me. I couldn't leave the criminal court. Judge's orders."

"You should've called Audrey and me. We could've gone out to get her."

"You were at school. And Audrey's got a successful grief-counseling practice. She can't just drop everything the minute I call. She had a full day of appointments."

"Why isn't she coming tonight?" Zoe complained. "I haven't seen her in two whole days."

"She's having dinner with her father. Just the two of them."

"Really? Why? I thought they didn't get along." Zoe rushed on without waiting for his answer. "Is Aunt Julia pissed off that you didn't come pick her up? It really sucks that you sent a complete stranger out to get her on her first day in town." She suddenly smiled. "Even if he's more smokin' hot than about any guy I know. My girlfriends think he looks a little like Edward. Dreamy." Zoe clasped her hands together and seemed to go into some kind of rapture.

"And Edward is?"

"Dad, don't you know anything?" Zoe shook her head, shocked and disbelieving and displaying it with the drama that only a fifteen-year-old girl could sustain. "*Twilight*? Bella? True love?"

"Oh yeah, that's the vampire thing you're always watching on video? What is it? Some kind of werewolves or bears in the woods, right?"

"Dad, Dad, you're so old sometimes. *Twilight* is absolutely sublime."

J.D. decided to ignore the *old* part. At least she was paying attention in English class. He'd never heard her use the word *sublime* in a sentence before. But he'd watch that movie, if he could stomach it, just to gain her approval. Maybe Audrey would watch it with him. She liked romantic stuff.

On the other hand, he didn't like Zoe noticing older men or calling them hot, or even knowing they were hot. He hesitated, then decided to let that pass, too. He didn't want Julia to walk into a big dad-daughter tiff. "I got hold of Julia about an hour ago. And she's not mad at all. She's already been assigned a case. She said she'll probably be out here around six thirty or seven."

Frowning, Zoe went back to her iPod and called up whatever pop band she was listening to at the moment. Used to be some idiotic group called Black Eyed Peas, of all things. Now it was probably that boy with the weird hairdo that she liked—the Biebs, or whatever his name was. He made Zoe and her friends swoon, according to Zoe. But Zoe was not sneaking out with boys, or sassing him much—yet another thing he could thank Audrey for. Speaking of Audrey, he hoped it went well tonight at her dinner. She and her dad had had a rocky relationship for many years, which had caused her so much anguish, but this private dinner was a step in the right direction. How anybody could push away a woman as sweet as Audrey, J.D. couldn't imagine.

Tired from sitting around for hours waiting to be called to the stand, he jerked off his tie and unhooked his hip holster. Hell, it was worse twiddling his thumbs all day than working on a case. He placed his weapon in the gun safe in his bedroom closet, and then relaxed in his worn leather recliner in front of the television set. About an hour later, a knock at the door pulled Zoe up from her loud-music morass. She ran to the door with J.D. right behind her.

"Aunt Julia! It's so cool you're staying with us! I made pizza! All by myself!"

His sister embraced her niece and smiled at J.D. over Zoe's shoulder. Jasper was jumping around barking, and Zoe dropped down on her knees and gave the dog a big hug. His tail was beating the floor like crazy. Next thing J.D. knew, Zoe was going to want a bloodhound, too.

"I'm glad to finally be here," Julia was saying

to Zoe. "Wow, you look awesome in that outfit."

J.D. examined his daughter's outfit, not really having noticed what she had on. Purple capris and a loose pink top that had some red sequins and stuff all over it. He guessed it was all right—at least she didn't wear those too-short tops and shorter-than-short denim skirts anymore. Fact is, now that she was dressing a little more conservatively, he thought Zoe always looked pretty. Even first thing out of bed in the morning when she was so grouchy. She was a gorgeous girl. Same went for Julia. In fact, they looked a lot alike. His daughter seemed to take more after Julia than she did her father. He watched Julia hold his daughter back by the shoulders and admire the lopsided red, sequined heart on the front of her shirt. "I love your top, Zoe. Where'd you get it?"

"There's this little store in the mall that has the most awesome stuff like this. Me and my friends love to hang out there. It's the coolest place in town."

Zoe was smiling, very happy; all three of them were. Zoe and Julia had hit it off big-time since Julia had visited them a couple of times for her interview process at Chattanooga PD. "I can't believe you're really going to live here in town, Aunt Julia. That's so cool. We can do things together all the time. Go to the mall, walk Jasper, go to Audrey's gym and work out. You and Audrey and me."

"Thanks a lot," J.D. said.

"You're not a girl, J.D. And you know you're pretty much a stick-in-the-mud."

Zoe laughed at Julia's remark. J.D. walked over and gave Julia a big hug. "So I'm a stick-in-the-mud—that's what you think?"

" 'Fraid so, but a lovable stick-in-the-mud."

They all laughed. J.D. sat down. "Well, welcome to Chattanooga. Sorry again about not picking you up. That blasted trial is driving me up a wall. I'm next up, then no, never mind, we've got to put so-and-so on first. It's crazy over there. Lots of recesses and bench conferences. Tam and I have been sitting around all day with little to show for it, except for heartburn."

He listened to the two girls talk for a minute or two, and then he had to ask. "So, Jules, how'd you like Will?"

"He's okay, I guess. Pretty funny guy, made me laugh, at least until we got to the crime scene. Then he turned into Mr. Solemn."

J.D. said, "That sounds like you."

Zoe seemed to quiver all over. "OMG, Will's such a hottie. Presley and all the girls think he's McDreamy. Everybody thinks so, even Audrey."

J.D. frowned. "Audrey thinks that?"

Julia and Zoe laughed at him. Zoe said, "Yeah, J.D., but then she said nobody's as handsome as you."

"Ooooh," Julia teased him. "You've got her

crazy about you already. What do all your other girlfriends say?"

"He doesn't have any other girls, Aunt Julia. Can you believe that? Even that awful Holly that he used to hook up with all the time. Audrey's got him hook, line, and sinker. Even he admits it."

J.D. felt sheepish, verging on silly, but everything Zoe said was true. Audrey was not like any other woman he'd ever met. Still, he didn't like these fifteen-year-olds talking that way about older men. "Where have your friends even seen Will Brannock, Zoe?"

"Oh, here and there, when you bring him around with you. Like you did on your last case." She grinned mischievously. "Actually, they all think you're hot, too."

"Well, then that's okay."

Zoe and Julia laughed together again. He loved to hear them laugh. He loved to see them together. Happy as a lark, Zoe raced off to the kitchen. "I'm gonna put in the pizza. It's got everything on it that I could think of. Hope you like it, Julia!"

"Oh, I will. I like everything. Ask your dad."

After Zoe was gone and happily clanking around in the kitchen, Julia and J.D. shared a smile. "She's just a great kid, J.D. I still can't believe you have a teenage daughter. Man, what a surprise that was."

"Yeah, tell me about it." He'd had a casual affair with Zoe's mother but hadn't known she had

had his baby until she was dying of cancer years later and called him about his paternity. After she died, Zoe came to live with him. It was rocky as hell at first, but things were good now. "She's really special, Julia." It had taken awhile to admit that, but now—now he didn't know how he got along without her, teenage angst, the Biebs, and all.

"So the trial's going badly?" Julia asked, unhooking her hip holster and placing it on the coffee table. She sank down on the couch and waited for his answer.

"Not so much that. It's pretty much open-and-shut. Just long and drawn out."

"Did Will tell you anything about the new case we got today?"

"No." J.D. paused. "Wait. What do you mean, *we*?"

He sat down on the couch beside her, and Julia kicked off her shoes and leaned back against the cushions. She sighed. She looked a little tired, but as pretty as ever. Again he marveled at the resemblance between Julia and Zoe. Now he could see it more than ever. All that long, straight black hair. Julia was taller, around five seven, but Zoe would probably be that tall or taller once she reached adulthood. Julia's eyes were large and golden brown and intelligent, but at the moment, they looked worried.

"Chief Mullins assigned me as Will Brannock's liaison. Tam will come aboard as soon as she's free. It's a bad one, J.D. A federal judge was murdered, right in his own house."

"I knew a murder case came up today, but Phil Hayes didn't have time to fill me in on the details. What judge are you talking about?"

"Lucien Lockhart. You know him, right? I remember your mentioning him."

J.D.'s frown darkened. "Can't say I'm surprised somebody finally got him. He's about as corrupt as they come."

"He's known for corruption?"

"He's known for worse than that. There are rumors of collusion, inside jury tampering, all kinds of illegal things."

"Well, that's interesting. You're not the first one to mention that."

"Hey, in there," called Zoe's excited voice. "Do you like black olives, Julia? Say yes!"

"Black and green both," Julia called out, winking at J.D. "Love 'em!"

"You got it! I do, too!"

Julia glanced around the living room. "So where's Audrey tonight? Working late?"

"She had a family obligation. She said to tell you she was sorry she couldn't be here to welcome you to town."

"So I take it you're still all gaga over her?"

"That makes me sound ridiculous."

"I think it makes you sound sweet."

"Oh God, that's even worse."

J.D. couldn't help but think that there was a lot of smiling going on since Julia got there. "Seriously, Jules, I'm so glad to see you. It'll be great to have you around all the time. A lot better than only seeing you at Christmas now and then, or playing phone tag the rest of the year."

"Yeah. I needed a change."

J.D. knew what Julia was talking about. She'd lost her partner three years ago. Bobby Crismon had been killed in action, right in front of Julia. The two of them had been surprised by an enraged husband high on meth. She'd had a tough time dealing with it. She was better now, looked better and felt better, and he hoped this change of scenery would really help her. Maybe someday she'd sit down with Audrey and talk it through.

"You uncover any leads yet?" he asked Julia about her new case. She was a hell of a good detective; had won more commendations than he had. He was proud of her and let everybody know it.

"Lockhart had a call girl out at his house last night. Brannock and I are going to interview her first thing tomorrow morning."

"Man alive, you've had to hit the ground running. How about this? You can have my bedroom while you're here. I'll sleep on the couch."

"She can sleep in my room," yelled Zoe from the kitchen.

"Oh yeah, I forgot to tell you. Zoe has ears like an elephant," J.D. said in exasperation.

"I heard that," Zoe yelled, and then they heard her laughing at him.

"See?"

Julia smiled. "I might crash here for a day or two, but you really don't have room for me. Zoe needs her privacy here and so do you. I've got a friend in Chattanooga who lives somewhere out on the Tennessee River. She has an apartment she'll let me live in until I get my feet on the ground and decide what I want to do. No charge, either."

"Who's that?"

"Cathy Bateman. Her last name's Axelrod, now that she's remarried. You remember her, don't you? I got to know her when we went through K-9 training in Nashville together. We got to be really close friends. She and Charlie Sinclair both handled the K-9 units in this area, so I've already got some good friends living around here."

"Well, you're welcome to stay here. You know that, don't you? We'd love it." J.D. hesitated and lowered his voice. "I may not be living here much longer. In fact, you could end up getting this place, if you're interested."

Julia smiled knowingly. "Why not? As if I didn't know."

J.D. grinned, too. "She's the one, Jules. I never thought I'd say that again, not after my divorce, but she's an angel."

"You're good together. I could see that the night she had us all over to her place for dinner."

"So hurry up and pop the question, J.D.," yelled Zoe from the kitchen. "You big scaredy-cat!"

Julia laughed and J.D. shook his head. Zoe was something else.

"Pizza's ready," Zoe announced from the doorway. "And I made homemade coconut cream pie for dessert. Audrey makes the best coconut cream pie in the whole world, and I got her to give me the recipe. She gave me the pizza one, too, Julia. She's teaching me to cook. Did I tell you?"

J.D. followed his sister and daughter into the kitchen. His own stomach was growling, and Zoe's cooking did smell good. Now he had all the women he loved in one town, where he could take care of them and make sure they were all safe and sound. Life was good—it sure was, and getting better all the time.

Chapter 4

Pulling up at the entrance of his driveway, Will Brannock swiped the card on his security box and waited impatiently while the barred gate slowly opened. Despite the fact that he was dead tired, he didn't expect to get much sleep. Not that insomnia was anything out of the norm. He drove the Hummer up the long, black-topped driveway to the house, wondering what Julia Cass would think of his place. The big house on Chickamauga Lake was his one refuge. He loved living on the water—any kind of water, river or ocean or lake, just so he could take a boat out and get away. Water skiing and fishing and swimming, all of it. He had the money to possess this kind of private sanctuary where he could be alone, relax, rest, and rejuvenate, without constantly having to watch his back. Once he'd checked for intruders, that is.

He'd worked with Julia Cass all day long, and if he ever decided to bring her around, which he probably wouldn't, he expected she would wonder how he afforded this kind of place. But so what? What did he care what she thought? Why was he even thinking about her being there? Or thinking about her at all? Now that they were temporary partners, their relationship was strictly professional. Julia Cass would never pass through his gate. None of his friends or colleagues had ever been here, not even J.D. And that was for their own good. Nobody else was going to die because of him and the vicious people who wanted to see him dead.

As soon as he reached his large three-car garage, he searched for pry marks and glanced up at the windows for movement, but saw nothing out of the ordinary. Turning his head and waiting as the garage door rolled up, he gazed out over the lake, looking for any suspicious boats, any flash of light that might indicate binoculars or a high-powered scope. After all these years, he was still a hunted man. It paid to be cautious and always on the alert.

Inside the garage, he pressed the button and waited for the door to come down and lock into place before getting out of the truck. He stepped down from the cab, checked the lock on the inside door for signs of tampering, and then entered the back hallway. He listened for any sounds but heard only the loud clicking of claws on the red-oak hardwood floor as his three dogs scrambled to get to him. Somebody had dumped two of them out on the road near his gate and he'd picked them up, fed them, and they'd been with him ever since. Spot and Rover, both lovable little twelve-inch beagles, were always glad to see him, no matter what kind of mood he was in. Kneeling down, he petted the hysterically baying beagles, rubbing their ears the same as he had Julia's beloved Jasper. He knew how she felt. He loved his dogs, too.

At the end of the hallway, his other dog finally showed up. His mother's haughty and fairly maniacal white miniature poodle. Afraid it would be bitten by a scorpion at her desert home, she had asked Will to keep the prissy little dog where she'd be safe. The other dogs tolerated her and so did Will, but just barely. The shrill yap sometimes put him on edge, but she was a good watchdog because she hated everything and was more than vocal about it. As if she was doing him a favor, she ambled up to him and waited for him to acknowledge her. He picked her up, his palm cradling her little chest, and she pushed up against his fingers when he scratched her ears.

After a moment, he put her down and checked out the house, the three canines clicking around in his wake. Once he was satisfied there were no signs of illegal entry or intruders, he unbuckled his hip holster and placed it and his nine-millimeter on the brown granite island in the large kitchen. Floor-to-ceiling windows overlooked the pool and the lake beyond. He loved it out here, where it was quiet and wooded and private, where he could think and safely let down his guard.

Inside the fridge he found some deli ham and cheese left over from the night before, and he made a sandwich, slopped on enough mayo to make it worth it, pulled out a Bud Light, and took the food out on one of the decks overlooking the lake. Dusk was falling. The heat was letting up some, now that the sun was down. He slapped at a mosquito on his arm; they'd be out in full force soon. His orders were to form a task force. He needed to think about the case, think about what kind of person could have committed such a horrendous crime. Severed tongues were not run-of-the-mill mutilations. This was a case that was going to be messy, dangerous, and he had a distinct feeling they'd only found the first body out of God-knows-how-many to come.

Again he found his thoughts wandering back to Julia Cass. The way he understood it, she'd been lead on most of her cases in Nashville, but she'd pulled back today, giving him complete authority and waiting for his direction. They could work well together. He liked women like her, women who were cool and calm and smart. The fact that she looked like Catherine Zeta-Jones didn't hurt, either. And hell, a woman who liked dogs was always a good thing. He'd always had dogs himself. He caressed Spot's head. Rover was on the deck with his tennis ball, waiting for him to throw it. Both were good little watchdogs and loved to run the rabbits and squirrels in the woods on his property, and the poodle yipped and carried on if Will looked at her sideways. Here in Tennessee, they were his only family.

Right now he had to think about the murder. Lockhart was a federal judge, for God's sake, and he'd been mutilated in his own backyard in the middle of an exclusive neighborhood of Chattanooga. This was no simple break-in and murder, no house invasion, no robbery gone wrong. This was a targeted killing with a definite message put out for investigators to decipher.

Half a tongue balancing stacks of dimes on a scale. *ONE* written in blood. They had to figure out what it all meant. Julia Cass already thought it was the work of a serial killer. Will agreed.

Fetching a second beer, he walked through the quiet house to his computer room and sat down just as the security lights flared on all around his property. Maybe this wasn't the first case in which a killer used a severed tongue, dimes, and scales as his MO. He needed to search all the FBI databases, which the TBI had access to, and see what he could turn up. It wouldn't be hard to find another murderer this depraved, here or any-where else in the world. He took off his Reeboks, popped the beer tab, and keyed in the web addresses for the Quantico databases. This was going to be a long night, and so were a lot of others before they caught this guy.

The Elite Escort Service didn't look so elite to Julia Cass. Will had picked her up at her brother's house at seven thirty on the dot. Now that his red-haired, clingy lovebird had flown the coop, he was prompt personified. She had been ready for an hour before he got there, champing at the bit, even. Raring to go was putting it mildly. Unfortunately, it looked like the so-called classy call girls weren't so classy after all. Ginger and her ilk were apparently housed in a circa 1930 shabby redbrick warehouse in a deserted industrial area near downtown. She leaned forward and looked up at the building's facade. Faded yellow letters across the second floor spelled out Smith Toilet Company. Wow, what more could a hooker ask for.

She glanced over at Will, who hadn't said two words to her on the way downtown. He was dressed today in a very nice charcoal-gray suit—expensive, Julia would say, if she knew anything about men's designer suits, which she didn't. The crisp white shirt, blue silk tie, and spit-shined black shoes didn't look too shabby, either. He looked good, of course, but somehow she liked him better yesterday in his Alabama T-shirt and jeans. She had on black pants and a white polo shirt. Both of them had buckled on their matching guns. Will had a brown leather hip holster. She did, too. They were quickly becoming *Starsky and Hutch* and a good title for a TV movie: *Twin Guns Visit Ginger the Call Girl.*

"I spent most of the night going through law enforcement databases," Will said, shoving the gearshift into park. "I found no reference to other cases that involved severed tongues and dimes and scales. At least, not all three in the same case."

"I spent time on the Internet, too. Nada. Tongues, maybe. But the dimes and scales are a unique twist. Our perp likes to be different."

Will leaned against the steering wheel and stared at her. He was so serious, no kidding around, no flirting. *Would the real Will Brannock please stand up?* Julia thought.

"Our gang database said that cutting out tongues is a practice of several U.S. gangs," Will continued. "One of them operates out of Chattanooga. The Battle Street Ten gang. You ever heard of them? They are known to cut out tongues as retribution for betrayal."

"Yeah, I've heard of them. So you're thinking this is gang-related? What about the dimes and scales?"

"Who knows? Criminal gangs adopt all kinds of weird practices and initiation rites. I think it could be their work. Maybe they were sending a message."

"Want me to look into CPD's records of gang activity here in the city? See if I can come up with a name known for mutilations?"

"Yes," Will said. "When we talked to Maria Bota yesterday, did you notice the tat on her left ring finger?"

"No, I didn't see any tattoos. Is it a trademark?"

"Yes, a triangle made of six red dots."

"And the significance?"

"Any female wearing that symbol is the initiated woman of a Battle Street Ten gang member."

"So we've already got a definite tie to that gang."

"Damn right."

"So we interview her again?"

"You got it."

Traffic was nonexistent in the warehouse district, probably because everybody in Chattanooga had enough sense not to come down there. They got out of the Hummer and crossed the narrow street. Julia pressed a doorbell affixed to a heavy, black metal door that looked like a horde of Mongols had tried to ram their way through it.

"They don't appear to be spending much money on curb appeal. Maybe a potted philodendron would be more friendly, or cheerful yellow paint on the security bars," Will said, a bit of yesterday's jokester shining through for almost one second. They both glanced up at the barred windows on all five stories. An iron fire escape clung to the front like some giant insect's skeletal remains. Escape hatch for fleeing floozies?

"I suspect they don't get many customers down here," Julia replied. "These girls probably prefer to meet their beaus elsewhere. I worked vice awhile in Nashville. I know."

Will grinned down at her. "Nab any Nashville political types?"

"A few. Most of those guys are way too careful. I never saw a politico who risked having a prostitute come to his house, like our naughty judge. Most of the men we ran into met their paid dates in ritzy hotels."

"Judge Lockhart must have felt pretty confident in his power."

Julia said, "His first mistake."

"Yeah, and his last."

A familiar, raspy, deep female voice drawled out from the speaker next to the doorbell, "Yes, who is it?"

Will leaned close. "TBI Special Agent Brannock and CPD Detective Cass. We spoke on the phone yesterday."

"Just a minute, please."

It was more like five minutes before the latch released from the inside, and Will pulled the door open. He looked inside for lurking armed assailants, and then stood back and allowed Julia to precede him. She did so, but warily. The stairway inside was steep and narrow and unadorned, with banisters affixed to both walls. The door at the top of the steps was closed, but it opened when they were about halfway up.

"Hello. I'm Ms. Daisy. Please follow me."

Julia felt as if she were in some kind of Tom Cruise spy movie. She stepped out into a hallway and watched Will come out behind her doing a James Bond impression, casing the room as if they were about to be attacked by the aforementioned Mongol horsemen at any moment. Charming Ms. Daisy was also in character. Judging by her attire, she was modeling herself on Daisy Duke of Jessica Simpson fame: wavy bleached blond hair, long tanned legs, red spike heels, and impossibly white teeth. Her short shorts were denim and even shorter than required to work there, and she had on a halter top at least two sizes too small. Will Brannock seemed to notice. Will Brannock seemed to like what he saw.

Will spoke first, all business after his first thorough appraisal. "Hello, Ms. Daisy. We'd like to speak with Ginger, if she's available."

"Yeah, I know. She's waiting in the back."

"Are you employed here, too?" Julia asked her.

Ms. Daisy laughed, a little trill that sounded like a robin in a Disney movie. "Oh no, I'm not an escort. Donatella says I'm too young and flighty for our wealthy clientele, but Ginger's teaching me to be like her."

"What do you do here then?"

"I answer the phone and take appointments." She looked funny for a moment, then added, "Everything's on the up-and-up here, you know. Purely legal. No laws are being broken or nothing."

"Of course," said Will.

Yeah, of course, thought Julia.

They followed behind Daisy Mae, who did a sort of prissy sashay down the white-carpeted, wainscoted hallway. Oh yes, Ginger was working her charm school on Daisy, all right. Upstairs, though, it looked like an elegant and lovely apartment with taupe walls and white woodwork. Track lighting on the ceiling shone down on various reproductions of modern art with all its cubes and staring eyes and misplaced body parts. No photographs of Ginger and her clients having a good party, though.

"Here you go, Officers," said Ms. Daisy.

Again Will stood back, plenty polite today, it seemed. Julia had a feeling that behind that charming smile of his, he was planning an FBI raid on the Elite girls in a couple of hours. On the other hand, he was being quite a gentleman now that they were inside. Julia preferred gentlemen, so it was fine by her.

As it turned out, in person Ginger was long and lean and beautiful and glamorous. She was reclining on a dark green velvet settee in front of a barred window, probably so the sunlight would turn her hair into that fiery red-gold corona for her visitors. She was a looker, all right. When they approached her, she unwound some very long bare legs and stood up. She had on a short black skirt and an emerald-green blouse that would have been alluring if it wasn't completely see-through. She was barefoot, but a pair of purple bejeweled sandals was lying beside her lounging couch.

"Hello, I'm Ginger Jones. Donatella said you wanted to talk with me."

Will said, "That's right. I'm Special Agent Will Brannock and this is Detective Julia Cass."

They both flipped open their badges and proved it.

"I know who you are," she said offhandedly. "I had nothing to do with Lucien's death, if that's what you're here about. He was alive when I left. Look on his surveillance cameras if you don't believe me."

"Mind if we sit down?" Julia asked courteously.

"Please do," Ginger said just as courteously, if not more so. She gestured at the matching couch across from her. They sat, and Ginger made no secret of her interest in Will and lack of interest in Julia. She watched him out of big, exotically lined blue eyes. Julia waited for her to bat them provocatively, but Ginger just stared at him as if he were a tall hot fudge sundae, waiting and drooling and moistening her already übermoist red lips.

Will was not returning the lust, thank goodness. "Thank you for seeing us, Ms. Jones. We believe you're the last person to see Judge Lockhart alive. We need you to tell us everything you can about the time you spent there."

Ginger's smooth brow furrowed, but most prettily. "I'm so sorry this happened to poor Lucien. He was a super-nice man who treated me with respect. We were friends. He tipped me good money."

But of course, he did, Julia thought, but she said, "Is he a frequent customer of yours?"

"Yes, ma'am."

That *ma'am* made Julia feel a bit long in the tooth, but maybe Ginger Jones was just a very polite type of gal. "How often?"

Will leaned back, apparently interested in letting Julia conduct the interview. Julia was pleased to oblige.

Ginger replied, "Oh, once every couple of weeks, depending on what was going on with him. He was a busy man."

"Did he act any differently this time? Get any calls or uninvited visitors? Act nervous?"

Shaking her head, Ginger gave a little shrug. "Not really. We had dinner. Talked. You know, a regular evening. We didn't go out, though. We stayed at his house in Woodstone Circle the whole night."

"Do you usually go out?" Will interjected.

"Not really. Sometimes he arranged a private room in a restaurant or hotel where we would meet. He was considerate of his wife in that way."

Yeah, real considerate, Julia thought.

"What about his wife? Was she aware of his relationship with you?"

"Uh-uh. He was careful. Said she was very jealous and would freak out if she caught him."

"Do you think she knew?"

"I can't imagine how she didn't. Their maid was there every time I came and went."

"Maria?"

"That's right. She sometimes cooked dinner for us. She makes wonderful fajitas."

Ginger didn't look like a woman who succumbed to fajitas very often, or any other kind of nourishment. She looked to be around five foot ten and weighed maybe a hundred and ten pounds, tops. Runway material.

Brannock leaned forward, voice intense. "Did the judge ever tell you that he'd been threatened?"

Flipping her long, coppery hair around like she had a hornet caught in it, Ginger answered, "Oh yes, all the time. Bad guys were always threatening to get him for throwing them in jail. I never thought they would, though. Is that what happened? Somebody paid him back?"

"That's what we're trying to find out," Julia informed her, still courteous. "Now, Ms. Jones, I'm going to be perfectly frank here. We know what you do. We know it's against the law. We're not here about that right now, but it could come to that if you don't tell us exactly what we need to know. What do you know about Judge Lockhart that will help us find his killer?"

Ginger looked at Julia, then at an expressionless Will Brannock, then down at her hands. "He was into some kinky stuff. Nothing really dangerous but not the run-of-the-mill stuff, you know."

Will and Julia waited. Julia had found that sometimes staying quiet and staring silently at the witness opened them up to dialogue more than badgering did. Of course, badgering had its place, too.

"He liked to handcuff me to the bed, tickle me, you know, with feathers and little fuzzy tassels."

Julia glanced at Will. He remained stone-faced. So she did, too.

"And sometimes he wanted me to dress up like Cinderella. Go figure."

"Right," Julia said. "What time did you arrive?"

"Eleven thirty."

"And you left at?"

"Four thirty."

That all checked out with the cameras. "What was he doing when you left?"

"He had put on his bathing suit and was going to swim laps. He swam laps for exercise. He did sixty laps every morning. He was in pretty good shape for his age."

"Did you see Maria last night?" Julia asked.

"She cooked dinner before I got there. It was beef stew and sweet corn bread. Blackberry cobbler for dessert. Lucien loved all that kind of stuff."

Will asked, "After dinner did you see her?"

Ginger shook her head. "No. I guess she cleaned up the kitchen and then she went to her room out back. She has a little kid. He's a cute little thing. Sometimes the judge lets him swim in the pool with us."

Now that was an interesting development. "Who's the boy's father?"

"I have no idea. The judge never said. I think he took Maria in after she got in trouble about something in his courtroom. He was good about things like that. Real nice to people down on their luck. He helped me out once when I needed some quick cash."

Will glanced at Julia. She got his message loud and clear, leaned back, and let him take over the interview.

"Okay, Ginger. Tell me this. Did he mention anything or anyone who might have wanted to do him harm? Any specific defendant that had it in for him?"

"Like I said, he told me he had lots of enemies who didn't like his judgments. He usually just laughed it off. He was well protected for the most part—the dogs and the gate and the cameras. I guess he wasn't as safe as he thought."

"We didn't see any dogs on the premises."

"That's right. He told me they were with his wife in Louisiana."

Ginger ran her fingers through her hair. She certainly looked good for having had such a long night over in Charlotte. She carefully avoided their eyes, which told Julia right off that she knew more than she was letting on. She was probably debating whether or not to tell them.

Julia said, "If I were you, I'd go ahead and tell us whatever it is you're trying to hide right now."

Will and Ginger both looked at her.

Ginger did some sexy shrugging with her shoulders. "Oh, okay, he did mention that he'd had a stalker of sorts, somebody who was angry about one of his rulings."

"Who?"

"I don't remember the name. He didn't really go into it much. Just said he'd caught him following him a couple of times, but that it hadn't really amounted to anything. He didn't seem scared or anything."

"You do know it's very important for you to remember the name, don't you?" Will suggested, still being a gent.

That was the understatement of the year, but something told Julia that if Ginger knew, she'd tell them. Especially Will. Yes, whether Will knew it or not, his charmometer was turned on high and working big-time with Ginger.

"I know," Ginger said, leaning toward Will, and oh-so-earnest now. "Maybe if you give me your card, I can call you if I remember something."

Whether Will caught her meaning or not, Julia did. He retrieved a card and handed it to her without a boatload of urging. Ginger tucked it down the front of her blouse as an exclamation point to her Will-Brannock-come-and-get-it invitation. She smiled at him. Julia could almost read the card through the sheer fabric of Ginger's blouse.

They spent another thirty minutes with her, trying to exact more information, but she didn't give them anything else. She didn't remember if the judge told her what kind of car the stalker had, if it was a man or a woman, if it was recently or ten years ago. Maybe the judge had been tickling her too hard with Maria Bota's feather duster. Whatever, Julia didn't think Ginger had anything to do with the murder. Unless she had a jealous boyfriend, which she'd denied, and which her plain as day, *mucho* obnoxious flirtation with Will Brannock rather negated.

Chapter 5

Outside, in front of the battered black door, Will paused and looked down at Julia. "Well, what do you think of Ms. Ginger's story?"

"I hate to admit it," Julia replied, "but I think she likes you better than me."

"Why do you say that?"

"Umm, let me see. Maybe the drool wetting the front of her peek-a-boo blouse?"

"Oh, come on, Julia."

Before she could answer, Will felt his phone vibrate inside his breast pocket and quickly pulled it out.

Julia said, "Don't tell me. It's Ginger, missing you already."

Ignoring that, he listened intently as they started

across the empty street. As Julia rounded the front of the Hummer, he opened his door and braced a hand on the top. "Guess what? Iris Lockhart is home from her mama's house in the French Quarter and ready for us to interview her."

"Great," said Julia, stepping up and sliding into the passenger seat.

They took off and found their way with all due haste to Woodstone Circle.

Stopped at a red light, Will decided to give credit where credit was due. "You're extremely good at interrogation. I'm impressed."

Julia looked at him in surprise.

He shrugged and said, "I call a spade a spade. You did a good job with her. You got more out of her than I could have."

"Thanks, but I rather doubt that. Not judging by the way she was admiring your manliness. Unfortunately, she didn't seem to know much, except that you were going to be her favorite next client."

"It's not me. She's an escort. That's what they do."

Julia didn't respond. A block later, she said, "Do you really think Iris Lockhart is totally ignorant of her husband's infidelities? His fun times seemed pretty in-your-face to me."

"Yeah, I suspect she knows exactly what's going on. Some women will accept infidelity. Some won't." Will waited for a pickup truck to get out of his way, then took a right onto a down ramp. "Maybe she's hiding her head in the sand?"

"Or just an innocent little trusting soul?"

Will glanced at her. "Is there such a thing anymore?"

"That's a little cynical."

"I've been in this business a long time." Will glanced both ways and took another right. "Are you telling me you're not cynical after so many years working homicide?"

"I try not to be," Julia admitted. "Sometimes it's hard not to be, you know. I'll give you that. I've seen too many things I don't like to think about."

Will turned in time to catch the telling expression on Julia Cass's face. It was fleeting, but he saw enough to clue him in. She'd experienced something pretty bad in her past. He wondered what it was, and then he wondered if he really wanted to know. God knew he'd seen enough terrible things with his own two eyes. A mental picture of his little brother flitted across his mind, but he forced that awful memory down and locked it away, as he'd done a million times before. He no longer allowed himself to think about what had happened. He had a feeling that's exactly what Julia was doing, too. Right now. Apparently they both had their demons, but what experienced law enforcement officer didn't?

Twenty minutes later, they pulled up in the

driveway of the judge's big Scarlett O'Hara house. The crime scene crew was long gone, but the yellow police tape was still up. A white stretch limo sat under the porte cochere at the side door. The trunk was open, and a white-uniformed chauffeur was retrieving matching white luggage. A butler was waiting to carry it inside. There was no sign of Mrs. Lockhart.

Will found himself eager to interview the woman. He had a feeling that she just might know something that would give them the lead they needed. As he'd told Julia, she was a better investigator than he had expected. Why he hadn't had much confidence in her abilities puzzled him now. He guessed it was her youth, but then again, she wasn't that much younger than he was. Three or four years, at the most. He should have known she'd be good, with J.D. for a big brother.

Maybe it was the antagonism she'd shown him at first. She hadn't been exactly fall-all-over-him friendly when he first met her, but she'd loosened up quickly enough. She'd been serious today, but so had he. This crime was committed by a seriously disturbed psychopath. They had to find him before he did it again, because he was going to do it again. They were working together now, and they'd have to cooperate to get the job done. That's what was important to him at the moment. It seemed that was what was important to Julia, too.

"You want me to question Iris Lockhart?" he asked. "Or do you want to do it?"

"It's up to you. You're the boss." She smiled, and he marveled at how pretty she was. And those dimples. "You certainly do seem to have a way with the ladies."

Will studied her face a moment, looking for sarcasm, but couldn't see it. But he had a feeling she was jabbing him, just a little. She wasn't going to forget Pam Ford, not anytime soon.

"I'll start us off," he said. "Jump in whenever you want. We'll share. Just like with Ginger."

"Thanks. I'll do that. What do you know about the wife?"

"Not much. I've seen her on television with her husband a couple of times. She looked like a nice enough lady. She didn't say much, just stood there behind him and smiled."

"Don't they all?"

A short time later, Will knew he was dead wrong about the nice lady thing. Iris Lockhart was not a nice lady. Farthest thing from it. From the minute she entered the spacious room where they'd been deposited by an equally haughty butler, Iris looked down her long, aristocratic nose at them like they were two bedbugs crawling out of her thousand-thread-count sheets. Julia didn't look exactly pleased at the woman's demeanor. He had a feeling that Julia was not the kind of woman who'd just stand there and let somebody put her down. If and when Iris made the mistake of over-doing her obvious disdain for police officers, he might just enjoy sitting back and watching the fireworks.

At the moment, Iris Lockhart sat across from them in her giant, overdecorated, plush Lockhart living room. All white or off-white everything: chairs, walls, couches, fireplace, Iris's hair, Iris's skin, Iris's snowy linen pantsuit that probably cost at least a thousand dollars. Hell, he and Julia were the only spots of color in the whole damn place, meaning his blue tie and Julia's black pants. They sat side by side on a camelback cream brocade sofa that looked like nobody had pressed down on its springs since 1952. On her own spotless chaise longue, Iris cuddled ad nauseam her three miniature Pomeranians, all with lots of fluffy white hair and manicured poufs on their tails. The air-conditioning was set to about twenty degrees, the room icier than an Alaskan glacier, and Iris had ordered the gas logs turned on. She cooed at her canine babies for at least five or six minutes before she put cold blue eyes on Will and said, "Okay, what can I do for you, Officer?"

Will gave a sidelong glance at Julia Cass. She shared his disregard for the condescending woman; he could see it in those big, gold-brown eyes of hers. He decided to let her go for it.

Julia took the bait like a starving bass. "You are aware that your husband was murdered in this house, not twenty-four hours ago—right, Mrs. Lockhart?"

Iris looked rather annoyed—more than rather, actually. "Of course, I do. Chief Mullins was good enough to call me at my mother's house in New Orleans and let me know all the particulars. That's why I had to cut my holiday short."

"With all due respect, Mrs. Lockhart, you don't sound too torn up by the news of your husband's demise."

Mrs. Lockhart looked at Julia, very cold, very controlled, and very despicable. "My husband was a degenerate and a bastard, my dear detective. What was your name again? Cass, wasn't it? For your information, he enjoyed humiliating me and putting me through hell on earth for the entire thirty years we were married. Pardon me if I don't shed a single tear for that SOB. I'm better off without him. In fact, I'm glad he's dead. I've been praying for it for years."

Shocked speechless at first, both Will and Julia could only stare at her.

"You should be careful what you say, Mrs. Lockhart," Will suggested in a low tone. "What you just said might sound like a motive to law enforcement officers."

"I was in Louisiana, and I hosted a cocktail party for twelve of my dearest friends on the night that Lucien was murdered. They will all vouch for me, every single one of them, as will my mother's household staff and the caterers." She paused, kissed one of her dogs on the mouth, and seemed to enjoy the good and sloppy licking the animal gave her for the next few seconds.

Damn, he loved his dogs, too, but he didn't want to make out with them. Will sneaked a peek at Julia, wondering if she let Jasper lick her like that. The idea of licking her appealed to him. Julia Cass did have that cute little mouth that turned up at the corners. It had to entice every guy she met to wonder what those lips tasted like. Himself included. Unfortunately. At the moment, however, Julia just looked at Iris with revulsion. And she was a dog lover.

"So you and the judge were estranged?" Will asked, afraid of what Julia might say next, if the expression on her face meant anything.

Iris finished her kissy-face tomfoolery with her dog and gave Will a supercilious smile. "We put on appearances, of course. We have a certain social standing, but we led separate lives. Surely you understand that. We went our own ways. End of story."

"Do you know anyone who might want him dead?"

"Other than myself and most of his girlfriends, all of whom he treated like trash? Of course, most of them *were* trash. Except for my sister, who betrayed me with him, not a week after our wedding day."

103

Julia said, "Your husband had an affair with your sister?"

"That's right. He seduced her. I can't entirely blame her. She was only fifteen at the time, and drunk. She drinks way too much and loses all inhibitions with men, even back in those days. I haven't seen or talked to her for years. She stays away at her place in Saint-Tropez, thank God."

"I see." Julia seemed a bit nonplussed by the heartlessness of the woman.

Will had never seen an icier, more bitter and undemonstrative woman—well, except when she was kissing her dogs. She was all over those poor dogs. From what he'd seen so far, the woman treated the dogs better than her help. For the first time, Will had a twinge of sympathy for Lucien Lockhart.

"Have you received any calls, any kind of threatening messages, had any strangers hanging around?" Will asked the woman.

"No. Although Lucien did mention something about somebody or other being angry. Something about an outburst in court and that he sentenced the guy to five days in jail for contempt. You ought to go downtown and ask his clerk. She'll know. She'll know a lot of things about my husband."

Snide, yes. Contemptuous, yes. Insinuating, yes. "What exactly are you trying to tell us, Mrs. Lockhart?"

"I think you know, Special Agent Brannock. And if you don't, I'm sure your little friend here does."

"I'm not his little friend, ma'am. I'm his liaison partner and a homicide detective at the Chattanooga Police Department. But you're right, I do understand your insinuation. And guess what? I don't like insinuations; I like somebody to tell me the truth when I ask them a question and quit playing silly guessing games that waste my time. So, spit it out, Mrs. Lockhart. If your husband and his clerk had an affair, who is she, when did it happen, and is it still going on?"

Well, that shut up the woman in white linen for a couple of seconds. Her dog, Flopsy, whined and looked at Julia as if she'd stolen his last gourmet doggie treat. So did Mopsy and Topsy. "Well, I declare, *Detective,*" Iris said sarcastically, "you've got a cheeky mouth on you. I really don't care for women who forget they're ladies."

Will interjected before Julia pulled her weapon and bloodied up Iris's pretty white living room. "Detective Cass is right. We're here to find out who murdered your husband and why. So let's quit all the recriminations and get down to business. What's the clerk's name?"

Iris didn't look chastised. She didn't look like she was a warm-blooded human being, either. She looked like she might shed her skin at the end of the summer. "Her name is Jane Cansell. She's been his charity lover for going on twenty years. She's pathetic and needy and has that motive you mentioned a moment ago. He's treated her worse than he treated me, and that's saying something. She still dotes on him, whereas I learned to separate my feelings and emotions concerning him. He is nothing to me. His death means nothing to me, other than a lot of trouble and ugly publicity. I'll be much better off without having to deal with him and his nasty concubines."

"Who is his latest concubine?"

"I stopped asking years ago. Maria can probably tell you. She was usually here when he had his trysts. He never brought women into this house when I was in town. I put my foot down about that a long time ago, and I will say that he honored that request. Of course, my walking out on him would've caused a stink and sunk his chances for the federal judgeship he so coveted. He finally bought his way into that, but he didn't get to enjoy it very long, now did he?"

"Bought his way in?" said Julia.

"That's right. He knew exactly who to wine and dine. My dear departed husband was as underhanded as the day is long. Bribes, graft, whatever, you name it. He was just too clever for anybody to catch him. Maybe that will change now that the FBI's in on this case. Good luck to both of you. I have a feeling you're going to get more than you bargained for before this case is wrapped up."

Will and Julia didn't comment, but Will couldn't say he was shocked by the revelation. There had been lots of rumors through the years that Judge Lockhart was into dirty politics and other felony crimes. He'd heard the whispers himself. As his wife intimated, the judge knew how to cover his tracks.

"Now, Officers, if y'all will excuse me. I've got to see to my husband's funeral arrangements. His position gave him a certain gravitas hereabouts, and I will have to make sure he's treated with respect, no matter how much he doesn't deserve it. If I had my way, I'd cremate him and be done with it, but I have always done my duty as the wife of a judge, and I'll do it now."

"You are truly remarkably cold and uncaring," said Julia.

Iris gave her a long look, then laughed with utter disdain. "You have no idea, my pretty little girl. No idea at all."

"You'll need to stay in town until this investigation is done," Julia told her with remarkable restraint.

"Maybe I will. Maybe I won't. Don't threaten me. I don't care for it."

"You will, or be faced with an arrest warrant," Will told her quietly.

At that, they took their leave. Outside, Will walked swiftly to the truck, jaw set, fists clenched. Pissed off big-time. Julia got in without comment, but once the doors were shut, she said in a tight voice, "I believe she's the most disgusting woman I've ever met. At least your sexy little Ginger Snap had some color in her cheeks."

"Lay off the Ginger cracks, okay? And you're right. Iris won't win any prizes for Sweetheart of the Year, that's for sure."

"What do you think? Is she involved?"

"I don't know. I think she probably wanted him dead and is glad he is, but doing it herself doesn't seem her style. Might mess up her snowy carpet."

"No, it doesn't." Julia adjusted the vents to direct the air-conditioning toward her face, still flushed with anger. "Her alibi will be easy enough to check out and will probably hold up. She's the type who would hire a thug to kill him for her."

"Maybe. She seems amenable to maintaining her lavish lifestyle. Bitter, hard as nails, and superior, but she did her own thing for years. If he's had that many other women during his marriage, why would she suddenly want him dead and rock her boat of plenty?"

Julia ticked off some reasons. "Insurance money? Freedom to marry somebody else? Maybe she's got a lover stashed down on Bourbon Street, some lifeguard or pool boy that she wants to marry."

"Could be. Go ahead and check it out. And check out her daughter, too. Her name's Tanya. She lives out in Seattle. You can get the number from Willie Mullins. He was the one who notified her, poor girl. Imagine having a mom like Iris."

"Will do. Did Willie tell you anything about her?"

"Just that she moved as far away from her parents as she could get. Pretty much hated their guts. But who wouldn't."

"I'll call her and get the interview today."

"Good. Right now, I think we need to pay a call on Jane Cansell down at the courthouse."

Tam Lovelady was sick to death of the trial. More than that, she was sick and tired of reliving terrible, long-ago memories that the Rocking Chair Murders brought down on her and her best friend, Audrey Sherrod, and lots of other innocent people. She didn't ever want to think about it, much less remember all the details, especially those concerning Audrey's stepbrother, Hart Roberts. She could hardly believe he was really gone, *murdered*. She had loved him for so long, those feelings hidden deep inside her heart. And their child, the child she conceived with him so many years ago and aborted when she was only eighteen. She lived to regret that decision, but knew it was her only choice, because she and Hart could never have been together. She'd never gotten over it. Never. Hart's death had hit her hard, even after all the years that had gone by, even after she had married Marcus, the kindest, most considerate, most wonderful man in the world.

Agitated by the deep and painful thoughts resurrected inside her, Tam rose from the wood bench in the hallway outside the criminal courtroom and paced the length of the marble floor to the windows overlooking the street.

J.D. was testifying again. He had been on the stand for three hours. And she wasn't even next in line on the witness list. She turned around and leaned against the windowsill. They'd break for lunch soon, thank goodness. She was tired and wasn't sleeping. She missed Marcus. They'd been separated for almost a year. Her idea, because of Hart, of course; it had always been about Hart. But she missed her husband since the first day she'd left their home. Her idea. He didn't want her to go, but she had temporarily moved back home with her parents. Her heart hurt, grieved over their separation.

She had cut Marcus out of her life, but not out of her heart. She truly loved him. More now. She'd seen him a couple of times. Not often. He'd given her the space she'd said she needed, and at first, she had welcomed the time alone, still struggling with her love for Hart—wanting to help Hart overcome the demons that had possessed him since he was the blond-haired, blue-eyed boy she had fallen so desperately in love with. He had been mentally unstable even back then, drowning in drugs and alcohol and living to forget the bad things in his life.

Across from her, the elevator doors slid open and a tall, handsome man and a woman stepped out. Pleasantly surprised, she hurried toward them. It was her new partner, Julia Cass, and J.D.'s fellow TBI agent, Will Brannock. Tam had first met Julia when Julia interviewed for detective, and had been impressed with her knowledge and experience. Will Brannock she had always gotten along with. He was a good agent, but ultra-private, the kind of guy that nobody ever seemed to know very well, not even J.D., who worked so closely with him. Closemouthed but nice enough.

"Hey, Julia," she called out as they turned in the other direction and hurried off down the shiny corridor.

Both turned around, and Julia smiled and waved. Tam really regretted being tied up at the trial, so eager was she to get back to work and partner up with Julia. Especially on this new case, yet another murder involving a member of the Chattanooga legal community. People were going to wonder if anyone in the courthouse walked the straight and narrow anymore. Once the details of the killing leaked out to the press and general populace, Judge Lucien Lockhart's death was going to be a raging media sensation. Tam wished she could help solve it before that happened.

Will said something to Julia, waved at Tam, and

then strode off toward Judge Lockhart's private chambers. Julia headed back to her. Smiling, Julia said, "You're still waiting to testify, I take it."

"That's right. I'm about to climb the walls. Why are y'all here?"

"We've come down to interview Judge Lockhart's staff. Will's gone to see if they're available."

"The clerks are all here. I saw them earlier today. They seemed in total shock. Especially Jane Cansell."

Julia glanced around and lowered her voice. "Do you know her?"

"Not real well. Why?"

"Iris Lockhart told us straight out that Jane was in a longtime affair with her husband. Know anything about that?"

"Yeah, who doesn't? It's been common knowledge around the criminal courts. And she's not the only one he was messing around with."

Julia shook her head, frowning. "Good grief, who did this guy not sleep with?"

Tam grinned. She really liked J.D.'s sister. They were going to be great friends; Tam felt it. "How's the investigation going? Wish I could help out."

"How much longer will you be down here?"

"Who knows? The defense is constantly delaying the proceedings. The judge is getting ticked off big-time. So is everybody else."

"This Lockhart case is going to be a doozy. Has your dad told you the details?"

"No, but I have clearance to join you as soon as I'm done here, so you can tell me everything."

They moved over to a deserted corner, and Tam listened intently as Julia ran the case for her in low tones. The mutilation of the body shocked Tam. "Oh God, his tongue was cut out? And what the hell's the deal with the dimes?"

"We're not sure yet. We're just getting started, but nobody we've interviewed seems to know anything. Except that Lucien Lockhart had lots of women on the side, and his wife hates his guts. You ever meet Iris Lockhart?"

"Hell no, she sticks her nose in the air when she runs into peons like me." She glanced down at the courtroom doors, but no one was coming out yet. J.D. was still on the stand. Lucky him. "I've heard rumors. He was a flirty guy. He came on to me a couple of times. Pretty lightweight stuff. I ignored him, but he's well-known for liking the women."

"Sounds like Will Brannock, huh?"

"Will?" Tam had to laugh at that. Will was so private that few people knew anything about his love life. She sure didn't. Not that she wouldn't want to. She bet it was as hot as everything else about him. "I haven't heard that one. What? Did he come on to you?"

"No, not exactly, but I saw him in full throttle, lady-killer form when he picked me up at the

113

airport. Flight attendants galore and all of them eating out of his hand."

"I know his sister's a pilot with Delta, but that's about all I know about him. He seems like a good guy, but he's so private it's almost creepy. At least, that's what J.D. tells me. Will is friendly and is easy to talk to, but when you get done talking, you don't know a single thing about him that you didn't know before. Are you two having trouble working the case together?"

Julia shook her head. "No, not at all. We're getting along fine. He knows what he's doing. Actually, I've been pretty much wowed by him. He was sort of flirty and silly at first, but man, once we got the case, he was all business."

"He and J.D. were the ones who saved the last victim of the Rocking Chair killer. Did you know that? She's here. See her, down there? She's the girl in the black suit and white blouse. Her name's Somer Ellis, and she barely made it out alive. She told me the other day that Will was the guy who untied her and carried her out of that awful church basement where the victims were taken. She said he was very kind and comforting and even came to see her in the hospital a time or two."

"He hasn't discussed that case with me yet. Like I said, he teased around with me some when he was driving me to J.D.'s house, but he's been serious since we were assigned to this case together. He's very thorough, and he doesn't give me that superior act that some special agents put on for the locals."

Down the hallway, Will had reappeared and was motioning for Julia to join him.

"Will's ready to start the interviews, Tam. I'll catch you later."

"Yeah, keep me posted, will you?"

"You bet."

As Julia moved away, a thought occurred to Tam. "Hey, Julia! Audrey and I are having lunch tomorrow downtown at the River Street Deli. How about joining us?"

"I'd like that, but I'm not sure I can get away. I'll let you know, okay?"

"Sure. You've got my cell number. Talk to you later."

Tam watched Julia hurry off. Yeah, J.D.'s sister was okay. J.D. was right about Julia and Zoe, but the resemblance was not just in looks, with all their dark hair and delicate features, but in other ways as well. She looked forward to getting to know Julia better. Actually, that couldn't happen too soon. She watched Will and Julia disappear into Judge Lockhart's chambers, and then she sighed and went back to the interminable waiting.

Chapter 6

Pleased that she'd bumped into Tam Lovelady, Julia had a feeling that in time they were going to be a great homicide team. She had never worked with a female partner, but they seemed to fit together well. She hoped Tam would soon be available. The task force could use her help. Even after this short time, she was feeling more than comfortable teaming up with Brannock, too. Their investigatory techniques were pretty well matched. At least, so far, and a lot more than she had thought they would be when they'd first met. Despite the fact that not much was adding up yet, Will was running a tight ship.

"Jane Cansell's ready for us. They said we could use the judge's private office for the interview," Will said as soon as Julia reached him.

"Okay, let's just hope this lady's more forthcoming than his wife was," Julia answered. "She can't be any more unlikable."

Once they reached the portal to Lucien Lockhart's private inner sanctum, it didn't take Julia long to locate Jane Cansell. Loud weeping could be heard through the door. Once inside, she and Will found Lockhart's clerk/lover/mourner sobbing like crazy in the judge's high-back chair, her face hidden in her folded arms where they rested on top of his magnificent mahogany desk. Will and Julia looked at each other. This was not the most optimal moment to interview the woman, but sometimes roiling emotions left a person less guarded in their revelations. Maybe Jane would be one of them. First off, they needed to get her to turn off the waterworks and settle down. That was the trick.

When Jane sensed their presence, she lifted her head and stared at them as if they had their weapons out, their laser target indicators focused on her forehead. Puffy, bloodshot eyes—blotchy, pale skin—disheveled, tinted blond hair—nope, she did not look picture-perfect. She looked like she'd been crying all night, or all year. It occurred to Julia that Jane Cansell was the first person they'd met who showed any real sadness for the judge's grotesque mutilation and violent death. Maybe that was the most telling thing they'd found out yet.

The poor woman was truly distraught, however, and Julia walked around the desk and placed a gentle hand on her shoulder. "Ms. Cansell, if you're not up to this interview, we can wait awhile. Until you feel better and are up to talking. We understand this is an extremely difficult time for you."

"No, no, I'm okay. I know why y'all are here. I want to help you. Please sit down."

Will and Julia took the two comfortable,

117

chocolate-brown upholstered chairs across from the desk. Jane sat up and ran both hands through her short, highlighted brown hair. "I just can't accept this, I really can't."

Jane Cansell was attractive and very petite, probably barely five feet tall, and she looked younger than she really was. Court employment records obtained by Will stated that she was forty-nine, but her tear-ravaged skin was clear and unwrinkled—whether thanks to good genes, face-lifts, or Botox, Julia didn't know. Jane looked haggard now, the loss of sleep showing on her face. But her emotions seemed genuine. She was grieving for Lucien Lockhart, all right. It seemed the man did have one person in the world who cared about him.

"My name is Julia Cass. I'm a detective with the Chattanooga PD."

"You're new, then. I know most of the officers down there." Jane was dabbing at her tears with a tissue now, smearing her heavy black mascara but trying her best to gain control.

"Yes, I just started. After this case, I'm slated to work with Tam Lovelady."

"I know her. She's Chief Mullins's daughter."

"That's right." Julia nodded and gestured at Will. "This is TBI Special Agent Will Brannock. He's in charge of this investigation."

"We already know each other," Will told her. "I'm sorry for your loss, Janie."

Janie? Julia wondered if Jane used to be a flight attendant, and therefore right down Will's landing strip. Somehow she didn't think so. In fact, she wasn't at all sure anymore that he was quite the lascivious Lothario she'd first branded him. If he was, no one around him seemed to know it.

Jane said, "Tell me, Will, do you know anything yet? Who could do this awful, awful thing?"

"That's what we're here to find out. Do you have anything you can tell us?"

Jane averted her eyes, looking guilty, an obvious sign that if she knew anything, she wasn't sure she wanted to tell them. "He has enemies, true. All judges do. But to do this kind of thing to him. Oh my God, I can't believe anyone could be so, my God . . . be so . . . savage." She looked back at Julia, tears springing up again. "Is it true, Detective? What they're saying? That the killer cut out . . ." Her voice fading, Jane couldn't finish her question.

"We're not at liberty to discuss that aspect of the case right now, Ms. Cansell," Julia told her. "But we really need you to be honest with us. It's very important."

Tugging another tissue out of the blue Puffs Plus box on her lap, Jane tried again to gain control of her grief. "It's just such a shock to me, all of it. Out of the blue, you understand?"

Will said, "Of course we do, Janie. But I'm

afraid I'm going to have to speak plainly to you. Is that okay? You do understand why we have to ask you these questions, right?"

"Yes." Despite her answer, she looked wary and afraid, as though she wished she were somewhere far, far away from her two interrogators. Tibet, maybe.

"We were told that you've been having a long-term sexual affair with the judge. Is that true?"

At Will's blunt words, shock suffused Jane Cansell's face, followed by a swift rush of blood-red color. Tears swiftly went on hold. "Will, who told you such a thing?"

"Iris Lockhart."

"Is it true?" Julia asked again.

Appearing mortified, Jane stared down at her hands. She was engaging now in a lot of wringing of hands and squeezing of fingers and twisting of the four expensive diamond rings she wore. One was a wedding band. "Yes. It's true."

"How serious was it?" Julia asked.

"I loved him. I tried to break it off many times, but I just couldn't do it. I'm so weak when it comes to Lucien. He was like cocaine to me. An addiction I couldn't break. Oh, my husband's going to be so hurt if he finds this out."

"You are aware that he had other women?" Will asked her, but he looked and acted sympathetic, maybe even embarrassed at having to ask these questions.

"Yes, he liked to tell me about them. Making me jealous amused him."

Not just a jerk, but a cruel jerk, Julia thought, disgusted. There were going to be dozens of suspects in this case, mostly abused and spurned women. Any one of them could have finally had enough, snapped, and gotten even with Lucien Lockhart in a very deadly way. Even gentle, heart-broken little Jane, sitting so distraught before them. Maybe she came off so distraught because she had just cut out her lover's tongue in a fit of rage and now wished she hadn't.

"Where were you night before last?" asked Will, seemingly right on cue.

"Oh my Lord, y'all don't think I had anything to do with this? That I would hurt him, butcher him, like people are saying?"

"It sounds to us like he enjoyed hurting you, saying things to make you angry and unhappy." Will stared down at her. "Everybody's got a breaking point. People snap. Even good and decent people."

"I'd never hurt him. I loved him. And he loved me, in his own kind of way."

Julia was thinking it was in his own kind of nasty, selfish, and manipulative way, but she smiled encouragingly. This woman was extremely fragile. Maybe not particularly bright or emotionally stable, but fragile. "Was your affair current?" she asked.

"Yes. Things weren't like they were at first when we spent every weekend together. It had come to maybe once a month, when he'd ask me to meet him at a hotel and spend a few hours there. Like you said, Iris knew all about me. She didn't care. All she cares about is the prestige she got for being his wife."

"What about your working relationship, here at the court?" Will asked.

"It was good. I took care of all his judicial paperwork. He doesn't trust anybody else in the office. He doesn't—I mean, didn't—trust much of anybody."

"Why not?"

"He's not the most, well, not the easiest person to work for. He treats people as if they were his own personal property. Just ask around. Nobody likes him here at the criminal court."

Will leaned forward, searching her face. "Yet you protect him and make excuses for his behavior."

"No, I don't. I don't make excuses. I know what he is . . ." Her tired eyes overflowed. "Was. I couldn't help it."

"Are any of these coworkers capable of killing him?"

"Some speak openly about how much they hate him."

"Who?"

"The bailiff, for one."

"The name?"

"Charlie Sinclair."

Julia stiffened when she heard the name. Will noticed and sent her a questioning look. She intentionally relaxed her tensed shoulders but couldn't stop the rush of anger at Jane Cansell's implication of her old friend. Charlie Sinclair was the guy who had trained both Cathy Axelrod and Julia to work with service dogs. He was a nice guy, a good friend. If he disliked the judge, the judge deserved it. By all counts, Charlie wasn't the only one. Julia had heard he had taken a job as a bailiff after he retired from the Tennessee State Police. He had taught both Julia and Cathy everything they knew about dog handling. There was no way he could have been involved in such a horrific crime. No way.

Eager to defend her friend, Julia jumped right in. "What makes you think Charlie Sinclair could be a person of interest?"

"Just his attitude toward the judge. They clashed constantly, but for some reason, the judge seemed to cut Charlie some slack. No matter how outspoken Charlie got."

"Did Charlie ever make a verbal threat?"

"Not in so many words. He just made it known that he didn't think the judge handled criminal cases very well. Went so far as to question his integrity. You'd think he was an attorney the way he argued law with the judge."

If Charlie had training in the law, Julia had certainly never heard anything about it. Charlie was another bright spot in her move to Chattanooga. She loved the guy almost like a father, and he was still actively training and boarding service dogs. Cathy was working part-time for him. If anyone could give her the truth about Lucien Lockhart, it was Charlie Sinclair.

"Was there ever any kind of physical confrontation between the two men?" Will asked, slanting Julia another curious look.

"Oh no. Both of them were too smart for something like that. In fact, I suspect they respected each other in some bizarre alpha male sort of way."

"What about the judge's cases? Any of them go down with any notable or particularly violent threats?"

"There was one. A gang member on trial for armed robbery. He yelled curses and said Lucien'd get payback for railroading him. Lucien slapped him with several days in jail for contempt."

"What gang?"

"I don't recall. It had the name of a street in it. And a number."

Will looked more interested. "Battle Street Ten?"

"Yes, sir. That's it, I believe."

"What's this gangbanger's name? Do you remember?"

"Jesus Ramos. He was sentenced to fifteen years in prison, no chance of parole."

"He's in prison now?"

"As far as I know."

"Were there any reprisals against Judge Lockhart by the Battle Street gang?"

"I don't know. There were a bunch of them who came to court for the trial. They all sat in the back together in their black pants and hoodies and their tattoos and black head scarves. We were all a little scared. Not Lucien. He stared them down, not the least bit intimidated."

"And now he's dead," Julia pointed out.

"I had a feeling gangbangers might be involved," Will said. "We'll check it out as soon as we get done here."

"Anything else you want to tell us?" Julia studied Jane's face. She was in control now, but her eyes were strained and troubled and horribly red.

"I just want you to catch whoever did this to Lucien. He didn't deserve to die that way."

Will took over again. "What do you know about Lucien's relationship with his wife?"

"You mean, was she capable of murdering him?"

"Yeah."

Jane hesitated, looking from Julia to Will and back again. "I think she's a mean, ruthless bitch who probably caused him to look for comfort with me and other women. Could she have killed him? I think she could. I think she could take a knife and carve up anybody without batting an eye. Except for those ugly little dogs of hers. She treats them better than the people in her life."

So there you go, Julia thought, *honesty at its most caustic.* "What about the housekeeper? The girl named Maria Bota? How does Iris treat her?"

"Like crap. Lucien was always having to protect that poor child from Iris's cruelty."

"Is Maria also Lucien's lover?" Julia asked.

"I don't know. I doubt it. She wasn't his type."

Julia thought that nearly anyone and everyone appeared to be Lucien Lockhart's type, with a few extra points for large breasts and extra-mini miniskirts. "What about your coworkers here at the court?"

"He didn't socialize with many people. The other judges liked to have lawyers in their chambers, to talk and joke around and gossip with. Lucien never did that. Believe it or not, Charlie was the one that he spent the most time with. You know, at lunch or during jury deliberations. I think he just liked to jab at him. But Charlie gave him back everything he could handle. Charlie is a highly intelligent man."

That was true. Charlie was nobody's fool. He would be able to tell them the truth about what was going on here at the criminal courts. Other than him, Julia wasn't sure she could believe anything anybody had told her so far.

Charlie Sinclair sat waiting in the back row of Judge Lockhart's empty criminal courtroom. He had seen Julia Cass go into Lucien's chambers. He also knew Jane Cansell was in there, blubbering and moaning for that bastard while she waited to talk to the police. He'd been eager for Julia to show up all day. Once he'd heard the news that Lucien had been murdered, it had just been a matter of time. He was anxious to see Julia again. She had always been one of his favorite students; a good girl, a good cop, and a good dog handler. She had gotten Jasper from him when the blood-hound was a puppy around eight weeks old. That old dog was now the best working canine that Charlie had ever seen. Julia had trained him well.

Under Julia's tutelage, Jasper had become one of the most decorated police dogs in the country. Julia was a born canine handler, better even than he and Cathy were. Having her working his dogs was going to be great for his business, and for her. If he could get her to sign on with him. True, she had never been quite the same since Bobby Crismon died. Blamed herself for his death, but that was Julia. She had been getting cozy with the guy, just starting to think about dating him, when he was shot to death right in front of her. She had barely survived the incident herself. That had been nearly three years ago. But sometimes he could still see the shadow of that night haunting her eyes. He knew how she felt. Sonia had been gone for over a decade now, but he still thought about her, still reached across the bed when he awoke during the night to pull her close, only to grasp cold and empty sheets.

It was strange that the three of them, he and Julia and Cathy, had all ended up together in Chattanooga. Cathy had left Nashville when she'd met and married Lonnie Axelrod. And now Julia had come to town, too. He knew it was mainly because of J.D. Cass. Her brother was well-known and well thought of in the Chattanooga law enforcement and legal communities. Charlie knew him a little bit, and he had seen the similarities between him and his sister right off the bat.

Ten minutes later, Julia appeared in the doorway leading into the courtroom from Lucien Lockhart's inner offices. He waved, and she headed in his direction. She looked as good as ever, trim and fit and pretty as a picture. All that long hair was caught back in a tight bun, which was the way she usually wore it when working. She reached him, gave him a tight hug and kiss on the cheek, and over her shoulder he saw Will Brannock's face dissolve into surprise, quickly followed by a frown. Charlie knew Will, too—another crack TBI special agent, but a man who kept to himself and didn't have a lot to say. Unlike J.D., who was always friendly and ready to sit down and shoot the bull with Charlie.

"Man, it's good to see you again," Julia was saying to him. "How have you been?"

"I'm good. A little shocked about the judge. Nobody can believe it actually happened."

"Yeah, it happened, all right. I got assigned to the case within an hour of leaving the airport."

"No joke? Lucky you, right? You got Jasper here yet?"

"Oh yes. He's at J.D.'s house at the moment, but I'm going to live out at Cathy's place where Jasper can run free and enjoy the fresh air."

"I heard about that. In that apartment she's got over the boat dock, isn't it?"

"Yes. She said it's stayed empty since her husband's mother passed away a few years ago. She insisted I move in, and I didn't want to crowd J.D. and Zoe, so I took her up on it."

"Tell you one thing—it's damn beautiful out there on that part of the river. Lonnie inherited the place from his family. I believe Cathy said it's been in the family, why, I think for four or five decades. A long time, anyway. Long before waterfront properties got so pricey."

When Will walked up, his frown had been replaced with a neutral expression, but he still didn't look pleased by Julia's familiarity with Charlie. Charlie looked up at the bigger man and said, "Hello, Will. How you doin'?"

"I'm fine. I need to ask you some questions, Mr. Sinclair. You have the time?"

"You bet. I'm ready. Go ahead, and call me Charlie. Everybody around here does."

"I didn't know you and Detective Cass were such close friends." Brannock looked from one of them to the other, not exactly suspiciously, but something was there. What was it? Jealousy, maybe? Already? Charlie wouldn't be surprised. Julia had a way of charming men before they knew what hit them. Himself included.

"Yeah, we go way back together."

"Charlie taught me everything I know about dog handling. He's one of my best friends." Julia hugged his shoulders again.

"Then maybe I better do the questioning," Will said without much tact.

Charlie thought Julia looked a mite chagrined by that somewhat suggestive remark, but she merely nodded. "You're in charge, Brannock. I'll just sit back, listen, and learn."

Charlie heard the mild sarcasm, but he knew Julia well. Will Brannock didn't seem to notice. Even if he did, he probably was the kind of man who wouldn't show it.

"Have a seat, Mr. Sinclair. This won't take but a minute."

"No problem. Court's called off until Lockhart's cases can be reassigned. I'm just killin' time and twiddlin' my thumbs."

"All right. First off, Ms. Cansell in there told us that Judge Lockhart had a confrontation with a Battle Street gangbanger. Name is Jesus Ramos."

"Yes, he sure did. That little punk cursed him all the way to the holdin' cell."

"Direct threats?"

"That's right. He was yellin' in Spanish, tellin' him he was goin' to die, that his homeboys would get him, among other more vulgar remarks."

"You speak Spanish?"

"Yes, my wife was from Puerto Rico." Charlie glanced at Julia. "Bet you didn't know that. San Juan. I met her when I was in the navy."

She shook her head but didn't respond. Charlie immediately knew what she was thinking. Will Brannock was in charge at the moment, and being the newbie, she wasn't going to make waves. She was a smart gal, always had been. She knew when to keep her mouth shut and her thoughts to herself.

"Tell me, Charlie, do you think this gang could have done this?"

Charlie considered Brannock's question a moment. "Of course. They're brutal. The rumor out in the hall is that the judge got his tongue cut out. That true?"

"I'm sorry. I can't divulge the details of the crime."

131

"Well, if it is, I know for a fact that the Battle Street Ten boys are known to do that to people who cross them."

"How do you know that?"

"I read the papers. It happened somewhere over around Charlotte. I hear they're thick as thieves in North Carolina."

Will didn't comment. "What about Jane Cansell? You think she's capable of killing the judge?"

Charlie laughed—couldn't help it. "I think she'd slash her own throat before she'd harm a hair on his head. He treated her like a piece of garbage, and everybody knew it. She's a good-lookin' woman. I don't understand why she let him put her down like that."

"Are you interested in her?"

"How do you mean? Like a girlfriend?"

"Yeah, like a girlfriend."

Somehow Will's tone antagonized Charlie. "Nope. Actually, I haven't been much interested in women at all since my wife died."

"I'm sorry. When was that?"

"Nine years, ten months, and twenty-six days ago."

"I'm sorry, Mr. Sinclair. I do have to ask you these questions."

"I know that, Brannock. Please, ask away."

He saw Brannock glance at Julia, who looked away. She remained silent. Charlie had a feeling she'd probably give Brannock an earful when they were alone. Then again, the TBI agent was only doing his job.

"Have you ever had a run-in with the judge?"

"Near every day. I guess you could say we had one of those love-hate relationships. More like a like-dislike relationship. We liked to shoot barbs at each other but spent a lot of time together."

"Are you saying you hated him?"

"I hated the way he treated people. I hated his arrogance and elitism and superior attitude. But so did everybody else in this building."

"Do you remember any other cases where somebody threatened him?"

"Probably about a hundred or so. He had a way of insultin' nearly everyone he ran into. His contempt citations became a joke down at booking."

"That means we'll have to go into his files and read the transcripts."

"Good luck. Jane might be able to pull the ones she remembers getting nasty."

"Yeah. Anything else you want us to know?"

"Nope."

"By the way, where were you night before last?"

"Home, mindin' my dogs and my own business."

"Alone."

"Yes, sir, except for my dogs. They're my family. Julia can attest to that."

Julia nodded agreement.

"You have neighbors who might vouch that you were there?"

"I have neighbors. Not close ones, though. I don't know what they'd vouch to. You can ask them, if you want. They might've seen me comin' or goin'."

"I'll do that. Thanks for your time, Mr. Sinclair. If you think of anything else that might help us get to the bottom of this, please let us know."

Charlie took the card that the big TBI agent handed him and stuck it in his shirt pocket. He shook the hand that Brannock held out to him, and he gave Julia a big hug.

"Oh, by the by, Julia, guess who I ran into the other day? Mr. Max Hazard, in the flesh. He was askin' about you, wantin' to know if you were still single. I told him you were movin' to town."

"Well, I hope you didn't tell him anything else about me."

"Who's Max Hazard?" Brannock interrupted.

"Oh, he's an obnoxious private eye that I arrested a couple of times," she said, shrugging off the subject. "He and Charlie are old friends."

Charlie chuckled, but he was astute enough to notice Brannock's interest in her past relationship with Max Hazard. He watched the two detectives walk out of the silent courtroom. And if Brannock was contemplating a romantic interest in Julia, he should be worried. Max Hazard was still

134

carrying quite a torch for Julia and didn't mind people knowing it. He was one cool guy who just might give Brannock a run for his money. What's more, Julia rather liked him, too, even if she wouldn't admit it.

Chapter 7

Julia was worn-out. It had been over a week since she landed in Chattanooga, and she had been on this case almost from the moment her plane set down. Will Brannock was turning out to be rather intense. In fact, he was a veritable slave driver when it came to the Lockhart investigation. They had interviewed, and were still interviewing, everybody whom Lucien Lockhart had known or seemingly ever spoke to, especially the ones he'd locked up for contempt. At least, that's what it seemed like. But that's okay. That's the way she liked it. Get on it, solve it. Get it done, the sooner the better. The case was gruesome, and whoever had mutilated the victim had thoroughly enjoyed himself. He'd planned it down to the minutest detail and executed it to perfection.

Jasper was sitting in the backseat of her dad's old '68 Dodge Charger, and he had been very glad to get out of the confines of J.D.'s house. J.D. had a nice place, true, and Signal Mountain was a nice area, but the last thing J.D. needed, now that he was seriously involved with Audrey Sherrod, was his little sister moving into his house and causing complications in his love life or in raising his daughter. She had loved being around Zoe, of course, and she planned to spend a lot more time with the fifteen-year-old, but that wouldn't happen until they solved the Lockhart case.

Cathy Bateman Axelrod lived somewhere up along the Tennessee River. Julia hadn't been there before, but Cathy had given her directions. She was passing by lots of luxurious homes. Apparently, the area was inhabited predominately by the rich and famous and infamous of Chattanooga. As Charlie had told her, Cathy's new husband, Lonnie Axelrod, and his family had owned a good-sized acreage on the river for years. From what she understood from Cathy, it originally had been a family farm but had ended operations when his father died. Apparently, Lonnie Axelrod had been offered well over a million dollars to sell out to a multimillionaire who wanted a spectacular river view. He'd refused. Lonnie liked the view, too, more than he liked money. Rare indeed, but admirable. So, good for him. One didn't see principled men like that much anymore.

The mailbox was brand-new, shiny aluminum with MR. AND MRS. LONNIE AXELROD and the numbers 443 printed in black on the side, inside a heart. *Newlyweds,* Julia thought, amused.

Julia took a right turn and followed a gravel road down a bit of a hill through some seriously big oak trees and lots of thick and dusty underbrush. The property was surrounded by dense, deep woods, but when she came out of the leafy canopy of trees, she saw that Cathy's house was a really nice log cabin with a wide, screened-in front porch, a green tin roof, and a magnificent view of the river beyond the grassy front yard.

Cathy was sitting on the front steps, waiting for her. Julia smiled and brought the Charger to a stop next to the lamppost at the end of the front walk made of bricks arranged in a herringbone pattern. Cathy was a vivacious, green-eyed girl, with lots of freckles, lots of wild auburn hair, lots of energy, and lots of personality. Tall and fit and slender, Cathy was one of Julia's best friends, and she'd missed Cathy since she had married Lonnie and moved away from Nashville.

She opened the door to release Jasper from the backseat, and he bounded out of the car and down the sidewalk to meet Cathy. He loved Cathy as much as Julia did. After all, she'd had a hand in training him. And she was Julia's dog sitter extraordinaire when they had both lived in Nashville. Laughing, Cathy leaned down and hugged the excited dog. Hearing Jasper's barking, four of Cathy's dogs shot around the side of the house. All were German shepherds, all trained service dogs, and they set up a din that got Jasper started with his delighted baying. Yes, their dogs were friends, too.

"Just like old times, right?" Julia said, giving Cathy a big hug.

"It just didn't happen soon enough."

Julia glanced out at the wide, swift-flowing river in front of them. "Wow. This place is phenomenal. You may never get me out of here."

"Yeah, I know. Lon just loves this place. Says it fills him with peace when he looks out over the river."

"That sounds like what I need. And it looks like your dogs like it, too. Where's Tasha?" Julia looked around for the snow-white Akita that was her favorite of all Cathy's dogs.

"She stepped on a sharp rock out in the woods. Split the pad on her left front paw. Charlie doctored her and is keeping her at his place until she feels better."

"I saw him today."

"You did? Out at his place? Talk about a layout. He's got an A-frame up on a high bluff that overlooks the woods and pastures, and a big babbling creek running through it all. Lots of room for his dog runs."

"No, I saw him down at the criminal courts. I haven't had time to visit him, but I will. Same goes for not getting out here sooner. I picked up a major murder investigation right after I got here."

"Are you serious? You're already on a case?"

"Yeah, and it's a big one."

"Darn, I was hoping we could hang out for the next couple of days, swim and sunbathe, make up a big batch of margaritas, and catch up on everything."

"That's what I was planning, too, but looks like it's a no-go for now. The TBI's involved. And the special agent that's my liaison is gung ho, to say the least."

"No kidding. Can you tell me anything about it?"

"Not yet, but the newspapers are bound to get hold of it soon. It's high-profile, very high-profile."

"Now you've got me curious."

Both turned around when they heard a man's voice coming from the front porch. "Hey, girls. I thought I heard a party going on out here."

Julia watched the man walking toward them. He had a white towel hung around his neck as if he'd been working out, and was wearing a pair of long denim shorts and a white T-shirt. He wore tan boat shoes without socks. She hadn't seen Lonnie since Cathy's wedding reception, but he was still gazing at Cathy with the same *I adore you, I adore you forever and ever* look. This guy idolized his wife, no doubt about it.

"She's finally here, Lonnie," Cathy called out to him. "I can't wait to show her the boathouse."

139

Lonnie Axelrod was around six feet tall, with a stocky build that looked like he had lots of strength in his body. He had dark brown hair but was balding in front, graying on the sides, and he wore old-fashioned wire-rimmed glasses. Julia knew he was retired from the air force, and he looked the part. Cathy put her arms around his waist, and he squeezed her close against his side.

"My wife's been counting the days until you showed up," he said to Julia. He had a nice smile that crinkled the corners of his eyes and put double creases in his clean-shaven cheeks. He had made Cathy very happy after several years of pure misery that she'd suffered after she'd divorced her first husband. Julia hadn't seen her friend this content in a long, long time.

"And who is this fine-lookin' fellow?" Lonnie said, kneeling down and putting his hand on Jasper's back. Jasper took to him at once, leaning up against Lonnie's knee and pushing his head under his hand for more petting.

"That's Jasper. He likes you already, I do believe."

"I usually have a way with dogs. Can't say exactly why. Well, welcome. It's good to have you here. We can't get enough dogs around here to suit Cathy. Jasper's going to love running around our property. It's fenced and posted, so you can just let him go. I doubt if he'll try to swim the river."

"No, he won't."

All the same, Julia wasn't sure she was going to let Jasper roam to that extent, but he was well trained in any event and wouldn't wander off on his own. Yep, he was going to love it here. Julia already did. The rushing sound of the river alone was soothing and must be great to go to sleep by. She loved the water, loved just sitting and looking out over it. "I love your place, Lonnie. I can't tell you how grateful I am that you're willing to let me stay here for a while. Just long enough to find a house that I like."

"Anything that makes my wife happy makes me happy."

Julia liked that, and the warm way Lonnie smiled down at Cathy almost melted Julia's heart. They were extremely compatible, and the happiness emanated from them like fragrance from a rose. Cathy deserved it. She'd had a rough go-round the first time. Her first husband had started taking dope, gotten addicted, and ended up in prison. He was still there, doing hard time. He was bad news.

"Let's go down to the boathouse. I know you're going to like it."

"You bet I will," Julia said to Cathy, then held out her hand to Lonnie. "Nice seeing you again, Lon. Again, thanks for your hospitality. I'll be glad to pay whatever you want."

"No, no, of course not. That old boathouse has

sat empty since my mom died. It'll be good to see somebody enjoy it again. I couldn't bring myself to clear it out. Still can't. I like to go there sometimes when I get to missing her. It makes me feel better."

Julia and Cathy made their way to the Charger. Julia opened the door and waited while Jasper jumped up on the backseat. Cathy climbed into the passenger side, and Julia started the engine. The motor had been missing some now and then, and she hoped she wouldn't have to take it into the shop.

"Well, looks like you got a good one there," Julia said as she put the car in gear.

"I'm so lucky. He's everything I ever wanted." Cathy was actually beaming.

Julia laughed at Cathy's in-love sigh. "I'm glad to finally get to move in out here. I want to get settled. I'm still tired, though. J.D. and I have been staying up late and talking about the good old days when we lived in Memphis."

"How is he? I run into him once in a while when I go down to the courthouse to see Charlie."

"He's fine. Finally found himself a woman to love."

"No way. I thought you said he'd never settle down, not with so many women chasing him."

"I was shocked, too, believe me. But he's got it almost as bad as Lonnie, the poor guy."

"Well, I'm glad you're here, and I hope you

never move out. I've got lots of plans for us. You still like to fish?"

"You know it. Is there good fishing along here?"

"I caught a whole string of catfish this morning. I'll cook them up tomorrow for the three of us. Hush puppies and fried potatoes. Sound good?"

"My stomach's growling, just thinking about it. Heard you're still training dogs with Charlie."

"Yeah. We get by on Lonnie's retirement, but he encouraged me to continue with the dogs if I want to. He's supportive like that."

Julia followed the gravel road down through more towering trees, some overhanging the river, their leafy limbs touching the water in places. A few minutes later, she saw her temporary new home. It was pretty much a miniature version of the main house, with the big brown logs and green tin roof. She couldn't wait for the next rain so she could hear it drum on that roof. The house in Memphis that she'd grown up in had a tin roof, and thoughts of it brought back some pleasant memories. The boathouse also had a large screened-in porch that faced the water, and a side screen door facing a forked path that led to the driveway and down to the river. Underneath the apartment was a boat dock with an old runabout speedboat and a johnboat moored inside.

When they got out of the Charger, the two

friends stood looking out over the river. "I gave this place a real good cleaning just this week," Cathy told her.

"So Lonnie's mother lived here?"

Cathy grinned. "Yes, and it's pretty much the same as she left it. Lon's sentimental about his mother's belongings. You can put some of her stuff away, though, if you want to. Just pack it in boxes and I'll take it down to our house. Lon won't mind as long as it's safe and sound."

"I sold most of my things. And my car. I'd had it awhile, and I decided if I was going to start anew, I'd go all the way."

"That white Mustang of yours was pretty slick, if I recall."

"That Mustang and I had a lot of good times together, but this time I'm getting a four-wheel-drive truck that'll get me around better in the winter. Or a Jeep, maybe. A red Jeep."

They walked up the path to the house together, and by the time they climbed the steps to the screen door, Julia already felt at home. Sweet-smelling red roses climbed trellises along the porch, and inside was a white iron daybed with a feather mattress, pushed up against the house under a large plate-glass window. A white wicker swing hung from the rafters at the other end of the porch. There was also a small wicker table with a glass top and four red-cushioned chairs around it. All the screens had long matchstick blinds that were rolled up now but could be closed for privacy.

"This is fantastic, Cathy. You'll have to pry me out of here with a crowbar."

"C'mon in. You may change your mind once you see the decor."

"I doubt that."

Inside, Julia saw what Cathy was talking about. Smiling, Cathy stood back and watched Julia's expression. True, it did seem as if they were stepping back into the distant past. How far? Maybe the 1950s or early 1960s, maybe even the World War II era. But that was fine with Julia; she loved the way things were back then, so slow and calm and family-oriented. There were only four rooms: a living room, kitchen, one bedroom, and a bath—all fairly small but fully furnished and cozy.

The living room was decorated in what Julia always called shabby chic, although she wasn't much into interior design jargon or the home decorating channels on TV. There was a pink-, blue-, and yellow-flowered chintz couch draped with several colorful handmade quilts. There was a giant white wicker rocker with a matching chintz cushion, a vintage Motorola cabinet radio that had no doubt seen the Axelrod family gathered around it to listen to Franklin Delano Roosevelt's fireside chats, and an equally old blond-wood console TV.

Julia was pleased to see that along with the central heat and air, there was a white brick fireplace, too; one with a wood-burning insert, which would make the place warm and snug on cold winter nights. Intricate doilies were pinned on the backs of several easy chairs, which were covered in chenille except for one that was upholstered in dark blue velvet. The coffee table was scarred from years of propped-up feet, tea parties, and children's crayon markings. A large, round crocheted doily; a large, white family Bible; and a thick family photograph album sat atop it.

"See what I mean?"

"I love it, Cathy. I can understand why Lonnie wants to keep everything this way. I had some trouble letting go of my dad's things after he died. I still have some of them. So does J.D. That Charger out there was Dad's. Wish I still owned our old childhood house in Germantown."

"I know. Lonnie's like that, too. Family means everything to him."

"Well, that's one reason I'm here. J.D. and I never saw each other anymore. Only on holidays."

"Well, I tell you one thing—J.D.'s thrilled you're here. Lon and I ran into him at Walmart the other day. He nearly talked my arm off telling me about your moving here and all the family things he's planning."

"I know. But it's not all about me. He's in a

relationship that makes it hard for him to keep a smile off his face."

"Audrey Sherrod, right?"

"Yes. You know her?"

"She's a grief counselor. Lonnie's mentioned her. He saw her awhile back when his daughter died in a car wreck."

"Oh, I'm sorry."

"It was around ten years ago. He's better now. Sometimes he has a little down spell, thinking about her. Most of the time, though, he's happy and upbeat. He spends a lot of time out back. He's got a studio out in the woods behind the house."

"That's right, he's an artist."

"Yes. He paints and sculpts. Come on in the bedroom. I'll show you one of his pet projects."

The bedroom had a window facing the river and another facing the woods alongside the house. It was also decorated in vintage old lady. Lots of quilts, lots of doilies, lace curtains on the windows, and a chaise longue upholstered in a rather beautiful pink-and-white toile with lots of images of French peasants with pitchforks gathering wheat in rolling fields. Julia knew it was toile because her college roommate had a bedspread with a similar design. Otherwise, she wouldn't have a clue. There was a very old dressing table with pink lamps on either side of a huge round mirror.

"Lon made this bed. Isn't it beautiful?"

147

The bed was made of wood, but the headboard was forged in a beautiful and intricate intersecting design of roses and delicate rosebuds climbing a diamond-shaped trellis.

"Wow, that's beautiful, Cathy. Does Lonnie show his work? Or sell it?"

"Not really. He made this especially for his mother because she loved roses so much. You saw all those climbing roses beside the porch door. You'll smell them all summer when you're out on the porch."

"I like this place better and better all the time."

"The kitchen's relatively new. I'll show you."

Julia was pleased with that because she liked to cook. The gas range and refrigerator were both stainless steel. There was a dishwasher, thank goodness, and a bar with three stools, which separated the living room from the kitchen. The bathroom had an old claw-foot tub with a hand-held shower attachment on the wall. A circular brass rod held a white lace shower curtain for privacy, and there was an old-fashioned cabinet with glass doors, and wall hooks for towels.

"This couldn't be any more perfect, Cathy. You've got to let me pay you something."

"Don't be silly. I knew you'd like it. How about coming down later and having some of that fish? You too tired?"

"That sounds great. I've got my stuff in the car.

I shipped the rest of it to your address. I hope you don't mind."

"That's fine. It sounds like you're going to be busy for a while on that case."

"Yeah, it's going to be rough. I'll probably be gone all day tomorrow. And every other day, too, until we get this guy. You'll keep an eye on Jasper when I'm gone, won't you?"

"Sure, I love that dog. If you shut the gate to the access road, he can get down to the house and play with my dogs. Don't worry, he'll be fine."

Cathy gave Julia another warm hug and headed down the road to her house and her devoted husband. Julia stood on the front porch and stared out at the water. Somebody had a big dock on the opposite shore and what looked like a river restaurant. Oh yeah, she was going to like it here just fine. In fact, she was probably not going to want to leave, even for work, even partnered up with somebody as smokin' hot as Will Brannock, as Zoe liked to say. And having Cathy nearby was just too good to be true. She smiled and headed for the Charger to get her suitcase, Jasper hot on her heels.

The killer was surprised that there was so little outcry about the death of One. He'd scoured the newspapers, listened to the local news. A federal judge was dead, murdered, so where was the outrage, the media investigation into Lucien

Lockhart's corrupt and evil judgments? The crime had been reported, true, but not with all the gory details about what he'd left behind to whip the media into a frenzy. The police were giving no news conferences. But that's okay. The facts would eventually come out. He'd see to it.

What's more, the authorities and media didn't know yet that the judge was only the first of many. They wouldn't know that the killer was sitting here in the cold darkness, ready to plan for number Two. Eager to get started on that task, he pulled his jacket closer around him. The cave was always very cold, no matter how warm it was outside, but yesterday's rain had made it dank and damp. He pulled the Murder Book in front of him and stared down at One's smiling face and the piece of his tongue. He still marveled at how easy it had been to get to Lucien Lockhart and keep him at his mercy. Then again, he prided himself on his cunning and his training. He knew exactly what to do and how to do it.

After a moment of reflection, he turned the page and gazed down at his second victim. Number Two. This one would be even more gratifying to send to hell. He shut his eyes, his mouth forming a tight, compressed line as he remembered the terrible things the man in the photograph had said and done to others. Awful, hurtful things. Words that felt like hard physical blows. But Two was going to pay dearly for his villainy and evil deeds. All of them were going to pay. He took a deep breath, and then counted out thirty more dimes from the basket and placed them in a large drawstring bag. Next he put in the brand-new pair of pliers and the fillet knife he'd honed to a new razor edge not an hour ago. Two was probably spouting his vile words even now, at this very minute, destroying somebody else's life, some other happy and loving family. Very soon Two would spend his last day on this good, green Earth. His filthy, vulgar voice would be silenced forever.

Chapter 8

Inside the Tennessee Bureau of Investigation's downtown office, Will Brannock sat at his desk, staring thoughtfully at his computer screen. It was early in the morning, well before eight o'clock when the rest of the staff would arrive, but Will liked some quiet time before the office buzzed with conversation and activity. He needed to continue his search of the databases for known gang activity in the Chattanooga area. He had done it several times already, but he needed names and addresses. He stopped and rubbed his eyes, trying to clear his head.

Last night at home, he had been restless. Sleep eluded him as he tossed and turned and tried to figure out which way the investigation should go. As Will had found out right off the bat, Judge Lockhart had enough enemies to keep the entire task force busy for months. The one bright spot in the case was Julia Cass. He had changed his mind about being saddled with a CPD detective dogging his heels. Julia worked hard, backed him up, didn't complain, and didn't question his authority.

Whether the last part was completely okay with her, he didn't know, but if she resented being second in command, she didn't show it.

Weary, tired to the bone, he sighed and massaged the back of his neck. Annoyed with himself, he admitted the complexity of the case wasn't the only thing that was keeping him awake. He was thinking way too much about J.D.'s kid sister. More than he should, or even had a right to. Truth be told, he'd felt the attraction from the first time he'd laid eyes on her. It hit him about the time she had stared scornfully at him out of those amazing golden-brown eyes. Not only did Julia Cass have that striking natural beauty, she didn't even seem to know how desirable she was. Unintentionally sexy, that's what she was, and that's what turned him on. On top of that, she was smart, well trained, in control, and worked as hard as he did.

Grimacing with self-annoyance, Will twisted in his chair. He got up and poured himself more coffee from the coffeemaker on his credenza. What in the devil was the matter with him? He'd only known Julia for a matter of days. He sure as hell didn't like the way he was feeling about her, didn't like this quick rush of admiration and other more potent things. He had been the one who always scoffed at the idea of love at first sight. It wasn't his style. In fact, he never jumped the gun. Hell, he never let any woman get close enough to even consider them a couple. And Julia was a partner, temporarily, and the sister of a colleague, to boot—all reasons why he couldn't let himself get involved.

Determined to wrest her out of his mind last night, the image of those big brown eyes of hers kept intruding. He found himself wanting to see all that dark, shiny hair cascading down around her shoulders again, instead of pulled back in that severe bun she always wore. Once they had started working together, he had pushed her away, stayed silent for the most part, and kept things professional; nothing like the flirting and having fun that went on between them on that first day. Well, it looked like he was just going to have to try harder to keep her at arm's length. To quit thinking about her at all. Give her the cold shoulder. Nothing but business, no small talk, no personal contact at all. Just professional courtesy, that's what it was going to have to be.

Good God, he thought, putting down his coffee mug. *This is completely absurd.* Frustrated with himself, he was glad when some of the office assistants began to drift in, talking together in little groups, holding their own fragrant, steaming-hot cups of Starbucks coffee. *Get back to work. Solve this case.* He was damn sure that was what Julia Cass was doing. She wasn't showing any undue interest in him. He had to do the same. Conquer his attraction to her.

Redirecting his full concentration on the computer monitor, he resumed scrolling through the FBI gang database. He'd already found out the history of the Battle Street Ten group, and that they'd shown recent efforts to establish themselves in Chattanooga. The report Julia gave him indicated that just under thirty members had been arrested by the Chattanooga PD for various crimes—carjacking and theft apparently being the gang's main endeavors. Other Battle Street gangbangers had been picked up for intimidation, public brawling, and for various felony drug charges. He tapped in Maria Bota's name and watched the computer screen impatiently while the search was being made.

After several seconds, her photograph popped up. It was Maria, no doubt about it. She was younger in the police image and looked bolder than she had when he and Julia interviewed her.

Scanning her vitals, he found that the data revealed her to be a member of the Battle Street Ten group out of Memphis. The data indicated the woman had been born in Mexico and come into the States illegally with her parents, had ended up in Tennessee with her Battle Street Ten boyfriend, and then had gone into hiding after unknowingly talking to an undercover police officer about secret rites performed by the gang. He frowned. If she was undocumented, that could be why she wanted to stay under the judge's protection. It would also explain why she didn't go to the police after she got into trouble for revealing gang secrets. Whatever the reasons, Maria Bota was a dead woman once the gang got hold of her. Will better find her first, and find her fast.

"So, tell me, Will, what'd you think of my little sister? Truth now—she drivin' you crazy yet?"

J.D. Cass was standing in the doorway, grinning. He was dressed for court, in a brown suit and conservative brown-and-white striped tie, and Will knew without asking that J.D. was highly frustrated with spending his days loitering outside the courtroom like some kind of felon. Testifying was part of the job, but J.D. wasn't exactly known around the office for his patience. More important, J.D. Cass was known to be overprotective of the female members of his family. Which included Julia.

Will leaned back in his swivel chair and

gestured for J.D. to come in and take a seat. He said, "She's smart. She definitely knows what she's doing. You taught her well."

J.D. sat down and took a drink from the coffee mug in his hand. "I didn't teach her anything. She's worked hard on her own to get where she is."

Will nodded and picked up his own coffee cup. "I can't say she likes me much, but it's not getting in our way."

"She says you were getting it on with some flight attendants out at the airport."

"Yeah? So?"

"She thinks you're a womanizer."

"Well, she's got it wrong, then."

"Or maybe she doesn't. That could've described me, before I met Audrey."

Will didn't answer. J.D. was probably right. Will liked casual relationships, no strings, no commitments. He guessed that could qualify as womanizing. He didn't hide it, had no reason to. Everybody knew it. "She's not letting her personal feelings about me interfere with our job. That's the important thing."

"No, she'd never do that."

Will was already damned uncomfortable with this much discussion of his private life. He never discussed personal matters with anybody. Time for a change of subject. "How's it going at the trial? You and Tam hanging in there?"

"It's endless waiting. The attorneys are arguing

156

over every single detail. They get me on the stand, then call a recess. Hopefully, Tam and I will be finished sometime this week or next week." J.D. glanced around. "Anything I can do to help you and Julia on the Lockhart case?"

"Not really. Unless you can keep the media jackals off us. They've caught wind of the details somehow and are all over the place."

"Yeah, I've been watching the news. I'd like to know who leaked it."

"Me too. I just now found out that Lucien Lockhart's maid was a member of the Battle Street Ten gang in Memphis, at least until she spoke out of turn to a police officer. As soon as Julia gets here today, we're going back to Lockhart's house to pick her up for questioning."

J.D. turned and looked out the windows that faced the front parking lot. "She was pulling in when I was getting on the elevator. Yeah, here she comes now."

They could see Julia through the glass wall of Will's office where she had stopped across the hall to say hello to J.D's administrative assistant. She was smiling down at the woman at the desk, talking animatedly with her hands. Will had already noticed that she got along well with other women, perhaps with the exception of Iris Lockhart and Ginger Jones. She had a damn nice smile, too—one he couldn't say he'd seen much of, but one that showed those seriously deep dimples. As had happened before, he found himself wanting to do or say something to make her smile, just so he could see them. Scowling, he pushed away from his desk.

J.D. had walked outside Will's office to greet her. Will watched through the glass as J.D. gave his sister a big hug. Julia had a happy smile ready for J.D., too. They were obviously extremely close, despite the fact that they had lived in different cities for a long time. For a brief moment, Will let himself think of his own sister and the reason he had been forced to stay away from her so long. And the rest of his family, too. He missed them, missed hearing their voices and spending time with them. He tried not to think about them much, but as time went by, and although it had been his own decision to keep them at bay, he felt intensely lonely of late. It couldn't be helped, but maybe it was time for him to visit his family. Such trips had been few and far between, but it was definitely time. As usual, it would have to be done with precautions, all of them careful who they told that he was coming. But first he'd have to solve this case. That was the most important thing right now, and he'd do well to remember it.

Julia showed up in his doorway a few minutes later, stopped, and didn't say anything. Her face was serious now; no smile for Will Brannock. "Good morning, Special Agent Brannock."

"Call me Will, would you, please?" he said, impatient with her formality. Impatient with everything else about her, too, or so it seemed. He calmed himself down and said more civilly, "You manage to get any sleep last night?"

"I woke up plenty of times. I just can't get this case off my mind. You did, too, judging by your bloodshot eyes."

"I came in early this morning and found a connection to the Battle Street Ten gang."

Julia walked around the desk and leaned down beside him to examine the data on his computer screen. Close enough that he could smell her hair. Vanilla, with a little coconut, maybe. Smelled like being on Maui.

"Maria was a gang member?" Very close now, Julia searched his face. "So you were right about the triangle of dots on her finger."

"Yes. And she inadvertently was a police informant for a while, with an undercover ATF guy, until the gang found out and she was forced into hiding. After that, ATF pulled their man out of the gang, so we don't have any current information."

Julia walked back around the desk and sat down across from him. Today she had on a trim black pantsuit with a light blue T-shirt underneath the tailored jacket. No jewelry, no makeup except for maybe a little lip gloss. She didn't need it. Her skin was soft and tanned with natural color in her cheeks. Her eyelashes were as jet black as her hair. Giving himself an irate internal shake, he thrust those kinds of thoughts out of his head. What was it about her, anyway? *Give me a break, for God's sake.*

"So, what are we waiting for?" she said. "Let's find her and see what she knows."

Will stood up. "We'll take the Hummer."

The drive out to Woodstone Circle took about ten minutes. As Will took the turn into the subdivision, he broke the stilted silence that had encompassed them since they got into his truck. "So, did you get all settled in your new house?"

"Pretty much. The rest will have to wait until the moving van shows up. I'll have to store most of it until I find my own place."

"You like it out there on the river?"

At that, she did bestow a smile on him. He frowned. "I love it. It's got a great view of the river but is still really private. I like quiet places where nobody bothers me."

Ditto, Will thought. *Make that double ditto.*

Julia continued, speaking easily, apparently not fighting against any giant sexual attraction the way Will was. "I slept outside on the screened porch that overlooks the river. The rush of the current lulled me to sleep in nothing flat. Unfortunately, I kept waking up."

"Where exactly is your place?"

"It's pretty far upstream, but I like the drive. It's out north of Booker T. Washington State Park. Around Vincent Road."

While Julia gave him the exact directions to her friend's property, Will realized it didn't appear to be too far from his own place, but on the other side of the river. "That's a pretty pricey area, if it's where I think it is."

"You're right. I passed quite a few la-di-da houses along that road. Cathy said Lonnie's family has owned their property for decades. Lonnie's father and grandfather wouldn't sell to the developers and neither would he, so it's stayed in the family. He's got a big acreage, but it's built up all around him."

"I bet it's worth a pretty penny right now."

"Apparently, with that kind of view. Lonnie doesn't care about being wealthy, it seems. He likes things just the way they are. You know, family tradition and all that sentimental stuff."

"I take it that Jasper likes it, too?"

That got Will another brief, sidelong smile. "He's in hog heaven. I could barely get him out of bed this morning, he slept so well. He's not a morning dog, you see. But Cathy raises service dogs. German shepherds and Akitas. So he'll probably play with them all afternoon."

By the time they reached the gate of Lockhart's house, the media was out in full force. Satellite trucks lined the shady street, and attractive

161

newscasters were all over the place, primping and preening before they appeared on camera for the morning update. Nothing like a sensational murder to draw them like flies. Will flashed his badge to the Lockhart security guard stationed at the entrance and waited for the electronic gate to slowly swing open.

"Is Mrs. Lockhart here?" Will asked the officer.

"No, she couldn't take the media barrage, so she said she was going to spend the night with one of her friends."

"Which friend?"

The question amused the guard. He was a young guy, blond hair cut in a military buzz, wrap-around sunglasses, and a black polo shirt and black pants. He looked like an off-duty Marine. "Mrs. Lockhart doesn't tell us common folk anything. Just open and close the gate and keep your mouth shut. That's what she told us to do."

Will wasn't exactly surprised. Iris Lockhart would not win any Miss Congeniality satin sashes. The woman was more than unlikable—verging on contemptible, in Will's book. But he did wonder if that friend of hers was male or female. The judge had had his share of women on the side. He had a feeling that Icy Iris did, too. It was something else to check out.

"What about the housemaid? Maria Bota. Did she and her son go with Mrs. Lockhart?"

The guard shrugged. "Who knows? If she did, I

162

didn't see her. The limousine has dark-tinted windows."

"Thanks. Good luck with the news morons. They'll eat you alive if they get a chance."

"So I've been told."

"You think Iris might have taken herself a lover?" Julia asked the minute Will rolled up his window, obviously homing in on the same track as Will. That was happening a lot nowadays.

"It's possible, if she could actually find somebody who could stomach her."

Julia's laugh was genuine and amused. "Maybe she has this slow-witted lover boy who whacked her husband while she established a convenient alibi way down yonder in the Pelican State."

Will couldn't stop his grin. But he ended it pretty damn quick. *Keep it professional,* he told himself. Arm's length at all times. "That's something we'll need to check out," he said seriously, ignoring her attempt at humor.

Pulling up under the columned porte cochere, Will and Julia got out and walked down along the east side of the house. Unlike the day they'd first found the body, today it was extremely quiet and the property was deserted. The morning air was still cool, some of the shaded shrubs still wet with dew, and the soothing chirps and whistles of birds rustling around high up in the oak trees were the only sounds. They walked past the pool and came upon the crime scene, which was still taped off, dark smudges from the TBI finger-printing process still noticeable. The judge's mutilated body was gone, moved downtown to the morgue. Will wondered again, for the thousandth time, what kind of monster could do such a horrific mutilation, and a better question: Why?

"If this murder is gang-related," Julia said softly, no doubt affected by the depth of the still-ness, "what was the motive? Because the judge helped Maria by giving her a job and a place to live? Seems to me they would just take her out as a warning to others and not risk murdering a federal judge. That's not going to help a criminal gang stay under the radar."

"I know. Unless they just wanted to scare her and he got in the way."

"Which they did. She's scared to death. But if she's a traitor, why leave her alive instead of making an example out of her? Why didn't they kill both of them?"

"Good question."

When they reached the guesthouse out back, Will rapped a knuckle on the door, and then stood back to one side. He put his hand on his weapon strapped to his belt. He noticed that Julia did the same. She had all the procedures down pat, and Will was feeling more comfortable about her instincts with every hour that passed. More so than with some of his fellow TBI guys. He hated to say it, but some of them didn't always follow procedures as precisely as they should. Something told him that Julia might have run into an unwelcome and dangerous surprise sometime in her past law enforcement career. Not that she exhibited fear or reluctance, just good common sense and caution. Which was a good way to be. That's the way he was, the way he had been since that long-ago day when his life had changed forever.

No answer came from inside. Will reached out and tried the handle. It gave, and he pushed it inward. Iris Lockhart had given them permission to search the property the day they'd interviewed her. The living room was empty. He called out to the maid.

"Maria, are you here? We need to talk to you."

His voice died in the complete silence until they heard a distant shout from somebody from the media installed outside on the street.

"Nobody's home. Let's toss the place and see what we can find," Julia suggested.

The two of them entered with guns drawn, *Law & Order*–style. No sounds from inside the house, but the interior of Maria Bota's apartment was no longer neat and orderly. Now it looked as if a whirlwind had barreled through it at a hundred miles per hour. Drawers were open, many empty, others with clothing hanging out. Inside the bedrooms the sheets were disheveled, and the dirty dishes still sat unwashed in the kitchen sink.

Julia opened the door to the second bedroom. "It looks to me like she took her son and left here in a big hurry."

"She's on the run, all right."

Will pulled out his cell phone and put out a nationwide BOLO on the woman and her child. They needed to find Maria ASAP and see why she was running and from whom, and if she did know who killed Lucien Lockhart. "I'm going to check out the Battle Street gang members around here, see what they know about Maria."

Julia nodded. "You want me to go with you? One thing I'd like to check out is the scales left at the scene. They're unusual. Maybe I can get a lead on the killer if I find out where he got them."

"Good idea."

"What about the lab? Have you heard anything from the medical examiner yet?"

"Yeah. Phil Hayes gets things done. Death was by hanging: asphyxiation. The other wounds were made before he died. They're still doing tests on the body. This case is priority, trust me. Dead federal judges wake up people downtown, big-time."

"The coins mean something, and the killer left them for a reason. He's sending us all kinds of messages, like the *ONE* on the floor. We've just got to figure them out."

"I hope something clicks soon. We're getting nowhere."

166

● ● ●

After Will dropped Julia off at the Charger, she drove home and took her laptop computer out onto the screened porch. The spacious and shady outdoor room had already become her favorite spot in the converted boathouse. Apparently, Jasper had settled in, too. He lay beside her on his side of the daybed, snoring slightly, very, very relaxed. She smiled and scratched his ears, but she was thinking about her research. Her Internet searches hadn't gone so well, thus far. Julia was computer literate; she had a knack for electronics in general, something that came in handy in her line of work. She had asked forensics to blow up the photograph of the scales left at the scene. It was propped up against the lamp in front of her. So were all the other crime scene images.

The technicians had made close-ups of the parts of the scales: the chains, the two baskets, and the crossed-swords finial, but there was no manufacturer's mark, no evidence of a maker, a date, or a place. She had already visited dozens of websites advertising similar scales, with no results. There was the possibility that the scales were cheap products brought in from overseas. The perp could have ground off all identifying marks, but there was no sign of that kind of abrasion.

Julia sighed and rested her eyes by gazing out at the water. It was really pretty here on the

Axelrod family's neck of the river. She felt good about the move so far. It had been a bit scary to pull up stakes and start all over again, but it was turning out all right. It was great to see her friends and J.D. Even Will Brannock was turning out to be less of a pain in the neck than she thought he'd be. He was different, all right, but he'd been on his best behavior. No longer did he appear to be that shallow woman-chaser that she had first branded him. He was serious about his work, a thoughtful and thorough investigator, and sometimes even halfway pleasant. Not the witty, fun-loving guy who'd driven her home from the airport that day. He had turned that off since they'd become partners. He was being professional. She admired that about him.

There was something else about him that she noticed right off, other than how good-looking he was. Unfortunately, she now readily admitted that Will Brannock was one hot hunk, but he was also closemouthed about himself and his life. Almost to the point of being secretive. There had to be a reason why. Otherwise, he seemed like a fairly normal guy. But he was always unnecessarily cautious: always looking around at his surroundings, at anybody who happened to be in the vicinity or approaching him, almost coiled and ready like some kind of big jungle cat, as if he expected trouble to come at him at any moment. Of course, all law enforcement officers feel that way most of the time. But something was up with Will, and she was curious to know what. She intended to find out, too.

Jasper snorted, then rolled up onto his feet and jumped off the bed, a sure indication she had company coming. His sense of hearing was almost as acute as his sense of smell. She watched the road, and it wasn't long before Lonnie Axelrod showed up on the path edging the riverbank, with two of Cathy's panting German shepherds.

"Hey, anybody home up there?" he called from out on the driveway.

"I'm working on the porch. C'mon in."

Lonnie entered the door with the dogs, and Jasper ambled over to meet them, his tail wagging. Jasper was going to love all this canine companionship. He usually just had Julia to play with.

"Hope I'm not interrupting anything important, Julia."

"No, you're fine. I'm just doing some research on my case."

Julia hoped he didn't ask her a bunch of questions about the Lockhart murder, because he wasn't going to get anything out of her. To her surprise and pleasure, he didn't broach the subject at all.

"I didn't see your car come by, so I thought I'd take Jasper out for a run with Cody and Jack."

"He'd love that. It's a nice day for it."

Lonnie glanced around. "How are you settling in down here?"

"Fine. This's a great place. I really appreciate your generosity."

"My mama loved this river, loved that dock down there. She liked to fish and go out in the boat. She was happiest when she was right here, enjoying the outdoors. And she did it till the very end."

"I can see why. What's Cathy up to today?"

"She's down at the house, catching up on paperwork on the dogs. Charlie Sinclair's coming by and picking up a couple of the dogs for shots and flea dips. You want him to take Jasper along for a treatment?"

"Yes, he's due this month. When's Charlie coming?"

"Sometime this afternoon. He's out fishing today and said he'd drop by in his bass boat and pick up the dogs on his way home."

"Wish I was out there with him."

"Me too."

Lonnie smiled at her, and after he'd taken the dogs and disappeared into the woods behind the boathouse, she settled back, this time in the porch swing with the laptop across her knees.

She pulled up the photos of the coins. The first photo showed them on the scale, stacked on top of each other in two neat piles. Fifteen each. Thirty dimes. Three dollars. What was the significance of thirty dimes? There had to be some kind of connection. Some kind of message or clue left behind for them. Julia picked up the second photograph, in which the coins had been laid in rows on a sheet of white typing paper at the lab. She studied it for a long time, then picked up the third picture, which duplicated the rows of dimes but with each turned to the opposite side. Nothing clicked. What the hell did it mean?

Standing up, she moved into the kitchen and got a cold can of 7UP out of the fridge. She popped the cap and stood looking around her new apartment. It never failed to amuse her, but in a good way, with all its antiques and antiquated machines, but it made her feel comfortable, too. There were pictures all around, and she picked up a frame with a photograph of a little old white-haired lady standing with Lonnie on the dock. His mother, she assumed, and she looked like quite a lady. She had on wading boots, a red-and-black plaid lumberjack shirt, and jeans. She had her hair pulled back in a bun. She reminded Julia of the granny in the old Tweety Bird cartoons. Lonnie had his arm around her shoulders and a great big smile on his face. Other photographs showed a younger Lonnie with a pretty young woman and two little kids, all holding fishing poles. The river had been a big part of his life. No wonder he refused all those lucrative offers to buy his property.

Back out on the porch, Julia sat down again and spread the pictures of the dimes out in front of her. She studied them one at a time. By the time she was finished examining each one, she was pretty sure she knew what the killer had meant. The coins all had different dates, but every one had been minted before 1964. If she recalled correctly, that was when the government stopped using pure silver in dimes. That meant thirty pieces of silver, and in Biblical terms that meant betrayal. The perp was exacting revenge for some kind of betrayal. The tongue-slashing could be revenge for something the judge had said to or about the killer. She checked the 1964 date on the Internet and confirmed that she remembered right about the silver in the minting.

Excited, she picked up the phone and punched in Will's number. He picked up at once.

"Yeah, Julia? What?"

"I think I just figured out the meaning of the coins."

"Hit me with it."

Julia told him, almost positive now that she was right.

Silence for a few beats, and then Will said, "That makes perfect sense. Good work, Cass. Now all we've got to figure out is who and why."

No calling her Jules anymore. No joking. Special Agent Serious as Sin. "So what about the Battle Street gang? You find out anything?"

"Yeah. I talked to a couple of our guys who work undercover for us, and they verified that the gang will kill Maria if they get to her. They're going to try to find out more on her background. Ask around with some of the gang members."

"That's good. Hopefully she'll show up for us before they get her."

"God, I hope so. She's got a little kid."

Julia had enough experience with gangbangers to know they wouldn't hesitate to kill a mother and her child. She thought of Maria's darling little boy with his big, innocent dark eyes. Her heart clenched, and she hoped Maria had found a good place to hide.

"Keep working on the scales. I'll see you tomorrow morning, bright and early."

"Right."

About an hour after she'd ended that conversation, she heard the low buzz of a boat's motor. She walked outside and down the steps to the dock. Charlie Sinclair was approaching her dock in his old black-and-gold bass boat. He was alone, and he saluted her. She watched him expertly maneuver the craft up alongside the well-maintained dock. He looked good to her. His gray hair was cropped very short, his mustache and goatee neatly trimmed. In the Marines he'd been a veterinarian for service dogs, and still used that training in his veterinarian practice and dog-boarding business. He was just over five foot ten, muscular, agile, and strong; and a dog whisperer, if ever there was one.

"Welcome to my new home," Julia said, taking the yellow ski rope he threw her and looping it around the piling.

"You're a sight for sore eyes, girl," Charlie said, looking up at her. "Lonnie called and said you might want me to take Jasper back to my place for a checkup and shots."

"Yeah, I'd appreciate it." Julia eyed his rope and remembered the last time she'd seen a yellow ski rope. "Where'd you get this rope, Charlie?"

"The ski rope?" He paused, thinking about it. "I think I bought it on sale at Home Depot. Why?"

"I was just wondering."

"Don't tell me you're taking up skiing on the Tennessee River?"

"Nope, not yet." She smiled. "C'mon up and have a soda. I have beer, too, if you'd prefer it."

"Don't mind if I do. I'll take the beer. Bud Light, if you've got it."

"I do have it. Lonnie's got Jasper and his dogs out for a run. They'll be back any time now. That'll give us a little time to talk."

Up on the porch, they sat across from each other at the glass-topped wicker table. Charlie cracked open his Budweiser and took a deep slug. He wiped his mouth on the sleeve of his tan, long-sleeved shirt. "It's good you're here, Julia. Just

174

like old times, ain't it, with all of us livin' out here within hailin' distance?"

She smiled. "Not quite hailing distance, but close enough. You know what, Charlie? For some reason, I feel like I've come home, even though I've never lived in Chattanooga before. It's just, well, comfortable and peaceful, and like I'm right where I ought to be. Cathy's the best friend I ever had, and I've missed her more than I thought."

"And I am?"

"Well, you're a good friend, too. And you know it. You're more like my K-9 mentor, my dog guru."

"Kinda like Yoda?"

"Sure, especially in the looks department."

They laughed together. Charlie's grin faded, and his face grew somber all of a sudden. He scratched his graying goatee and placed a troubled gaze on Julia's face. "Any word on who killed the judge?"

"We're working on it."

"He wasn't exactly the Mother Teresa of the Hamilton County criminal court system, but if the rumors are true, he died pretty hard."

"I can't really discuss it, Charlie. You know that."

"Right. I'm not pressing you. It's all anybody's talking about downtown. They're goin' crazy trying to reschedule his docket. Jane's distraught, but everybody knows she was in love with the judge. It wasn't hard to see."

"And he loved her, too?"

"If he did, he sure didn't show it at work. He treated her as disrespectfully as he did everybody else."

"How'd he treat you?"

"About the same as he did other people. Just a lot of condescension and hatefulness. If you made a mistake or said something wrong, you know, incorrect English and whatnot, he'd put you down for it, in front of everybody if he could manage it."

"I'm sorry, Charlie. You don't deserve that."

"That's why I've worked with dogs all these years. They love you unconditionally and never talk back."

"Why'd you sign up as a bailiff?"

"It came open when I was wantin' something to do. I thought it sounded interesting and like something I could do and still keep my vet work part-time while I trained my dogs. I've been really lonely since Sonia died. I don't mind admittin' that. She was the best thing that ever happened to me."

"Yeah, she was special, to be sure. Is it still lonely, even with all the dogs around?"

"Not so much anymore. Lonnie's gotten to be a good friend since he married Cathy and I got to know him some. We fish when Cathy's got something goin' on. I'm pretty much just layin' back enjoyin' life right now. Just takin' things slow and easy as they come along."

"Speaking of dogs, I think I hear them coming."

Moments later Lonnie showed up, all three dogs running out in front of him. Julia caught Jasper and snapped on his leash and got the directions up to Charlie's place, then stood watching the two men herd all three dogs into the boat and take off. Lonnie's dock wasn't far upstream, and Charlie would drop him off, then head home. She watched them until they were out of sight; she already missed Jasper. She could pick him up at Charlie's in the next couple of days, though, and she did need to do more research on those damn scales. Maybe she could even get into some of the judge's old cases and find out if any of them were particularly controversial. If it was revenge that motivated this kind of mutilation murder, she suspected more than one convicted felon would hold a grudge against a judge like Lucien Lockhart.

Chapter 9

Julia opened the front door of the Cracker Barrel at Lookout Valley and scanned the gift shop looking for Will. He had called and asked her to meet him there. Why, she did not know. She finally saw him where he was standing and reading a newspaper near the hostess station at the back of the shop. When Will looked up and saw her, he waved her over, and she wound her way through about twenty customers browsing around the island shelves or checking out the nifty gift items at the cashier's station.

"Thanks for meeting me here," he said, placing the folded newspaper under his arm. "I thought we could discuss the case over lunch and fill each other in on what we've been doing."

"Sounds good to me."

Will asked for a table for two, and they followed the waitress into the noisy dining room with its wood tables and chairs and giant colonial fireplace. Julia liked the food at Cracker Barrel; good, old-fashioned, Southern home cooking, especially the chicken and dumplings.

Yum. Her stomach took notice of the delicious aromas wafting out of the kitchen.

"You ever eaten here before?" Will asked her.

"Who hasn't?" she answered, sliding into the wooden booth near the front windows while Will took the side facing the door.

The waitress took their drink orders; both ordered sweet tea with lemon. Will placed his menu aside. "I always order chicken and dumplings," he said. "They're not as good as my mom's, but they're good."

Julia's antennae went up. Did Will actually mention his family? No way. *Well, well,*

Brannock, what a momentous first in our relationship. Of course, she jumped on it. "So your mom's a good cook?"

Will instantly looked disconcerted. Julia could almost read his thoughts: *Oops, I mentioned my mother to Julia. Quick, call in the cleanup crew.* Frowning, she watched him squirm. What in the world was his problem with all this silly secrecy with which he surrounded himself? Julia wasn't a snoop or a busybody, and didn't really care how good his mother's dumplings were. On the other hand, she was the suspicious type—detectives usually were—and she'd never known anybody who could shy away from questions about his past as skillfully as Will Brannock could.

After a ridiculously long pause during which Julia stared unblinkingly at him, Will finally said with totally feigned nonchalance, "Yes, she is. Some of her dishes put Paula Deen to shame."

"Then she's a pretty damn good cook." Julia closed her menu and placed it atop Will's. "I just bought a Paula Deen skillet. An orange one. It's great for frying chicken. Does your mom live around here? I'd love to meet her."

"No." Will looked away from her rapt gaze and checked out the nearby tables. As was his wont, he quickly changed the subject, slick as a whistle. He picked up the *Chattanooga Times Free Press* and tossed it down on the table in front of her. "I guess you've heard that the

179

media's coined a name for our perpetrator?"

Picking up the paper, Julia looked at the giant headlines: WHEN WILL THE TONGUE SLASHER STRIKE AGAIN? CHATTANOOGA WAITS IN FEAR. She grimaced and lowered her voice. "Well, why don't they just send him an engraved invitation to kill again? They might as well. And yeah, I heard it this morning on CBS. Catchy, huh? Pretty apropos, though. How do you think they found out about the tongue?"

"Who knows? Probably somebody with an agenda or in need of quick cash leaked the details. We'll probably never know. Phil's trying to find out. How did your search of the scales go?"

Thus, another of Will's usual and abrupt 180-degree changes of subject, casual but effective. She had a feeling he'd had lots of practice perfecting the technique. The little dickens thought he was getting out of telling her about his family. Wrong. Some serious digging was now in order. "Tell me, Will, do you have any family in Chattanooga?"

Will's brow creased noticeably; he was obviously annoyed with her persistence. Did she hit a nerve, or what? It was certainly an innocent enough question. What was the big deal with him?

Neither of them said anything while the waitress put down two frosty glasses of iced tea and scribbled down their order. Chicken and dumplings for her, with fried okra, fried apples, and green beans on the side. Will had the same but with macaroni and cheese and corn, and opted for the fried apples, too. All good food and exactly the same, no matter which Cracker Barrel in what city.

But Julia wasn't going to let him adeptly slippery-slide himself out of answering her questions this time. "So, what is it? Anybody related to you live around here or not, Brannock?"

He gave in. "No. I don't have much family. None around here."

"Well, I can relate to that. J.D.'s all I have now."

Will sipped his tea and kept up his intense surveillance of the premises, like he was expecting a swarm of killer bees to wing their way through the windows. He looked at her. "We still haven't gotten a hit on Maria Bota's whereabouts. She's gone underground with her son."

"Or the gangbangers already snatched her."

"If that's the case, she's probably dead."

From what Julia had pulled up on the Battle Street gang, she didn't doubt that. The idea was sobering. "Maybe she'll turn up soon. If so, I can't wait to reinterview her."

"Yeah, me either. Anything new on the scales?" he asked again.

"Nope, not yet. It appears to be a unique piece, but I haven't searched all the websites yet. None of the big manufacturers list it in their catalogs."

"He could've picked it up at a flea market or a garage sale."

"Maybe. I've been thinking that he might be connected with the legal system somehow. You know, the scales of justice, and all that. It would fit right into our scenario. The victim was a judge, after all. It could be something like that."

"Yes, definitely. Or the killer could be one of Lockhart's multitude of lovers, someone he jilted or abused. By the sound of things, he had plenty of them."

While he spoke, Will's eyes were darting from the people eating around them to the entrance and back to the exit, examining each and every customer, as if to get the jump on the one with the belt of live grenades. She looked around, too. Oh yeah, maybe that little eighty-year-old granny with the white hair, navy-blue polyester pantsuit, and white sneakers was having lunch with her grandkids because she needed a break from her domestic terrorist bomb-making.

Julia scanned all the other tables. Unfortunately, being around Will so much was beginning to make her into a Paranoid Patty. Maybe while she was working with him, she should strap an extra .38 snub nose to her ankle. "Or that could be the motive," she suggested. "His wife's as frosty as a snowbank. Yes, I can see her exacting revenge. You know, the poor-little-me, mistreated-and-abused-wife routine."

Will halted his heretofore steady surveillance of Cracker Barrel diners and caught her gaze. "You really think a woman like Iris Lockhart could mutilate her husband's body like that?"

"I think anybody is capable of just about anything, given the right opportunity. Especially to right a wrong they felt was perpetrated against them. I'm sure you've seen that kind of thing in your tenure at the TBI."

"I have, but why would Iris act now? She's put up with him for years. And from what I could tell, she's doing exactly what she wants to do, and did so even before he was murdered. There's a three-million-dollar life insurance policy that she'll get, but she already has access to all the money they have. Both their names are on everything."

"Did you check into her love life, if she's even got one? My bet is that she'd probably have to pay a man to take her out." Julia decided to inject a bit of humor; it seemed Will could use a hefty dose of ha-ha lately. "Hey, maybe we ought to look into the Elite Escort Service. They probably have some guys who'd squire her around for, say, ten million dollars."

Will didn't bite. Didn't smile, either. "I doubt that. I have agents checking out her mother and friends in New Orleans. So far, they're all upstanding citizens and beyond reproach. I still think the gang angle is more probable. Iris wouldn't dirty her hands."

What in heaven's name had happened to that happy-go-lucky guy with all the clever banter she'd first met? Had making her acquaintance turned him into a zombie? Or does the smiley Will Brannock go into hibernation until the weekends? More pertinent of all, perhaps: Does Will Brannock have a split personality?

"Everything okay with you, Will?"

He looked back at her, surprised. "Yeah, why?"

"Well, all work and no play makes Jack a dull boy—you know the drill."

"Are you saying I'm dull?"

"No, just distracted and sort of, well, wary of everything."

"Aren't you?"

"Yes, I am."

"Okay, then."

Brannock wasn't going to tell her anything concerning himself—even if he had a knife sticking out of his chest he wouldn't admit it, so she might as well give up with the inquiries. At least she knew his mom could cook. "I was talking to Charlie the other day, and he told me that Judge Lockhart had lots of controversial cases. Some of them that Charlie says were rumored to involve payoffs to the judge."

"I've heard the same thing through other sources. You and Charlie Sinclair are good friends, I take it?"

"Like I told you, he trained me when I first

started with the Nashville K-9 unit. I learned just about everything I know about dogs from him. So did Cathy. We went through the initial K-9 training courses together. Later, he made both of us instructors."

Will nodded and seemed to ponder things for a moment. "It could be some past defendant, or maybe some kind of personal hit arranged by a criminal element that he betrayed somehow."

Both remained quiet as the waitress arrived with their food. She hovered a moment to refill their tea glasses. Julia watched Will pick up a corn bread muffin and slather it with real butter. Good, she liked people who actually ate and enjoyed their food. As far as she was concerned, there was way too much emphasis on being superskinny. She had never worried much about her weight. She was naturally tall and slender, but nobody liked food as much as she did. She picked up a biscuit and broke it open. It was fluffy inside and still warm.

She added butter, took a bite, savored it a moment, and said, "I know we've talked about this, but I still can't quite figure it. If the Battle Street guys are involved in this because of Maria Bota, why would they murder and mutilate the judge and give her time to run? Why wouldn't they just off her and end it?"

"I know. Slashing the tongue could have been a warning to her, but why use the judge to send the warning?"

"Unless he'd been coming down hard on one too many of their members."

"I'll let you check that out, too," Will said, forking one of those delectable dumplings into his mouth.

"I'll get on it today."

They continued to discuss the case while they ate, making sure to keep their voices low. Except for the tongue removal, the pertinent facts of the murder hadn't hit the news yet, but it was only a matter of time. Problem was, they had lots of leads but no real clues. That was not a good thing. She needed to come up with something concrete, or she and Will Brannock would still be discuss-ing the same possibilities over chicken and dump-lings a month from now. Something was bound to break, something hiding in plain sight that she'd been missing. She'd go home, get out the crime scene photos, and study every detail. All night, if she had to. She was missing something significant, but that didn't mean she couldn't find it.

"Well, well, lawsy me, if it isn't the prettiest little detective this side of San Diego," said a man's deep voice close behind her.

Julia jerked around and found Maximilian Hazard standing right behind her. He grinned down at her, looking as handsome as ever, all tall and broad-shouldered in his loose blue- and yellow-flowered Hawaiian shirt, flip-flops, and long khaki shorts. Charming and devil-may-care, Max had sun-bleached blond hair long enough to tuck behind his ears, blue eyes the exact color of today's August sky, a square chin, clean-shaven cheeks, and a sensual mouth that was always smiling or laughing. He used to make her laugh like nobody else. Too bad he lived up to his last name.

"Hello, Max. Funny meeting you here. Are you following me again?" He had followed her around, once upon a time in Nashville when they were investigating the same murder. Since he lived in and investigated out of Chattanooga, she hadn't seen him since that case had ended nearly two years ago.

"Mind if I join you?" Max said, and without waiting for an answer sat down beside her, forcing her to scoot over.

"Yes, I do. This is a private conversation."

"Please, please, don't tell me you're married to this guy," Max groaned, giving Will a considerable once-over. "It'll break my heart if you are, Julie girl. I won't survive it, I tell you. I'll die."

"What do you want, Max? I thought I made it clear I didn't want to see you anymore."

"But that was then, and this is now. And I am here, and so are you. So who's Mr. Grim across the table? He doesn't like me one bit—I can tell."

No wonder Max thought that, Julia decided,

judging by the hard look Will was giving him. Will's dark eyes didn't waver.

"Who is this guy, Julia? Is he bothering you?"

"You bet I bother her—hot and bother you, right, sweetheart?" Max reached across the table, extending his hand to Will. "Maximilian Hazard, private eye. M. Hazard Detective Agency. East Brainerd. Glad to make your acquaintance, Julia's Stern Lunch Companion."

Julia suppressed a smile. Will looked at Max's hand as if it were a large, hairy spider, and then back at Julia. She shrugged one shoulder, but she wished Max would go away. She watched Will break down and shake Max's hand, albeit with distaste. "Will Brannock."

"You stealin' my girl, Brannock?"

"Shut up, Max, would you? Will's a special agent with the TBI, if you must know. We're working together on a case."

Max turned to Julia and put all his attention on her. "I'll shut up, if you'll go out with me tonight."

"I'm busy."

"How about tomorrow night?"

"I'm busy."

"How about any night between now and the day you die?"

Julia laughed and shook her head. Will stared unblinkingly at Max, this time as if he was thinking about heaving the guy bodily over three or four of the nearest tables. He was probably big enough to do it, too. The idea made Julia laugh again.

"Get out of here, Max. I mean it. We're talking business. You're interrupting us."

One thing about Max, he always knew when to stop. It was an acquired knack of his. Usually right up to the point where he was about to get punched in the nose or thrown out by a bouncer. "Okay, sorry about that, but I saw you and almost passed out from the sheer joy of being so close to you again, so I had to come over. I couldn't stop myself. I mean it. Charlie told me you were moving to Chattanooga, and here you are. He gave me your cell phone number again when I saw him yesterday, so I'll be calling you soon. Decide where you want to go on our future first date, and I'll make it happen. Anywhere you say. Anywhere at all. Anytime at all." He gave her a quick peck on the cheek and then gave a sarcastic salute to Will. "Nice to meet you, Mr. Brannock. Take good care of my girl here."

Max strode off with his usual cocky saunter, saying something to their waitress that made her laugh out loud.

Silence reigned at their table.

"So, who's the clown?" Will asked, his eyes following Max's retreating back.

"He's okay. Just likes to goof around. He's pretty good at his job. I ran into him on a mutual case a couple of years back. Had to arrest him for trespassing. Twice, actually. He's been asking me out ever since."

More quiet. "And have you gone out with him?"

"And you're interested in that, why?"

Will looked nonplussed by her question. "Never mind. You're right. It's none of my business. No need to get so touchy, though."

Well now, me *touchy? Will Brannock's one to talk. He is the king of touchy,* Julia thought, but she said as pleasantly as she could, "I'm not being touchy. I've never gone out with him, but I might someday. He can be entertaining enough when he wants to be. He's good at his job, but not above bending the rules now and then. That's his negative point."

"He looks like a California beach bum to me. I bet he's got a surfboard hanging on his living room wall."

"That pretty much nails him. That's where he's from. San Diego. LA before that."

"Here, I'll treat," Will said, conversation now obviously over. "I've got to get going. I'm supposed to meet somebody. I don't want to keep her waiting."

Julia immediately stood up and grabbed her brown leather purse. As he put down a tip, she bid him so long, not waiting for him to go to the cash register and pay the bill and walk outside with her. As she left the front doors and stood on the big veranda with the rocking chairs, she wondered who the *she* was that he was in such a hurry to meet. Well, there was probably a myriad of choices in the Will Brannock Magic World of Maniacal Privacy. Why, heavens above, it could be Pam, the redheaded airport bombshell, perhaps, back in town for another romp in the hay. Or Ginger, the vampiest vamp of the Elite Escort crew, who let it be known loud and clear that she was even more available than available could be. But probably for a price—or maybe not, considering Will's hot factor.

Somehow Julia didn't like the idea of him meeting up with either one of those women. Her thoughts hit the stop button and skidded to a shuddering halt. Oh my God, she thought, what was this all about? Surely she wasn't starting to fall for him. Surely his good looks, face and body like a Greek god, and overwhelming masculine sex appeal didn't affect her. Surely not. But, oh no, yes, it did, Julia realized with not a little trepidation. One thing she did know: she certainly didn't like the idea of taking a running jump onto the Will Brannock Love 'Em and Leave 'Em Fan Club bus with the arena full of other women who found him just as attractive and desirable. Uh-uh, that would not do, not for one teeny little minute. She was going to have to step back and give herself a biting lesson in self-restraint, corral the troubling thoughts of sexy Will that were beginning to run wild and reckless through her mind of late, and bid those roiling romantic notions a fond adieu. Will was her partner right now—off-limits, and that was that. *So get a grip on yourself, boiling hormones.*

As Audrey Sherrod drove into the Lookout Valley Cracker Barrel's parking lot, she felt a long shiver course down her spine, and tried not to think about the horrible scene she had experienced the last time she had been summoned to this particular restaurant. It was the day they'd found Jill Scott's body. Jill was the Rocking Chair killer's second victim. The poor girl had been propped up in one of the country restaurant's porch rockers, and in her arms was a child's tiny skeleton wrapped in a blanket. She swallowed hard, remembering. Those murders had happened over a year ago, but it had affected her in so many terrible ways, revealing deeply hidden secrets in her own family that had come back to haunt her and turn her world upside down.

Trying again not to dwell on the past, she got out of her cocoa-brown Buick Enclave. No, the idea of eating at the scene of a previous murder wasn't particularly appetizing to her. But she wasn't there to eat. She was there to visit the gift shop, and she never would have set foot in the place if it hadn't been for Zoe. The teenager had begged her to pick up a specific T-shirt that she wanted to wear to the surprise party that Audrey was planning, to welcome J.D.'s sister, Julia, to Chattanooga. Tam and her mother, Geraldine, had thrown a surprise party for Tam's father's birthday at the Read House in downtown Chattanooga the year before, and it had been a great success. It would be the perfect place for Julia's party, too.

Grabbing her Coach bag, she got out and hurried across the parking lot, avoiding the end of the porch where the poor girl's body had been found. All the wooden rockers in that area had been removed, replaced by long benches under the windows. No one sat on them. She wondered if everybody else remembered that day as vividly as she did. Trying again to put it out of her mind, she pulled open the door to the gift shop.

The only good thing about that day, of course, was that she had also met J.D. Cass, right here in this parking lot. Not that she had liked him one little bit at the time. No, at first glance she had considered him a condescending creep. A man she had later learned was alienating his own darling daughter, Zoe. But then, as the case progressed and she'd spent more time with Zoe, and therefore with J.D., she had seen the true man. They'd been together for a year now, and she was ready to commit. She'd told him once that if he hadn't proposed to her in six months, she would do the honors. So it was long overdue, and another happy reason to have a party.

Once inside the busy eatery, she was surprised to find J.D.'s colleague, Will Brannock, walking quickly toward the exit. She smiled and held out her hand. She liked Will a lot. He had been the TBI agent with J.D. the night they'd finally captured the Rocking Chair killer as he attempted to smother his last victim. Will seemed like a nice man, not that she knew all that much about him—except that, in J.D.'s words, he was one hell of a TBI agent.

"Hi, Will. It's good to see you again."

"Yes, it's been awhile." Will Brannock kept looking around at the other customers. Who was he looking for? "Are you meeting J.D. for lunch?" he asked her.

"No. He's still waiting around at the trial."

Will gave her one of his half smiles. He was a very handsome man, she decided, but she'd always thought so.

"I guess that tells me what kind of mood he's in," Will said.

"He's no happy camper, that's for sure." It was Audrey's turn to glance around. "Are you here alone?"

"Julia Cass had lunch with me, but she took off a few minutes ago."

"Really? Well, that's a coincidence, because I wanted to talk to you about her."

"Me?"

Audrey grinned up at him. "So, what's it like

working with her? J.D.'s always bragging on her, telling me what a great detective she is."

"He's right. We probably ought to try to get her to defect over to the TBI."

"She's very pretty," Audrey noted then, watching for his reaction. What a cute couple they would make, both so tall and good-looking.

"I haven't noticed."

Audrey laughed at his obvious lie. She knew enough about Will Brannock to know that he would have noticed something like that first thing. "Yeah, I'll bet."

He looked uncomfortable with the subject, and she decided he had definitely noticed Julia's beauty.

"What's up about her, Audrey?"

"First, you have to swear yourself to secrecy. I don't want her to find out about this."

Will hesitated, frowning a little. "Okay, I guess."

"I'm going to have a surprise party for her. You know, to welcome her to town. It was Zoe's idea, and I'm inviting all our friends and colleagues. J.D. says she won't have time to make new friends very fast because she has a tendency to obsess about her cases. Do you think that's true?"

"Yeah, I'd say so. I can't find fault with that, though. That's what makes her so good."

"True. J.D.'s the same way. I'd like to invite some of her friends, too, if she's got any here in town. J.D. gave me a few names. Do you know if there's anyone she might want to have there?"

"She's staying at a friend's house. Cathy Axelrod is her name. Her husband's name is Lonnie. Charlie Sinclair down at the courthouse is an old friend of hers."

"The bailiff? I know him. He's so nice. But I didn't know he was friends with Julia."

"Don't know of anyone else. She saw a guy today, here at the restaurant, a man named Maximilian Hazard, but I'm not sure she likes him much. J.D. probably knows more about her friends than I do. Julia and I haven't known each other very long."

"I've already asked him." She hesitated, gazing up at him. He was even taller than J.D. "I have another favor to ask you, Will."

"What's that?"

"Would you mind picking up Julia and bringing her to the party? We're having it downtown at the Read House. Just think up any excuse that makes sense. J.D. can probably help you out with that."

"No problem."

Somehow, however, Audrey sensed that he wasn't thrilled with the idea. "Will, I'm getting a funny vibe here. What's wrong? Don't you want to bring her?"

Will shook his head. "No, it's not that. I'm just not sure Julia Cass is the kind of woman who likes surprises. I could be wrong, but that's the way I see it."

"Why?"

"I don't know. I just get that feeling. You might ought to ask J.D. if he thinks a surprise party's a good idea."

"I'll do that. He didn't say anything negative when I first brought it up."

"Okay. Just let me know when, and I'll think of a way to get Julia there."

They chatted a few minutes, and then Audrey watched him walk swiftly away. It hadn't occurred to her that Julia might not like such a surprise. She had better discuss it a bit further with J.D. and make sure it truly was a good idea. Turning, she headed inside the gift shop, hoping they still had the T-shirt that Zoe had described in such detail to her: black with lots of sparkly sequins in a red-and-silver fleur-de-lis design. Zoe was already like a daughter to her, and she hoped that relationship would become a reality, sooner rather than later. She smiled to herself. And it would, if she had anything to do with it.

Chapter 10

It was nearly nightfall on a hazy and hot late August evening, the heat finally beginning to let up over the city as the sun went down. Downtown Chattanooga was still fairly busy, people straggling out of office buildings, trying to get home in time to cook dinner, make that Little League game, or watch the Atlanta Braves play the St. Louis Cardinals.

City buses, cars, pickup trucks, and SUVs whizzed by in both directions along the street where the Tongue Slasher had parked his vehicle and waited patiently for his next victim to show up. He welcomed the falling darkness, but he seriously doubted if anyone would recognize him. The late-model white Ford Fusion he'd rented for the occasion was suitably nondescript. No one would be expecting him to be there, lying in wait, dressed impeccably in a brown UPS uniform and cap. A large UPS package sat on the passenger seat beside him.

Resting the back of his head against the seat, he tried to sit still, to relax completely and remain calm. It was hard to do, but it took that kind of focus to kill efficiently. He was so eager to do it again, finish off the despicable man that he'd chosen as number Two. How he hated this man, this foul-mouthed, ignorant, biased, filthy, rotten SOB. He clamped his teeth hard, felt his muscles tense up and grow rigid. He wanted so bad for this guy to die, wanted to make him suffer, make him beg, make him crawl. He was going to enjoy every minute of it, even more than he had enjoyed Lucien's terror and choked-off screams.

He had picked his second victim because he

had been the one who'd said the most salacious and vile things back then. Two had caused such pain and heartbreak, such utter despair. He was going to pay, pay dearly, and soon. It was strange, this hardness inside his heart. He had always considered himself a sane man, a rational man, a good man. Maybe he wasn't so good. Maybe he never had been. If he were, he'd regret what he'd done, what he was going to do. But he didn't regret anything. He looked forward to the next killing with a pleasure, a kind of sheer ecstasy, that he'd never before felt in his life.

Tired of waiting, bored, he took off his aviator sunglasses, folded them, and slid them into the case he'd attached to the visor. Turning his head, he gazed across the busy street. His next victim worked downtown in a prestigious and beautifully designed chrome and glass building, but even its luxury didn't measure up to the apartment the bastard lived in. Yes, Two's apartment building was pure luxury, all champagne and caviar and top-of-the-line everything. It must be nice to have the kind of money that would buy that kind of lifestyle. Only the highest paid, the most elite of Chattanooga's wealthy could even dream of setting foot inside that spacious marble lobby. The tall doorman in his spotless black uniform and a cap that sported gold trim and a patent leather visor guarded the portal at all times. He made sure that no mere commoner dirtied the shiny, pristine floors of the rich and arrogant.

And yet, a demon lived in the penthouse in that high-end place with its spectacular view of the river and the Walnut Street pedestrian bridge. Yes, his next victim had a good life up there in the clouds, could afford anything he wanted, anything at all, and for what? For spewing nasty garbage over the airwaves about innocent people, every single day of the year. But it would all end soon. His victim had an old friend waiting to make things right. An old friend with a razor-sharp fillet knife.

It took twenty minutes before Two showed up at his workplace. The slasher watched him climb out of a long black stretch limousine, his door opened by his personal chauffeur. He swaggered over to the doorman's post, ignoring the poor guy's greeting as if the doorman were a filthy insect to squash beneath his heel. What a condescending jerk, a loudmouth, a liar, a manipulator, one who lived only to hurt and humiliate people who couldn't fight back. But not tonight. Tonight he would finally encounter somebody who knew how to fight back. Tonight he would die a horrible death.

Closing his eyes, the Tongue Slasher again tried to relax, but his fingers were squeezing the steering wheel, harder and harder, until his knuckles turned white. His victim's caustic, hateful language came back so clearly, echoing up from the deep, cold cellar of the past, each word like a stiletto jabbing into his heart. This man, this savage, was about to die. Lucien Lockhart had hidden his poisonous ways behind his black robe and ivory gavel and bought-off judgments, true. He'd had to die. But this man, this scum of the earth didn't hide anything; he luxuriated, wallowed in his vileness. But he wouldn't for much longer. His time on the Earth was almost done. It wouldn't be long now. He started up the Fusion and pulled out onto the street. He took a deep breath, calming himself, and then flipped open his inexpensive, untraceable TracFone. He punched in a number and waited.

Shock jock Roc VanVeter was having a very good day. He was sitting in his plush studio, waiting for the current round of commercials to finish so he could continue taking calls. The ratings of his radio talk show had gone through the roof since Lucien Lockhart had breathed his last. The news media had finally gotten hold of all the nasty details, and all day long Roc had managed to get Lockhart's enemies on the air, deriding the judge as a liar, a corrupt and vindictive animal, and worse. Much worse.

Of course, Roc knew that firsthand. He had often raked the judge over the coals for some of his rather, shall one say, questionable rulings. Yes, they had colluded illegally more than once, but this murder was fodder that would give Roc one good bump in salary in light of the recent through-the-roof ratings. He had been the one who had christened Lockhart's killer, on air, coming up with the name Tongue Slasher after an anonymous caller had leaked the news about Lockhart's severed tongue. Brilliant, sheer genius on his part, and the television and newspaper reporters had all picked it up and run with it. Sometimes his knack for creating chaos and notoriety surprised even him.

A satisfied grin curving his mouth, Roc waited for the green light to come on so he could connect with the next caller. The last woman had gotten so irate that she had lashed out at him with a string of profanities so vulgar that his producer had to shut her down. Roc could do that to people—enrage them, make them totally freak out and lose all control. He loved it, too. And that was exactly what his boss wanted him to do, and what his listeners wanted to hear. He always gave it to them. The nastier, the better—that was his personal motto. He had talent, all right; he could find the tiniest chinks in people's emotional armor and exploit the hell out of them. Oh yes, that was a definite skill he possessed. On top of that, he truly enjoyed infuriating people.

Chuckling to himself, he saw the green light flash and punched the button. "Hello. You're on the Roc VanVeter Show. How do you feel about

Judge Lockhart? Do you think he deserved to have his tongue brutally slashed out of his mouth?"

A short silence ensued. He had shocked the caller to silence. Good. That's what he was here for, what he lived for. He just wished he could see the look on the listeners' smarmy faces when he did it.

"Hello, caller. You still there?"

"I'm here." The voice was muffled; sounded like the caller had his hand over the receiver. Roc wasn't sure at first if it was a man or a woman. Probably afraid their spouse would hear and get ticked off that they called into a show like his.

"Well, caller, tell my listeners: What'd you think of the judge's murder?"

"I think a fraudulent tongue shall be cut out."

Roc grinned. It was a guy, all right, and one Roc had a feeling he could make explode in a fit of crazy anger. "You're saying the judge was fraudulent. Do you have any proof of that?"

"The fraudulent tongue shall be cut out."

"Okay, okay, we got it. You think the judge deserved it. What? He mess with your wife or daughter? Or both at once?"

Roc waited, thinking the guy had hung up upon the mention of his female family members. The low voice spoke again. "He deserved what he got. As you will deserve what you get."

"Uh-oh, now that sounds suspiciously like a threat. You threatening me, sir?"

203

"The fraudulent tongue shall be cut out."

"Well, thanks for your call. Afraid we don't have time to go on, if all you're going to do is say the same thing over and over."

Roc flipped the switch and went on to the next caller. Some people were just so damn lame. Thank God, most of his callers had been out boozing and had a few too many drinks in them —that always loosened up inhibitions. He had to keep this Lockhart frenzy going. Maybe he should make up something to get the audience angry and vindictive. Maybe one of them would do some-thing outrageous and cause headlines. That's what Roc needed. Maybe he could play up that veiled threat he just got. Yeah, maybe if he was a target, he could get even more mileage out of it. Bump up his ratings even higher. That's what he'd do. He laughed out loud. This murder couldn't have happened at a better time. He was going to have a heyday with this one.

As soon as the show ended, Roc wrapped up his instructions to his production assistant, summoned his limo, and headed home. There was a private party over at Studio Zero, and he intended to hook up for the night with an exotic dancer there, a woman with long, silky legs and big boobs and no morals—none whatsoever. His favorite type gal. As he arrived at his apartment building, he noted again that his doorman was a moron who grinned constantly and looked a lot like a grown-up Opie from that old Andy Griffith TV show. The man even had freckles. He rode the elevator all the way to the top, strode quickly down the hallway, and let himself into his apartment. He was in a big rush, for obvious reasons. He was horny as hell. And the naughty Aurora Bright was waiting for him with her whips and chains and full, ripe mouth.

Flipping on the recessed lights along the hallway, he entered his bedroom, jerking his blue T-shirt off over his head. He would dress up a little, take Aurora out for drinks and dinner. God, he was so ready for her, and she was always just waiting to jump on him and wrap her legs around his waist. She was a slut, true, but she turned him on like no other woman he'd ever met.

In the other room, the doorbell rang. Roc cursed under his breath and walked back through the foyer. He raised the shield on the peephole and saw a man wearing a UPS uniform.

"Yeah, what d'you want?"

"I've got a package to deliver to Mr. Roc VanVeter."

"Okay, wait just a minute."

Accustomed to receiving FedEx and UPS packages from fans and sponsors, Roc turned the dead bolt and pulled the door open. He barely saw the stun gun before the deliveryman jabbed it against his chest. He went into spasms, the pain excruciating, almost more than he could bear. He fell backward and hit the floor, his arms and legs jerking spasmodically. His assailant came quickly inside, shutting and bolting the door. He had some kind of club in his hand and a big pair of pliers. Roc saw them coming down hard. The blow hit the top of his head, and everything went dark.

Later, when Roc began to regain consciousness, he was so groggy that he couldn't think, his head thudding like crazy. For a moment, he couldn't remember what had happened. Something terrible, he knew that much, but what was it? He forced his eyes open and blearily made out the furniture in his bedroom. It was shadowy; only one light was on, a track light on the ceiling that was focused on him. His bedside table was pulled up beside him. Several objects had been placed on the table. What were they?

Blinking his eyes, he tried to move and realized he was tied to a dining room chair. Panicking, he fought to focus his vision and saw that one of the objects was a small set of scales, a set of scales with intricate crossed swords on top. Beside the scales was a length of neatly coiled yellow ski rope, a large fillet knife, and a bloodstained pair of pliers. Oh God, oh God, were those the things the Tongue Slasher used on Lucien Lockhart? He began to struggle desperately against the bindings, but he was tied much too tightly, his neck to the back of the chair, his wrists to the arms, and his ankles to the chair legs. He could barely move. He froze when a low and muffled voice came out of the shadows. The voice from the threatening caller. The words were low and calm and deliberate.

"Don't say a word . . . don't tell more lies . . . for the fraudulent tongue shall be cut out."

When the killer moved into view and picked up the knife and the pliers, Roc began to scream . . .

Julia didn't think she was ever going to find Charlie Sinclair's new place. Was it out in the boondocks, or what? She had the directions, but it was high up on the mountain somewhere. She was going out there to pick up Jasper and to visit with Charlie. It had been great to see him the other day. Too bad he hung around with Max Hazard. Max was incorrigible. And a pest at times. Other times, he could be charming; yes, he could.

Charlie lived on Lookout Mountain, across the Georgia state line. It was quite a drive. No wonder Charlie liked to come visit her in his boat. She had no idea where he put into the river, but he certainly had enough choices. When she finally found the right dirt road and wound her way through a heavily wooded tract, she glimpsed a couple of spectacular views of the tranquil valley lying below. The A-frame house came into view after about ten minutes. Charlie liked isolation for himself and his dogs, but this was downright ridiculous.

Julia pulled up at the rear of the structure and parked. The back of the house had an entrance, but the door was locked. She walked along a large, planked deck that was built around the cabin. She ended up at the front porch and found herself pretty much perched atop a cliff. But the view, oh my God, it was beautiful. A lovely patchwork of green fields and woods below, with the shaded blue mountains of Tennessee in the background.

She looked around. The house itself was rustic, something else right down Charlie's alley. There were six large plate-glass windows set in the A-frame that faced the valley, and she could see a giant stone fireplace inside the front room. Wow, how gorgeous would it be up here during the winter snows?

Trying the storm door, she found it locked, too, so she headed back around to the back porch. Realizing that Charlie was probably down at his clinic located somewhere out back, she headed off toward where she heard dogs barking. She could see the structure in which he had his veterinarian business in a clearing at the edge of the trees. Long, shaded dog runs stretched into the woods behind it.

The door had a WE'RE OPEN sign, so Julia walked inside and called out Charlie's name. He was nowhere to be found, but her voice brought out the loud baying of Jasper. Smiling, she headed into the back. Man, had she ever missed her dog. He was going crazy in his pen, and she unlatched it and let him out. They spent about five minutes loving on each other, and then she snapped on his leash and began to wonder about Charlie.

Outside again, she called out Charlie's name and listened. Only stillness, except for the barking of the penned dogs. It was strange. Charlie wasn't one to leave his dogs untended, and his Ram truck was sitting right outside, his bass boat still on a trailer behind it. Jasper was pulling her in the direction of the woods, and she gave him his head. What if Charlie was hurt? Lying somewhere in the woods with a broken leg?

Worried, she followed Jasper across the rocky ground and down a dirt path that led deeper into the woods. Jasper stopped where the mouth of a cave gaped in the leafy greenness of the woods. It was part of a high craggy outlook, but Jasper only sniffed momentarily at the entrance and then moved on down the trail. After about ten more minutes, Julia breathed a sigh of relief when she saw Charlie walking toward her, his red T-shirt vivid against the green undergrowth.

"Hey, Charlie. I was getting worried about you."

Charlie looked up and saw her where she stood at the top of the trail. He was carrying a little puppy in his arms. "Hey, Julia. I've been out huntin' for this little rascal here. He decided to do a bit of explorin' on his own."

When Charlie got up to her, Julia took the brown-and-black sheltie pup out of his arms. "Well, aren't you the cutest little thing in the world? I bet you were scared when you couldn't find your mama, weren't you?"

"Not to mention facing the bobcats around here." Charlie looked at Jasper, who was sitting contentedly at Julia's feet. "I think Jasper is ready to go home. Those sad eyes of his nearly got to me. I almost brought him back to you yesterday."

"He's all done, then?"

"Yep, he's ready to go. I'm gonna miss him. I tell you, I love that dog."

They walked together back to the house, first dropping off the puppy at the clinic.

"C'mon in, girl. Sit awhile. Can I get you something to eat or drink?"

"I'll take some of that homemade lemonade you always used to have."

"You got it. Go sit down while I rustle it up."

Julia moved into the living room with Jasper. As usual, Charlie had a swing hanging in the living room, one that faced the view. Julia sat down in it and swayed back and forth, warmed by the sunlight flooding into the living room from the large front windows. Charlie had sold his former home because everything in it reminded him of his deceased wife. He had simply worshipped the ground she walked on and mourned her still. On the fireplace hearth, she could see that he'd set up a little altar with a silver-framed photograph of Sonia, a crucifix, and a white pillar candle.

"Here you go, kiddo."

Julia took the glass he held out to her and tasted the sweet and tangy lemonade. It tasted good after the trek in the heat to find Charlie. "So how do you like it, way up here on the mountain?"

"I like it fine. Like to look out over the view. I feel at home."

"So do I."

They shared a smile.

"It's good to see you again, Charlie. Even if you did sic Max Hazard on me."

"I like old Max. He makes me laugh. He's still got the hots for you."

"I don't think so. He pretty much has the hots for everybody."

Charlie laughed. "He's coming up here for some hunting later today. Want to hang around and see him?"

"I guess I'll be leaving now."

Chuckling, Charlie shook his head. "He's not so bad. He likes to go down in those caves out back with a twenty-two and hunt for bears. He's going to find one someday, and I'm afraid of what's gonna happen then."

"God, I hope he doesn't find one." She smiled but grew serious. "Charlie, have you heard any-

211

thing else about the judge's murder? Anything that could help our case?"

"I've been listenin', trust me on that. It's just that nobody seems to know anything. It sure has thrown all of us down at the criminal courts for a loop."

"I know."

"You got any suspects?"

"Yeah, a few. I can't discuss it with you, though. Sorry."

"I know that. I need to ask around among some of the troopers I used to work with. They all agree with my opinion of Lucien, and they all had their stories about trials they'd been involved with when he was in charge. Not one of them had a good thing to say about him. That's awfully sad, in a way, don't you think? A guy dies, is murdered, and nobody can think of one nice thing to say about him."

"Yeah, this whole case is sad. Brutal and sad."

Charlie changed the subject. "Hey, I've been meaning to ask you. How would you like to train some of my dogs for me—you know, part-time? Maybe later, after you're done with this case? What d'you say?"

Tilting her head, Julia considered the idea. "Maybe. On the weekends. I certainly don't have time now. No way. I barely had time to come up here and get Jasper. I just missed him so much, I couldn't wait any longer."

"You've always been a softy."

"With Jasper? You bet I am."

They talked some more while they finished their lemonade, but soon after, Julia gave him a hug and loaded Jasper into the Charger. She waved to Charlie where he stood on the porch, watching her. Somehow, she felt he was still very sad over his wife's death. How lonely it must be so far up in the mountains. Then again, Charlie had all his dogs to keep him company. And his old bud, Max Hazard. And that was one guy who could keep a person from getting bored.

Chapter 11

"You sure he said to meet him at the Read House?" Will asked Julia, pulling into the parking lot of one of Chattanooga's most popular places.

"Yes, this is it. He said he and Audrey want to treat me to dinner."

Will said, as nonchalantly as he could manage, reluctant as he was to have a hand in Audrey's little plot, "Mind if I come in with you? I need to talk to J.D. for a minute."

"Sure, if you want to."

Will was not a good liar, and he didn't like helping to pull this stunt on Julia. As he'd told Audrey at the Cracker Barrel, he didn't think Julia was going to like it, not at all. He opened the door. "It looks pretty busy tonight. Hope they got reservations."

"Knowing J.D., he didn't."

Julia smiled at him, and he smiled back before he could stop himself. He was growing more and more attracted to her—*fascinated* might be a better word, but that would not do. He had been trying his best to be as professional and stand-offish as possible, certainly not encouraging any personal small talk. She had noticed, even called him a dull boy, and she was probably wondering why, especially after the fun they'd had on the way home from the airport. Nope, they weren't having much fun anymore, and he didn't like the stilted atmosphere when they were together. He had a feeling she didn't, either.

"Don't sell J.D. short," he said as he opened the front door of the restaurant. "I've seen him do a lot of nice things for a lot of people."

"Oh, I have, too. Especially now. Audrey's been great for him."

"She's a nice woman. Classy."

"I haven't really had a chance to get to know her as well as I want to. But I like her."

"Maybe you'll get to tonight."

Will walked alongside Julia across the crowded lobby, but he was still not sold on her being exactly thrilled with what was about to go down. She just didn't seem like the *yeah, please jump out and scare the hell out of me* type. And she was still wearing her weapon under her tan blazer. She'd probably be gracious after the fact, especially since Audrey meant so well. He'd be the one she'd probably get mad at. Still, he felt like he was leading a lamb into a lion's den, albeit an armed and dangerous lamb.

Inside, the place was hopping. It didn't take long for Will to pick out J.D.'s six-three figure at the back of the restaurant. J.D. motioned them back to the private room they'd reserved.

"There's J.D.," he said to Julia.

Julia took the lead, and Will trailed her, all kinds of misgivings going through his mind. Hell, maybe he was wrong; maybe Julia was going to laugh and smile and clap her hands in delight, completely comfortable in the limelight. Right. Well, he'd find out in exactly one minute.

"Hi, sweetheart," J.D. was saying to his sister. "I'm glad you could come tonight. Audrey's going to be so pleased. We've got a private table. Audrey's back there waiting for us." He turned to Will and winked. "Hey, Will, nice to see you. Why don't you join us?"

Will felt like a jerk. J.D. stood back and let the two of them precede him into the darkened back room. Two seconds after Julia appeared in the doorway, the lights flamed on with about thirty people yelling and flashing camera shots. Julia was caught by surprise, all right. She went down in a law enforcement crouch, hand on her Glock,

215

and might've drawn on Audrey's guests if he hadn't caught her arm in time. Worse, he saw the initial look of shock and fear on her face before J.D. grabbed her around the waist and swung her around.

"Surprise, Sis! This is all for you! Audrey and Zoe put it together to surprise you."

Just as Will had feared, Julia glared up at him accusingly. He shrugged. "I'm just the delivery-man. Don't blame me."

Luckily, her answer was interrupted by Zoe's excited and effusive arrival at a run. She grabbed Julia in a giant bear hug. Probably a good thing for the teenager to show up when she did. He had a feeling he was going to get hell for not clueing Julia in on the surprise. He couldn't blame her. He probably would've shot somebody, too, if they jumped out of the dark at him like that. He eased into the background of the party, kept his back to the wall, and watched Julia. He no longer liked crowds, not even in nice, safe, friendly restaurants. He watched J.D. and Audrey move around the crowd with Julia, introducing her to all their friends. She was over her first shock now and seemed to be enjoying herself. More than he could say about himself. He hated parties. Hated crowds where he couldn't keep his eyes on everybody.

After a while, Audrey showed up at his side and took him by the arm. "C'mon, I've saved you a seat at our table. Thanks again for getting her here. I'd say we surprised her, wouldn't you?"

Will stopped her, glancing at Julia, who was moving toward the head table arm in arm with Zoe. They did resemble one another. Zoe was going to be a knockout someday, just like Julia was. But that was J.D.'s problem. He turned to Audrey. "Did you get the feeling that Julia was more startled than she should've been?"

Audrey stared up at him, her smile fading. "Yes, I must say I did."

Audrey was the licensed grief counselor, not Will. Still, he wondered if maybe there was something in Julia's past that he didn't know about. "Has she suffered anything traumatic that you know of?" he asked. "Maybe something that went down bad when she worked in Nashville homicide?"

"Well, we never mention it in front of her, but she did lose her partner about three years ago. I don't know much about it. J.D. thinks she and Bobby Crismon were more than just partners, but she doesn't talk about it so we aren't sure. Has she said something to you?"

"No. It makes sense, I guess, her losing a partner."

"I think they were answering some kind of a domestic disturbance call. They walked right into it."

"I guess that explains some things."

"Maybe now that she lives here, she'll come in and see me," Audrey said. "I've been waiting for the right time to broach the subject with her."

"She's a good cop. She can handle the job. I found that out the very first day."

Audrey gave him a knowing look. "Will Brannock, you held out on me. Are the two of you getting together already?"

"No. Not at all. We just work well together."

"So you are getting along? No dueling jurisdictions? I've heard J.D. complain about that at times."

"Not with Julia."

Audrey laughed. "You can't fool me, Will. I know you like her more than you're letting on. And who wouldn't? She's gorgeous. Come along—they're waiting for us."

Yeah, I do, Will thought. *Damn it, anyway.*

It did take Julia several minutes to recover from all those people yelling and screaming at her out of a pitch-black room. It had been so unexpected that she didn't have time to prepare herself. She used to love surprises, parties, crowds, everything like that, and J.D. knew it. But not anymore. Tonight, when it happened, frightening images of the worst day of her life came barreling back and hit her like a malevolent wind. She and Bobby were on a homicide call, canvassing the neighborhood for witnesses to a drive-by shooting. They'd heard a call come in for a domestic altercation that was going on down the street from their crime scene. Then, just like that, Bobby was gone from her life forever. Dead and buried, just when they were beginning to fall for each other.

Julia was ripped by a cold chill, just thinking about it; even to this day, it unnerved her. Nightmares and flashbacks, they still happened, too. Shaken, she tried her best to erase the terrible memory. She was going to enjoy the party that Zoe and Audrey had been kind enough to plan for her. She took some deep breaths, got herself under control, and glanced around the room. There was quite a crowd, most of the tables full, but her gaze stopped on Will Brannock and Audrey Sherrod, who looked to be having a serious conversation on the other side of the room. Will had been looking in her direction, and he nodded then looked back down at Audrey. What was going on?

"Oh, Julia, isn't this the coolest party ever! Look at all the people who came, just to meet you. Aren't you excited? C'mon over and see all my friends! Everyone that I invited came. Isn't that awesome? They're all here to meet you! They think it's really cool that you're a cop, just like those cool girls on *CSI*!"

Zoe was the excited one, so happy that her smile lit up her face until she veritably glowed, and Julia knew then that she probably couldn't deny this kid anything. Zoe grabbed her hand and pulled her along. "Don't tell J.D., but my boyfriend's here, too. His name's Colin. J.D.'s almost ready to let me go out on dates. Isn't that the most awesome thing? Audrey's been working on him about it. You know, she means if she takes us, like, to the movies and picks us up, and stuff. Maybe you could put in a good word, too? He thinks you're really smart and with it and cool about stuff. What d'you think? Am I old enough to date? When did J.D. let you date?"

"Oh, no you don't, Zoe. You're not dragging me into this. I will say, though, that I wasn't all that interested in boys when I was your age."

Zoe stopped and stared at her, as if stunned speechless. "Then what were you interested in?"

Zoe's pretty little face looked so incredulous that Julia had to laugh. "Well, at that time, I liked target shooting better than boys."

"Are you serious? Did you really? Better than the guys?"

"Well, maybe I was a little bit interested in boys, too. J.D. didn't like the idea then, either. He was protective, but he gradually eased up on me." *He was just afraid I'd date a boy like he was back then,* Julia thought to herself.

Zoe looked relieved, but they'd reached a table full of teenagers, who were dressed like typical high school kids but also looked like fairly clean-cut, regular fifteen-year-olds. She met Jacy, Reesa, Brittney, Tyler, Travis, Ethan, and Jeremy, and of course, Zoe's best friend, Presley. Julia readily picked out the special boy in question, Colin, even before Zoe introduced them, just by the slight flush on Zoe's face when she darted a surreptitious glance at him. Ah, young love. Nope, Julia didn't know a thing about it. Hell, she had trouble with old love.

"It's very nice to meet all of you. Hope we'll see each other again soon," she said. "Just not at the police station." The kids all laughed, and Zoe sat down beside Colin. When Julia caught sight of the Axelrods sitting at a nearby table, Cathy stood up and waved. Charlie Sinclair was sitting with them, as well as another couple Julia had not yet met. Max Hazard sat across from Charlie.

"Hi, guys," Julia said, sliding into a chair beside Charlie. "I'm so glad to see some familiar faces. This is pretty overwhelming."

Cathy said, "It sure is. Will and J.D. both told Audrey that she might ought to invite us. None of us would've missed it for anything. Even Charlie took time out from fishing and running his dogs to celebrate your coming to town."

"And he invited me, since you gave me the bum's rush at Cracker Barrel," said Max as he slid over into the chair beside her.

Charlie Sinclair nodded. "That's right, Julia. We already know a lot of these folks, of course. Seems like most are connected to the legal community in one way or another. I've never seen so many cops and lawyers. And one private eye."

They all laughed and looked at Max, but then Charlie spoke aside to Julia. "You looked a mite startled when the lights came on."

"I was." She met his eyes. "It's a miracle I didn't shoot somebody."

"Yeah," Cathy said, "I'm surprised J.D. didn't realize scaring an armed officer to death wasn't the best idea to come up with."

Julia nodded. "But I think it's really sweet of Audrey to think of it."

"That it is," agreed Lonnie. "She's good at her job, too. She's a very good counselor. I know people that she's really helped cope."

"J.D. says the same thing."

Cathy grabbed her hand. "You're going to love it here in Chattanooga. I just know it, because I do, and we're so much alike. God, I've missed you a lot."

"You know, I think you're right. So far the move has been a good one."

"It's an answer to my prayers, I can tell you that," said Max, leaning close and nuzzling her hair. "God, you smell good, Julie."

"Oh, stop it, Max," Julia said, pushing him away, but they exchanged a smile. Max was the only person who called her Julie and wouldn't stop no matter how many times she asked him to. He looked good tonight, in a white linen suit and a blue shirt that matched his eyes, and was on his best behavior. So far. And for a nice

222

change. She wondered how long that would last.

Cathy glanced around. "Which one's Will Brannock?"

"He's standing over there by himself against the wall by the door. The big guy in the white shirt and red tie."

"Oh, my God, Julia, is he the hottest guy alive, or what?"

"No, he's not," Max remarked. "I'm sitting right here."

"Yes, me too. Thank you, dear," Lonnie joked, looking at his wife with fond indulgence.

Julia spoke quietly to Cathy, making sure that none of the men could hear them. "Yes, Will's good-looking, all right. You should've seen him at the airport when I first got here. Bad thing is, he's a regular Pied Piper when it comes to flight attendants."

Cathy smiled, a wicked gleam in her eyes. "Not just flight attendants, not judging by the way he's been watching you since you got here. I noticed that right off and wondered who he was."

Julia glanced over at Will. He was still watching her. He gave her another polite little nod, probably afraid she was ticked off because he shoved her into a dark room with dozens of screeching, camera-toting well-wishers. She looked back at her friend. "Was he really looking at me?"

"You bet he was. Couldn't take his eyes off you."

"He's just afraid I'll get him back for throwing me to the wolves. And I will."

"I still think he's sexy as hell."

"Yeah," said Charlie, leaning close to them, his eyes twinkling. "He's sexy, you're cute as a button, and you two look good together, especially when you're toting guns and flashing your badges and rounding up the bad guys."

"Good grief, you guys, enough already about Mr. Perfect TBI. He's my major competition for Julia," Max complained, frowning. "Talk about my virtues for a while, for God's sake. C'mon, Julie, let's dance."

Max dragged her out of her chair and onto the dance floor with the other couples. She didn't want to dance, but she didn't want to make a scene, either. Max thrived on making scenes—the more outrageous, the better.

"You dance as good as ever," Max said, smiling down at her.

"We've never danced before, and I don't want to dance now. Let's go sit down."

"Can't. Wouldn't get to hold you like this if we weren't dancing. But we can stand still and keep the embrace, if you want to."

Julia just glared up at him without comment.

Max lost his grin. "Actually, I just wanted to get you alone so we could talk."

"About what?"

Max took her down in a long dip that was extra

embarrassing, then whirled her around. "About your investigation. How's it coming along?"

Max liked to play dumb and make other people believe he was harmless. She knew for a fact that he was not dumb or harmless. In fact, he was smart enough to persuade all kinds of people to do all kinds of things to help him with his investigations. She didn't trust his motives, not for a minute. "So now the truth comes out, huh? You're digging for information about the killer."

"So do you have any clues as to the identity of the killer?"

"And you're interested why?"

"I'm a private investigator, and we always nose into things that aren't any of our business, you know that."

"Just a one-time warning, Max. Stay out of it. This is a state investigation, and Will Brannock won't put up with any interference. He'll lock you up and throw away the key, trust me on that." She glanced over at Will and found him in the same spot, his eyes locked on her and Max. This time he didn't give that agreeable little acknowledgment and didn't look away. He just stared at them.

Max said, "Okay, I get it. I'll back off, but on the other hand, maybe I got a lead that'll help y'all out."

"Then let's hear it."

"You gotta promise to keep my name out of it."

"I'm not promising you anything. And enough

of this mystery-novel stuff. Tell me what you know. Or I'll let Special Agent Brannock ask you, and he doesn't fool around."

Max danced her over to the edge of the floor, stopped, and looked around for eavesdroppers. "It concerns the judge's housekeeper."

"Maria Bota?"

"That's right."

"Go on."

"I hear she's holed up in Las Vegas with her little kid. That she's looking for a job in the casinos."

"Where'd you hear that?"

"A confidential source. A friend of Maria's. Can't tell you her name."

"Can't or won't."

"Both."

"Maybe a subpoena would help you out with that."

They considered each other. Julia said, "Tell me why you're so interested in this case."

Max glanced around at the other dancers again, then took her arm and led her off to a quiet corner. "Okay, Julie, here it is. Lockhart's daughter, Tanya, asked me to look into this for her."

"How do you know her?"

"She used to bring her mom's dogs out to Charlie's for shots and stuff. That's how I met her. Charlie and I sort of took her under our wing. She had two lousy, obnoxious parents who were always on her case. We really felt sorry for her."

"She's not here in Chattanooga yet, is she?"

"Nope. She called me right after she got the bad news." His face was serious now. "She's afraid this psycho is going to go after the whole family, herself included. She's afraid he's gonna show up at her house."

"There's no indication of that kind of threat. Why didn't she mention that to me when I interviewed her over the phone?"

Max shrugged. "She trusts me. She asked me to find out what I could, so that's what I'm doing."

"Maybe Will and I ought to have a sit-down with her when she gets to town."

"She's not coming. Said she hated him and couldn't stand the thought of being around her mother. She hasn't been back here for five years."

"She seemed pretty upset when I talked to her."

"He's her father. He just ignored her. Her mother abused her. Anyway, that's why I'm interested in this case and that's how I found this lead."

"You need to tell me who this friend of Maria's is, Max."

"No can do. Put me in jail, if you have to."

"I've done it before."

"Yeah, you sure did. And it turned me on, especially the second time when you slammed the cell door yourself."

"Shut up, Max. This is serious."

"I know. That's why I'm helping you out.

Thought you'd want to alert the Las Vegas police that she's out there and they need to look for her."

"We've already got a BOLO out on her. But this will help. They can canvass the casinos. Thanks, Max. I think." She frowned. "This better not be another of your cons."

"Me? Heaven forbid. I'm just trying to do you a favor and win your personal regard."

Julia laughed a little at the feigned hurt expression on his face but headed back to the table, eager to tell Will what Max had found out. Anything that would help get their investigation moving forward was welcome news. She and Max returned to the table with their friends, and Julia sat listening to their conversations, but her mind was back on the case. When the food was delivered to the long buffet table at the rear of the room, guests slowly began meandering over to get in line for the steaming pans of lasagna and spaghetti and pasta primavera, hot crusty garlic bread, and lots of other Italian goodies. J.D. knew her favorites, all right. That's when Julia caught sight of Tam Lovelady sitting at a nearby table. She decided to go over and say hello.

"Hey, Tam, how're you doing?"

Tam turned and looked at her, and Julia knew at once she had caught her CPD partner at a bad time. There was the sheen of tears in Tam's eyes, tears that she quickly wiped away with the back of her hand.

228

"Oh, I'm sorry. Did I interrupt something?"

"No, no, of course not. Let me introduce you to my . . . husband. Julia, this is Marcus. Marcus, this is my new partner, Julia Cass."

"How do you do," Julia said, feeling like a fool. She had obviously disturbed a private conversation—even worse, an emotional, personal one.

Marcus held out his hand. He was a nice-looking man with kind eyes and an easy smile. His handshake was firm and warm. "You must be J.D.'s sister. He speaks very well of you."

"Yes, he's my big brother. He overlooks my faults. At least, most of the time."

Marcus grinned. "J.D. and I have gone to a couple of Memphis State basketball games together." They chatted a few minutes longer, and Julia sensed at once that Marcus cared deeply for Tam, if only by the longing way he looked at her.

"Tam's been telling me about you," he said to Julia. "She's looking forward to joining you on your new case."

"Me too. I could use some help. There's not a lot to go on yet. The city's all riled up because of the media's hysteria about the Tongue Slasher. That's not helping us. There might just be the one victim. We have no evidence that it's a serial killer." *But my gut still tells me it is,* she thought. She turned to Tam. "When do you get to testify?"

"I'm next on the list, thank God. But J.D. and I can't leave because we're on the standby list."

Marcus said, "How about letting me escort you two lovely ladies to the buffet table? I don't know about you, but I've been working all day, and I'm starving."

Tam smiled at him, and even though Julia understood they were separated, or had been, she knew instinctively that they were well on their way back into each other's arms. At least she hoped so. According to J.D., they made a perfect couple. Julia wasn't sure what had caused the strife in their relationship, and she certainly wasn't going to ask. On the other hand, she knew for a fact that police work wasn't exactly conducive to happy marriages. She hoped that J.D. and Audrey would fare better, if and when they got married.

The party was going well, her friends back at their table. Julia was supposed to sit at the head table, so she took her plate and headed there, eager to talk to Will. She sat down where her place card was, between Will and Audrey.

"You mad at me, Jules?" Will asked, but he was grinning. He hadn't been cracking many jokes since they'd picked up the Tongue Slasher case, but what's amusing about severed tongues and yellow nooses? And he called her Jules only when he was in a teasing mood.

"I'll get you back, Brannock. Just wait and see. I'll strike when you least expect it. Like the Phantom."

"I'll keep my eyes open."

He seems different tonight, Julia thought, and wondered why. But she liked him when he was relaxed and enjoying himself. She liked him, period. Unfortunately.

"I see your beach bum friend is here."

Will was watching her closely now. "Yes, he and Charlie are good friends. They hang around together a lot."

"I also saw him whispering in your ear and leading you off to a dark corner."

Will was a regular Chatty Cathy now, smiling, even. Maybe that was because he was armed and his back was to the wall.

"It wasn't dark, and he took me there because he gave me a lead on our case."

Will turned serious really quick. "Is he working on this case, too?"

"Yes. Tanya Lockhart's afraid the killer's coming after her and her brother."

"I don't think so. She should have told us that when we talked to her."

"Probably was afraid we were as corrupt as her daddy."

"What's the lead and where'd he get it?"

"He won't say where, but he said Maria Bota's looking for work in the Las Vegas casinos, and we should get the Las Vegas police looking for her."

"What else?"

"Nothing. I told him to stay out of it."

Brannock didn't say another word but pulled

out his phone and headed out to the lobby. Within minutes, he was back. "LVPD's going to search for her. Keep your fingers crossed."

The food was good, and everybody seemed to be enjoying it, as well as the liberally flowing wine. Julia enjoyed the sweet interaction between Audrey and J.D. For heaven's sake, J.D. smiled around like some kind of sappy, lovesick puppy dog when it came to Audrey Sherrod. But why wouldn't he be so besotted? She was an elegant and gracious lady whose eyes absolutely glowed when she looked at him. Yep, he was pretty much a goner. So was Audrey.

As the night wore on, Julia tried her best to meet all the friends and coworkers who came up to introduce themselves and welcome her. It was a touching gesture, and Will actually carried on a conversation that didn't include fillet knives, gangs, and autopsies. He made a crack or two about Max and the wisdom of staying away from a private detective fishing for information. And another about Max stalking her. Perhaps this new attentiveness of his had more to do with Max Hazard than it did with her. She smiled at that idea. As Audrey tapped on her wine goblet with her knife, Julia leaned back in her chair. The room gradually quieted.

"First off, I want to thank all of you for coming here to meet J.D.'s sister." She raised her glass toward Julia. "Here's to our beautiful Julia.

We're all so happy to have you here with us."

Julia nodded and smiled. Will saluted her with his wineglass and whispered, "Now we can all sleep better at night with you on the job." He laughed a little at Julia's discomfort when Audrey told everybody about Julia's law enforcement decorations and sharpshooting trophies. Yes, she was going to have to kill him. He was having way too much fun at her expense, but maybe that was a good thing. Both of them had been so intensely concentrated on finding Lockhart's murderer that letting off some steam was probably the best medicine for both of them. As soon as Audrey took the spotlight off Julia, Julia raised her goblet and drank deeply.

"You keep drinking like that, and I might have to carry you home," Will said.

"I don't think so."

"I could overpower you. I'm pretty strong."

"So am I. And I know where to kick you."

"Well, maybe you can carry yourself home. Just so Max Hazard isn't in the picture."

They quieted and listened as Audrey continued speaking.

"There is another reason I invited everyone here," Audrey said to the crowd of their friends, a big smile on her face as she turned to look at J.D. "Since everyone we love is here in this room, I think it's the perfect time for me to make good on a threat I made to J.D. last summer."

Julia looked at J.D. He appeared surprised, clearly in the dark about whatever was coming next. So, Julia wasn't the only one getting a surprise tonight. Julia leaned close to Will. She could smell the faintest scent of some kind of citrus aftershave. She liked it. "What's this all about?"

Will shrugged. "She didn't fill me in on this one. I bet it's going to be good, though. Poor J.D."

Audrey had walked over to J.D. She took his hands and pulled him up until he towered over her. "If you'll remember, J.D., I told you that I'd give you six months to propose to me, before I took matters into my own hands and proposed to you."

The room exploded in a roar of laughter and clapping. Zoe's voice rang out from the end of the table. "Well, finally!"

That brought more laughter, even from Will. He had a deep laugh that matched his voice, a pleasant sound that Julia hadn't heard much of since they'd seen Lucien Lockhart hanging from a rafter on his back porch.

J.D. was grinning, too. Pleased as punch. He gave Audrey a bow and waited. "Well, go ahead, hit me with it," he said, to the crowd's delight.

Audrey laughed, too, and said, "J.D. Cass, will you marry me, or not?"

"I do," he said, eliciting more laughter.

234

Then he sobered and took Audrey's hands. The crowd quieted again, then oohed and aahed as J.D. went down on one knee. "I will," he said. "That's why I brought this ring along tonight. You just beat me to it."

Now it was Audrey's turn to look stunned. She watched as he flipped open a small black velvet box. He took out a large diamond ring that flashed and sparkled in the overhead lights. "Will you marry me, Audrey Sherrod?"

"You bet I will, J.D. Cass."

There was murmuring throughout the crowd as J.D. slid the ring on her finger, and they hugged and kissed as the whole room cheered.

"Well, I'll be damned. I never figured J.D. for a romantic," Will whispered, close enough to Julia's ear to send a cold chill racing down her arm. "Looks like there's going to be a wedding. If that transpires, I guess you know you'll actually have to drop your tomboy persona and put on a dress."

"I've had a dress on, Brannock. Once. And that was once too often," Julia answered, but that wasn't true, of course. As she watched Audrey and J.D. kissing, she got a big lump in her throat and tears burned her eyes. *Good grief,* she thought, *what in the world is going on here?* But in her heart, she knew. She was just happy, so happy for her brother to have finally found the love of his life. And, by the looks of things, Audrey Sherrod was definitely his soul mate. Embarrassed, she surreptitiously dabbed at a tear. Will noticed. He placed his hand over hers, where it lay in her lap, and gave it a comforting squeeze. She looked at him, and even before he spoke, she could see the understanding in his brown eyes.

"I know. It's because you're happy for them."

Swallowing hard, she looked down at her hand covered completely by his long, tanned fingers. So Will Brannock could be nice and comforting and compassionate, too, as well as all that super-sexy and crazy-masculine and more-attractive-than-humanly-possible stuff he possessed in such gargantuan quantities. On the other hand, he was still her partner and pretty much hands-off. *Well, that's just great,* she thought, irked to high heaven. *I finally find a guy that turns me on and causes ripples to shiver over my flesh, and he's off-limits. Wow, how lucky can one girl get?*

Her gaze connected with Will's concerned eyes again, and she smiled to herself. Then again, they wouldn't be partners forever, now would they? Another reason to catch this psychopath Tongue Slasher as soon as possible. Maybe then, but only then, the time would be right for her and Will Brannock to hook up and see what would happen.

Chapter 12

Sweat pouring, breath heaving, blood pumping, Cathy Axelrod kept the fast jogging pace she'd set all the way to the end of the road that paralleled the river. Her German shepherds raced along with her. The Akita, his paw sufficiently healed to have returned home from Charlie's, lagged behind as if he knew Cathy would just turn around and come back. He was the smartest dog, after all. Cathy had been a star cross-country runner in high school and college, with lots of ribbons to prove it. Since she'd joined the Wilderness Trail Running Association, she never missed a morning run, rain or sun, sleet or snow. It had a way of clearing her head, making her happy just to be alive, especially on a beautiful summer morning. She and Julia used to run together a lot when they were in their first K-9 training academy with Charlie, but she'd had to drag Julia out of bed if it was before seven o'clock. Dawn was totally out. Julia did like to sleep in. She smiled at the thought of the times she'd jumped up and down on Julia's bed, forcing her to get up. And Jasper, of course, still a growing puppy back then, helped by yapping and licking Julia's face. She was so thrilled her friend was in Chattanooga and actually lived right next door. Just like old times. She hoped they'd soon become as close as they once were.

It would be good to have someone like Julia for some serious heart-to-hearts, especially right now. Lonnie was truly struggling with his clinical depression, and she wanted desperately to help him get through the bad times. Those times didn't happen very often, but when they did, he was so deeply sad that she suffered along with him. Anytime one lost a family member, it was very hard to survive. Lonnie's loss had happened in late summer, around this time of year, many years ago, and Lonnie always sank into an introverted, depressed state when the last week of August rolled around. She was determined to help him snap out of his melancholy, and maybe with Julia around, he'd be more apt to talk. He had done well at Audrey Sherrod's party, better than she had expected, and had actually cheered up a tad.

Charlie had been the one who had not seemed himself that whole night. Even with his old friend, Max Hazard, joking with him, Charlie had barely spoken to anyone until Julia appeared at their table.

Apparently, what Lonnie needed was friendly social diversions. Maybe she should plan a dinner party herself, and soon, just to cheer him up and get him out of his studio and back into the swing of things. Yes, that was exactly what she'd do.

Slowing down, about ready to turn back, she watched a black-and-chrome Hummer truck turn off the highway and onto their road. It was unusual for anyone to come visit, especially this early in the morning. Moments later, she recognized the driver as soon as he rolled to a crunching stop on the gravel beside her. Will Brannock, in the flesh, and some flesh it was. She'd met him last night at Audrey's party, only briefly but he seemed very nice. Maybe a mite reserved, as Julia had described him, certainly a watchful and quiet man, but he had said nice things about Julia. That was good enough for Cathy.

"Well, fancy meeting you here, Mrs. Axelrod," he said in his deep voice, rolling down his window and grinning at her. Wow, he was indeed a good-looking fellow. She was happily married, but she wasn't immune. She noticed men who looked like Will Brannock, all right. Just like most other women did.

"Mornin', Will. And please, call me Cathy."

"You look bright-eyed and bushy-tailed this morning. Don't tell me you're a die-hard early-bird-who-always-gets-the-worm kind of person."

Cathy laughed because the adage fit her so well. "Thanks, I think."

"It's a compliment. Nothing like watching the sun come up over the river. That's what I always say."

"Oh, so you live near the river, too?"

Will looked away and then changed the subject. "You're the lucky one, with a place like this. It's beautiful out here. Julia mentioned that this property's been in your husband's family for years."

Cathy noticed that he didn't answer her question. An inquisitive sort since she was a child, Cathy wondered why. She didn't push it, though. "Yes. He still gets offers now and again, but he's never gonna sell this place, you can rest assured of that."

"Well, I can see why. It's nice to have these woods surrounding your house. Does he hunt?"

"Sometimes. Deer and squirrels. Not so much since we got married."

"Well, I won't cool you down from the rest of your run. J.D. called this morning and asked me to pick up Julia out here. He forgot to tell her that he wants to come by later and pick up the Charger for a full diagnostic overhaul. Couldn't get her on her cell."

"She probably forgot to charge it. She's bad about that."

"Yeah, I noticed. J.D.'s putting on all new equipment for her, including four new tires. Says they've needed changing for a long time, but he kept putting it off." He looked up the road toward Cathy's house. "I take it I'm going in the right direction?"

"You sure are. We live in that log house up there

240

on the left." She turned and pointed up the narrow gravel road. "Julia's staying in the boathouse about half a mile farther along the river."

"Okay, I think I can manage that." He patted the dashboard. "And this baby's got GPS, if I get lost."

Cathy laughed. She rather liked him. And he was such a hunk. He'd be perfect for Julia. Nice-looking, good profession, everything pointed to a great match. "Hey," she said on a sudden impulse. "How about joining Lonnie and me for dinner on Saturday night? Julia will be there."

Will Brannock didn't hesitate a second. "Thanks for the invite, Cathy. That sounds great. Count me in."

They chatted for a few more minutes, during which time he asked what he could bring to the dinner party, and then Will Brannock bid her good-bye and rolled off in his truck toward the boat dock. She watched him go, smiling after him. Julia had been alone ever since she lost Bobby Crismon in that awful domestic-dispute call; had hardly dated anybody since. And that had been three years ago. Maybe Julia was finally ready to move on, and Cathy decided right off that Julia and Will Brannock made one kickin' couple— movie-star striking, both of them. Yeah, Julia needed a new man in her life, and perhaps Cathy could be the one to nudge that relationship up to the next level. She was one heck of a good matchmaker, just like her mother. Delighted with her new quest, she whistled for the dogs and turned back toward the house. She took off with her usual last hard sprint. Lonnie would be up soon and ready for breakfast. And she had a romantic dinner party to plan.

The house was dark, everything quiet except for the terrified screams. Julia pressed her back against the wall. Her breaths were coming fast and hard. Bobby was across from her, pressed against the wall on the other side of the front door. The woman inside was yelling bloody murder, calling hysterically for help. Then, abruptly, the screaming stopped and silence dropped over the night like a heavy, thick blanket. The call had been a domestic dispute, the husband a known felon with a penchant for violence and rage.

Bobby put his forefinger against his lips and signaled that she should go low when they went in. Her heartbeat went crazy inside her chest. Her weapon was out and pointed down, but she kept her finger very close alongside the trigger. She was tense, more so for Bobby than for herself. They had broken the departmental rules, begun to get romantically involved, and both would be reprimanded, possibly even demoted, if the chief found out.

"Let's do it," Bobby mouthed as the woman cried out again. He stood back, then kicked the door open. He went in high; she, low. It was pitch-black inside, but she could see light coming from an open door down a side hall. That's where the woman was. Julia could hear her moaning now. They crept across the room, edging along opposite walls toward the light and the victim.

Julia froze as the sudden, loud blam of a gunshot blasted her ears. Bobby went down to his knees, blood blooming on the front of his light blue dress shirt and tie. A second bullet slammed into the wall beside her head, and then she heard the sound of a gun jamming. She got off a shot into the bedroom behind Bobby, and then another as the shooter came at her from the darkness, grab-bing her by the hair, unfazed by the bullet in his body. Her heart hammered out of control as he shoved her up against the wall, knocking the breath out of her. They grappled for her weapon, and then he had his thumbs on the front of her windpipe, squeezing, squeezing, squeezing the breath out of her . . .

Will stopped the Hummer outside Julia Cass's weathered boathouse, got out and looked around. She had definitely lucked into one idyllic little riverside nest, very private, almost isolated. The river flowed by, very close to the house. The constant rush of the water was soothing, the fluttering leaves of the old oak trees peaceful, and the twittering song of real early birds getting real worms was all over the place. He held the drink carrier from Starbucks in one hand and the box of doughnuts in the other as he climbed the steps to the screened porch.

Hands full of breakfast, he kicked the bottom of the screen door a couple of times with his toe, rattling it loudly on its old hinges. Startled, he watched Julia shoot up to a sitting position on the daybed pushed against the back wall. Her black hair was all tousled around her shoulders, the way he had always wanted to see it, those incredible eyes heavy with interrupted sleep. Unfortunately, she also had her weapon in her hand and trained on his chest. He ducked instinctively, nearly knocking both coffee cups off into the rosebushes.

"Whoa, whoa, Cass! It's me! Put that gun down!"

"What the devil are you doing here?" she snapped, lowering the Glock. "Trying to get yourself shot?"

"Good God, do you sleep with your weapon?" he said, slightly unnerved by her extreme reaction to the unexpected noise. She could've shot him dead.

"Yeah, don't you?"

He did, but decided not to admit it. He had better reason to, though, or at least he thought he did. They stared at each other for a moment. Her voice was still hoarse with sleep as she placed the weapon on the side table and threw back the faded blue-and-white patchwork quilt. Shapely bare legs swung over the edge of the bed. "You should know better than to sneak up on a cop and bang on the door when they're sound asleep. What time is it, anyway? Crack of dawn?"

"It's six thirty, and J.D. asked me to pick you up. He's taking the Charger in for a tune-up and new tires today. He tried to call you. So did I."

"No, he didn't, or I would've been ready. Why didn't he just let me take it in?"

Will hitched a shoulder. "How should I know? But it's okay. I've been wondering where you lived. Pretty neat place you got here."

Julia frowned as she stood up, obviously not pleased with his unexpected visit or being rousted out of bed so early. Will tried not to stare at the way her breasts mounded provocatively underneath the thin pink cotton T-shirt, but he couldn't drag his eyes away. The shirt was short, too, and the same went for those long, tanned legs of hers as she padded barefoot across the porch and flipped up the hook on the screen door.

"I brought you coffee," he said, stepping onto the porch. "Take it as a little thank-you for not blowing me away a minute ago. By the way, do

245

you always draw your weapon if somebody knocks on your door?"

"I was having a bad dream, if you've got to know. The banging on the door played into it." Julia eyed his grin as she took the Starbucks cup he held out to her. "Black, right?"

"You bet. Just the way you like it. I do try to please, Jules. It's pretty clear to me at the moment that you're not going to win any awards for Most Cheerful Morning Police Officer."

"No, I'm not, and so what? I, for one, can't stand anybody so chipper and smiley this early in the morning." But she gave him a faint smile as she ran her fingers through all that tumbling, silky, black hair of hers. She hooked her flowing hair behind her ears. "What, no doughnuts? What kind of partner are you, Brannock?"

"You sell me short, Cass," he countered, holding out the box of goodies.

"You better have some jellies in there." She shook her head. "I can't believe you're out here at six thirty a.m. Early birds, jeez, I can't figure what makes you guys tick. Cathy's the same way. It's disgusting. Anyway, you should've given me a call."

"And you should keep your phone charged."

Julia was smiling now, though, and Will followed her inside the boathouse, thinking that he did like those deep dimples in her cheeks. He wished she'd smile more often, and wear thin cotton T-shirts more often. In fact, he wished she was a flight attendant and not the partner he had to work with every single day. And despite his earlier complaint, he also liked the fact that she slept near her weapon. He had learned to do that the hard way. He wondered if her other partner's death had triggered that habit.

Stopping just inside the door to the house, he glanced around the room while Julia pulled on a short, white, terry cloth robe that, lucky for him, still showed those great legs of hers. Good God, this place was antiquated, to say the least. Antique city, to be exact.

"Who lived here last, Cass? Grandma Moses?"

Julia pulled her sash tight and frowned at him. "What's it to you, Brannock? I think it's got a nice homey feel. Comfortable and well taken care of."

"Yeah? Maybe if you're eighty years old. What's that smell, anyway? Vicks VapoRub?"

"Very funny. Can't wait to critique your house." Julia sat down in an old-fashioned, white wicker rocking chair and placed her paper cup on the coffee table. She gestured for him to take a seat on a colorful chintz couch across from her. "Where is your place, anyway, Brannock? You live in your truck, or what?"

Will opened the tab on his coffee, still unwilling to answer that question. Nobody knew where he lived and wouldn't anytime soon. Especially Julia

Cass. But he found himself wanting to tell her; to tell her everything she wanted to know about him. She had asked him a few questions earlier, casually, but he knew she was curious, maybe even suspicious. Hell, she was a detective, a damn good one. He'd incurred her interest, and she wasn't going to stop digging. He took a sip, savored the caffeine kick, and brushed off her question. "Sometimes it sure feels like it."

"I'm beginning to think you're hiding stolen property at your place. Or maybe you've got a kid-napped flight attendant handcuffed to your bed?"

Ignoring the flight attendant jab, Will flipped back the lid of the box, took out a chocolate cake doughnut with white icing sprinkled with chopped pecans, then offered the breakfast pastries to Julia. Let her think he was a real womanizer. Maybe that would put the brakes on his growing attraction for her. Hell, growing? He wanted to throw her on that daybed, jerk off that little robe of hers, and kiss her until neither one of them could breathe. Damn, what was it about her? It was a good thing she kept pushing him away, because he was weakening big-time. *Keep it light, keep it easy, Brannock,* he told himself. "Take your pick, Cass. I got two of everything so you wouldn't freak out if I took your favorite."

Julia wrinkled her nose at him, then leaned forward and picked out the biggest jelly doughnut. His second favorite. She took a bite, and Will watched her tongue flick out and catch a bit of raspberry jelly on her full lower lip. Then she slowly wet her lips—innocently, but still one of the most erotic things he'd ever witnessed. Will's masculine sensibilities jumped up and took note —okay, maybe it was more like a jolt of pure lust, enough to make him shift positions on the couch. Julia Cass was one desirable woman, especially at the moment. Not many women looked this good when they had just got up, with no makeup and long hair all tangled and wild around their shoulders. Natural beauty. He realized the way he was thinking and stomped hard on his carnal brakes.

Man, what in the hell was his problem? He was acting like an idiot. She wasn't interested in him, and even if she was, she wouldn't any more act on a mutual attraction with a partner than he would. Partners just didn't get involved. It was an unwritten rule. She'd already broken that rule once, with tragic consequences. She wasn't crazy enough to do it again. Worse, she was J.D.'s sister, and J.D. was ultraprotective about his female relatives. Another good reason for Will to keep his distance. On the other hand, they weren't really partners, technically speaking, and never had been.

"So what's on the agenda today? Must be something important, since we're starting work before the sun comes all the way up," she grumbled, taking another bite.

"The sun's up. See, look outside. Enjoy the morning."

Will dragged his eyes away from her mouth and watched Jasper amble out of the bedroom, yawning so widely that it looked almost painful. When he saw Will, he loped over and bounded up beside him on the couch, sniffing at the box of doughnuts. Will laughed and rubbed the floppy ears and fed him a generous bite.

"Admit it, Cass. Your dog loves me."

"Yeah? Well, I never said he was bright, just loyal." She propped her bare feet on a grandma-ish stool covered with an intricate needlepoint image of a white cat sitting in a rocking chair with a big ball of red yarn. "It's probably just the doughnuts. He's a bloodhound, you know, known for his nose. The smell of jellies always draws me in, too."

"Jellies are the way to your heart? I'll have to remember that the next time I tick you off."

"You might have to buy a Dunkin' Donuts franchise for that." But she smiled, a real one that showed those damned dimples again. He stared at them until her smile faded and she said, "So, anything new on the case?"

"Not yet. We really need to get a break soon. This guy's going to strike again. It's just a matter of time."

"Nothing's come in on Maria Bota?"

"Not yet. I still think she could be connected to

the murder somehow. It's worth pursuing, in any case. Something just doesn't add up about her working at the judge's house, then disappearing the way she did."

"I still haven't gotten any hits on the scales. Maybe we ought to publicize a picture of it and see if we get a tip."

"That's not a bad idea. The media would salivate to get anything, now that they're calling him the Tongue Slasher to jump-start their ratings." Will finished off his doughnut and wiped his fingers on a napkin. "I think we need to check out the rest of Lockhart's girlfriends. Starting with Jane Cansell. With a little prodding, a jealous woman might be apt to point the finger at her rivals for his affection."

"You speak like a man who deals with lots of jealous women."

"Cass, c'mon, give it a rest, already. You do know you've got me pegged all wrong, don't you? I date some, just like any other guy, but I'm no Casanova type, trust me."

"Could've fooled me that day out at the airport. But hey, it's none of my business."

"What about you? You got a boyfriend that you pull a gun on first thing every morning?" He grinned, that visual amusing him. Especially if it was Max Hazard.

"Nope, but I just moved here. The best ones haven't found me yet."

Will laughed. That was probably true. He wondered about her past love life. She was in her midthirties. She was a drop-dead gorgeous woman. There had to be lots of men, other than Bobby Crismon, who'd been interested in her. Like Max Hazard. He was finding her almost as secretive as he was. Ironically, her reticence annoyed him.

Julia stood up, stretched, and yawned as big as Jasper had. The stretch brought the robe up to dangerous levels. Same thing with his heartbeat and other things prone to rise up and be known.

"Okay, Brannock, I'm going to take a quick shower. Try not to peek. And don't let Jasper eat too many of those doughnuts. He's got a delicate stomach. And don't snoop around, either."

"Me? You wound me, Cass."

Will watched her until she disappeared into the bedroom and shut the door. He heard the lock turn. There was just no denying it. He was interested in her, very much so and no doubt about it. God, next he'd be having dreams about her. Okay, so be it. Maybe someday, maybe after they solved this ugly case and went their separate ways, he to the TBI, she to the CPD. Then they wouldn't be colleagues, exactly. Maybe he'd ask her out. Maybe she'd go, maybe she wouldn't. And that would end it. Time would tell. Meanwhile, he needed to concentrate on the case and not her legs or her dimples or that rockin' body of hers. He fed Jasper the last bite of his cake doughnut, then picked up a glazed one. When he heard the shower come on, he walked back out on the porch and sat on the big swing facing the river. He ran the case through his mind. Over and over; how many times he couldn't begin to count. Leads weren't exactly pouring in right now, and it was frustrating as hell.

A few minutes later, his cell phone dinged. It was his boss, Special Agent in Charge Phil Hayes. He answered, said hello, and then listened as Phil filled him in on the latest development. Frowning, he finished the call just before Julia showed up in the doorway, dressed in a dark blue polo shirt and jeans. Her Glock was buckled to her belt, along with her badge, and she had a lightweight white jacket in her hand.

"Cass, you ever heard of a guy named Roc VanVeter?"

"That jerk radio guy? Sure, who hasn't?"

"Well, he's dead. Found hanging on the balcony of his high-rise downtown apartment. Guess what the killer left behind?"

"Scales?"

"You got it."

"Tongue and dimes, too?"

All business now, Will nodded and opened the screen door. "Let's go. We've got ourselves a serial. And a whole lot more trouble."

Chapter 13

Roc VanVeter lived in a ritzy high-rise in the downtown area near the Walnut Street pedestrian bridge. It seemed that foulmouthed, crude, and vicious radio commentators did very well for themselves. Yes, VanVeter was the local shock jock that took low-life shots at anyone and everyone in the news. His radio and television shows consistently harassed and humiliated people who had the misfortune of catching his attention, especially anyone involved in sensational court cases or celebrity missteps.

Julia shook her head as she and Will Brannock got out of his Hummer in a taped-off zone at the canopied entrance.

"You do know that when the media gets wind of this, all hell's going to break loose," she said to Will as the uniformed police officer checked their ID and let them enter the building. "They were giddy enough about Lockhart's murder. There'll be celebrations in the pressroom with this one."

"Let's just hope it doesn't happen for a few days."

"When it's Roc VanVeter? Dream on, Brannock."

"Where is he?" Will asked the policeman.

Julia didn't know the CPD police officer, but he was a young, muscular African-American, clean shaven, tough, a man who looked like a prize-fighter. Probably a rookie, judging by his fresh-faced, eager response to Will's inquiry.

"Top floor. Penthouse apartment. Nothing's been touched. They said to wait for you to get here."

"Good work. What's your name?"

"Officer Shane Williams. CPD."

"Who found the body?" Julia asked him.

"Some old lady who lives in a high-rise just south of here. Said she likes to watch people through her telescope and called CPD when she saw a man hanging by the neck on a balcony. She thought it might be some kind of joke, but my partner and I checked it out and it wasn't any mannequin. The victim was dead, with blood all over the place. That's when we called it in to Chief Mullins. We're still waiting for your forensic team to show up."

As the elevator whisked them up to the top floor, Julia handed Will a pair of latex gloves and paper booties that she'd brought in from the truck. They donned the protective gear, both serious about what they were about to walk into, well aware that a serial killer stalking the streets of Chattanooga was not something they wanted to deal with. When the doors slid open, they stepped into a silent hallway with dark gold

255

travertine tiles and pale yellow walls set with gold glass sconces. Julia decided it definitely did not fit Roc VanVeter's style. Nope, nasty graffiti and blood spatter was more in keeping with that guy's personality.

Another cop stood outside Roc VanVeter's door. Young, looking to be around twenty-five, and clean-cut, he seemed to recognize Will Brannock. "He's outside on the balcony, Will. Brace yourself. It's gory as hell in there."

"Thanks, Ryan. Julia, this is Officer Ryan Karns. Ryan, this is Julia Cass. She's just started in your homicide unit."

"Yes, I heard about that. Nice to meet you, Detective. Welcome to the CPD. You're starting out with a real messy case."

"Yeah, I'm finding that out. Nice to meet you, too."

Julia was pleased to know another new colleague by name, but she braced herself as Will opened the door to Roc VanVeter's apartment. It did not look like the elegant, traditionally decorated hallway outside. It was as sparsely modern as modern could be, done all in black and white with a touch of red; geometrics and stripes and chrome and mirrored everything. It was quiet, the air conditioner turned down to very cold.

"Good God, it feels like Antarctica in here," Will said, inspecting the room. "It doesn't appear that anything's been touched inside this room, but we'll let forensics sweep the place and hope to hell they find something to help us."

There were three long leather couches, two white and one black, identical otherwise, each with three oversized red cushions, and very modern with low backs and no arms. A black fireplace was the focal point on one wall, the other walls painted white. Paintings were everywhere, all in large black frames, all nudes made of curving slashes of black paint. The carpet was thick white plush with zebra-skin throw rugs and one large red leather recliner near a wall of plate-glass windows that looked out on a fabulous river view.

"Well, there's our victim," said Will. "Good God Almighty."

Roc VanVeter was hanging outside on a long, wide outdoor balcony. He had been strung up by the neck, his feet dangling about a foot above the ground.

Julia inhaled deeply and let her breath out slowly, preparing herself. "Let's check out the rest of the place first."

They walked down the interior hall into VanVeter's bedroom and quickly identified the actual location of the grisly murder.

"He must've killed him in that chair and then moved him out onto the balcony."

Julia followed Will's pointing finger. There

was a huge glass door that led onto the balcony, and a trail of blood stained the white carpet from the death chair through the outside door. "He cut his tongue out in here, then took him out there to hang him. Why would he do it that way?"

"Who knows? The guy's crazy," offered Will. "Okay, let's get this done."

Outside on the open-air balcony, the August heat hit them like an oven blast after the frigidity of the interior of the apartment. VanVeter was swinging slightly in the hot wind off the river. He had on black trousers and gray New Balance sneakers without socks. The killer had removed the man's shirt and left it on the bedroom floor. Tattoos of every shape and color covered VanVeter's torso, among them a big eagle with spread wings and a geometric design that looked like the sacred cultural tattoos of Hawaiians and Samoans. More inked pictures decorated his arms, with one that said MOMMY DEAREST inside a heart. His eyes were open and staring, blood staining his face and chest red from when the tongue was removed. *TWO* was written on the floor in blood.

"Looks like the killer left us some more messages," Will said.

Julia turned and looked at Will where he stood with his back to a different plate-glass window, one through which Julia could see a second bedroom with red walls and a huge round white bed. On the glass wall separating it from the balcony, more words had been scrawled in blood, probably written with the victim's tongue: *PROVERBS 10:31.*

"Are you familiar with that verse, Will?"

"Not offhand."

"I'll pull it up on my phone."

It just took a second or two to pull it up. Julia read the Bible verse, then looked at Will. "Are you ready for this?"

"Shoot."

"Proverbs chapter ten, verse thirty-one, says, 'The mouth of the just brings forth wisdom; but the fraudulent tongue shall be cut out.' "

Will stared at her. "Fraudulent tongue. So we're right about the revenge thing. VanVeter finally went after the wrong guy."

"Unless the slasher's pitching a false lead and trying to throw us off."

"In my book, cutting off the tongue points to an act of revenge for something someone said."

"Maybe he wants to be caught."

"Or is just toying with us," Will said. "We need to check out the databases again and see if we can find a similar MO."

"I've already done that, and so have you."

"There's got to be a connection between these two victims. Something they were in on together, something that wronged the killer."

Will stared at the man hanging from the

balcony. "Both are high-profile and in the news a lot. He might just want victims that will cause a frenzy in the media. People who can catapult his murders into fame and history, make him famous like Ted Bundy."

"Yeah, well, that's already happened."

No sooner had Julia spoken than they heard the *thut-thut* of rotors and a news helicopter swept into view from across the river. She'd heard the Chattanooga CBS affiliate had recently gotten a chopper but hadn't seen it in action yet. It soared toward them, and they watched helplessly as it hovered above the building, a cameraman hanging out the door, his camera trained on them and Roc VanVeter's mutilated body.

Will tried to wave them off, holding up his badge, but the forensic unit had not arrived yet to put up the privacy shields. They couldn't cut down the victim, not until the ME arrived and released the body, so there was little they could do. Julia just hoped the news team wasn't working on a live feed.

"Wait a minute. I'm going to check out what they're saying on VanVeter's TV."

Inside the living room, she turned on the giant seventy-inch LCD flat-screen television and caught the latest news report. Her worst fears were realized when she saw the scene on the balcony unfolding before her eyes and for all of Chattanooga to see. She watched as Will continued to try to shield the corpse from the camera.

He was on his cell phone now, trying to get the helicopter ordered out of downtown airspace.

The female news anchor was still talking, still winging it so early in the story. "It appears the victim is Roc VanVeter himself, who, we have recently learned, lives in the penthouse apartment that we now have on camera. The man on the balcony looks to be a law enforcement officer but has not yet been identified. From what we've seen, it looks like the infamous radio personality has hanged himself. Although we can't verify that at this point, it appears that is the case from our reporters arriving on the scene."

Julia grabbed a folded black velvet throw off the couch and headed outside. Will grabbed one end of it, and they stretched it across the crime scene as best they could. It worked, or Will's attempts to call them off did, because the helicopter hovered only a few more minutes before banking left and heading out over the river.

Fortunately, it wasn't too long before Will's TBI forensic team showed up with a standing screen that would conceal the body from air surveillance or vantage points from surrounding buildings. The team got right to work, and when Peter Tipton, the medical examiner, showed up, Will and Julia stood with him while they waited for the photographer to take his still shots. Another technician was filming the crime scene process from beginning to end. They were top-notch and everything was done by the book. The longer Julia was on this case, the more respect she had for the Tennessee Bureau of Investigation.

Pete shook his head. "By the amount of blood on the body, the killer severed the tongue while the victim was still alive. Did he take the tongue this time, too?"

Will said, "Yes, but only part of it, just like at the Lockhart scene."

"It's the same guy. It has to be," said Julia. "There's not been enough news coverage yet for a copycat. No one knows this many details about the crime scene, anyway."

"True," said Will. "But now that the news media's got hold of the fact that it's VanVeter, it's going to go viral."

"Great, just great," Julia muttered under her breath.

Behind her, the television reporter was still talking about the murder. "We've just gotten word that Roc VanVeter's death is actually a murder that may be tied to the recent killing of Judge Lucien Lockhart . . ."

"Oh no," Julia said, looking at Will.

". . . We've heard from a reputable source that both victims had their tongues removed."

The male commentator chimed in, seemingly excited about the shocking nature of this new information. "If that's true, then the Tongue Slasher has struck again, just as we feared, and he's still on the loose, maybe even stalking another victim. These two tragic murders just might be the first and second of many mutilation murders in this city."

"I can't believe they can get away with this kind of reporting," said Peter Tipton.

"And who leaked information about the tongue mutilation so soon after Lockhart was killed?" Julia said. "We need to find out and prosecute them."

"This is not good, and getting worse," said Will.

Peter Tipton walked behind the privacy screen and began to examine the body. He felt the front pockets and pulled out a key chain with two keys on it. "Looks like a car key and probably the apartment door key. There's a book of matches."

"Does it have a logo on it?" Julia asked quickly.

"It says Studio Zero."

"What's that?"

"It's a nightclub two or three miles from here," Will told them. "I checked it out when I was researching the Battle Street Ten gang. They like to hang out there."

"That could be the connection we're looking for," Julia said.

"We'll soon see. As soon as we get done here, we'll check out his coworkers and see if he has any personal connection with Studio Zero. That goes for the judge, too. It'll be interesting to see if they frequented the same nightclub."

• • •

"So you are Mr. VanVeter's personal assistant here at the radio station?"

The young woman raised her face and looked at Julia, eyes flooding over with tears that dripped down her flushed cheeks, taking a lot of black mascara and thick eyeliner along with it. She looked like a little punk rocker or an addicted Hollywood starlet, take your pick. She had long hair, dyed so dark there was no shine left, just a flat, dull black like a dead man's eyes. Two nose rings, six earrings in each ear—and as she spoke, Julia caught sight of the silver stud in her tongue. Tattoos decorated her pale skin—not as many as they'd seen on her boss's body, but her arms were blue with ink in every pattern you could think of. There was even a fancy, curlicue illustration of Roc VanVeter's name, and his face.

"This sucks so bad. It just sucks, sucks, sucks."

Okay, it sucks, we get it, Julia thought, in no good mood, but the child obviously didn't speak standard English. Julia tried to mollify her. "Yes, it sucks big-time. I know it's shocking to you, but Special Agent Brannock and I are here to find out who did this to Mr. VanVeter."

The girl wiped tears off her cheeks with impressively ringed fingers. Heavily ringed—twenty, thirty perhaps. "Did they really, like, really, like, cut out his tongue?" Her hands flew up to cover her mouth, and huge blue eyes, outlined in black kohl like Cleopatra's, stared at Julia in true horror.

Like, yes, Julia thought, but she did feel some sympathy for the girl. She seemed like such a child, and she had to work closely with Roc VanVeter. What could be worse than that? "We really can't get into the details of the case, Gigi."

"How old are you, Gigi?" Will asked, obviously riding the same train of thought that Julia was. That was happening more and more lately. Julia wasn't sure if that was good or bad. The two of them on the same wavelength all the time. He was certainly growing on her, although his Jekyll and Hyde routine was still throwing her for a loop. This morning he was Will Jekyll. Now he was Will Hyde. So there you go.

"Eighteen. I have to be, if I'm gonna work here on the show. I promise, I am."

That indicated to Julia that Gigi might be sixteen and fudging on her job application. Probably with Roc's approval and encouragement. Everyone they'd interviewed at the radio station thus far looked like high school sophomores. Certainly no older than Zoe.

"Do you know anyone who might have wanted Mr. VanVeter dead?" Will asked the weeping girl.

Both Julia and Gigi gave him incredulous looks. Gigi answered, "Is that a joke? Everybody hated him except for all of us guys who work here."

Julia said, "He means is there anyone who

threatened him lately or showed up here angry and demanding to be let in. You know, somebody throwing around ugly threats."

"Jeez, that happens near, like, every day. But we got big guys out in the lobby that keep 'em out. You know, like, security guys."

"But Roc didn't have a personal bodyguard?" Will asked.

"Yeah, he did. Clark Sorensen. But sometimes he let the guy go home and see his kids. You know, Clark didn't live at the penthouse. They thought Roc was safe up there."

"Why?"

"Because there was that big doorman and the elevator. How could any bad guys get past all that?"

How indeed, Julia thought. That was the pertinent question, to be sure. One that she and Will were going to have to figure out ASAP. The doorman hadn't seen anyone unusual, but there were lots of apartments with lots of visitors and friends and deliverymen coming in and out. The burly doorman had intimated that at busy times, crowds came through the door, more than he could check out. And there were a couple of freight entrances in the back. The perp could have entered anytime that day and hidden out somewhere in the building. Will already had task force members reviewing the security tapes.

Will's eyes were intent on Gigi's face. "Have

you ever heard of a club called Studio Zero?"

Gigi nodded but looked guilty about it. "Yeah, why?"

"Did Mr. VanVeter frequent the place?"

"What d'you mean, frequent the place? I don't know what that means."

Julia took over. She and Will had turned into a tag team worthy of the WWE. "Did he like to go there? You know, get down, party, and all that kind of thing?"

"Sure, it's an awesome place. That's where he met me. I did some dancing."

Will frowned. "You worked at Studio Zero?"

"Yes, sir."

"What kind of dancing?"

"Any kind I wanted. Latin dances—you know, the kind they do on *Dancing with the Stars* on ABC. You know, like, the ones where those girls really shake their booty and have on those sexy dresses with lots of fringe that shakes around. It'd be bad news, like, if those little straps ever broke."

"You ever seen any gangbangers down at that club, Gigi?" asked Will.

Gigi immediately lowered her eyes, obviously knowing who she could safely squeal on and who might cut her tongue out if she talked about them.

"Nobody will know you've talked to us, Gigi. You can speak freely," Julia told her. "This is strictly confidential."

The teenager licked her ruby-red lips and darted her big eyes around, nervous as the devil in a cathedral. "Well, okay, yeah, they like it there. Yeah, they show up all the time. It's got a lot of salsa dancing, and all that."

Will said, "Roc enjoyed it?"

"Yeah, he sure did. He knows the guy who owns the place."

Julia said, "Who's that?"

"Everybody calls him Hap—you know, short for Happy, 'cause he smiles all the time. He's got real white teeth. His real first name's Juan, I think."

"What's his last name?"

"DeSoto. Hap DeSoto."

"Did Roc get along with him?"

"Yeah, we used to sit with him in his private booth a lot. It's up near the stage. They got into it once, though, not too long ago."

"What happened?"

"Roc was, like, flirting around with one of Hap's strippers, and Hap didn't like it."

Julia said, "Did you ever see Judge Lucien Lockhart there?"

"Yeah, nearly every time. He came with his maid, Maria. I don't think she liked it, though. She always looked scared of everybody, but there's never much trouble down there. Hap's bouncers are tough guys. Like, nobody ever messes with them, not even the Battle Street boys."

On the way out of Roc VanVeter's studio, Will stopped. "Looks like Lockhart and VanVeter had a lot more stuff in common than we first thought."

"Yeah, especially the fact that they're dead and their tongues have gone bye-bye."

"Not a good club to be in."

"The killer's not waiting long between murders. You think he'll strike again soon, Will?"

"I think you can count on it. He's only just begun."

"Next stop is Studio Zero, I take it, and a talk with its happy little owner."

"You got it."

Chapter 14

The killer sat at his table watching the taped news broadcast on his smart phone. They were still calling him the Tongue Slasher. Damn, they just didn't get it, and neither did the two detectives that the six o'clock news crew had caught standing on VanVeter's balcony. He took the tongues to send a definite message. He'd spelled it all out in blood, plain as day, given them a clue they couldn't ignore. It had been easy so far, the murders, the getting to and from the victims' houses. Now that the media was involved and reveling like jackals in the murder and mayhem, maybe what he'd done to Lockhart and VanVeter would put the fear of God into the other people in his Murder Book. Once everybody understood what he was doing, maybe they'd deem him the Punisher or the Avenger, as comic-book as that sounded. It fit the crime much better; fit what he was trying to do. Everyone on his list deserved to die, to suffer as he had suffered. All the people named in his book of shame would soon join his first two victims burning in hell. On the smart phone's screen, they were now showing VanVeter's body where it dangled by the neck on his fancy balcony. The cameraman in the heli-copter zoomed in on the shock jock's face, on the rivulets of blood covering his vulgarly tattooed chest. The male detective was waving them off, holding up his TBI badge. The female detective had disappeared inside, and he wondered if they had any inkling who had done the crime, and why. He doubted it, but they needed to know why, needed to figure out what VanVeter and Lockhart had done to deserve to die. They needed to make sure the whole world knew. Maybe he had to help them out. Virtually spell out everything for them in black-and-white.

Rising to his feet, he walked across the cave to where he had placed his small video camera. He chose a DVD and meticulously wiped it clean of fingerprints. Maybe they needed to see for themselves, maybe everybody did, maybe they all needed to see why his victims had to die, why he was righteous in what he was doing. He picked up a second DVD, wiped it clean, too, and inserted them both into mailing envelopes. Soon the world would know what he knew about the godless evil of his victims and the ones to come.

Opening the Murder Book, he looked approvingly at the two tongues glued under the photographs of Lockhart and VanVeter. Neither tongue would ever spew hateful lies about people. Never again. The third page showed the picture of a woman: blond hair, brown eyes, no soul, no compassion, no conscience. She was next to die, and she was as despicable as the others; even more so in some ways. She worked for the evil, condoned their misdeeds and lies and evildoings. She would not live much longer. He had already been watching her. Now that the investigation was on, the detectives on his trail, time was of the essence if he was to be success-ful in finishing his job. Two down. Ten to go.

Gloria Varranzo tried not to smile as she left the shocked uproar inside the courtroom where she'd just won her latest trial. She stopped outside the door and let relief and pure pleasure flood her. Sometimes it was almost too easy to get her guilty clients off; sometimes she amazed even herself. Yes, it was scary how good she was. She especially enjoyed her job on days like today, when she could prove without a doubt to everyone in the courtroom that the police were inept and had mishandled the evidence. Yes, O. J. Simpson's dream team had opened up a whole new era of challenging every single step of police procedure. Her client was a bastard, that was for certain; a loathsome excuse for a human being, a rapist, drug addict, and distributor. God, she couldn't stand to be around him for longer than fifteen minutes. He actually made the hair on the back of her neck stand up. But today he was a free man, and what was more important, she had a hefty seven-figure paycheck to deposit in her already bulging bank account.

The corridors were busy. Lots of trials were going on. Criminals didn't take vacations, lucky for her. She stopped at a mirrored pillar near the elevator and fluffed up her newly highlighted dark blond hair. Her nails were done, immaculate with a perfect French manicure, one that cost her fifty bucks. She looked great for her age. Yes, she was a month away from her fifty-sixth birthday and she looked no older than her late thirties. Thanks in part to the expertise of her New York cosmetic surgeon and the monthly Botox injections. She still dated younger men, men who were half her age, but that was fine by her. She could handle them, enjoy their hard, young bodies until she grew bored with their lack of wisdom and experience. They were a dime a dozen, especially the young lawyers interested in sleeping their way into her prestigious firm.

"Here, allow me," said a voice behind her as the elevator doors opened.

The man prevented the door from closing, and she entered. She smiled at him, and he smiled back. He was too old for her taste, but any man over thirty was. He looked vaguely familiar, and she tried to recall where she'd seen him. They stood silently together, side by side, as the elevator began its descent.

"Have we met before?" she suddenly asked him, curious where their paths had crossed. It irked her when she couldn't remember things. She prided herself on her sharp memory.

"I think I would've remembered you," he said, presenting her with a very pleasant smile. His remark was suggestive. She liked that.

The guy had something attractive about him. "You just look so familiar."

"Lots of people say that. I guess I look like a regular Joe."

Yes, he did. Rather nice-looking but nondescript. She nodded at him as the doors slid open on the ground floor. She hurried out, eager to meet young Trent at her place and get him into her bed. He was sexy in every single department, and he knew how to please her. Of course, she had taught him what to do, when and where and why, and he had taken to it like the proverbial duck to water. As she left the criminal court building, she paused a moment as the August heat assailed her. She raised her face to the warm sunshine. Then she turned to her left and walked quickly toward the parking garage and her brand-new silver-gray Mercedes.

Intent on thoughts of Trent Casey and his newly acquired bedroom expertise, she didn't look behind her, didn't notice that the man from the elevator had turned in the same direction and followed her at a discreet distance.

Studio Zero was quite a place—quite a disgusting place, true, but still quite a place. Zero was a pretty good appraisal, too, if one were to judge the classiness of the joint on a scale of one to ten. It fronted on an alley in a particularly questionable part of town, and Will and Julia both flashed their badges at the muscular, bald, heavily tattooed gatekeeper who was outside the entrance, picking and choosing who could and could not gain entry to this seedy Shangri-la. He let them pass without comment, but when Will glanced back, he was on the phone warning somebody inside that law enforcement officers were entering the premises.

"Gee, what a neat place to hang out," Julia said to him. "The mingled aromas of weed and beer make it seem so homey."

"Yeah, the rap sheets on these guys would probably stretch to Seattle and back."

274

"I think I'll keep my weapon out with my finger on the trigger."

"Don't shoot anybody. Not unless you have to, of course."

"I'll try to control myself. It'll be hard, but I'll try."

Will grinned a little, but his eyes were searching the dark, smoky interior for Juan DeSoto, aka Hap DeSoto, the owner of the grand establishment. His rap sheet was fifteen pages long, full of everything short of murder, starting when the guy was nine. There was an untalented band playing on the stage, lots of scantily clad women gyrating and strutting their stuff and twirling themselves around stripper poles for the rowdy, drunken patrons. Gigi had mentioned a specific booth Juan used for his personal guests, and it didn't take Will long to find it.

"There he is. See him? The guy in the zebra shirt and black leather fedora."

"I see him. Well now, he's a regular Michael Kors, is he not? Think he's got enough women in the booth with him? Maybe you'll luck out and six or seven of them will be Delta flight attendants."

"You aren't ever going to let me live that down, are you?"

"It was just so impressive. That fond farewell lip-lock is forever imprinted on my mind."

Will frowned as they pushed their way through

the crowd. He wasn't the unscrupulous playboy Julia obviously thought he was, and it annoyed the hell out of him that she continued to think so. He hadn't been with a woman since he met her, but maybe that's what needed to change. Maybe he needed to hook up with somebody, make love to Pamela Ford for about a day and a half, and forget Detective Julia Cass. And this bloody, frustrating case.

"Juan DeSoto?" he said when they reached the owner's booth. "We'd like to talk to you, if you have a minute."

DeSoto was small and wiry and swarthy. He wore a sleeveless white T-shirt under a zebra-striped silk shirt, a large gold crucifix around his neck, and lots of leather bracelets on both wrists. He wore a little black goatee that made him look like a pirate; that and the black scarf he had tied backward around his shaven head under the fedora. He had a tattoo of a teardrop under his left eye. He looked up at them as they flashed their badges. "Woo hoo, we got both the TBI and the Chattanooga cops in here. I feel so special. Call me Hap—everybody does."

"I'm Special Agent Brannock and this is Detective Cass," Will said, pulling back his jacket to show he was armed.

"Maybe you should feel special enough to send all your girlfriends back to their dancing poles and answer some of our questions."

That was Julia. Not exactly the patient sort, he'd found. Often straight to the point, no wasting her time on polite chitchat, not while on a case. And, yeah, he liked that about her, too. And she did have her right hand resting on the butt of her weapon. There you go, more to like. She had his back, and yes, that was endearing, as well. Especially in a place like Studio Zero.

"No need to get ugly wit' me, sweet cakes," their new friend, Hap, said to Julia. "Hey, maybe you might wanna moonlight down here with my girls sometime? You sure got the nice tight little bod for the pole. You be crazy hot for a cop. Whooee." He feigned wiping sweat off his brow and gave a low and appreciative whistle, just to get his point across.

"Thanks, but no thanks. I'm not into taking off my clothes and prancing around. It makes me feel like a Clydesdale."

"Too bad. I'd like to teach you some moves myself." Hap DeSoto's appraisal of Julia was utterly lascivious and rubbed Will the wrong way, big-time. But then DeSoto laughed and shooed his six bikini- and high heel–clad women out of the booth with an insulting, dismissive wave of his hand. Will and Julia slid in on each side of him, just as a new dancer entered the stage in a leopard outfit that would fit comfortably in a teacup and slithered her way to the pole on her belly, in far slinkier fashion than any poisonous snake Will had ever seen.

DeSoto concentrated his attention on Julia. "Okay, what can I do for you, sweet cheeks?"

Julia ignored the remark. Will breathed easier. He didn't want to have to pull her off the punk. He jumped into their titillating conversation. "We want to ask you some questions about Roc VanVeter."

"Yeah, I heard about that guy." Hap placed his hand over his heart. "He was a good friend, man. God, he was here just the other night, drinking and partying, and now he's dead on the slab."

Julia said, "You wouldn't happen to know who killed him, would you? Sure would make our job a breeze."

DeSoto threw back his head and laughed heartily for two seconds, cut it off on a dime, and frowned at Julia. "Nope. I keep my nose clean. I got a legitimate business here to run. I don't get mixed up with criminal types."

"Yeah, right."

Will decided he'd better join in, keep things more on the civil side. "Was Roc here alone that night?"

"No, he always brings that cute little assistant of his. I do love all her body piercings. What's her name? Gigi?"

"How often did he come here?"

"A lot."

"We hear that you and he got into an argument a couple of weeks ago. What was that all about?"

"Nothin', really. He got a little rough with one of my girls. Slapped her around. I don't allow that kinda thing. My girls are my meal ticket. I take good care of them."

Julia said, "Wow, you're a class gentleman, aren't you?"

"Yes, ma'am, Detective Cass. That turn you on?"

"What do you think?"

Will said, "We heard Roc bad-mouthed you on the air. Called you a two-bit pimp. Maybe you got angry, decided to teach him a lesson."

"Nope. I'm an honest businessman. That ain't the worst thing I ever heard said about myself. I ain't sweatin' it."

"How about Judge Lucien Lockhart? You know him?" asked Julia.

"Yeah, but not as well as Roc. He got whacked, too, didn't he? It's getting downright dangerous around this town. Maybe you two oughta start doing your jobs a little better." He grinned and showed a lot of sparkling Crest Whitestrips teeth.

"Did he frequent this place?" she asked.

"Sometimes. Brought that cute little maid with him. One of his better-lookin' lovers."

"Maria Bota?" Will asked.

"Yeah."

"They were lovers?"

"Yeah. So?"

"Have you seen her here lately?"

"Nope."

Across from them, a table of gangbangers got into a shoving match with some drunken college guys in the next booth. DeSoto raised his arm and signaled to a couple of beefy bouncers who immediately moved in to break it up and make some memorable bruises for the guys to take home.

"You cater to the Battle Street Ten guys?" Will asked him.

For the first time, the sarcastic grin faded off DeSoto's face. He shook his head. "I don't know nothing about them, either. We card customers, but we don't make 'em tell us their life stories. Hey, you about finished here? I've got business to attend to."

"If you see Maria Bota, tell her we'd like to talk to her."

"Sure thing. I'll make a point of it."

"He's a real jerk," Julia said as they made their way outside. "I don't believe a word he said."

"Me either."

"Let's go. I want to go home and take a long, hot shower. That place was nasty."

Will nodded, thinking a long, hot shower sounded pretty good to him, too, especially if it was with her.

Chapter 15

The savory aroma of chicken pot pies floated through the kitchen of Audrey Sherrod's Walnut Hill town house as she pulled a baking sheet out of the oven loaded with perfectly browned homemade yeast rolls. Zoe was busy around the kitchen, eagerly helping her prepare the meal, and Audrey was pleased that J.D.'s daughter was well on her way to becoming a very good cook. What was more, the child seemed to truly enjoy it.

At the moment, Zoe was making a raspberry vinaigrette for Audrey's luncheon guests. There were just the four of them at her house, and Tam and Julia were already seated at the dining room table discussing the Tongue Slasher case in hushed tones. Shuddering at the moniker with which the news media had dubbed this newest killer soon after Lucien Lockhart's murder, Audrey stopped what she was doing and stared out the kitchen window. She still had bad dreams about the Rocking Chair and Baby Blue Murders, and now there was another killer on the prowl, terrifying all of Chattanooga. She sighed, then decided she wasn't going to let that ruin her party.

"Okay, everything's ready, ladies," she said brightly.

Carrying a silver tray with four white ramekins of flaky-crusted pot pies, Zoe headed for the dining room. Audrey followed her with the yeast rolls and fresh salad. An icy pitcher of sweet tea was already on the table, and a red velvet cake sat on a white cake pedestal on the buffet. Zoe had decorated the white icing with Red Hots and red sprinkles, so dessert was ready and waiting.

When they were all seated and beginning to pass around the salad, Audrey told them the reason for her get-together. "I wanted all of you to be here today so I could ask you an important question."

The other women halted what they were doing and looked questioningly at her. "I want to announce that J.D. and I have set a date for our wedding."

Smiles and congratulations erupted all around the table. "And," Audrey continued happily, "I want to ask each of you to be in the wedding party. Tam, you've been my best friend forever. I'd love it if you'd be my matron of honor."

Tam laughed. "As if I'd ever say no. Of course, I will."

"And Zoe and Julia, you'll be my bridesmaids, won't you?"

Zoe clapped her hands. "Can we get strapless dresses, Audrey? Red ones. I've been dying to wear a red strapless gown, fire truck red, but J.D. wouldn't ever let me."

"We'll pick out the dresses together. I promise." She looked at J.D.'s sister. "What about you, Julia? Can we count on you?"

"Of course. You know you can. I'm just so glad that you've made J.D. so happy. He's turned into a different man since he met you."

Audrey was touched and very pleased. She liked Julia very much and wanted them to become as close as real sisters. J.D. absolutely adored Julia and played quite the big brother now that she was in town. "Thank you so much. J.D. will be pleased."

"So when's the big day?" Julia asked, spooning a liberal portion of the raspberry vinaigrette over her salad greens.

"December fifteenth. That's a Saturday. Eight o'clock in the evening. Unless there's some kind of major conflict with any of your schedules."

Everyone agreed they'd be available, and they chatted and asked her questions about her colors, which were going to be red and black and white. Audrey looked around her dining table and felt a new kind of joy welling up inside her. She was so pleased, so gratified that everything had turned out all right between J.D. and her, that the horrors of her past had been laid to rest. Her father was even coming around; their dinner together had been good, with both of them more comfortable in each other's company, more so than anytime she could remember. She hadn't asked him to walk her down the aisle; not yet. But she felt good about asking him, and she felt fairly certain that he just might say yes.

Life was close to being perfect right now. Zoe was happy again, acting like a typical teenager, with her bright and lively eyes, so eager to begin her young life. Most of the rebellious, defiant attitude she'd exhibited when she'd first come to live with J.D. had now gone by the wayside. J.D. doted on her, just like he obviously had always done with his little sister. She watched Julia laugh at one of Zoe's girlish remarks, then take a sip of her iced tea. Julia did seem a bit distracted today, but Audrey knew the murder case she was investigating had to be troubling to her. J.D. was the same way when he was on a difficult case. In fact, the two siblings were a lot alike, and she was observing it more and more as she got to know Julia. And Julia wasn't so much a tomboy as J.D. had intimated. She was a police officer, but she managed to be feminine and graceful at the same time. She was going to look absolutely beautiful in the red strapless bridesmaid dress that Audrey had decided on a few minutes ago. After hearing Zoe's plea, how could she choose anything else?

"What?" Julia said, noticing Audrey's contemplative gaze.

Audrey thought Julia had the most incredible

284

eyes; their brown color was almost golden. Julia was really quite lovely, with her chiseled bone structure and thick black eyelashes. It was amazing how much Zoe resembled her. Each blessed with all that flowing black hair and a tall and slender athletic build.

"I was just thinking that you remind me of J.D. in lots of ways."

"I'll take that as a compliment, unless you're talking about his quick temper and goofy sense of humor." But Julia was teasing and Audrey knew it.

Zoe piped up. "He's a lot more laid-back now that he and Audrey are finally getting married. He's even letting me go to the mall today to meet my friends."

"She's right. You've been good for him, Audrey," Julia told her. "Not that he's ever been a bad guy. Let's just say he wasn't exactly domestic-bliss material until he met you."

Audrey's lips curved up. "He was quite a ladies' man, as I understand it."

"Yeah, it must be a TBI macho thing."

Tam looked quickly at Julia. "And you're talking about Will Brannock, I take it?"

Julia shrugged a little. "I saw him in action at the airport. It's hard to forget."

"Well, no wonder. He's a real hottie," Zoe chimed in, clasping her hands together in feigned ecstasy. "I wish I was old enough to go out with him. I'd even ask him to go to the movies on Saturday, if I thought he'd go."

Audrey quickly said, "Better not let your dad hear that."

They all laughed, and the luncheon continued on a light note with everyone enjoying themselves and the bountiful array of food. While they were serving the cake, Zoe excused herself to take one of the endless phone calls she received night and day. And when it wasn't a call, it was a text. Audrey had never seen anybody's fingers move so fast on a touch screen. It wasn't long before Zoe was back, cell phone still in hand.

"The girls are waiting for me at the food court. Could you drop me off there, Audrey? Presley's mom is picking us up at four o'clock. J.D. already said I could go to the movies this afternoon with them."

"Let me drop her off, Audrey. I'm going right past Hamilton Place Mall, anyway." Tam grinned sheepishly. "I'm meeting Marcus, since the trial's in recess until tomorrow morning."

Audrey couldn't hide her delight. "Does that mean you're getting back together?"

"It looks that way. We're having dinner together almost every night. We're trying to work things out. I miss him, more than I ever thought I would. Guess I didn't know a good thing when I had it." Her eyes met Audrey's. "We're going to do whatever it takes to make it work this time."

And Tam was thrilled about that. Audrey knew her well enough to see the pleasure in her eyes, and that made her happy, too. She knew Tam had been lonely since her separation, and every time Audrey had seen Marcus he had looked absolutely miserable. She loved them both, and this was just one more blessing in her life for which to be grateful.

Audrey and Julia bid Tam and the excited Zoe good-bye, and then they sat down together at the table over coffee and cake and smiled at each other.

"There go two happy campers," Julia said.

"What about you, Julia? Do you think you're going to be happy here, now that you've settled in a bit?"

Julia nodded. "I do like it here. I love seeing J.D. and you and Zoe so often. You know, having family around is pretty awesome. It's been a long time."

"What about Will? Do you like having him around?"

Julia met her teasing gaze. "He's a good detective. We work well together. I like that about him." Her delicately arched dark brows lowered slightly in a frown. "But he's so secretive. It's, well, it's almost as if he's hiding something."

Surprised, Audrey examined Julia's serious face. "What do you mean by secretive?"

"Well, we've been working together all day nearly every day for quite a while now, and I don't have a clue as to where he lives, where his family is, or what he did before he landed here at the Chattanooga TBI office—nothing. If I mention something about his personal life, he changes the subject or ignores the question. Don't you consider that a little odd?"

"Now that you mention it, I don't think I know anything about him, either. I haven't ever thought much about it."

"And neither does J.D. I've already asked him."

"Maybe he's just one of those extremely private people. There are lots of them around. Maybe you ought to Google him."

Julia smiled. "I already did, I'm ashamed to say, but it turned up very little. Mainly just listed some cases he's worked on here in Chattanooga. No address, no phone number, which is very strange. I know it's intrusive to do something like that, but, Audrey, it almost seems like his slate has been wiped clean. I just wish he'd tell me on his own volition. Or maybe it's better I don't know."

"You're probably right about that. The Internet doesn't know everything about a person, anyway, unless we're talking Facebook. My God, I can't believe what the kids nowadays put out there for anybody to read. J.D. and I are strictly monitoring Zoe's Facebook page. Luckily, she doesn't seem to mind anymore."

"I'm pretty sure Will doesn't have a Facebook

page." Julia chuckled to herself, obviously thinking the idea pretty absurd. "I just don't know many people who hide where they live from their own partner. Sometimes he acts almost, well, almost like a wanted man would."

Audrey frowned. "What do you mean?"

"I mean, watch him sometime, Audrey. He always sits with his back to the wall—not just occasionally, but every single time. Wherever we are, he's constantly watching the entrances and exits and the people coming in and out. He looks uncomfortable if I even touch on anything personal about him or his life."

Audrey chuckled. "Sounds like J.D. And I've seen you do some of those things, too, Julia. Could it be just a cop's habit?"

"Granted, all of us in law enforcement learn to watch our backs. Will acts like he's being stalked."

"Well, I do know one thing about him. He likes you."

Julia picked up her glass, swirling the ice around. She kept her eyes down. "How do you know that?"

"He told me that you were exceptional at your job." Audrey hesitated, not sure she should bring up his concerns, but she wanted Julia to know that both she and Will were there for her, if she ever needed them. "Please don't take this in the wrong way, Julia, but Will and I both noticed the way you reacted when we surprised you the other night. I apologize if I caused you pain or brought up any unpleasant memories."

Julia kept her eyes focused on her glass for another moment. At first, Audrey thought she wasn't going to speak to the issue, but then Julia looked up. "It was an incident when I worked homicide in Nashville. I was attacked by a guy high on drugs. My partner was shot and killed. I'm just jumpy sometimes, is all." She laughed. "You guys surprised the hell out of me that night."

"I understand."

A rather uncomfortable silence settled over them after Julia's admission, but Audrey didn't want Julia to leave before offering her professional help. "If there's anything I can do to help you work through that terrible night, Julia, I hope you'll let me know. If you need to talk about it, or talk about the way you feel about what happened, anything at all, I'll be there for you. Sometimes going over it with someone who understands how a trauma can affect you is very helpful in working through your emotions."

Julia raised her eyes, and Audrey easily read the pain in them. J.D.'s sister still suffered from the death of her partner and her own attack at the hands of a brute. "Thank you, Audrey. I know you're a grief counselor. I appreciate the offer. Maybe sometime, after we get through this case, I will want to talk it out. Right now, the Tongue Slasher murders are all I seem to think about."

"Okay. Just so you know. I'm here anytime you need me." She smiled. "Night or day."

They chatted some more about the people Julia had met at the surprise party as they cleared the table and put the dishes in the dishwasher, but nothing else personal was said, nothing more about Julia's past. Audrey bid her future sister-in-law good-bye at the door and gave her a hug, but as Julia ran down the steps and headed for the old Charger, Audrey couldn't help but wish that J.D.'s sister would confide in her now rather than later. Audrey had been in the counseling business long enough to sense when someone was struggling with emotions, possibly even repressing some memories. In her professional opinion, Julia was doing just that.

Julia got into the Charger and pulled the door shut. She sat with her hands on the steering wheel, unsettled by the fact that Audrey had brought up her concerns about Julia's state of mind. That awful night when Bobby died was the one thing she never, ever discussed. That was something she handled on her own and in her own time. She'd gotten a handle on it a long time ago, and unless startled by a similar situation or a terrible dream, she was dealing with it okay; at least, so far, she was. She sat silently in the car for a while, thinking about it. Thinking about how Bobby had bled to death in her arms. How she'd heard him take his last breath. How his last word had been her name, his dark blue eyes riveted on her face. Her breath caught, and she quickly forced that image out of her mind, the way she always did. It was over, past, done with, don't think about it.

Turning the ignition key, she pumped the accelerator a few times and let the old engine run a bit. She was going to have to make buying a new car a priority or she'd never get it done. She knew that J.D. planned to give the Charger to Zoe someday, when she was older and able to appreciate the car's sentimental value. That was one reason he was still working on it, trying to get the motor and body in top-notch, pristine condition. Julia just hadn't had the time to go car shopping, not with a killer slashing his way through Chattanooga. Maybe she'd get a truck like Will's. Jasper would love to ride around in that. Yep, she would like that, too. And she'd get it in white because she played for the good guys' team.

Heading home, she planned to do more research on Roc VanVeter's life and career. Tam was done with her part in the trial now and had offered to take over the search into the judge's past cases. Julia had already run a search for Roc VanVeter and Judge Lockhart, trying to find a connection between the two of them, but hadn't got that many promising hits. There were many news articles mentioning that Roc VanVeter had blasted Judge Lockhart on some ruling or another, but nothing that really might lock them together in a killer's crosshairs. She intended to keep looking until she found a good lead. There had to be something that was connecting the two murders. There was no way these crimes could be random. This was the exact same MO, the same carefully constructed crime scene, with just a few varying factors. She just hoped to God that the murderer didn't kill again before they identified him.

When she neared a grocery store on her right, she realized that her fridge was basically empty, the cupboards bare, so she pulled into the parking lot. The store was busy, lots of people buying their weekend supply of ground beef and hot dogs, buns, sodas, and chips for Saturday's cookout on the grill. She picked up some salad greens, tomatoes, and cucumbers, a few frozen entrées for nights like tonight when she didn't have the time or energy to cook for herself, a case of bottled water, 7UP, and a few other staples she needed.

The store was unusually crowded. Everybody was rushing around like they were on a racetrack—carts rattling, many customers talking loudly on their cell phones—so she cut the grocery shopping short. She went through checkout and pushed her cart of groceries out to where she'd left the Charger.

Audrey had insisted on sending some leftovers home with her, and Julia wasn't one to argue with a free and already exquisitely prepared meal. She considered herself pretty good in the kitchen, too. She had pretty much run the household when she and J.D. were left alone after their daddy's death. But on the days she spent hunting down a psycho-path, a mutilating killer, she just wasn't up for handling raw food. Drink, maybe, if it was something strong. The only other home-cooked food she was likely to get in the near future was at Cathy's when she and Will joined the Axelrods for dinner. Which reminded her, she thought belatedly on the drive home, she had forgotten to pick up the bottle of wine that she had decided to take to the dinner party.

So that meant yet another stop. She pulled up to an upscale package store along the way and decided on a bottle of Beringer white zinfandel; not her favorite, but she did know it was Cathy's. She made a few more stops, picking up her dry cleaning, checking in for a moment at her desk at police headquarters down on Wisdom Street, where she dropped off some paperwork for Chief Mullins. CPD was pretty deserted, so she headed home, anxious to hit the Internet for a more thorough search.

When she passed the Axelrods' log cabin, all was quiet and deserted. Lonnie's car was gone and so was Charlie's bass boat, which had been there earlier, so she suspected Charlie had returned home and Cathy and Lonnie were out running errands. When she reached the boathouse, Jasper was parked inside the screen door, wagging his tail, as pleased as punch to see her. She grabbed her groceries and let him run out the screen door and prowl around down by the river, very feisty after being cooped up all day. She unpacked the milk and fresh fruit and put them in the fridge, then walked back outside for the dry cleaning and wine. As she gathered up her clothes, she saw a UPS package sitting in the back window of her car. She hadn't noticed it before, but she knew for a fact that it hadn't been there when she'd left the boathouse earlier that day on her way to Audrey's town house on Second Street.

Immediately alert, she unsnapped her holster and pulled out her weapon, her gaze quickly searching the yard and surrounding woods. She stared out over the swift current but detected no boats anywhere on the river. Who had put the package inside the Charger? And when? Where? Instinctively knowing it had something to do with the Tongue Slasher, she sheathed her gun, grabbed a pair of latex gloves, and snapped them on. Keeping a wary eye on the thick undergrowth alongside the riverbank, where Jasper was now sniffing out a squirrel, she opened the door and got her first good look at the package.

When she saw what was written on the front of the tan mailing envelope, she tensed and again searched her surroundings. PROVERBS 10:31 in black marker. The Tongue Slasher was sending them another message, one he wanted to make sure they received in person. He had been inside her car. The idea made her stomach turn over.

Taking care, she picked up the package and examined the wrapping. It was a used UPS box, left unsealed. When she opened the end, she saw the DVD inside. Oh God, she hoped the killer hadn't filmed the murders for them to watch. The sinking sensation in her stomach, however, and her sixth sense, told her that was exactly what they were going to find recorded on that DVD.

Pulling out her cell phone, she punched in Will's number. He picked up on the second ring. "Yeah, Cass? What's up?"

"Where are you?"

"At home."

"How quick can you get to my place?"

"What's wrong? You okay?"

"Yes, but guess what the killer left in my car?"

"Oh my God, what? Not part of a tongue?"

"A DVD with *Proverbs 10:31* written on the front of the mailing envelope."

"You sure he's not still around there? He could be watching you."

"I've been looking, believe me. I don't think anybody's out here creeping around. Jasper would've let me know a long time ago. He doesn't like strangers."

"I'll be there in ten minutes, fifteen tops."

Julia carried the DVD inside, very carefully handling the evidence. Forensics would have to dust it for prints, but her hunch told her they weren't going to find anything usable, at least not usable in court. If the perp had managed to clean up the gory crime scenes without leaving a trace of himself, he sure as hell wasn't going to be careless enough to leave fingerprints on a package that he delivered in person to the police.

It wasn't long before she heard the sound of a boat's motor coming upriver. She hurried out onto the porch, thinking it might be Charlie. He visited Lonnie often, but it didn't sound like a bass boat. It sounded like one of those big racing speed-boats that passed her place from time to time. A minute later, she was shocked to see Will Brannock fly into view, in one of said big, sleek racing boats. He maneuvered the long black-and-red craft beside her little dock with expert ease, tied up, jumped out, and ran up the steps.

"Any sign that he's been here?" was his greeting. "Do we need to call in forensics?"

"No. It doesn't look like he placed it in the car out here. If anybody ever came up my road, I'm sure Cathy and Lon would've seen him pass their house. I'll ask them, but I don't think he'd take that chance."

"Have you played it?"

"No. I figured you'd want me to wait. Maybe

assemble the rest of the task force before we watched it."

"Where was it in your car?"

"In the back window."

"Don't you lock your car?"

"No."

He gave her a disapproving frown. "Well, you should. You have any idea when he put it in?"

Julia shook her head. "Not a clue as to where, but I'm fairly certain the package wasn't there when I left for Audrey's this morning. I can't say anything else for sure. I stopped at several places on the way home. He could've done it then. He could've done it when I was parked outside Audrey's house, for all I know. We can look at the parking lot videotapes at the grocery store to see if he did it there."

"We will. Where else did you stop?"

"After the grocery store, the dry cleaners, and a wine and cheese shop."

Will was frowning, eyes intently roaming the surrounding woods. "I don't like him getting that close to you."

That surprised Julia, all right, but she could see that the concern in his eyes was real. "Well, I don't, either, trust me. Rest assured, nobody's going to sneak up on me out here, not with Jasper around. He'll bark the minute he hears anything."

"Yeah? Well, Jasper's not always awake. He didn't bark at me the other day when I showed up

298

out here early in the morning, if you'll remember."

"True, but I am a trained police officer. I can take care of myself."

Will's frown deepened. "I got all the way to your front door the other day."

"True, and I had my weapon pointed at you before you got inside."

Surprisingly, Will didn't argue with that. "I know, but this guy's a psychotic killer, and he's picked you out to deal with. That makes you a target. He's obviously been tailing you. I don't like this. Especially when you didn't suspect you were being followed."

Will was right, and Julia couldn't deny the implications. "Don't worry. I'll be careful from here on out. What about the DVD? You ready to watch it?"

Will hesitated. "Yeah, where is it? Maybe he's gone and made a big mistake this time, pulling this kind of dangerous stunt."

"I wouldn't count on him making stupid mistakes. He's been a clever boy so far."

Inside the boathouse Will put on the gloves Julia handed him and pushed the DVD into the slot on her laptop with one finger. "Get ready, Cass. My gut tells me that this is not going to be pretty."

"Tell me about it."

Will hit the play button, and they sat side by side, saying nothing, just watching the static that appeared on the screen. The picture flashed on a couple of seconds later. It was a video of one of the murders, all right, just as they had feared. Judge Lockhart was bound to a white iron chair on his back veranda. He was sitting upright, forehead strapped to the tall back of the chair, his eyes bulging wide and filled with fear. Rivulets of sweat streamed down his face, and he seemed to freeze as a voice came out of the darkness behind the camera. The voice was distorted electronically, sounding hollow and gruff and inhuman: "Don't say a word . . . don't ask me for mercy . . . the fraudulent tongue shall be cut out."

Then the camera panned down the judge's naked chest, past his white swim trunks and bound legs to the floor of the porch. There, set out in precise order, lay the metal scales, a big pair of pliers, a well-honed, twelve-inch fillet knife, and a coiled length of yellow ski rope. Julia cringed and had to force herself to watch as the actual murder went down.

"He's showing himself," Will said, leaning closer to the screen.

Julia watched the killer move toward the camera. He was dressed in black, his face hidden by a black ski mask. He held up the tongue in one black-gloved hand for the camera to record, cut off the tip, and then placed the other part on one side of the scales. He carefully stacked a handful of dimes on the other side. The screen went back to static.

Will ejected the DVD and looked at Julia. "He wants us to find him. He's helping us. I think he's frustrated that we haven't yet."

"Or he wants us to know why he's doing this. Maybe we're not catching on to his clever little enigmatic clues the way he thinks we should. Maybe he wants us to follow the leads in a certain way, go through this exactly the way he set things up. Could be that he's not exactly happy with us or the news media's take on his murders."

"He's got his own murderous agenda, Julia, and he's carrying it out one step at a time. He knows who we are. He has already contacted you. That puts you in danger. You've got to be careful. This man is seriously deranged.""He seems pretty deliberate to me. I think he's out for revenge, getting rid of one perceived enemy at a time. All we have to do is tie all this together and we'll get him."

"There's got to be a common denominator here somewhere. But it's a needle in a haystack thing."

Julia felt sure that she was right, but now that she'd actually seen the guy wreak his cruelty, his savagery, on a helpless victim, she had a terrible feeling that the killer had already chosen his next victim, maybe more than one. He might have already killed again. He wasn't wasting time between kills, as some serial killers liked to do. He wasn't picking people at random, also not typical of most serials. But that was good. If he had a specific agenda with specific targets, they just might get lucky and identify him sooner rather than later. Whatever the case, they weren't going to stop until they found the key.

Chapter 16

Gloria Varranzo regained consciousness, aching all over, head pounding, mouth dry, lips parched and parted. She couldn't remember anything at first. She had come home from the Hamilton County criminal court, taken a quick shower, and heated up a bowl of tomato soup. Then the doorbell had rung. She had answered it, hadn't she? Had Trent showed up early? She was expecting him later tonight, wasn't she? No matter how hard she tried, she just couldn't decipher her jumbled thoughts. Squeezing her eyes shut, she tried to raise her hands and massage her aching temples. But she couldn't move. Oh God, why couldn't she move?

Finally she forced her eyes open but blinked painfully under the glaring light trained on her. She tried again to see, jagged pain crashing around in her skull like a spiked steel mace. Except for the one light, the room was dark. Where was she? She finally realized that the light was coming from one of her Pottery Barn copper bedside lamps. It was lying on its side, the bulb pointed at her face. She tried to think.

Okay, that meant she was at home, and then she remembered the man. He'd been standing outside her door. The man she'd met in the elevator. Yes, that's right. At first, she'd thought he was flirting with her, that he'd thought her attractive and followed her home. Men noticed her, lots of them, even though she was past her best years. His attention didn't surprise her; she'd kept her trim figure with lots of grueling workouts and distance jogging, and she paid close attention to her hair and nails, and especially her skin. She didn't have a wrinkle on her face. Thanks to cosmetic surgery and Botox, true, but not a single one.

But what had happened at the door? She tried to remember, tried to get past the excruciating, thudding pain in her head. *Think, think.* The man had hit her on the head. She remembered that now, although it was all a blur. Now she was tied up. Was this a sexual assault? Oh God, where was he now? What was he planning to do to her?

"Are you scared, Ms. Varranzo?" came the man's low voice.

Should she say yes? Would that make him feel sorry? Make him think her vulnerable? Or would it be better to say no, pretend to be brave. But she wasn't brave. She was so scared that she couldn't answer either way.

"I think you are. I think you're a coward when you aren't telling lies in front of a jury, or making the victims of the crime feel awful about themselves, or making the victim's family live through the horrific things done to their loved ones, or taking pleasure in making their loved ones look like criminals, smearing their names, torturing their grieving families."

Terrified, she tried to summon some kind of bravado, tried to make her voice strong like she did in the courtroom. "What do you want? You'll never get away with this. Never."

"Shh, Gloria, don't say a word. Don't expect mercy. All you've ever done is lie and accuse and damage innocent people with your cruelty."

"Please . . ." Gloria got the word out somehow, all vestiges of courage fading to hollow horror. "Please don't hurt me."

"You've gotten by with inflicting so much pain. So much suffering imposed on others."

"I'm sorry. I'll do whatever you want. Anything. I've got money, lots of money. I'll give it to you. All of it."

"I don't want your money. I want you to pay for what you've done to me."

"What did I do? I don't know you. I don't know you!"

Gloria bit her lip and struggled against the ropes binding her. The man came out of the shadows. He had a set of scales in one hand. He held a long, thin knife in the other. The steel blade shimmered in the light when he moved it.

"See these? They're my scales of justice. You've never worried about justice in all the years you've been defending murderers and rapists and criminals, have you? Well, Gloria. Now it's payback time. I'm the one you've got to face now. This is your final judgment."

"Please, no . . ."

" 'The mouth of the just brings forth wisdom; but the fraudulent tongue shall be cut out.' "

"No, no, please, please, I beg you . . ."

The man walked forward with the knife. Gloria began to scream, and then her screams were cut short . . .

Julia sat on a tall bar stool inside Cathy Axelrod's kitchen, watching her friend take a glass baking dish of delicious-smelling chicken parmesan out of her oven. It smelled so good that Julia resisted the urge to pick up a fork and take a bite. Cathy's mom was a great cook, out of the old Italian school, which meant having some kind of pasta nearly every night, and lots of it. In Julia's opinion, Cathy could now give the chefs in Rome and Naples a run for their euros, no doubt about it. Lonnie was busy setting the table on the open-air rear deck and had refused Julia's offer to help, instead pouring her a glass of the wine she'd brought and bidding her to sit down and keep his wife company. Will Brannock had not shown up yet. She wondered if he planned to stand them up. Julia was still surprised Cathy had invited him.

"So tell me, Cath, why's Will coming tonight? You hardly know him."

"To get the two of you together, of course. Why else would I have him over?" Cathy smiled impishly. She'd had her long, auburn hair cut short recently, and she looked really good, freckles and all. "You've been alone way too long. I bet you've forgotten how to kiss a man."

"C'mon, Cathy, stop it already. Nobody's going to want to kiss me tonight, anyway, not if there's garlic in that chicken." She smiled, but Cathy was pretty much right on. Julia hadn't kissed a man since Bobby died, hadn't been out on many dates, either; just hadn't wanted to. Not until Will Brannock came along, but why did it have to be him? Another cop. Another partner. She had lost one man she cared about because he was a cop. How could she get involved with another one, another man who faced danger and death every day? Well, she couldn't. Wouldn't. It was not going to happen.

"You're alone too much. In fact, you're alone all the time. Lonnie and I worry about you."

"Well, you shouldn't. I'm doing fine. I'm here, aren't I? Having dinner with my friends. And you shouldn't have invited Will. Nothing's going to come of it. We're partners." Julia swallowed, and the next words came out hard. "Partners don't need to get involved. You know why."

"You're not really partners. As soon as this case is over, you'll be with Tam, and Will will team up with J.D. That means a green light. That means a go. That means a wedding next year."

Julia rolled her eyes at Cathy's persistence. "Stop this, I'm telling you. It's not going to happen. He isn't even interested in me in that way."

Cocking her head, Cathy stopped buttering the loaf of French bread and looked at her with that same knowing grin. "He sure accepted our invitation quickly enough. Maybe he's more interested in you than you think."

Maybe he was. The reverse was certainly true, as hard as that was to admit. There was just something about him that got to her, especially when he was in an open mood and kidding around, laughing and teasing. Rare occurrences, of late. And there were those other things. Yeah, he was almost too good-looking, too tall, too strong, too smart, and last but not least, too addicted to redheaded flight attendants. Oh yeah, and he wouldn't tell her a single thing about himself, his family, his life, or his past. Yessiree, that was exactly what she needed at the moment. A man of mystery. Not. Of course, said the good little angel perched on her other shoulder, he hadn't shown that kind of womanizing behavior since that one time in the airport. And everybody who knew him said he wasn't like that. And why shouldn't he go out on dates? She did. J.D. did. Audrey did. Everybody did. Oh God, her resolve was dissolving big-time.

The doorbell rang and Lonnie got up from where he was now watching a Braves baseball game on TV and went to answer the front door. They heard male voices speaking together, then a laugh.

"He's he-e-re," Cathy singsonged. "Is your heart going crazy?"

Maybe it was, but so what? And Cathy would never know it. Neither would Brannock. She was having enough trouble keeping her hormones under control.

"Hello, Mrs. Axelrod," Will said from the doorway. "I brought you some wine. Chardonnay. Hope that fits your menu."

"I beat you to it, Brannock," Julia told him.

"That's okay," Lonnie said, coming into the room. "There are four of us. That's half a bottle each."

Will laughed. "I'm not much of a drinker. Found out early on that wine and whiskey can get a guy in trouble."

Everyone laughed, but Julia wondered what kind of trouble he was talking about.

"Here, everything's ready and hot. Let's take the food out on the deck. Will, would you take the bread? Julia, you bring the salad and salad dressing."

Cathy had seated Julia and Will side by side, across the table from Lonnie and her. Julia noticed how close their chairs were. As she sat down, she moved hers a little farther away.

"Would you bow your heads for grace?" said Lonnie, folding his hands.

Lonnie had been a chaplain in the military for many years and was still very devout. So was Cathy, which made them an even stronger match. After the blessing, Lonnie took their plates and served the chicken parmesan as they passed around the rest of the food. Will fit in very well, asking Lonnie about his years in the service, but Julia noted that he didn't volunteer any information about his own military service, if he'd had any. Maybe it was time to find out exactly what he'd done.

"What about you, Will?" she asked pointedly, turning in her chair to look straight at him. "Were you in the service?"

He smiled and shrugged, easier with the question than she'd thought he'd be. "I'm afraid I can't divulge that information without unidentified forces coming after me."

"So you were in the Special Forces?"

"I plead the Fifth."

"Yeah, surprise, surprise."

"Sounds exciting," Cathy interjected, no doubt

sensing Julia's frustration. "But we won't put you on the spot, will we, guys? Can you tell us how long you've been with the TBI?"

Julia thought Will didn't look like he wanted to tell them zip about himself or anything else. To her surprise, he said, "About ten years now. I've only been in Chattanooga for a year and a half."

"Where were you before?" Julia asked him.

"Afraid I can't say."

Julia turned to Cathy. "You ask him, Cathy. I think he responds better to you."

Cathy and Lonnie laughed. Cathy said, "Oh, no way. I think he responds a whole lot better to you."

Well, that was blunt and embarrassing as hell. Why didn't Cathy just get down to brass tacks and say that the two of them were so intensely attracted to each other that it was a miracle there hadn't been a sexual attack committed by one or both of them?

Will gave his easy laugh, Sergeant Sociable all of a sudden. "We make a good team, that's for sure. Julia is quite a detective."

Lonnie nodded. "That's what Cathy says, too. She said you were great with the K-9 units, but that you're even better in homicide."

"I try," Julia said, feeling silly. Truth was, she didn't like talking about herself and her past anymore than Will did. Yet another trait they had in common. Two privacy freaks.

"This is the best chicken parmesan that I've

ever tasted," she said enthusiastically, in an awkward attempt to change the subject.

"I agree," said Will. "Thank you for inviting me, Cathy. It's good to get away from the case a bit. That's about all Julia and I have been thinking about."

Well, that was partially true. They were checking out every single lead, twice, even three times, and so far they were getting almost nowhere. Lots of connections, lots of false leads, lots of shady people who were probably lying. And a serial killer who was probably hanging his next victim from a yellow ski rope while they all cheerily clinked glasses and partook of great Italian food and crusty bread.

"I brought dessert," Julia said, not liking the direction of her thoughts. Will was right, they needed to clear their minds, think about other stuff for one night. Maybe then they'd remember something, see some little detail they'd overlooked. "It's pecan pie."

"How'd you know? That's my favorite," Will said quickly, giving her that great smile of his.

"Well, that's lucky." Julia wondered if he was buttering her up for something, and why, and if he really did like pecan pie. On the other hand, who didn't like pecan pie?

"You got my number, I guess."

"Yes, she certainly does," interjected Cathy, like the sly dog she was.

Julia gave her a warning look as Cathy scooted back her chair and brought out a pot of coffee. Cathy poured the brew, and Will ate two pieces of pie and politely complimented Julia on its deliciousness. She was stupidly pleased and chastised herself soundly. *Keep it professional, keep it professional,* she kept telling herself. *Partner, partner, partner, partner.*

"Oh yes, Julia's a better cook than I am. Lots of down-home Southern recipes from Memphis," gushed Cathy.

Jeez, what was Cathy going to do next, give Will a punched ticket into Julia's bedroom?

"My favorite kind of cooking," said Will. "That's what my mom does."

Aha, Julia thought, the most private one slipped up. "Where does your mom live?"

"She moves around a lot."

"Will the *Men in Black* come after you if you talk about your mom's cooking, too?"

There was another awkward silence for a moment. Cathy and Lonnie looked at her as if she'd asked Will how well he performed in bed, which she suspected he might be willing to describe readily enough. Oh no, he wouldn't. What had gotten into her? She was being ridiculous. He was a nice guy. Maybe that's what had her so upset. He was okay, which wasn't okay.

"My mother grew up in Alabama. She's a great lady. I miss her."

Well, now, let's peel down some more of that onion, thought Julia, delighted he was finally talking about himself. "What about brothers and sisters? Do you have any?"

"Yes." Will turned to Cathy. "Do you think I could take home a doggie bag? Everything you made was so good."

"Of course." Cathy was pleased. Julia could see it in her face, and Will's request got Cathy jumping up from the table and packing him a sack of goodies. Effectively ending any need for him to answer further questions about his family, brothers and sisters included.

After dinner they played cards. Hearts, men against the women. Will was very good. To her chagrin, the men won. Afterward, Cathy refused to let them help with the dishes, and when they were ready to leave, she shooed them out the front door like two teenagers on their first date. No doubt planning to peek out the bedroom windows like an overprotective mom.

Outside, on the long porch filled with comfortable chairs and couches, Julia looked at Will. "You did notice, of course, that Cathy's got this matchmaker complex. She just can't help herself. Sorry about that."

Will held the screen door open for her. "I like your friends. Lonnie, too. He's a nice man. We both root for the Braves."

They walked together out to his truck.

313

"Well, I guess I'll see you tomorrow," she said abruptly.

"Get in. I'll take you home."

"No, that's okay. I walked down here. I like to walk."

"Then I'll walk you home. It's the least I can do on our first date. Besides, Cathy there, who's watching us out the window, will be disappointed if I don't."

Julia laughed. "Okay, but it's not a date."

"I know. Just kidding."

He didn't act like he was kidding. Trouble was, it felt like a first date—discomfort, self-consciousness, stammering, and all. She had a feeling he was experiencing the same asinine Zoe-aged emotions. "Okay, I'll take the ride. Thanks."

"I really like it out here on the river," Will commented as they drove the short distance to the boathouse. "There's something about living on water that's soothing."

"Does that mean that you live on water?"

There was a slight hesitation, but this time he actually divulged a fact about his place of residence. Miracle upon miracle.

"Yes, but it's more of a lake."

"Around here?"

"Yes. Here we are. That took about three minutes flat."

Will turned off the ignition and then the headlights. They sat silently with the moonlight flooding through the windshield, painting them in a pearly, romantic light. "How about inviting me in for a nightcap?" he suggested.

No, no, no, no, she thought. "Okay," she said.

They walked up the steps, and Jasper came barreling out of the house. He stopped barking when he realized it was Julia and Will. "Have a seat," she told Will when they reached the porch. "I don't have much, just beer and water and 7Up."

"That sounds great. I'll take a beer."

Will took a seat on the swing, and Julia walked inside. She got two Bud Lights out of the fridge, twisted off the caps, and carried them back out on the porch. *This is not a good idea,* she thought. *Nope, it's a bad idea, in fact. Very, very bad.* This was feeling more and more like a date. Unfortunately, she liked the feeling. So did her body, judging by the way her nerve endings were all tingling and having a party inside her skin. Damn, she liked Will more than she should. A lot more, in fact. And if she was not mistaken, he liked her, too. They both knew better, but then again, crazy, insane, impossible-to-control sexual chemistry was hard to ignore.

Will was outside now, down by the river, leaning up against the picnic table on the bank. She walked down the hill to join him and handed him a bottle of beer.

"Here you go, nice and cold."

Will took the beer, tipped it back, and she stood beside him, looking out across the dark river at the lights on the far side, trying to ignore the quivering going on in certain intimate places. "This is a great spot," she said. "You can see the stars like nowhere else I've ever been."

When she looked at Will, his eyes weren't on any stars. They were drinking her in. They stared at each other, longingly, hungrily, and every nerve in Julia's body started dancing jigs. They were very close now, eyes locked, thinking about one thing and one thing only, and what it was going to feel like. He reached out and stroked her hair. "You just don't know how long I've wanted to touch you like this. You have beautiful hair, Julia, the blackest hair I've ever seen."

Then his fingertips caressed her cheek so lightly she could barely feel it. She felt all the caution, all the barriers she'd erected around her heart start to come down like a row of flicked dominoes. She tried to refreeze her inner fortitude, but his other hand was on her waist, pulling her up against his chest. Oh God. She didn't resist, and chastised herself silently for that, too, but it felt good. It felt so good to have a man's arms around her, to have Brannock's arms around her. He felt hard and warm and strong, and she leaned into him, wanting more, despite her better judgment. His lips found hers, hot and eager, and

316

she let herself go, just for this moment, just for this one kiss. She responded, sliding her arms around his neck, and Will made a sound of pleasure deep inside his throat and tangled both fists in her hair. Julia opened her mouth under his invading tongue, and then they were lost in the sheer sensations, tongues touching, their bodies on fire, both giving in to something they'd wanted since the first day they'd met but had fought off for days and days and days.

It took some time, but finally, she wasn't sure how long, Julia managed to pull her whirling, incoherent, unbelievably turned-on thoughts together, and realized what they were doing, what they shouldn't do, what she couldn't do. She thought of Bobby, of what had happened to him, of how she'd grieved so long and hard, and she stiffened in Will's arms and somehow managed to push her palms against his chest. She could feel the way it was heaving under her hands, could hear him panting, could hear her own breaths, shallow and quick and shaken.

"We can't do this," she got out in somebody else's voice. Somebody whose words were wavering like a frightened virgin's.

"I know. We can't." His lips attacked hers again. She fell against him, forgetting everything but the masculine taste of him, the way his hands felt exploring her body, finding his way under her shirt, his palms sliding over her bare flesh. Julia fought herself back to good sense.

"We can't do this," she tried again, very half-heartedly.

"No, this is a terrible idea."

His mouth found hers again. Julia fought for self-control, didn't find it for a while—quite a while, actually. When she did, she backed out of his arms, jerked loose, and put a few feet of distance between them. Will took a step toward her, his breathing harsh and his chest heaving. She took another step back, shaky, weak in the knees, weak in the head.

"God, I want you like I've never wanted anybody," Will muttered, breathless, too.

Julia moistened her trembling lips. She wanted him, too; was tired of fighting the attraction. "We're both pros. We're working on a murder case. We cannot do this right now. Later, it'll be a different story. It'll be acceptable then."

Moonlight carved dark planes and hollows in Will's handsome face as he stared silently at her. He didn't look exactly thrilled. He placed his hands on his hips, shook his head, then looked back at her. "Okay, I can live with that, I guess, if it's got to be. As long as we can finish this. Soon."

Julia swallowed hard. "I don't know anything about you, Will, except that you're hiding things from me. That makes me nervous."

"I've got my reasons for that."

Julia waited, surprised that he had admitted it,

but he didn't elaborate, didn't tell her why. "What is it? You don't trust me?"

"I trust you. I just can't tell you everything you want to know. Let's leave it at that."

That was all he said. That was all he was ever going to say. But could she leave it at that like he wanted to do? "Then maybe we should step back and pretend this didn't happen."

Will gave a low laugh. "Maybe you can forget the way that felt, but not me."

"I'm just saying, not while we're on this case together. It's too important. People are dying. We've got to find who's doing it."

"You're right. I know that. I've been living this case, night and day. Just like you have."

Julia looked out over the river. "I'm no prude, Will, but I don't go in for casual sex. I never have, and I don't intend to change that with you. And I like to know who I'm getting close to."

"It won't be casual."

Will reached out and pulled her back into his embrace. She could feel his heart beating beneath her ear.

"You need to go," she whispered, "before we do something we'll both regret."

"I won't regret it." He stopped speaking for a moment and just held her. "Look, I'll back off and go, sure, if that's what you really want, but don't think this is over because it's not. We're not finished."

"Maybe, maybe not."

"Oh, we're gonna finish this, all right, and I think you know it."

He was right, of course. They would finish it; she knew that only too well. She wanted him to stay, to kiss her all night long, forever if he wanted to, but she couldn't bring herself to give in to it, not yet.

"Then I guess I'll see you in the morning," Will said, still holding her tightly against him. He whispered, his mouth against her hair, "Good luck pretending this didn't happen."

He let go of her then, and Julia watched him walk off. He stopped halfway to the truck. "Thing is, Jules, I'm not at all sure you can keep your hands off me. It's going to be hard for you. You know that, don't you?"

"Yeah, right," she said, but she had to laugh at his joking, because his words were oh, so true.

"Go ahead, laugh. But you'll see. You'll want to kiss me again, and you'll be sorry about sending me packing like this."

"Would you just get out of here?" she told him, but the smile would not leave her face.

"You really know how to hurt a guy, Cass." He paused. "Lock your doors tonight. Keep that gun under your pillow."

Julia watched him get inside his Hummer, glad he had ended this episode on a light note. That would make things easier in the morning. He sat there for a few seconds, then the headlights flared on and the engine roared to life. He slowly turned the truck around and headed down the river road toward Cathy and Lonnie's house.

Julia stood in the darkness and looked around. The river was flowing along, just as if nothing momentous had happened, crickets singing full force in the woods. The stars were out; the breeze was nice and cool. She wished Will was still there. How could this have happened? Who would've thought it possible? She had thought him a playboy type from the day they'd met, had felt that attraction that so many other women had undoubtedly felt.

During all the time they had worked so closely together, hour after hour, day after day, week after week, he'd been strictly professional, had done nothing to make her feel that he was a self-absorbed cad. In fact, he had been a gentleman, a serious law enforcement officer on the job, and had certainly given her no indication that he was a sleazy guy on the make. Just the opposite, really. She trusted him now, trusted his instincts on the job. He made her smile, was easy to be with, was easy to fall in love with.

On the other hand, she had seen the way women looked at him. He was a sexy man, and she knew now that he was certainly adept at kissing a woman until she turned to jelly. He could have any woman he wanted. Why was he suddenly so interested in forging a relationship with her? Was she a challenge? Was that it? Down deep, she really didn't believe that. He had treated her courteously, given her great respect the whole time they'd worked the case. *Okay, Julia, calm down. Time will tell.* Thing was, he might be right. After tonight, and those overwhelming kisses that left her so breathless, she might indeed have trouble keeping her hands off him.

Later in bed, listening to the rush of the current, she relived the feel of his mouth again—those warm, eager, possessive, deep, penetrating kisses. Her body reacted. Furious with herself, she punched her pillow and flipped over. After about an hour of Julia's tossing and turning, Jasper apparently had had enough. She felt him get up, jump off the bed, and pad off to the living room couch, no doubt seeking some peace and quiet. Julia groaned and wished she could do the same, but it was not until the early morning hours that she finally got Will Brannock off her conscious mind and dreamed about him instead.

Chapter 17

When Julia arrived at the TBI offices early the next morning, she hoped nobody commented on her puffy, bloodshot eyes. This time Visine had not done the trick; not even close. Surprised to find the full task force assembled inside the conference room, she poured herself a cup of strong black coffee and joined them. Will was standing at the head of the table. When he saw her at the door, he glanced away without acknowledging her. Okay, he was doing exactly what she had asked him to do. Then why did it bother her so much? Good grief, this guy was driving her crazy.

"Hey, Julia!"

Julia turned quickly and found Tam Lovelady motioning and pointing to the chair beside her at the long, shiny conference table. Glad to have somebody else to concentrate on, she hurried over and took the upholstered chair beside her CPD partner.

Tam looked her in the face and said, "Are you feeling all right, Julia? Got allergy problems?"

"No, I'm fine. Just couldn't sleep last night."

"I know how that is. Good news is, though,

now that I'm finished testifying, the chief told me to get over here and help you guys out any way I can."

"Great, Tam. We can use you, especially in the research you're doing on Lockhart's judicial decisions. He was on the bench for nineteen years. That's a lot of files to go through." Julia was pleased her new friend had come aboard on the case. Determined not to look at Will again, she listened intently while Tam filled her in on the status of the Rocking Chair murder trial.

"Your brother still hasn't been called back, but they've told him they're goin' to, so he's got to hang around. Talk about somebody champing at the bit. Audrey's probably goin' to be called, too."

"J.D. told me something about Audrey's involvement. It was pretty awful. A complicated case."

"The Tongue Slasher is pretty terrible, too. Now y'all think he's a serial, right?"

"Yeah. He used the same MO and the same mutilations on both the vics."

"I know. I saw the crime scene photos Will's got up there on the bulletin board. This guy's a real psycho. What's this meeting about?"

"I don't know. Will didn't mention it last night."

Tam searched her face. "Last night? Are y'all goin' out? J.D. keeps saying that Will thinks you're really something special. That true?"

"C'mon, Tam. You know I can't get involved

324

with a partner. You wouldn't, either, now would you?" Julia could not believe the interest everybody was showing in her and Will and their relationship. Good grief. Please, make it stop. She was having enough trouble resisting the guy without everybody in town pulling for a romance.

"I'm your partner, not Will. He's just your liaison special agent on this case."

"Technically. In any case, we all need to keep our minds nice and clear so we can find this killer." She hesitated, not really wanting to continue any discussion of her or Tam's love lives, or lack thereof, but she felt like she should ask about Marcus. "So, Tam, how are you and Marcus doing?"

Tam's smile was quick, maybe even a bit self-satisfied. "I moved back into our house two nights ago. I was so glad to be home again. Living without a man is not all it's cracked up to be."

Tell me about it, Julia thought. Thank goodness she had Jasper, although he had deserted her last night, the dirty dog. "I know one thing. Audrey's going to be thrilled to death."

"I know. We go back a long time. Lots of history."

Both women stopped talking and turned to face the front when Will walked to the podium. He didn't beat around the bush. He was a straight-to-the-point-so-shut-up-and-listen-up kind of guy. Julia was getting used to that. Will Brannock laid things on the line, like it or lump it. Julia liked it. Julia liked him, period. Especially after what happened last night.

"There's now a third victim. From the initial report, everything points to the Tongue Slasher as the perpetrator."

A low murmuring erupted around the table. Nobody had expected another murder so soon; not even Julia. The killer was speeding up his agenda. Why?

"The victim is a white female, a fifty-six-year-old defense attorney. Most of you will probably recognize her name. Gloria Varranzo. The CPD officer who got the call describes the MO exactly the same as the first two, down to the thirty dimes and identical scales. Detective Cass and I need to get over there right away. Tam Lovelady has joined the task force, and Tam, I'm assigning you to Varranzo's law office. You need to question her partners and the staff before they get any details about what happened to Varranzo. We'll need for those of you on forensics to get over to the crime scene at Varranzo's residence ASAP. I've called the ME's office already, and Pete Tipton's probably already there, knowing him." He paused but still didn't look at Julia. "The rest of you continue with your assigned duties. We'll apprise you of the evidence gleaned from the scene as soon as we finish the forensic investigation. And keep this quiet. The media's salivating over this case since the CBS affiliate got that Lockhart murder video from the killer. Thank God, they only aired a little of it. They'll try to pry every gory detail out of you. Don't let that happen. Any questions?"

There were a few people who had questions about their assignments, and then the meeting was over. Tam stood up and said, "Call me later and fill me in on what you turn up at the Varranzo scene."

Julia nodded and then sat and waited for Will to finish giving orders to a couple of special agents at the front of the room. He then had a quick conversation on his cell phone, after which he hung up quickly and headed in her direction.

"Your car or mine?" she said, trying to act normal and keep her eyes off his mouth when he answered. She ought to be ashamed of herself, at her age. Really.

"Mine. C'mon, we need to get over there."

Will hardly looked at her. He was Brother Brusque this morning, no panting, no lusting, and all business, like nothing earth-shattering had ever happened between them. She wished she could do that kind of abrupt, brush-it-off thing, but she felt her face heating up, just being so close to him.

"When did the murder happen?" she asked him once they were inside his Hummer and fighting early morning traffic.

"Don't know yet. Tipton can tell us more after we get there. I suspect it's going to be identical to the first two, and that means no trace evidence." He slapped his palm on the steering wheel. "Damn it, we should have nailed this guy already. We're missing something. It's out there, we just can't see it."

"I agree. It's pertinent, of course, that it's another court-affiliated official. We got a judge, a jerk radio jock who covered trials, and now a defense attorney. I've never heard of her. What kind of reputation does she have around here?"

"Well, I know her. In fact, I've had the misfortune of being a victim of her relentless and underhanded grilling. She's a real barracuda." Will didn't look at her. He kept his eyes on the dark green Toyota Camry in front of them. "Want me to give you a couple of adjectives that describe Varranzo to a *T?* Well, here you go. Deadly, cutthroat, ruthless, unscrupulous. She attacked me with all guns blazing, but I've testified often enough to hold my own. It's the untrained people, witnesses to the crime, neighbors of the victim, young, inexperienced criminalists; they're the ones she really cuts to ribbons on the stand. I've heard that woman verbally eviscerate people in a way that should be a crime in itself. Trust me, she'll do anything to win her case and get herself a big, fat check."

"Well, that provides plenty of motives for

plenty of people. Does she get her defendants off?"

"Most of the time. Her clients are usually celebrities or mobsters, anybody who's got the big bucks and no scruples. And they're usually guilty, and everybody knows it. I don't see how she was ever able to live with herself."

Will seemed uncharacteristically angry. She stole a sidelong glance at him. His face was in profile, his eyes focused on the road, but there was a tic in his cheek as his jaw clenched and unclenched under his tanned skin. His fingers were squeezing the steering wheel.

"You okay, Will?"

He glanced at her then, his dark eyes flashing fury. "I'm sick of seeing severed tongues on a weekly basis. I want to find this guy and put a bullet between his eyes."

"You don't mean that."

"Don't I?"

"My, my, we are a bit cranky today, Special Agent Brannock."

"Then again, maybe it's just extreme sexual frustration. Seems like I've got myself a partner with ice water in her veins."

Lord have mercy. He was wound up tight, and was he ever. Maybe he didn't get enough sleep, either. And the ice water in the veins crack: if he only knew how laughable that one was. Calmly, she said, "I thought we agreed to wait until after this case was over."

"You did. It sure as hell wasn't my idea."

"We have to stay focused, Will. This killer's taking out people's tongues for souvenirs, for God's sake."

After that sobering remark, they drove along in an unhappy silence. Will was just venting. She glanced over to see if steam was coming out of his ears, but she knew exactly how he felt. Last night didn't help; it only complicated things, just as she knew it would. Sexual frustration was inside the truck, all right, slapping both of them around.

A few minutes later, Will said, his tone much more conciliatory, "Sorry. I didn't sleep much last night."

"If it makes you feel any better, I didn't, either."

Will frowned across the cab at her. "Good. I hope you paced the floor all night. Doesn't sound like you've changed your mind about anything, though."

Julia thought it better not to answer that. Truth be told, she wanted to change her mind and was fighting herself. They rode without speaking the rest of the way. Julia was already dreading walking into yet another gruesome crime scene. Will spent the rest of the ride on the phone with Phil Hayes.

As it turned out, Gloria Varranzo lived in a classic Victorian mansion on Lookout Mountain —on East Brow Road, to be exact, which was a

330

very high-end residential street overlooking the city. Julia wasn't familiar with the area, but Will managed to tell her that lots of attorneys and politicians lived in the vicinity. He wasn't gnashing his teeth anymore, either, so he was feeling better. The neighborhood was not gated, but it should have been. Julia had never seen so many Mercedes, Cadillacs, BMWs, and even one sleek, black Lamborghini.

A significant portion of East Brow Road was taped off. She bet that raised the hackles on all the uppity, well-to-do home owners. They were probably choking on their caviar at the inconvenience. Will pulled up to the driveway and stopped the car near the front door. The house was huge, probably six or seven thousand square feet. They got out and walked along low hedges lining the front sidewalk. There was one gigantic oak tree on the front lawn; the rest of the yard was well-maintained grass and shrubbery. The house itself looked like something out of a benevolent Grimms' fairy tale. The south side had a three-story round turret that rose above the wide porch. They could see Gloria Varranzo's body hanging outside from a white curlicue banister on one of the second-floor porches. She wore a belted white silk robe that was stained dark with blood. A lot of blood. She had on one white, high-heeled slipper. An identical shoe was lying on the grass far below her body. A tech was dusting it for fingerprints while another man was photo-graphing it and the brass scales sitting beside it. The dimes were stacked on the right-hand side, as at the other crime scenes. Part of Gloria Varranzo's tongue bloodied the other side.

"He's silenced another one of his enemies," Will said, shaking his head. "This could be the break we need."

"How so?"

"If we can come up with a case where Varranzo was the defense lawyer and Lockhart was the judge, we might isolate some leads on who's out for revenge."

Julia nodded. "That could be dozens of cases. They've both been in the Hamilton County court system for ages."

"We could get lucky."

"We'd better. Let's see what he left for us this time."

Inside, they found out. The Tongue Slasher left them a truckload of blood all over the place. More than at any of the other crime scenes. It seemed as if Varranzo had put up more of a struggle than the two male victims. There was blood in the main foyer, spattered all over the oversized black-and-white tiles. A giant crystal chandelier hung directly above a round marble-topped table, which was the only furniture in the room. A tall, expensive Lalique crystal vase sat atop it, full of fresh white orchids and white

English roses. A painting that looked like a genuine Monet hung on the curving, cream-colored wall along the glossy and intricately carved wood staircase.

"Is that real?" Julia asked Will, pointing to the painting.

"I would say yes. When I talked to her law offices this morning, they said her fees went six figures, and usually higher than that."

They spoke to the forensic techs on the stairway, where they stopped and slipped on their protective gear. Upstairs, a long hallway with white wainscoting stretched out in both directions. Will turned right. Julia followed, slightly spooked by the huge house that seemed to crouch down over them, totally, completely, creepily silent. Not even the forensic guys were saying anything.

"Did she have a family?" she asked.

"She's divorced. And she's got a couple of college-age kids. We'll have to interview them and her ex-husband. Probably by phone. None of them live in Chattanooga."

"There's blood all along here. He dragged her down this hall."

"Yeah. My guess is he clubbed her at the door with something. Looks like she put up a fight. She was the type who would. Once she was subdued, he dragged her up the steps and down the hall; thus the blood trail."

The bedroom they sought was at the end of the

hall. Double white doors stood open. They stopped at the threshold and observed the scene. Gloria Varranzo apparently had liked shades of blue. Her entire bedroom was done in pale blue and white: the soft plush carpet was cream, the bedspread and flowing canopy panels were blue damask, and the floor-to-ceiling drapes, now wafting in the breeze, were sheer and white. The techs in their white jumpsuits looked up, acknowledged them, and then went back to work.

Peter Tipton stood out on the balcony. He shook his head when he saw them. "Man, this's sickening. I hope this is the last time anybody has to die like this."

"Is it Mrs. Varranzo?" Julia asked.

"Yes. Actually, I knew her a little bit. She and my wife were on the Arts and Education Council together."

"Did your wife like her?"

"No, not at all. But nobody deserves to end up like this, not even detestable people."

Will was walking around on the small porch and looking at all the crimson stains. The word *THREE* was written in Gloria's blood on the white-tiled floor. More blood spattered the iron banister and the white fabric of the drapes. "She must've come to and fought for her life," he said, turning to look at Julia.

Pete Tipton said, "She was clubbed over the

334

head with something. I'd guess some kind of weighted sap. Maybe a hammer."

"Or a heavy pair of pliers." Julia moved over beside the photographer and looked down. Gloria Varranzo dangled there for all to see, her beautifully highlighted blond hair ruffling in precise layers in the gentle wind. Her arms dangled at her sides, her beautiful robe blood-soaked. One sleeve, the right one, was ripped at the shoulder, showing her tanning-bed bronzed skin.

"There's got to be forensic evidence somewhere in this house," she said to the tech from TBI. She had gotten to know Tim Neely during the case. He was a tall, blond-haired man, thin almost to gauntness, with a reddish-blond mustache and neat appearance. Will had told her that he was one of the best in the state and trained at Quantico. She was glad he was on the job. If there was anything to find, he'd find it.

Tim stood up, towering over her, almost as tall as Will. He had a pricey camera hanging around his neck. The TBI supplied their guys with the best.

"I think so, too," Tim agreed. "This lady must've fought him tooth and nail. But one thing's different: the other scenes weren't nearly as contaminated as this one. We'll find something, you can count on that. My bet's on DNA. If she fought him hard enough, we might even get a drop of his sweat."

"Great, Tim. Call us as soon as you get anything. You know, I'd call this a copycat, but the scales and dimes haven't hit the broadcasts yet. It's the same exact scale. I've done a million Internet searches. Next, I'm going to start checking the pawn shops and flea markets in Hamilton County. The scale's just too unusual for people not to remember. I keep thinking I've seen one similar to it somewhere, but can't place where it was."

"Ever tried hypnotism?"

Julia smiled at Tim's suggestion. "Not lately."

"There is another difference. He left the scales outside on the grass."

"It was still under the body."

"He hung the body up here. Why put the scales down there on the lawn?"

"Maybe it's another message to us," Will said, entering their conversation.

"But what? It's the same scale, just in a different place," Julia said.

Will said, "Unless he left something else, too, and somebody took it. Or a dog dragged it off?"

Julia thought about that a moment. "That's a good question for the guys you assigned to canvass the neighborhood."

"If there was anything left behind, our guys will find it," Tim told them.

"Who discovered the body?"

"Actually, it was a security guard on a drive-through," Will answered. "There have been some break-ins on this street during the last few months."

"Anything violent?" Julia asked.

"Burglaries for the most part. No one hurt. No one caught. Security says it's probably some teenagers out for the thrill."

"We'll have to check all of that out."

"I've already assigned it. Tim, if you're finished here, let's get this body down and laid out so Pete can release it to the morgue."

Will Brannock was dead tired. He hadn't slept much, and he'd gotten the Varranzo call just before dawn. He and Julia had been working the scene for going on six hours, helping forensics and questioning Varranzo's staff and neighbors. Will had been the one who had notified the ex-husband, a prime suspect until they learned that Austin Varranzo, a world-renowned architect, lived in London and had been at a play where he sat in a theater box with eleven other people. Any one of them could verify his presence there around the time of Gloria's death. Austin wanted to notify their two children himself, a son in college at Harvard; a daughter at USC. Will was only too glad to let him break that bad news.

Stooping to look again at the pattern of blood soaked into the thick, white bedroom carpet, he watched Julia Cass for a moment. She was tireless when working a crime scene. All the forensic technicians liked her already, admired her, and hell, so did he. In lots of ways. He had pushed it too far last night, had done it again this morning in the truck. She just wasn't ready, and she was right. He wasn't going to force the issue again. But she had enjoyed that intimacy on the riverbank as much as he had. She had opened her lips under his and welcomed him inside her mouth, and into her life. Across the room, Julia suddenly looked up at him, as if she sensed he was watching. She raised a quizzical dark brow when she found his eyes riveted on her.

His phone rang, and he was glad for a distraction. He pulled it out, touching the screen. It was the TBI Chattanooga office.

"Yeah, Special Agent Brannock."

"Will, you've got a call from the Las Vegas Police Department. Wanna take it now?"

Will's heart stood still for a second. "Yeah, patch it through."

"Special Agent Will Brannock?" said a deep voice on the other end.

"Yes. What can I do for you?"

"We just picked up a woman by the name of Maria Bota. You put a BOLO out on her, right?"

For the first time that day, Will smiled, a sense of relief running through him. "Great news. Is she still in custody?"

"Yes. We've got her at central booking."

338

"We've got to interview her for a multiple-murder investigation. One victim's a federal judge. Hold her until we get there."

"Then get here quick. We can't hold her forever without cause."

"We'll leave here ASAP. Can we get access to her later today or tonight?"

"Yeah, I'll pave the way at booking. They'll probably keep her down there overnight."

He pocketed his phone and headed straight for Julia.

"Pack a bag. They've picked up Maria Bota in Vegas. We're flying out there as soon as you can get ready."

"Why? If she's out of state, she can't be the perp."

"No, but she ran from us. That makes me think she knows more than she's telling us. My gut tells me she's hiding something."

"Okay. Take me to my car, and I'll meet you at the airport in an hour."

Will handed her his keys. "Take my truck, and pick me up back here. Make that thirty minutes."

"What about your clothes?"

"Don't worry about it."

"I'm not exactly worried about it, Brannock."

"I keep a change of clothes in my truck."

Will felt like squirming under the accusatory look in her eyes. He knew what she was thinking, but she was dead wrong. This wasn't the time to talk about it. He wanted to interrogate Maria Bota and bring her back to Tennessee, if need be. Julia walked off without another word. Will moved a few steps away and punched in another number on his phone. He smiled when he heard the voice at the other end, very pleased to hear it. It had been way too long.

"How do you feel about me using the jet to come out there?"

He listened a moment. "Great. Can you get me the suite? I sure would appreciate it."

After a brief conversation, he hung up and went back to work. He wasn't in the mood for a crowded passenger jet or for waiting around for two available seats. He needed a quiet atmosphere where he could think things through and plan for the interrogation. Maria Bota was hiding something, perhaps even a key that would help them crack this case. His inner voice kept telling him that, and one thing he'd learned throughout his years in law enforcement was to listen to his instincts.

Chapter 18

"What's this? Donald Trump joining us on the flight?" Julia asked Will as they walked out across the tarmac to the sleek maroon-and-tan private jet waiting for them.

"This is our ride."

Will strode on, but Julia stopped in midstride. "Wait a minute, are you serious? We're taking a private jet to Las Vegas?"

"That's right. C'mon."

Julia caught up with him. "Man alive, you special agents do like to travel in style. The rest of us peons fly tourist."

When they reached the jet, Will started manually checking the outside of the plane and doing all kinds of other pilotlike things.

Julia trailed along. "I hope you don't break any of this stuff."

Without comment, Will kept doing what he was doing. Julia frowned until he finished, stood back, and allowed her to precede him up the steps. "Just to be clear, this isn't the Bureau's. It belongs to a friend of mine. I can get access to it whenever I need to get somewhere fast."

"Wish I had friends like that."

Will gave her that splendid smile of his. Aha, he was loosening up about last night. "Maybe I'll introduce you someday."

"You? Introduce me to a personal friend? I think not. Trust me, I'm not going to hold my breath until that happens. You'll probably make him wear a mask and cloak."

"Don't forget the dagger."

Julia had to laugh. She'd never been on a private jet and had to admit it was pretty cool and überluxurious. The interior sported maroon and tan decor. The walls were tan with a maroon stripe at midwall. The carpet was maroon, and both couches and the six leather swivel chairs were tan. There was also what looked like a fully equipped galley in the rear, and even better, a wet bar with lots of bottles lined up behind secured glass doors. All very snob-o-licious and privileged. She felt mightily out of place. Then, of course, there was that good-looking, coppery-haired private hostess who hastily made her way out to Will's side. They air-kissed on each cheek, European-style. Yuck.

"Hello, Will. It's so good to see you again. How have you been?" Very heavy accent. Scandinavian, perhaps?

"Good. Everything okay with you?"

"Oh yes, I'm looking forward to my day off tomorrow."

"Well, you just got today off, too. Grab your things. We've got to get this baby off the ground."

Belatedly, he remembered to introduce them. *Tsk-tsk, Brannock, where are your manners?* "Julia Cass, this is Barbie Johanssen. Barbie, this is Julia."

Of course her name would be Barbie. What else would it be? Julia watched Norwegian Barbie twist her hips back down to the galley. She did indeed look like a Barbie doll: large breasts; long legs; tiny, waspish waist; and short black skirt.

"Wow. I'd say this friend of yours knows how to spell luxury. He also seems to know what kind of flight attendants you prefer. Redheads must really ring your bell, Brannock." She was kidding, sort of, and he looked annoyed, sort of. Yes, maybe his irk was rising back to the just-above-mild level.

"You're never going to let that rest, are you?"

"Probably not, if it gets this kind of rise out of you. But hey, I'm just kidding. Don't be so sensitive."

The pilot was next to appear. He exited the cockpit door and strode toward them, rolling a small black suitcase with one hand. He was an older man, probably in his sixties. He was deeply tanned, had a trim build, and was not much taller than Julia. He and Will shook hands and seemed to know each other very well.

"Julia, this is Jim Cooper. Coop, this is Julia Cass."

"Nice to meet you," she said, a little concerned when Barbie showed up with her own rolling bag and the two of them headed for the exit door.

"I thought we were in a hurry," she said, slightly alarmed when Will pressed a button that started the door closing behind them. "Whoa, wait a cotton-picking minute. Where are they going?"

Will didn't answer at first, just listened for the pneumatic hiss of the vacuum, then twisted the lever. He headed off toward the cockpit.

"Will? Wait a minute here. I'm not liking the looks of this at all." She followed Brannock and found him calmly strapping himself into the pilot's seat.

"Sit down," he said. "You get to be my copilot."

"Oh no. No way. I'm not going anywhere without a real pilot."

"I'm a real pilot. In fact, I've got more hours in the air than Coop does. You're safe with me." He looked up at her, amusement glinting in his brown eyes. "Trust me. You're in good hands. I promise."

Forcing down a swallow, Julia still hesitated. She watched him flip all kinds of switches and press some buttons, and then settle his headphones over his ears. She could feel her heart beating fast inside her breast, but she sat down in the seat and fastened the seat belt. Will Brannock was just full of surprises.

After a moment of clearing takeoff with the air traffic control tower, Will pulled off the headset and looked at her. "Don't be nervous. I know what I'm doing. I've flown planes since I was eighteen. Trust me."

"Jets this size?"

"Well, this kind, just since I was twenty-three. Relax, enjoy the flight."

"I do trust you, but maybe not so much at thirty thousand feet."

"Put on your headphones. Take a nap. We'll be there in three or four hours."

"Yeah, right. Believe me, I'm going to sit here and watch every move you make. I'm nervous flying anyway, so you'd better not be lying to me."

"Yeah, sorry, but I'm lying. I've never been in a cockpit before. I decided to try it out and see if it's as complicated as they say."

"Ooh, sarcasm is alive and well in Special Agent Brannock."

"You're going to owe me the biggest apology you've ever given, once we land safely at McCarran International."

"You act almost excited about this trip."

"I am. I love to fly, and don't get to do it very often. On top of that, my gut tells me that Maria's going to tell us something we need to know."

Julia tried to relax as they taxied out to the runway and awaited their turn for takeoff. He seemed to know what he was doing, and Will wasn't a moron. Surely, he wouldn't take the controls if he didn't know what he was doing. Still, she'd be glad when they got to Nevada. She might even kiss the ground like the Pope did.

"C'mon, Cass, relax. All that hand-wringing is making me nervous."

"Me, making you nervous. That's a laugh."

When they got the okay, Will maneuvered the jet out on the tarmac and slowly increased speed until they smoothly lifted off and gained elevation. Julia was gripping the arms of her seat as he banked in a long turn and headed west. He knew what he was doing, she knew that; he was displaying that, but still, it was only the two of them. What if he had a heart attack?

"What if you have a heart attack?"

"I'm going to, if you don't quit dissing my piloting skills. If it'll ease your mind, I've got some parachutes stashed in the back."

Julia narrowed her eyes. "Do you really?"

"Hell no. We're not going to need parachutes. Now go to sleep and give me a break."

"You're tired, too. What if you fall asleep?"

"I'll wake up when the plane goes into a nose-dive."

"Ha-ha, very funny."

But it was funny, and she had to laugh, be it a shaky one.

"Ah, that's more like it." Will glanced over at her. "Relax. You look like a Macy's window mannequin. Take a nap, figure out if you're going to let me kiss you again tonight."

"That's not going to happen."

"You never get tired of breaking my heart, do you?"

"You'll get over it soon enough. I'm sure you know more Barbies in Las Vegas."

"Yeah, you're right. I know at least fifty, or it might be up to sixty by now, but some of them are Barbs. A few more are Barbaras."

Smiling, Julia leaned her head back against the seat, a lot more comfortable than she thought she'd be. He handled the controls with ease and skill, and she trusted him to get them across the country in one piece. Sometimes he made her laugh, even when she didn't want to. A sudden vision of Gloria Varranzo's body sobered her, and she ran the case in her mind. It wasn't long before she took Will's advice and closed her eyes. And that's pretty much all she remembered about the flight to Las Vegas.

McCarran International was a busy place. Desert winds were buffeting palm trees, newlyweds were excitedly boarding hotel shuttles, and last-minute gamblers were trying their luck with the airport slot machines. Without much ado, Will and Julia got into the new black Lexus left for them by Will's mysterious friend and headed off to the Las Vegas city jail on Stewart Avenue. The LVPD booking center was a busy place, too, and as they arrived, several police cars were discharging drunken, mouthy prisoners who seemed to have been enjoying the Las Vegas nightlife a tad too much. Yeah, what happened in Vegas stayed in jail in Vegas.

Julia said, "Well now, this is a jumping hot spot tonight. Almost as much as the casinos, I'd say."

"You ever been out here in Sin City before?"

"Nope, but it's quite glittery and well lit, I must say."

"The lights never go out."

"That's not very energy efficient."

"This place has its own kind of energy." Will shoved the gearshift into park and opened his door. "Let's go. We're looking for Sergeant York."

Julia got out but questioned him over the top of the car. "You're kidding me. Like the World War One hero, Sergeant York. You know, that movie with Gary Cooper."

"I guess so. First name's Archie."

"I wonder if Archie's as good a shot. Sergeant York's my sharpshooting hero. I idolized him when I was nine."

Inside, they introduced themselves, showed their law enforcement badges, and asked for Archie York. He showed up a moment later and led them to the elevators. Several floors up, they passed some newly booked prisoners shuffling around in orange shirts and pants and flip-flops. Most of them were solemn, hangdog, and behaving themselves, but a few were yelling and screaming cop brutality behind heavy white steel doors. A few were beating their heads against the window. Their jailors didn't like that much. Four officers rushed a man going berserk in his cell and strapped him into a restraint chair.

As they passed by that commotion, Archie York looked at Julia. "We try to let them detox before we process them. Makes it easier."

"Yeah, so do we." Sergeant York was from Texas, she'd bet on it. The cowpoke accent was a dead giveaway. So were the tattoos on his arms. The first one read *Remember the Alamo* in fancy curlicues, and the other one was a very good rendi- tion of the Texas state flag. All he needed was a portrait of Davy Crockett to lock up the deal. "So what's this little Bota gal done back in Tennessee?"

"Nothing criminal," Will answered. "Not yet."

"She's been cooperative but acts scared spitless."

"Where did you pick her up?"

"On the Strip. In Circus Circus. A security guard recognized her."

Julia said, "Did she have a little boy with her?"

"No, and she wasn't registered at that hotel. We ran a check and couldn't find her name registered anywhere on the Strip. No room keys on her, either. Of course, she could've been using an alias when she registered."

"Did she tell you anything?"

"No, she clammed up once we got her in here."

York stopped in front of one of the quiet cells. A heavy, green plastic curtain covered the outside of the small window on the door.

"Take a look-see. See if it's your gal."

Will lifted the flap and took a peek. "That's her, all right. Can we talk to her inside?"

"Sure. But we've got interrogation rooms that you can use if you want."

"The cell's fine," Julia said. "As long as you don't forget to let us out."

Her quip was answered with a low guffaw. Yep, he was a Texan, no question about it. "Where are you from, Sergeant? San Antonio?"

"No, Amarillo. How'd you know?"

"Lucky guess."

York grinned at her.

"Okay, York, quit flirting with the detective and open it up." That was Brannock, displaying a bit of his testy side. Then again, he hadn't taken the airborne four-hour nap that Julia had.

Maria Bota sat up on the built-in white iron bench, and the terrified expression on her face indicated that she was not exactly overjoyed to see them. She scooted back into the corner as far as she could get, as if she thought they were going to drag her out by the long, black braid hanging down her back. She had on a pale green knit tank top with gold sequins around the neckline, denim skinny jeans, and a pair of tan low-heeled sandals adorned with plastic sunflowers. Her toenails were painted baby-girl pink. She looked cold. Julia leaned one shoulder against the wall and let Will do the talking. He obliged, and with gusto, at that.

"Hello, Maria. Nice to see you again," Will started off, real laid-back and pleasantlike.

Maria didn't fall for his TBI charm. "What you want with me? Why you follow me here? I do nothing, nada. I am innocent."

"Because you ran. That makes you look guilty."

"I do nothing, nothing. I was scared, scared for my *niño*."

"Where is your *niño*?"

Maria put her head down on her bent knees and wouldn't look at them. Julia had a feeling Will wasn't going to get much out of her. When he looked at Julia, she gestured to let her give it a try. Woman to woman. Will could be a little pushy, and his size alone was intimidating.

Sitting down on the bench beside the shivering young girl, Julia kept her voice low and non-threatening. There was a reason this girl was so frightened and had been since the judge had been murdered. She knew something, something they needed her to tell them.

"Maria, listen to me. We aren't here to hassle you, or hurt you, or accuse you of anything. We don't think you killed the judge. We know you're scared. We know you want to protect your son. Julio's all right, isn't he, Maria? You got him to a safe place, right?"

Maria looked up, her dark eyes blurred with tears. She nodded. "He's with *mi madre*, but do not tell no one. Please, I beg you."

Julia's voice remained quiet. "Who's after him? All we want is the truth. Just tell us."

No dice. Julia decided to tell Maria what they already knew. Maybe that would crack her reserve a little bit. "We already know your involvement with the Battle Street Ten gang. We know they're after you for talking to the cops."

"I did not know he was a cop. He was, how do you say it? Undercover man."

"Do you think they're after Julio, too? Is that it? Is one of the gangbangers Julio's daddy? Is that why they're looking for you?"

Maria shook her head. "I do not know what they want. I know they kill you if you talk to cops. They have cut out tongues. Many times, like Lucien."

Again, the fact that Maria and the judge were on a first-name basis bothered Julia. "Tell me, Maria, what kind of relationship did you have with Judge Lockhart?"

No answer. Maria put her head down on her knees again, hiding her face. Julia decided to change directions.

"Do you know a man named Juan DeSoto? Goes by Hap."

That brought Maria's head jerking up. "I do not wish to go to that place. The judge make me."

"Mr. DeSoto gave us the impression that you and the judge had more than an employee-employer relationship. Told us you were lovers."

Maria's teeth tugged at her lower lip. "He made me do it. The undercover man told him about me. Lucien say I stay with him, that I be safe. I thought kind man and want to help me." She shook her head and tears streamed down an otherwise stoic face. "But he came to me late in the night. He make me, make me be with him. He hurt me. He hurt me lots of times."

Julia looked at Will. Will's jaw was clamped, and he looked angry and disgusted. Maria's story was ugly and getting uglier by the minute. Then the truth dawned on Julia.

"Julio is Lucien Lockhart's son, isn't he?"

Maria wiped her tears on her sleeve. Sighing, she nodded. "*Sí*, and after Julio was born, he kept me like slave and not let me leave with my baby. He cruel to me. Senora Lockhart knew, and she hate me for things he make me do."

"Why did you run, Maria? Tell us. The judge was gone. He couldn't keep you there. Iris Lockhart kicked you out, is that it?"

Will went down on one knee in front of her. "Tell us the truth, Maria. There's something else, isn't there? Something you know. Please, you've got to help us. We need to find this killer. He's killed again since you left. Did you know that? Twice. A man named Roc VanVeter and a woman named Gloria Varranzo."

Maria's young face went white, bleached out as if her blood had instantly plummeted to her toes.

"Do you know either of them?" Will continued.

She shook her head and kept shaking it.

"He's a serial killer," Julia told her. "That means he's going to keep killing, keep mutilating bodies the way he did to the judge. Tell us what you know. Help us get him."

Now Maria really looked petrified. Even so, Julia was shocked at the next words that came out of Maria's mouth, in a whisper so low they could barely hear them.

"I see him."

Will stiffened, his face locked with intensity. "Saw who? The judge?"

"No, sir, I see the *diablo* who do that awful thing to him. This is why I run away, why I hide here. He do the same thing to me and Julio if he know I see him."

Will and Julia looked at each other, but Julia's heart was racing. "Did you know him?"

She shook her head.

"Would you recognize him if you saw a photograph of him?" That was Will.

"I think so."

Will pushed her, his voice excited. "Where did you see him, Maria? Can you describe him? Was it a man?"

"I think so. He wore hood on his head. And clothes were black. He not big as you."

"Where did you see him?" Will asked again, pretty much taking over the questioning now. Maria didn't seem to mind.

"Julio sick, a cold up here." Maria pointed to her nose. "He cry early when it just getting day. I was in kitchen, getting Julio juice. I heard sound like scream that stopped real quick, and so I look out window. I see man at pool. He look around, and I see his face, very clear. He in shadows, but I think he see me. The blinds, the slats were open." Her voice grew very low. "After I find Lucien I am afraid, afraid he come back and get us, too."

"Did you see him accost the judge?"

"No, I never see Lucien. I rock Julio back to sleep and stay with him. We both sleep till late. That's when I find Lucien, out on porch." She shivered all over, no doubt remembering how Lucien Lockhart had looked.

"If we get a suspect, will you come back to Chattanooga for a lineup, or pick him out of a photo lineup?"

"Do you know who man is?"

"No, but we can get photos of some of Lucien's colleagues and other suspects to show you. If we get you released, will you promise to keep in touch with us?"

Maria nodded.

Julia said, "You won't run again?"

"No, Julio safe with *mi madre* now."

"Does she have a phone number?"

"*Sí.*" She told them what it was and the address.

"Thank you, Maria. You are now a material witness. That's very important, and you can be arrested if you flee again. Do you understand that?"

Maria looked at Julia and nodded. "I so afraid. I thought you take me to jail and send Julio away."

"Why were you hanging around Circus Circus?" asked Will.

"I am maid. I want job." Maria gave a little sob. "I have no money. Julio still very sick."

Will frowned, then pulled out his wallet. "Here, take this. It should last until we get in touch with you again."

When Will handed Maria a wad of cash that looked like the king of Saudi Arabia had just made him a crown prince, Julia blinked, stunned. Well, Will better hope she brought her debit card, or they were going to have to spend the night under a bridge somewhere.

Outside, they arranged with Sergeant York to have Maria released, but she declined their offer to take her home. Will put her in a cab and watched her drive off, and they both felt a little giddy when they got back into the Lexus. It had been an eye-opening interview, to say the least.

"Well, you were right. She did know something. Good God, this is a big break. We've got ourselves an eyewitness."

"Yes, but she didn't see the actual murder," Will reminded her. "But anybody she can identify as the guy skulking around the grounds just

356

before Lockhart was murdered is pretty good circumstantial evidence."

"We're going to get him. We're going to bring this guy down."

"Well, let's not put the cart before the horse. We've got to find him first."

Will grinned over at her. "I want to show you something, Cass. You game?"

"That depends. Like what?"

"God, *cautious* must be your middle name."

"As if you're not. So what is it?"

"It's a surprise."

"I hate surprises."

"I know, I was there. But this is a much better one and nobody's going to jump out and scare you."

"By the way, you'd better hope I brought ten thousand dollars with me. How much cash was in that wad you gave her?"

"I don't know. A couple of thousand."

"That's right, I forgot. You always carry around thousands of dollars in your billfold."

"I guess you're going to criticize my generosity, too?"

Julia spoke from her heart. "No, actually I think what you did was pretty cool." She smiled, and Will looked pleased. "But not to worry, I have a gigantic wad of ones in my wallet. That should get us a half a night at Super Eight."

Will laughed and turned the car onto the Strip,

which was crowded with people this time of evening, gambling and already lining up for the casino performances. When they reached the three thousand block of Las Vegas Boulevard and the magnificent fountains of the Bellagio, Julia turned in her seat and watched in awe as the water shot up hundreds of feet in the air, then fell in graceful cascades, changing colors before doing an intricate crisscross design, all lighted up and spectacular in the darkness.

"I've heard about these fountains, to be sure. So that's the Bellagio?"

"That's right," Will said, turning onto a palm tree–lined drive. The wind was still tossing and rustling the lacy fronds. "That's the surprise. We're staying at the Bellagio tonight."

That got Julia's complete attention. "No way. Don't tease me about something that big."

"Believe it. So you've heard about this place?"

"Well, I saw George Clooney and Brad Pitt robbing it on *Ocean's Eleven*. And I saw Julia Roberts coming down an impressive staircase in a red suit looking pretty darn confident about her sex appeal." She peered up at the huge hotel. "Look, Brannock, fancy schmancy is great now and then, I have to say, but believe me, I don't have enough cash for a bottle of water in this place, much less a room. I bet the valets here have more elaborate uniforms than Prince William at his wedding."

"No, they don't. And this is on me. More to the point, I'm way too tired to fly halfway across the country again tonight. I'm exhausted, and you probably are, too. I like it here at the Bellagio. Let me show you a good time, just this one time. Call it our celebration for nailing down an eyewitness."

"Okay, very funny, ha-ha and all that, but get real. You can't afford this place, either. I know what TBI special agents make. J.D. told me."

"Well, I've got this rich friend, see? Remember him? He can get me in a high roller's suite at a special rate. You're going to be impressed, I guarantee it."

"This friend of yours—Warren Buffett or Bill Gates, by any chance? Or the Donald?"

"Not Trump. He puts his name on all his hotels, if I recall. Just relax, Detective, and prepare yourself to be highly impressed."

Chapter 19

Highly impressed, Julia was. Oh boy, and make that Highly Impressed with a capital *H* and a capital *I*. The Bellagio was quite the sight to behold, all right. The front entrance was a vaulted atrium with gigantic hanging lamps, but the lobby was all beige marble and patterned carpeted floors and giant chandeliers, accompanied by the riotous dinging of slot machines. Will strode through the casino like he owned the place, and Julia gawked around like all the other tourists around them. When an attractive blonde in the Executive Suite Lounge called him by name and handed him a room card without his saying a word, Julia knew something was up.

"Okay, Brannock, what is this? *Queen for a Day*, or what? If you're doing all this to seduce me, it'll probably work." *But it'd probably work in a Super 8, too, or in the backseat of the Lexus,* she thought, a bit ashamed of herself for those admissions. But last night, well, last night was a revelation.

"I told you last night that I wasn't going to pressure you. We've got a Grand Lakeview Suite, and you'll have your own bedroom and bath. You won't even have to see me, unless you want to. Like I said, my friend pampers me."

"Is she a redhead, by any chance?"

"Please stop with that."

"And exactly why's this friend so beholden to you, Will? You let him off an embezzling or kidnapping rap?"

"What a rude thing to say to an honorable TBI agent." But Will smiled as he led her through the casino and behind a beautiful balustrade to the bank of elevators.

"I was just starting to trust you, and then you

pull this rather bizarre, all-expenses-paid adventure in never-never land."

"Just quit complaining. Let's go up, clean up a little, and I'll treat you to dinner at the best restaurant in Las Vegas."

Will showed his card to the man guarding the hall to the elevators, and they walked to the nearest elevator and entered it. Julia found it pretty darn elegant, too. Rich wood panels with red-and-gold tapestry on the back wall. A well-groomed, gray-haired old lady was already on board. Julia looked at her pink Chanel suit and her miniature poodle in its pink bejeweled collar, set with real rubies, no doubt, and decided the lady looked a hell of a lot more at home at the Bellagio than Julia did in her jeans and red polo shirt. She should have put on her diamonds and red spike heels, too.

"Wow, you're quite the Prince Charming all of a sudden," Julia leaned over and told Will in a low, hushed voice. The doors slid together with a well-engineered sigh, and she lowered her voice even further. "Why am I feeling like *me fly, you spider* —you know, that come-into-my-parlor thing?"

"Cass, you have to stop being so distrustful. Then again, that's a good thing in our line of work. Think about it. We got a big break today. We're in Las Vegas for the night, with nothing else to do. We deserve a reward, at least till morning. What's wrong with that? Loosen up, and enjoy life for a change. It'll do you good."

Behind them, Coco Chanel smothered a chuckle behind her white-gloved palm. In seconds, they reached her destination, the doors slid open on the thirtieth floor, and she stepped out with her teensy dog in tow. She turned, looked back at Julia, and presented her with a wise and knowing smile. "Sometimes, my dear, being the fly in the parlor turns out to be quite a pleasant experience. I imagine you'll find that out soon enough."

"I like her. Smart lady," Will said as the elevator closed and rose with the barest of whispers. Julia watched more floors whisk by. "Are you kidding me? What floor are we on?"

"Thirty-six," Will told her. "Better views, just for you."

"And for high rollers with unlimited bank accounts, I bet."

"Them, too."

"Okay, I am suitably enthralled now and ready to step into your parlor."

"Great. Follow me."

Julia trailed him down the romantically lit hallway, all marble and beige and cream and pale blue, with embossed wallpaper and beautiful sconces. He stopped in front of a door, swiped the key, and stepped back. He gave her an expectant smile. "After you, my dear."

"This better be good, Brannock, with all this buildup and all-for-the-likes-of-me stuff."

As it turned out, it was better than good. Maybe even Taj Mahal–ish. They entered a spacious marble foyer, with its own powder room, no less.

"Do I have to take off my sneakers?" she asked Will.

"Nope. There's housekeeping service twice daily. Track in all the mud you want. These doors go into the bedrooms—take your pick. They're pretty much the same."

At the end of the foyer, they entered a huge living room and dining room. Soft mood music was playing somewhere in the background. "Do you think there's enough room for both of us, Will? I mean, I do like to spread out the stuff in my backpack."

"Five-diamond resort hotels think big. This suite's got about three thousand square feet."

"Is that all? I'm insulted."

Julia looked around at the wet bar with the mahogany credenza behind it, but it was the wall of four curved, floor-to-ceiling windows that really blew her mind. Will hit a switch, and the drapes and the sheers slowly drew open to reveal one of the most beautiful vistas Julia had ever seen. The fountains and lake below were breathtaking. She could see the lights of a helicopter coming in off the desert. Beige marble floors, crystal chandeliers, a long white sectional in front of a lavish gas fireplace, glass-topped tables with beautiful lamps. Artwork all over the place. A forty-two-inch LCD television with the works.

All done in muted tones of rust and tan and beige and green. She looked up to see if there was a reproduction of the Sistine Chapel ceiling. Nope, they forgot all about Michelangelo.

"Like it?" Will asked, obviously still fishing for compliments.

"It's okay, if we're only staying one night," she returned, but then she laughed. "I have to say, Will, you and that lady in the elevator got this one right. I just have one question: When do I meet Queen Elizabeth?"

"Let me show you to your room."

"Said the spider to the fly."

"Keep that up and you'll have to beg me to make a move on you."

Her room was almost as big as her entire boathouse, and a lot pricier, to be sure. Not a doily in sight. The decor was more beige and pale blue and soft brown. And a king-size bed that even the princess from "The Princess and the Pea" wouldn't object to.

"The bedrooms have his and her baths," Will said, pointing them out like a proud papa. "His has an oversize steam shower with a built-in seat. Hers has a whirlpool bath and Bellagio spa products and bathrobe."

"I think you've been memorizing the hotel brochure."

"I've stayed here a few times. I want you to enjoy yourself."

Julia couldn't help it. She kept looking around at all the goodies, so very lush and expensive and heavenly. "We both have a bedroom like this? You sure?"

"Yes, ma'am. Just across the foyer from each other."

"I'm not sure I'll know how to act in a place like this," she told Will. "I'm used to hotels that let Jasper sleep on the beds."

"Tonight, I'll have to do."

Their eyes met, held for a moment, and she had a funny feeling, despite all their objections to the contrary, that some kind of erotic die had been cast last night on that picnic table. They could ignore it, question its wisdom as long and hard as they wanted, but it was there. Pure D desire. And it wasn't going away anytime soon, at least not inside her betraying body.

She looked at Will, who was appraising her hopefully, very obviously trying to please her with this fantastic place. Her heart reacted, skipped a beat, then another one. Oh my Lord, was she actually falling in love with him? Already? How could she feel this way after such a short time? Not her. Will's eyes remained on her, alive and warm and naked with his own brand of suppressed need. She forced herself to look away, not sure she wanted him to recognize the same thing in hers. Were they really ready to go to that next step, a step that would be difficult to take back? Well, one thing was for sure: if they did, Will couldn't have picked a better setting for a seduction. The view alone was about as romantic as anything she'd ever seen or expected to see.

"Okay," Will said as the silence between them lengthened. "Let's clean up a bit and go downstairs for dinner."

"I didn't bring any clothes suitable for dining in this place."

"Look in the closet. There might be something there that'll fit you."

"You just happen to have women's clothes in my size lying around? Why doesn't that sound legitimate? Let me think."

"They belong to my friend's daughter. You're about her size. Suit yourself. You look fine just the way you are. Just make it quick. I'm hungry."

Actually, Julia was pretty hungry herself. She did take a shower in that luxurious, garage-size shower stall and put on the snowy white robe and complimentary house slippers. She found herself wanting to forget dinner and slip beneath those soft white sheets that probably came from some kind of rare Beijing silkworms, or something even more exotic. However, Will was treating her to some fantastic fun out here in Sin City. If he had some more tricks up his sleeve, she was ready to pull them out and enjoy the heck out of them.

Standing in front of the long expanse of windows in the living room, Will watched night settle over the desert and the lovely spectacle of the sparkling lights of the casinos along the Strip. He had changed into a blue dress shirt and trousers that he kept at the Bellagio, but he was more than impatient for Julia to come out of her bedroom. It was good to see her out of her detecting mode, becoming more relaxed. Just for this one night, that's all he asked. God knows, they wouldn't be able to think of anything but the Tongue Slasher case once they returned home. He found out last night, and in no uncertain terms, that he cared a hell of a lot more about Julia Cass than he had ever intended to. It had taken everything he had to let go of her and drive away in his truck. He had wanted more from her, more than those long and passionate kisses. And he had for a long time, if he really admitted the truth to himself.

It was a good thing she had come to her senses and pushed him away, or they would probably still be in her bed going at it. That's what he wanted to happen tonight; he had to admit that, too. Julia turned him on like crazy. Now that he was so blithely admitting his true feelings to himself, he could also admit that he had wanted her from the beginning, even though she'd turned up her nose at him at the time. He had liked her humor, even on that first ride, until she'd been assigned as his partner and both of them had thrown the brakes on any kind of personal involvement between them. Those brakes were wearing thin, almost ready to give, at least in his case.

"Okay, I'm ready."

Will turned and found Julia scrubbed fresh, without a trace of makeup, which he liked. She didn't go in for artifice, not in any way. And she was one woman who did not need a bunch of makeup to be beautiful. She had chosen to wear the short black silk dress and high heels. Beautiful, elegant, just like everything else about her. He couldn't drag his eyes off her.

"What?" She glanced down at herself. "Is it too short?"

"Nope. You'll do, I guess."

"Thanks a bunch for being so effusive. Now I really feel confident in these stupid shoes."

"C'mon, Cass, time's a wastin'." But Will felt happy to be alone with her like this. Happier than he'd been in a long time.

"You must be starving. Maybe I should carry a backpack full of snacks for your stomach pangs. Just to keep down all that growling."

"That's not a bad idea."

As they rode down in the elevator, Julia said, "So tell me, Brannock, how do I smell?"

He put his face down close to her, and it took all the fortitude he had inside himself not to press his lips to the side of her slender and fragrant neck. "You smell good enough to eat."

"That's good enough, I guess. Maybe I'll filch the rest of those fancy little spa bottles when we leave."

"I won't tell."

Downstairs they made their way through the casino and down the beautiful Via Bellagio, past some high-end shops and restaurants, at which time Julia seemed to begin to have reservations.

"I'm telling you, Brannock, I'm just a cop from Chattanooga, but I know five-star restaurants when I see them. You don't even have on a tie. They'll probably make you go buy a Ralph Lauren tie."

"Quit worrying. I know the—"

Julia interrupted. "Don't tell me. This mysterious friend of yours owns this restaurant, too, and you can eat here anytime you want and everything you want, and all free of charge, without a tie. Even without a shirt, if you want."

Will shrugged. "Well, sort of."

"Jeez, Brannock, is this guy single? I can't wait to meet him."

"Maybe you will."

Will led her up to the restaurant, and Julia stopped out front and stared up at the stained-glass fanlight over the cut-glass doors. "The Taste of the South? Are you kidding me? No way."

"Yes, this is the one. You've heard of it, I take it?"

"Well, of course, I've heard of it. There's one in Memphis, and New Orleans, and Chicago, I think, but I've never been inside one. I hear it's pricey, but the food'll beat even Paula Deen and both her sons."

"I think it's better, but I'm prejudiced."

Opening the front door, Will stood back and, with a gentlemanly bow, allowed her to precede him. He was jacked up himself. It had been a long time since he'd been here, and he was eager for Julia to meet his so-called friend.

The maître d' greeted him by name. "Hello, Mr. Brannock. Please go in. Your usual room is ready."

"Thank you," he said.

"Your usual room," Julia repeated. "Are you forgetting to tell me something else?"

"No, but I do have a surprise."

"I can't be any more surprised than this."

Inside, the restaurant was as crowded as it usually was. It was also beautifully decorated: mirrored walls, white silk drapes, the tables beautifully set with the trademark silver and crystal and white tablecloths, and the soft glow of white pillar candles. He led Julia toward the glassed-in private room closed off by paned, seven-foot French doors. Their table was set and ready, the candles lit, soft violin music playing. More French doors led to the balustrade over-looking the Bellagio fountains, now in full, glorious display before them.

"Wow, your friend even lit the candles."

Will laughed at Julia and pulled out her chair. She was loving this, he could tell. That made him happy, too. He was one happy fella tonight.

"This is feeling more and more like a romantic

tryst," she said, giving him a narrow-eyed glance. "Just a place to eat, same as McDonald's."

"Yeah, right. Guess I'll order a McRib and see if the waiter faints."

"It's not that stuffy here. You'll see."

"I do see, and it's pretty damn stuffy. But I like stuffy, sometimes."

"Don't be so critical," he told her, taking the chair beside her.

"I can't help but notice that there are three place settings," Julia remarked. "Is the governor joining us? Or the president of the United States? UN secretary-general?"

"No. My friend is, though."

"Great. Maybe he'll give me free passes to some other neat places."

"Maybe so."

Outside in the main dining room, a woman appeared from the kitchen wearing a chef's hat and white coat and apron. She was meandering among the tables, nodding and talking to her guests, getting a spattering of applause as she went along.

"The chef is taking bows."

"Yes. Would you like to meet her?"

"Sure. She looks pretty popular with the guests."

"Good, because she's coming this way."

The woman was tall and statuesque, with soft, curly blond hair that framed her pretty face. She looked as if she might be in her late fifties or early sixties. It took several minutes for her to reach their door, but then she entered, shut the door behind her, and beamed down at them.

Will pushed back his chair, stood up, and gave her a huge hug. He kissed her on the cheek, and she said, "It's about time you showed up, sweetheart."

Will grinned, very happy to see her. Julia was watching with not a little surprise and wariness. "Julia, please allow me to introduce my mother, Betty Brannock. She owns this place. Mom, this is Julia Cass, the woman I've been telling you about."

Julia's jaw dropped, literally. She wasn't one to be blindsided, but Will thought she had been this time. She had been complaining about his refusal to tell her about his past or his family, so he was going to tell her. He was more than reluctant to do that, of course, but he wanted her to trust him, wanted them to develop a deeper relationship, or at least have a chance to see what might happen between them. It had been a hard decision for him to make, but now that he had taken the first step, he felt good about it.

"Hello, sweetie," Betty Brannock said, taking the chair beside Julia. "You have no idea how glad I am to see you."

"Me? Really?"

"Really. If you're the gal who could get Will

out here for a visit, I want to shake your hand and cook you anything you want to eat. You deserve it."

Julia laughed, and the two women looked at him. "My parents own this franchise," he admitted. "Dad's out of town on business at our restaurant in Phoenix this weekend. I want you to meet them so you'll stop giving me grief about being so secretive."

"Well, this is quite a shock, I must say."

Betty turned to her. "So he's being close-mouthed about us again, is he? You'd think Will is ashamed of us."

"I'm sure that's not the case," Julia answered quickly, but she appeared uncomfortable with the subject.

"I've got a good reason. I'll tell you about it later."

At that, it was Betty Brannock's turn to look startled. "Well, I'll be. That's a first. You've obviously made quite a good impression on my son. God bless you for getting him out here. We miss him terribly."

Will said, "We're out here on a case, Mom, but I wanted you to meet Julia. She's J.D. Cass's sister."

Betty smiled. "I've heard a lot about J.D. I've seen his picture. He's a good-looking man. Will says he's a fine agent. Are you with the TBI, too?"

"No, I'm a detective with the Chattanooga Police Department. I'm a liaison on this case.

I'm new in town. I spent most of my career in Memphis and Nashville."

"We're originally from Alabama."

"It's quite a change living out here in the desert, I suspect."

Betty glanced over at Will. He didn't react. He knew his mother knew better than to reveal the reason behind their move. It was one of the hardest things his family had ever had to do.

"Yes, it was pretty drastic," his mother said, cryptically enough to suit him. "We're used to it now. Will's sister flies in often. A lot more often than you do, Will." She looked accusingly at him. "Did you know that Will has an older sister, Julia?"

"The pilot?" Julia asked. "I believe I'm wearing one of her dresses. Hope that's okay. Will said it was."

"Of course. Colleen won't mind at all. She flies for Delta. I'm surprised he told you about her. Will and his daddy are both pilots. Not me. I hate flying. I'd rather get in some awesome car and drive, any day."

His mother kept watching Will, her blue eyes twinkling with their usual mischief. "I heard your first impression of Will wasn't exactly stellar. He's never brought any other woman out here to meet us, if that makes you feel any better."

Will felt the heat rise in his face and quickly changed the subject. "How about us ordering now? What's the specialty tonight, Mom?"

"Anything you want, sweetie. You, too, Julia. I'm cooking for you myself. I'm glad to get the chance."

"When's Dad getting back?"

"Tomorrow night, if all goes as expected." She turned to Julia. "Our restaurant there is in Scottsdale. We have a condo there, too. At the Landings."

"I've heard lots of good things about your restaurants," Julia told her. "But I've never had a chance to have dinner in one."

"Well, you do now. You'll be my special guest. What do you think of your suite?"

"Yes. It's beautiful, Mrs. Brannock."

"Please, call me Betty. The owner of this hotel happens to be a dear friend of mine. He wanted one of our restaurants bad enough to give me exclusive use of a high-roller luxury suite as one of the contractual terms." She laughed. "He didn't mind. We're making him a fortune."

Julia smiled and returned her gaze to Will. "Will's just full of surprises today."

"Well, that's a shock. He usually hates surprises."

"I've noticed that he watches his back. He won't tell me where he lives, either."

"He has a tendency to be closemouthed. If you're here, I think he's beginning to come around to you."

"Hey, Mom, I am sitting right here, you know. Enough about me. Let's order. I'll have the biggest T-bone steak you have, steak fries, and a salad with your special house dressing. Chocolate peanut butter pie for dessert."

"And what can I make for you?" Betty asked Julia, smiling.

"What do you suggest?"

"The specialty tonight is chicken and dumplings. We've also got barbecued ribs and fried chicken. Mashed potatoes and white gravy. If it's Southern and mouth-watering, we make it."

"I'll take the fried chicken. Do you have bread pudding?"

"You bet I do. Homemade, with sunshine sauce on top. That's one of Will's favorites, too. Sit here and enjoy yourselves. It'll be right out."

Will watched his mother thread her way through the tables, again receiving applause. "Julia, you are not going to believe how good her food is. She's a genius in the kitchen. She does the cooking. Dad handles the business end of things."

Julia raised her stemmed goblet full of ice water and took a sip. She gazed at him over the rim. "Why don't you visit her more often? She seems like a very nice lady. She misses you." She gestured at the busy restaurant outside the French doors. "And you certainly live like a king while you're here."

"I have my life in Chattanooga. I come out here as often as I can. She liked it better when I worked at the LA field office."

"You worked in LA? I didn't know that. Then again, I didn't know anything about you until today."

"I'm a private person, but so are you. Admit it."

Julia looked down and traced a floral design on the white damask tablecloth. "True. About some things, anyway."

Will knew she was probably thinking about her partner's death. She was reliving it again, so he tried to change the subject. He knew how she felt. He relived the biggest trauma of his life, over and over again. It never stopped.

"So what do you think of the Bellagio so far?"

"I think it's way above my CPD expense account."

"Thanks to Mom and Dad, I get a free ride around here."

"Do you have an interest in these restaurants?"

"I'm on the board of directors. It's family owned, so there's just the four of us."

"I bet your parents wish you and your sister took more interest. Maybe they could make you a cook's apprentice."

"I cook better than you might think. I'll prove it to you one of these days."

"At your house?"

Will hesitated. He'd never taken anybody to his place in Chattanooga, not even J.D. Then again, he hadn't brought anyone to meet his mother, either. Julia was different. He had feelings for her, and he was tired of fighting them. They had a lot in common, more than she knew or expected. But he wanted to tell her the truth about his past, and maybe this was the place to do it, the night to do it. He did trust her, and trust sure as hell didn't come easy for him.

Chapter 20

The ebullient and effortlessly friendly Betty Brannock sat down at a table laden with her beautifully displayed and delicious home cooking and ate with them. Betty had removed her apron and chef's attire, and now wore a gorgeous copper-and-brown beaded shell under a black suit. Her high heels were the exact coppery shade of her shell. She wore a wrist-full of gold and diamond bracelets, and diamond studs and gold hoops in her ears. Julia noticed, though, that she wore only a particularly lovely wedding band and a sparkling diamond anniversary ring on her left hand. But no doubt about it, Betty Brannock was a very stylish woman. Judging by what had been said, Julia had a feeling that Will's parents had an excellent marriage.

Listening to Will and Betty talking about his dad, Julia took her first bite of the crispy, golden-brown chicken fried to perfection and almost slid off her chair in ecstasy. It had to be the best chicken she'd ever tasted. She told Betty as much, and Betty bestowed upon Julia that glowing smile of hers and patted her hand. Julia was hungry and let herself enjoy the meal. After all, she had some interesting company. Not to mention the personal revelations Will was throwing at her, right and left. Finally, finally, he was opening up, letting her really see him for who he really was. That's what she'd wanted since she'd met him.

As Julia watched Betty playfully kid around with her son, she found she really liked the woman. Even after this brief acquaintance. Betty absolutely adored Will, that was clear to see, and Julia could also sense how much his mother missed him. But tonight's Will was the biggest surprise. He acted like a different person with his mother. He was so much more at ease seated there in the Taste of the South; not so much on guard and alert to everything and everybody around him. He actually appeared relaxed; well, probably as relaxed as Will Brannock could ever be, anyway.

The evening wore on, and Julia found that she was enjoying herself, more than she probably should. Mother and son joked around and were openly affectionate, and Julia found that she, too, was smiling a lot, caught up in the banter and easy conversation. She watched Will cut into his steak, realizing with some shock that her feelings about him had evolved, become deeper and more heartfelt. She admired him as a partner, true, no question about that. And she'd vowed never again to get involved with a partner.

Bobby Crismon's face flashed through her memory, dampening her high spirits, bringing sadness. But even so, now it was too late to pull back and nurse her grief. Will Brannock had definitely invaded her heart. The way she'd let him touch her last night, the kisses—that was proof enough that she already cared more than she should about him. As much as she didn't want to admit it, none of that intimacy would have happened if she hadn't wanted it to. She had coveted it, all right, last night and lots of other nights. Savored the idea of it and lay awake thinking about it. He cared about her, too. All day he had done everything he could to show her. Why else would he bring her to meet his mother? And the warmth in his eyes when he looked at her was something that put butterflies in her stomach. Sometimes it wasn't just warmth; it was naked, undisguised hunger. She understood that, all too well. Sometimes she felt that ragged kind of hunger herself. She felt a shiver ripple over her flesh, with just the anticipation of what might happen between them, if she let it, if she could bring herself to forget what had happened when she'd allowed herself to get involved with Bobby.

The rest of the dinner passed with sociable chat and good spirits, and Julia felt relieved to have a respite from thinking about the murderous Tongue Slasher and his deadly crimes, if only for one evening. She had thought of little else since the first murder, as had Will. She was glad Maria Bota might be able to identify the killer, but before she could, they had to find him.

The three of them lingered over dessert and coffee and talked about the magnificent hotel and the sights and sounds of Las Vegas. More interesting, Julia listened to the stories Betty told, of Will as a child, of his childhood in Gulf Shores and Biloxi, but Julia also noticed that there was a shadow of sadness in his mother's voice when she related those childhood memories; sadness that Will tried to alleviate with a gentle hand on her shoulder or a squeeze of her hand. Julia was pleased to see his compassion, but she couldn't help but wonder what might have happened to cause such melancholy in their eyes.

They talked until late and finally left as the restaurant was closing up for the night. They walked Betty outside to the entrance and stood with her as the valet brought around her car. Julia smiled when she saw the large red 1959 Cadillac convertible with its huge fins and white leather seats. Will's mother pulled out a trendy brown-and-gold paisley silk scarf and a pair of big

381

stylish sunglasses. She put them on, be it night-time or not.

Apparently sensing Julia's thoughts, Betty said, "The lights on the Strip are bright enough for me to show off my new shades, don't you think?"

"Sure. Thank you for the wonderful evening, Mrs. Brannock. I am so glad I got to meet you."

"Now what did I say about that Mrs. Brannock stuff. It's Betty, you hear?"

Julia smiled, and Betty turned to Will. She gave him a long and heartfelt hug, and didn't release him for a few moments, as though she didn't ever want to let go. Then she gave Julia one, with just as much warmth and sincerity.

"Be patient with my Will, Julia, dear," she whispered in her ear. "Someday I suspect you'll know all his secrets. Then you'll understand."

"Thank you again," Julia said, truly meaning it. Betty Brannock's company was easy to enjoy. "I really had fun tonight."

"I know I'll see you again soon," Betty said with a conspiratorial smile. Then she turned back to Will. "Y'all come out again when your daddy's in town. And your sister, too. Colleen misses you. Why, she was complaining the other day that she hasn't seen you in months."

Julia looked at Will and started to mention his penchant for busty airline employees, but he looked a little sheepish so she remained silent. And enough was enough. No more teasing him about flight attendants. He gave his mother one last peck on the cheek, and she told them both to take care. Then Will and Julia watched his mother drive away, her scarf blowing jauntily in the wind.

"I like her very much," she told him with complete honesty.

"She's a great lady. I miss her a lot."

"Then why don't you come out here more often? The TBI doesn't have you on that tight of a leash, do they?"

"Depends on the case. It was lucky for me that Maria showed up here. You know, kill two birds with one stone, and all that."

Julia laughed. "That's not the best analogy when talking about your family."

"No, I guess it's not," he said, grinning a little. He had a great smile, but it didn't last long. He grew serious and said, "It's good to hear you laugh, Julia."

"We haven't had much to laugh about since we met, I'll grant you that."

Their eyes searched each other's faces, both solemn, both fully aware things were changing between them—had already changed. The kiss had proved that everything was different. Tonight was going to be a test, and Julia was afraid it was a test she might fail, despite all her best intentions. She broke eye contact and tried to forget the longing she saw in his eyes.

Their elevator ride to the penthouse was silent. Two young couples got on with them on the twenty-ninth floor and rode to the thirty-second, with lots of giggling and excited chatter. The four were having a wonderful time, and by the way they were groping each other, their night was headed to even more fun later on.

When they entered the Grand Lakeview Suite, Julia walked through the opulent marble entry hall into the living room. The view of the glittering lights of Las Vegas stretching out below was breathtaking. A couple of lamps had been switched on, giving a soft glow to the room. The fireplace was burning, and music was playing somewhere, soft and romantic. Julia wondered if Will had arranged that, anticipating his seduction. She hoped not. She hoped so.

Will strode into the living room and dropped the card on the table in front of the fireplace. "The maids always turn on music and turn down the beds."

That answered her question. "Very cool. This is quite an experience."

"How about a nightcap? Some wine, maybe."

"Sure. I guess I should check in with Tam, though."

"Do it tomorrow. She'll call right away if anything turns up. We're off the clock."

Julia hesitated. If there was one thing she wasn't used to, it was considering herself off the clock. The same could be said for Will. She knew that for a fact, from all the weeks working so closely alongside him. Oh God, she did want him in the worst way. She wanted a serious romantic relationship. She wanted him to grab her, crush her to him, and make love to her all night long. She had been fighting it, denying it, but now was the time. She was confused. Up until last night, he had been the one who had been stand-offish. They'd decided it had to be professional and that's all it could be at the moment. But then what did he do? Turned around and introduced her to his family and treated her to an overnight stay in heaven. What the devil was going on inside his head?

Will expertly opened a bottle of merlot and poured it into two stemmed crystal goblets. He handed her one and sat down across from her. They both stared into the fire. Julia frowned. She was not used to all this secretive drama and the kiss-me-like-crazy-then-run-like-a-rabbit routine.

"Look, Will, I'm not the type of woman who dances around problems. I think you know that. I think you know how I feel. You grabbed me and kissed me like I've never been kissed before, and then you treat me like the Queen of Sheba, or Beyoncé or somebody—bring me to meet your mama at the Bellagio, no less. Whom I really like, by the way. So, what's it going to be, Will? Is this strictly professional, or something else we're going to get into without much further ado?"

Will kept staring into the fire, for so long that Julia was about ready to slap him upside his head. Talk about a roller-coaster kind of guy. Since Bobby died, she'd tried to date a few times, but found she just couldn't risk an emotional attachment again. She just didn't want to get involved with anyone. And, true, she shouldn't get involved with Will, either. So why was she pushing it? What the hell was the matter with her?

When he finally spoke, his voice was so low that she could barely hear it. "I guess it's going to have to be strictly professional."

Julia stared at his chiseled profile, backlit by the darting orange flames. She felt absolutely foolish, ridiculous, dumbstruck; the truth was, she wasn't as insulted as she was disappointed. So, as it turned out, Will really was what she'd thought in the beginning—a man who went through women like water through a sieve. No deep feelings, no relationship, except for the physical act whenever he was in the mood for it. Anger shot through her. Burned through her body like caustic acid.

Okay, so be it, jerk.

Carefully placing her goblet on the table, she stood up. "Whatever you say, Will. You're probably right. It would be a mistake for us to get together tonight. We'd both regret it."

Will didn't answer, just set his jaw at a steely angle and stared moodily at her. She watched his

386

facial muscles working hard under his tanned skin as he gritted his teeth, but he didn't say anything else. Julia shook her head, turned, and walked into her bedroom. She shut the door quietly behind her, but she leaned against it and fought back tears. She should've slammed it like a hurt and jilted teenager. That's what she wanted to do. She felt so silly. She never came on to men. But, damn it, he had started all this with that no-holds-barred kiss, and then he'd come off this morning like he was angry that they hadn't gone further than a few kisses. She shouldn't be angry; she should accept this as for the best. But she *was* angry. She was furious.

Cursing him under her breath, she kicked off her shoes and stripped off the slinky black dress that should have turned him on and hadn't, and then slung it down on the shiny hardwood floor with as much strength as she possessed. Okay, if that's what he wanted, that's what he'd get: cold, cool, collected, on the case, no other thoughts in mind. Damn him, he'd started something, then cut bait as soon as she took it. Breathing in and out, nice and deep and steamy, she tried to calm herself, let the anger subside. *He's right, of course. That's the way it should be.* There was a vicious, cold-blooded killer on the loose in Chattanooga. That's what she needed to concentrate on; that's what was going to be her focus. They'd be professional. They'd do it exactly by the book.

He'd never lay a finger on her again—no way.

The palatial bathroom she chose was all mirrors and marble and glass doors. The shower was huge and luxurious, with enough shower-heads to bathe an elephant and its calf. She turned them all on, hot as her poor skin could take it, and stepped into the pounding water and cloud of steam and let it wash away the rest of her anger. Truth be told, a cold shower probably would've been more appropriate. She shut her eyes, made the water a bit cooler, and raised her face into the spray. One thing was for sure—a cold shower was in order with all the lurid thoughts she'd been having since last night.

It wasn't until Julia felt his hand on her shoulder that she realized Will was in the shower with her. She jerked around, and there he stood, right behind her, still fully dressed. The hungry look was back in his eyes, so intense that her lips parted. Regaining her wits, she put her palms against the wet shirt clinging to his molded chest muscles, stopping him where he stood, not sure what he wanted—what *she* wanted. He'd rejected her a minute ago, only to show up now. He didn't push forward against her, just stared into her eyes.

"I want you. I want you so badly I can taste it."

Julia swallowed, unable to move. "You just said you didn't want to do this."

"I tried to do the right thing. I can't do it anymore. I don't have the strength."

"If we do this now, there's no going back."

"I don't care." A long, torturous pause. Then he said the magic words. "I love you, Julia."

Julia melted a little inside. Now that was more like it. She cupped his jaw in her palms, felt the strength in it, but also the trembling as he held himself back. Then she leaned into him, giving him the permission he needed, and he was pulling her wet, naked body against him. She went up onto her toes, trying to reach his mouth, and their lips came together, hot, eager, searching. Her mouth opened to his tongue, and they let loose all the emotions that had been building up for days. Will went down on his knees, the spraying water wetting his hair, and she pushed it back as his warm mouth closed over her nipple. She cried out, the sensation ripping through her body and deep into her core, barely aware of the warm water streaming down over her bare flesh, his hands pulling her against him.

Then she was jerking his buttons open, and he impatiently stood and shrugged off his shirt. Hard, sculpted muscles flattened her breasts as their wet skin met and slid together, both his hands tangled in her wet hair. Her hands went to his belt, and then he was finally naked, too, and their bodies came together. She felt his palms on her thighs, pulling her legs up around his waist. He backed her against the wall, and their mouths attacked each other. Then he was inside her, and he took her with him down onto the marble floor. Warm water still streaming over them, Julia grasped him around the neck with both hands, holding on tightly, moving with each of his deep thrusts. Her eyes were squeezed shut, overcome by sheer pleasure, and she moaned in desire, clutching his hair with her fingers as he found his way to the side of her neck, his tongue licking at her wet flesh. His mouth moved lower, taking one nipple then the other into his mouth and sucking until deep, erotic, electrifying sensations streaked like flame along her nerve endings.

The pleasure built until she couldn't stand it, and then it happened. The climax gripped them both, their bodies going rigid as they held on to each other, letting it happen, letting the ecstasy go on and on until they shook with the sheer, wracking pleasure of it.

Afterward, Will held Julia on his lap and smoothed back her hair. They sat there without speaking, her head on his shoulder, their lips and tongues still exploring each other's faces and mouths, doing all the things they'd both dreamed of since they first met.

Finally they stood and washed each other slowly and gently with the scented soap, turning each other on again as warm water sprayed over their nakedness, sensual, slick, slippery. Their bodies slid together, joined again, and moved slowly, until the sensations climbed, climbed to that final, exquisite moment again, and the pure sexual gratification exploded inside them both, shaking them to their cores. Weak, overwhelmed by what they had experienced, they held each other.

Two hours later, they sat together again in the living room, on the white couch facing the huge glass windows where the fountains still shot white geysers high into the air. They both now wore the long, white terry cloth robes embroidered with the Bellagio logo. They clinked their champagne glasses together, sipped, then tasted the wine off each other's lips. Julia opened Will's robe and touched the scar she'd seen earlier on his shoulder, then kissed it. "This looks like a bullet wound. What happened?"

At her question, Will stiffened noticeably, and Julia drew back, surprised. He abruptly let her go, stood up, and walked away to stand in front of the windows, his back to her, all of Las Vegas glittering in the distance. Julia watched him, hoping he wasn't regretting their lovemaking. How could he, as wonderful as it had been? He couldn't have faked the tenderness he showed when he'd made love to her again in that big, soft bed—the gentleness, the whispered words of love. There had to be something else, something that was troubling him. So she sat silently and waited.

"I'm sorry, Julia," he said softly, turning around and facing her. At that, Julia tensed, set down her glass, and waited for him to continue. "I shouldn't have pushed you away earlier tonight. I didn't want to. But I didn't want to hurt you. I didn't want to put you in danger."

"What are you talking about? Tell me. Nothing can be that bad."

"You just don't know."

"Then tell me. Please."

"I'm trying to protect you. I don't want you to get hurt."

"So you don't want to continue this relationship?"

"Yes, of course I do," he said quickly. "This is what I've wanted for a long time. And it was everything I thought it'd be—more, a lot more."

Pleased by his words, Julia watched him. His words were coming out hard, as if he'd never given voice to his fears before. "Then why? What are you afraid of?"

"I'm afraid that the people who are trying to kill me will kill you instead."

Nothing he could have said could have stunned Julia more. "*Kill* you? Are you serious? There are people gunning for you?"

Will remained silent, but Julia could see the pain on his face. She asked again. "Are you talking about this case? The Tongue Slasher?"

"No, this has nothing to do with our case. It's about something that happened to me when I was a boy."

"Will, you're beginning to scare me. Who's

after you? Why?" But everything suddenly made sense to Julia: all his secrecy, his extreme caution, not mentioning his home, family, past life. He was finally going to tell her what was going on. Now, though, she was almost afraid to hear what he would say.

"I was only eighteen when it happened."

Julia's every nerve quivered on edge, now that he was on the verge of revealing all his secrets. It was going to be bad. Very bad. She could feel it.

"We lived in Mississippi back then. In Biloxi. Dad had a restaurant there, one inside a casino, one a lot like the Taste of the South. I worked there—everybody in our family did—cooking, waiting tables, or busing the dishes. Colleen was a hostess. I was learning the business. Dad wanted me to take it over when he retired."

The story was coming out very hard. Will did not want to do this, relive it, Julia could tell that, but he was going to. He wanted her to know. He wanted the secrets between them to end. So did she, but she felt terrible for him. The emotions flickering across his face were tortured, almost too painful to watch. She wanted to rush over to him, to hold him and help him get through it, but she didn't. He wouldn't want that. She waited for him to get himself under control.

"That night I was taking a break out back in the alley. I saw a murder go down."

"You witnessed it?"

"Yes, and that made me a material witness in a murder case."

"Oh my God."

Will gave a wry smile. "Yeah. Turned out that the hit man sang to the FBI, told them that the casino owner was behind the hit. His name was Oscar Kraft. The FBI charged him with conspiracy to commit murder, put them on trial together, and asked me to testify. So I agreed."

"And Kraft came after you."

"Yeah. They sent me threatening letters. You know, the usual intimidation tactics. So I had to go into protective custody until the trial." Pure agony took hold of his face, and Julia braced herself, sensing the worst was coming next. Whatever it was, it was a deep, festering wound inside Will, one that was killing his soul. So raw that even now it clogged his throat, making it difficult for him to get out the words.

"They got my little brother instead. Bryan. He looked a lot like me. A little shorter. One night when he was coming out of a movie theater, they shot him down like a dog. Shot his girlfriend, too. She survived. Bryan didn't. He had just turned sixteen when he died."

Julia's heart hammered out of control. Of all the things he had told her, this was the most horrific, and the last thing she had expected to hear. Again, her instinct was to get up and hold him close, comfort him, but something about the stiffness of his stance told her not to, that he wasn't finished. "I'm so sorry, Will. That must have been terrible for you and your family." She thought of Betty, the lovely, smiling, affectionate woman who had lost her innocent young son to violence.

"I testified anyway. I wanted to get that bastard. And I did." Will began to pace the floor in front of the fireplace, then stopped and braced a hand on the mantel, staring down into the flames. "After the trial was over, I still got threats. The Feds wanted me to go into witness protection and disappear for good. That's not my style. Not even back then was I willing to go into hiding. But I was afraid they'd go after me again and get my parents instead, or my sister. They're vicious enough to kill anybody in their way."

The hurt in his voice was so naked now, so heartbreaking that Julia had to go to him. She moved up behind him, put her arms tightly around his waist, and laid her cheek against his back. "You were afraid for the people you loved. I would've done the same thing."

"The only way I knew to keep them out of danger was to disappear, put out word through the FBI that I was dead, killed for my testimony. So that's what I did. I avoided my family, broke off with the girl I was dating back then, and joined the army. I volunteered for special ops and black ops missions for the next nine years. Once I opted out, I joined the FBI. First in Los Angeles and then St. Louis. And then I joined the TBI in Chattanooga."

Will pulled her to the sofa and sat down beside her. "So there you go, Julia. That's my life history, as sordid as it is."

"I'm so sorry, Will. I can't imagine how awful that must have been for you. If something like that ever happened to J.D., I don't know what I'd do. He's been my protector, my only family, for most of my life."

"Believe it or not, I used to be fun-loving, happy-go-lucky like my mom, but after Bryan died, I knew that anybody I associated with, anybody that I cared about, was a potential target. That's why I kept pushing you away. Trying not to get involved with you. Once we started working together, I was that much more determined not to involve you."

"Well, now I think I've seen the real you a couple of times." She smiled, thinking of the day they met. "The day we met, you were quite the charmer. But, Will, it's been so long now, surely they aren't still after you."

"They've already tried three times since I went into the army. That bullet wound you asked about a minute ago—that was the first time. They got me in the shoulder. The second time, they put a bomb under my car. Lucky for me, it ignited and burned up the car, but I got out before the gas tank blew. The third time, they missed me, but the high-powered rifle exploded the store window behind me and hit a customer in the leg. They'll keep trying. It's an honor thing with Oscar's family now. His sons are going to keep on trying until they die. If they find me again, they'll try again."

"Even now that you're with the TBI? I'd think they'd be afraid to mess with a special agent."

"It's helped. They haven't done anything for the last five years, but that doesn't mean they won't in the future. My family thinks it's over now because Oscar Kraft died in prison six years ago, but I'm not sure it is."

Rage welled up inside Julia, but when she spoke, she was very calm. "Then we'll go after them, Will. We'll get them first. I'll help you get them."

Will stared at her, then leaned back his head and laughed. "I should've known you'd say that."

"I'm serious. We can get them. We can go after them as soon as we solve this case. Let them worry for a change about who's going to show up. Let them watch their backs. But we'll do it legally, with a charge of attempted murder. We can do it together."

Will pulled her close and their lips met, tenderly, softly, until Will pulled back, held her shoulders, and looked seriously into her eyes.

"That's a hell of a thing for two law enforcement officers to contemplate, but I have to say, Julia, it's as tempting as hell."

Chapter 21

Early the next morning, Will rolled the linen-draped cart of breakfast foods he'd ordered down through the suite's foyer and into the dining area. Under the silver warming domes were scrambled eggs, bacon, buttered toast, biscuits, and every kind of breakfast pastry, including Julia's favorite, jelly doughnuts. He'd also ordered pancakes and fresh fruit, icy orange and grape-fruit juice, and a steaming pot of coffee. After the fireworks they'd set off in bed last night, both of them were going to need some serious sustenance.

Today he was in a good mood. Better than he'd been in years. Despite a major lack of sleep. He hadn't been able to keep his hands off Julia, and she had been as eager in their lovemaking as he was, and that was saying something. She was as energetic and thorough in bed as she was on her detective job. He smiled and poured himself a cup of coffee.

After so much struggling to keep Julia at arm's length, he felt relieved, like somebody had lifted a two-hundred-pound stone off his chest. It had been different with Julia, so different than any other woman he'd been with. She was the first woman he'd told about his past, the only woman he'd let into his private life. He didn't regret it. He was glad—glad he could be himself and quit worrying about her, at least for today, anyway.

"Good morning."

When he glanced up, he found Julia standing at the bedroom door. She had just gotten out of the shower, and he was sorry he had missed it. He'd surely never forget the shower they'd shared last night. She had on the white hotel robe and slippers, and he was pretty sure she wore nothing underneath it. His loins roused and took note, and that boded very well for the way they'd spend the rest of their time at the Bellagio. She walked over and sat down beside him. She smiled and entwined her fingers with his, and he was sure he had never seen anybody look so beautiful in his life. Oh God, he had it bad for her. Embarrassingly so. But who wouldn't?

"You fixed me all this for breakfast? What a guy."

"Of course. I come from a long line of chefs and restaurateurs, you know."

"Liar. I heard the room service guy come in. But that's okay. I'm starving. I'm still weak from last night. You worked me over pretty good."

"*I* worked *you* over? If I recall, and do I ever, it was pretty much the other way around."

"Are you complaining, Special Agent?"

"No, ma'am."

This time Julia smiled. "So you're as happy as I am this morning? No regrets? No turning back?"

"See this satiated smile on my face. See this fantastic breakfast I ordered up for you. You bet I'm happy."

Will poured her a cup of coffee and took another sip of his own. He lifted off the warming domes and some delicious aromas wafted out. "Heard anything from Tam this morning?"

"Not yet. I hope she's come up with something pertinent from Lockhart's files."

"Forensic reports should be back on Gloria Varranzo by the time we get home."

"I want to pick up her backlog of cases and see what I can find out. There's got to be a connection."

Will handed her a plate. "We'll do it at my place. I've been wanting to show you where I live."

Julia picked out a jelly doughnut. "Could've fooled me on that one."

"Now you know why I was hesitant. Want some orange juice?"

She nodded and tasted a strip of bacon. "This is delicious. You did good, Brannock."

"Wait until you taste my specialty. Homemade ravioli."

"You made that sound provocative."

Will laughed, and Julia did, too. "Turns out that you have a nice smile, Brannock. I'm glad I'm finally getting to see it instead of that serious frown of yours."

"Among other things."

"Oh yeah, we can't forget those other things."

They grinned at each other. Will's phone dinged and vibrated where he'd placed it on the coffee table. He picked it up and read J.D.'s name on caller ID. "It's your brother."

"Uh-oh. Tell him what a good time you're showing me in your personal little Bellagio luxury seduction suite."

"I think not," he said, feeling a bit uncomfortable with that idea. "We'll keep all this under wraps for a while. We'll choose the exact right time to tell him. After this case is over."

"Scaredy-cat."

Will ignored that. He punched the button. "Yeah, J.D.? What's up?"

J.D.'s voice sounded worried. "I'm looking for my sister. Can't get an answer on her phone. Are you with her?"

"Yeah. Her battery's probably dead."

Julia nodded yes to that explanation, and Will handed her the cell phone. While she talked, he dialed the office on the hotel phone and told Phil Hayes what they'd found out and approximately when they'd be flying into Chattanooga. Phil told him that the task force members had been interviewing Gloria Varranzo's partners and clients. He and Julia would need to interview the rest of her family and some of the neighbors as soon as they returned. Phil also said the woman had more enemies than Genghis Khan, just like the other two victims. Will hung up and watched Julia talking with J.D. There would be more unlikable victims hanging by the neck minus their tongues, and so far the task force wasn't having a lot of luck figuring out who was the killer or where he'd strike again. And he would. It was just a matter of time. The Tongue Slasher would kill until they caught him, but catch him they would.

Julia hung up but kept looking at the screen. "Tam just texted. Said we need to pick up Varranzo's digital files at her law offices. She's still working on connections between Lockhart and VanVeter."

"We'll stop by and get them and take them to my house. I'll help you go through them."

"All work and no play?"

"I am planning on some major play, count on it. In fact, playing might be high on my priority list from now on."

"I can go for that."

It was amazing how different their relationship had become, and so quickly. On the day they met, he never would have dreamed in a million years that it would come to this. In fact, he thought at first that she'd make a point to never lay eyes on him again. He had liked her even then, but she had been a hands-off, not interested, no dice kind of girl and didn't mind showing it. He just thanked his lucky stars that she'd changed her mind.

"You know, I think Bellagio serves even better breakfasts than McDonald's. But, I don't know, you can hardly beat an Egg McMuffin and hash browns."

"Think so, huh?" He took a bite of toast, then spread strawberry preserves on the other half.

"Egg McMuffins are hard to beat, you have to admit."

"Let's take a slow shower and talk about that. A really slow and hot and slippery shower. The plane won't be ready for hours."

Smiling in an extremely promising and erotic invitation, Julia held out her hand. Will took it, thankful he finally could.

Folger Parmentier had never been so pleased with himself. He had beaten the latest charges against him without breaking a sweat. He shouldn't have, of course. He chuckled to himself. Truth was, he had forced that college girl to have sex with him, had done everything the prosecution said he did. But the bitch wanted it all, every single thing he did, no matter what she said to the contrary. She wanted it hard and rough, like all women did. And he gave her exactly what she asked for, and with a great deal of enthusiasm, at that.

Gloria Varranzo had done a great job in court,

lying her head off, characterizing the victim as an immoral slut, just as she did every time he was accused of wrongdoing. Too bad old Gloria was dead now and couldn't represent him anymore. But her partner had finished up the closing argument for her, and Folger had walked, scot-free. Again. Of course, the five hundred thousand dollars his daddy had given Gloria up front had helped things along quite a bit. Man, it was good to be alive and kicking. He hadn't felt so power-ful in a long, long time. His dad was ill and wouldn't last much longer. Finally. Soon he could inherit the Parmentier estate and do whatever he wanted, without any parental restraints whatso-ever. As far as he was concerned, it couldn't happen soon enough.

Relaxing back into the comfortable black-and-white striped cushions on the lounge beside his pool, he cleaned his designer sunglasses on a towel, poked them back over his nose, and relaxed. He shut his eyes, glad that that little bitch Patti Ann had been bought off, once and for all, and would quit causing him trouble. Hell, she'd probably be calling him before a week was over, wanting to come over for more. She liked being tied up and whipped, among other sick things. She'd be back. They all came back. He paid them well enough.

Grinning lazily, he visualized how he'd make her beg him for it. She'd have to crawl on her hands and knees back to the whipping post he'd built in his secret basement room. She'd scream prettily, but then her screams wouldn't be so pretty, not with the instruments he intended to use on her. So deep was he into his deviant sexual fantasies that he didn't hear the killer's soft footfalls just behind him; didn't have a clue that he was about to become one of the victims in that infamous room he kept downstairs. He fought hard at first against the cloying effects of the ether-soaked towel pressed against his face, but the killer's grip was too hard and strong. Within seconds, Folger stopped all his struggling and blacked out, unaware that the horrors awaiting him would be even worse than the ones he had inflicted on others, with such unparalleled enjoyment.

The Tongue Slasher took all the time he needed. He unwrapped the leather cloth holding his deadly tools. An uncharacteristic rush of excitement flooded him. He was pleased, of course, at the deaths of his other victims. For years he had prayed unceasingly for their righteous punishment and painful demise, but to no avail. All of them deserved to die, every single one—to die horribly, for all the evil they'd done. But Parmentier, Parmentier was the Devil incarnate. The lives he had destroyed during his young life were incalculable. And he would not stop. He enjoyed his crimes.

The killer was interested in only one of Parmentier's many vicious crimes. Horrible as it was, he had gotten away with it, too. But now, no longer would he smirk and grin and pay off people for their silence and their lies. Folger Parmentier would pay the price today, right now.

The two of them were alone together in Parmentier's basement torture chamber. The killer had been impressed with the wide variety of whips and chains and blindfolds and handcuffs that he'd found neatly hung on the walls, not to mention the video equipment. Yes, Parmentier's hidden recreation room, designed for his deviant fun and games, was completely soundproof. Screams for help could not be heard. Perfect in every way, because now the sinner was all alone inside his own worst nightmare. He would be punished in the way he deserved. The killer placed the noose around Folger Parmentier's throat. The coins, the scales, the knife, and the pliers were lying on the table. It wouldn't be long now before the victim awoke. The killer looked forward to it with a vicious, vindictive eagerness that he hadn't felt before. This was the one who started it all. He would pay more severely than his minions and henchmen had.

Picking up Folger Parmentier's fancy sunglasses that had probably cost thousands of dollars, he went outside, placed the dark glasses on his nose, and relaxed on the lounge chair beside the pool.

The man who'd caused him the worst pain of his entire life was bound and unconscious in his own basement. He wasn't going anywhere. Patiently, he watched the faraway road down the hill that edged Parmentier's property. It was quite isolated out here. There was no hurry. No one was going to bother them so far out of town. He listened to the distant call of a blue jay. Yes, it was a nice, quiet place to live. Soon it would be a nice, quiet place to die. Parmentier had chosen this place so that his victims' screams couldn't be heard. He had chosen well. Parmentier would soon find out how helpless all the victims he'd brought here had felt as he raped and beat them. He leaned back and let the sun warm his skin, but the heat did not penetrate to his heart. His heart had been frozen, icy and hard, for the last ten years.

Julia drove home, finding it nearly impossible to believe what had happened between Will and her in Las Vegas. But it was so right, so meant to be. After hearing about the tragedy of Will's past, the loss he'd suffered as a boy, she understood him so much better, understood his pain, his fear that someone else he loved might lose their life because of him. This guy, Kraft, had not only ruined Will's life but had changed his personality, changed him into a cautious, emotionally remote loner. She was lucky he had allowed her into his private life. After she found out the truth, she decided that she suited him more than most women would. She could take care of herself and was usually armed and ready for trouble, especially now that she knew what was going on. She would be vigilant. No one was going to get to Will when she was around, not if she and her Glock had anything to do with it.

Stopping at Cathy's front sidewalk, Julia got out, slammed the Charger's door, and opened the picket gate. She'd left Jasper in Cathy's care, and she was eager to pick him up. As she walked up the marigold-lined brick path, she felt that Cathy would be pleased that Julia and Will had gotten together romantically. She'd been pushing hard enough for them to hook up, ever since Julia had arrived in Chattanooga. No one answered when Julia knocked, and the front door was locked. They could be at church, or perhaps they'd just gone out for dinner.

There was a huge fenced-in yard out back, and she walked around the house, looking for her beloved bloodhound. Jasper must have picked up her scent on the river wind, because he came barreling out of the dense glade of trees at about a hundred miles an hour. The other dogs were right behind him, all yapping and barking. She went inside the yard and shut the gate, kneeling down and hugging the lovable old bloodhound. She petted the others, too, gave them some of the baby talk that she used with Jasper, and then attached

Jasper's leash. She peered back into the shadowy woods, wondering if Cathy and Lonnie were somewhere out there; in Lonnie's private studio, perhaps. It didn't matter. She punched in Cathy's number, got her voice mail, and left her a message that she'd already picked up Jasper. Otherwise, Cathy would be worried about him.

Jasper was thrilled to see her and eager to get home. His beating tail proved it. He scrambled up into the front passenger's seat. She started the engine and headed home. Will was insisting that she spend the night at his place tonight. When she reminded him of Jasper, he said to bring him along. *A decision that Will just might regret,* she thought, amused. However, based on the way Will and Jasper loved on each other, they had already bonded. She grinned to herself, very interested in what kind of house Will had chosen. If she had to guess, it would be extremely isolated and well protected. *Probably has a moat, too,* she thought. But he had good reasons to be careful, and now she understood that.

Inside her house, she checked for messages. There was a call from Charlie Sinclair, and she punched redial but got no answer. She glanced at her watch, wondering where he was. Maybe he was feeding the boarded animals out back and couldn't hear his phone. Maybe he was out fishing with Lonnie and Cathy. Their boat was gone, now that she thought about it. Not to worry; he'd call back if it was important. Tam had called but hadn't left a message. Max Hazard had called and asked her out on a date again.

On the way back from the airport, she and Will had made a stop at Gloria Varranzo's law offices and picked up her digital files. They planned to go over them tonight at his house. Will had gone downtown to check in at headquarters so Phil could fill him in on anything else that had happened during the short time they'd been away. They also needed to e-mail more photographs of persons of interest to Maria Bota and see if she could identify the man she'd seen at the Lockhart crime scene. She found herself rushing around, throwing things in her overnight bag, so eager to be with Will again that she finally stopped, shirt in hand, and chided herself for the girlish giddiness. *For Pete's sake, Julia, act like an adult. Quit behaving like some trembling adolescent.* Still, the thought of Will's hard body and warm lips inching down over her belly sent all kinds of electric currents bouncing around over her flesh.

So when she heard Will's tires crunching over the gravel outside her window, she headed outside to meet him. Jasper had beat her to the door and started baying as Will walked down the path toward them. His step was lighter, he was smiling, and she hoped in her heart that his good spirits had everything to do with her. She opened the screen door, and he wasted no time grabbing her against him and giving her a long, satisfying kiss that lasted until Jasper decided enough was enough and jumped up on Will's back, barking.

"I forgot to tell you that Jasper's the jealous type," she told Will.

"Yeah? Well, so am I. Looks like we'll have to fight for your attention."

Will kept looking at her mouth, and she decided Will was going to beat Jasper at that game every single time. Attempting to get her mind on something other than the way Will felt pressed up against her, she decided she needed to get their minds back on business. They had all night to enjoy themselves in bed. The idea brought a ridiculous blush rising up her throat.

"Did Phil have anything else on the Tongue Slasher?" she asked him.

"Yeah. The killer cleaned up pretty well after himself this time, too. They did find a drop of blood that they presume to be the killer's, but the DNA hasn't matched it up to anyone in our databases." He hesitated. "They found something else at the Varranzo crime scene, too. A couple of dog hairs."

"I didn't see any sign of a dog at her place."

"She didn't have one. That's the significance."

"What breed?"

Will hesitated. "Actually, it's from a bloodhound."

They stared at each other a moment, both thinking the same thing. "So you think it's Jasper's?"

The bloodhound reacted at the sound of his name, lying down at her feet and presenting his belly for her to rub. She knelt and obliged, but she didn't like the idea that she may have been so careless that she contaminated a crime scene with Jasper's hair.

"I didn't say that. It could be from another blood-hound, some kind of transference. I've seen how careful you are before you enter a crime scene."

"I'm trained to do that, of course, but it can happen. It never has before—never, not once—but I guess it's possible."

"Send a sample of Jasper's coat over to forensics and find out. Don't beat yourself up until you know for sure."

"God, I hope it's not Jasper's."

Will glanced down at the CDs in her hand. "Are those Varranzo's files?"

"Yes. It looks like we're going to spend lots of time checking them out."

"Not as long as you think. I just put in some really awesome computer equipment."

"It's still going to take time. I want to get through it all tonight."

"What's that you said not so long ago? Something about all work, Jack, dull boy—remember that?"

"This case has to come first."

Will's smile faded as he acknowledged the truth of her statement. "I know, but we have to eat and sleep. And make love." He looked at her mouth again, with a lust he no longer even tried to disguise. He was going to have to stop doing that, or they weren't going to get anything done. Man, the rippling cold chills he could give her. "We've got to get to know each other better, Jules, and there's so much more I want to show you."

Julia knew exactly what he meant and was glad to hear it. Okay, the sexual tension was gone, but now that she knew what it was like in his bed—his hands all over her body, the desire she felt—the idea of making love with him again was even more titillating. Jeez, she was going to have to get a grip and lock up her carnal urges, not to mention corral Will's lusty bedroom appetite. She changed the subject.

"Are you sure you want me to bring Jasper along?"

"Sure. He can get to know my dogs."

"You have dogs?"

"Yes."

"What kind of dogs?"

"Two beagles," Will said, then admitted with a sheepish look, "and a toy poodle."

"You, Will Brannock, own a toy poodle? You've got to be kidding me."

"It's Mom's. When they moved to Las Vegas,

413

she was afraid a scorpion or snake would get her, so she insisted I keep her here. She said my life was way too lonely, anyway, and poodles love unconditionally."

"That sounds like Betty. What are their names?"

"The beagles are Rover and Spot."

"How ingenious. And the poodle?"

"Don't laugh."

"I can't promise that."

"My mother named her, not me."

"So, let's hear it."

"Baby Cakes."

Julia laughed out loud. The idea of a big, virile, strapping man like Will cuddling a little lapdog named Baby Cakes struck her as more than funny.

Will frowned. "Don't tell J.D., okay?"

"Oh, he and the other guys are going to have a heyday with this one."

"I'll have to think of a way to convince you to keep my secrets."

At that, Julia became serious at once. He was now opening up to her about every aspect of his life. She didn't want to do anything to make him reticent again.

"Why didn't you tell me about the dogs?"

"I tend to keep my cards close to the vest, remember?"

"You wanted to protect your dogs?"

"Don't you?"

Julia couldn't disagree with that and admitted she'd found yet another facet of Will Brannock's personality that she absolutely loved and that fit hand in glove with hers. *Tread carefully,* she told herself as she picked up the CDs and her backpack. She wasn't used to having a romantic relationship and neither was he. They were already close to getting carried away with the euphoria of it all.

As it turned out, Will lived out on Chickamauga Lake. His place was just off Gann Store Road, in a gated waterfront community not too far from downtown Chattanooga. His property was enclosed by a tall brick wall with KEEP OUT signs and BEWARE OF DOG warnings.

"Beware of dogs? Don't you mean beware of Baby Cakes?"

"Ha-ha. I don't like the idea of people sneaking up on me. I'm careful. And for your information, Baby Cakes yaps louder than the other two put together."

"The IRS probably couldn't even get to you out here."

"That's an added perk, true."

The gate was activated with a card sweep. A camera was positioned on the gate. "The president could stay here without the Secret Service and still sleep without a care in the world," Julia commented.

"I like my privacy."

"Well, at least you won't get any door-to-door salesmen. How much land do you own?"

"Five and a half acres."

The tarmac road wound up through a well-kept grassy lawn to a large contemporary house covered with dark wood siding and white brick. It was all dark except for a few lights on the ground floor.

"How big is this house? It looks huge."

"Eighty-four hundred square feet. Or thereabout."

"Is that all? Just a little bachelor pad, huh?"

"It's got four decks and lots of windows overlooking the lake. I like looking at the water, just like at your house."

"I just have one window."

"But it's got a good view of the river."

They drove around the house to the three-car garage. The view was beautiful to behold, all right, and a *House Beautiful* house to go with it.

"Wow, Brannock. You Daddy Warbucks, or what?"

"I bought this place for the security systems. It's hard to break in here."

"Well, you got whatever you paid for this place, and more. I guarantee it." She looked over at him as he hit a button on the remote attached to the visor above the driver's seat, and the garage door slowly began to rise. They drove inside, where she saw his black-and-chrome Mercedes motorcycle and red Corvette convertible.

"Okay, I have one question. Where do you park the Rolls-Royce?"

"No Rolls-Royce. Way too flashy."

"Are you kidding me? No Rolls-Royce. What do you take to the opera and all those posh charity galas?"

"I like vehicles, and I told you I'm part owner of the Taste of the South franchise. I'm not as rich as you obviously think."

"Yeah, right."

"That's a 2005 magnetic-red Chevrolet Corvette hardtop. What do you think of it?"

"I think you should sell it to me, cheap."

"Maybe I will."

"Maybe I'll take it in a New York minute."

"Maybe I'll just buy you a matching one. You know, his and hers."

"You're talking my language, baby."

Will laughed, but the beagles had heard the garage door and were outside Will's car door, barking up a storm and letting their master know they had missed him in the worst way. Jasper looked highly interested but was too well trained to go to pieces.

"Your guard beagles aren't going to attack my bloodhound, are they?"

"Nope." He opened his door but leveled a gaze on her. "At least, I don't think so. They don't attack Bab"—he cut that off, apparently not ready for another round of jokes—"the poodle. The

417

poodle might attack him, though. She thinks she's a Saint Bernard, or something. She's quite a handful."

Handful was right, Julia thought as they entered the house and the aforementioned canine slid around a corner with a great clicking of nails. The poodle was tiny, even for her breed, but her bark was as shrill as any ambulance siren. More so, in fact. Jasper looked like he wanted to lie down and put his paws over his floppy ears. Baby Cakes slid to a dancing halt on the glossy hardwood floor and stared suspiciously at Jasper.

"Stay, Jasper," she ordered. Jasper obediently sat, still eyeing the tiny pooch as if it were the creature in *Alien* and was just hankering to hook itself on his face and explode through his chest.

Still chaperoning the sniffing-and-summing-each-other-up dogs, she looked around the interior of Will's house. *Jeez,* she thought, *definitely no expense spared.* "The Taste of the South franchise must be doing one hell of a business, Will. You ever get lost in here?"

"C'mon, give me a break." He turned his head and raised an eyebrow. "Wait until you see my bedroom. You're going to like it, trust me."

"I'd like it if it were a cot and a horsehair blanket."

"Good answer."

Their laughs were easy and genuine, and they were getting more and more comfortable with their new closeness. That was good. Will led her into the great room, which had floor-to-ceiling windows with a fabulous view of the glistening lake; but then again, every room they passed through had that magnificent outlook. The kitchen had every conceivable convenience, Kitchen-Aid and Sub-Zero appliances, cherrywood cabinets, and black marble countertops. Anything and everything a cook could ever need.

"Well, I must say, I am mightily impressed. I bet it even echoes like the Alps when you yell from the top of that grand staircase."

"I yodel there every chance I get."

The idea of Will yodeling there or anywhere also amused her.

"I'm getting the impression you don't like my house."

"I love it, but where's the Olympic-size heated swimming pool? I must have my Olympic-size heated swimming pool, you know."

"It's down beside the lake. See? Look down that way. Not quite Olympic, but big enough for both of us."

"Wow, I'm speechless," she said, looking and wishing she were in it, or in the big spa feeding it with a warm, steamy waterfall.

"It's heated. Hop in anytime you want, winter or summer."

"I will, believe me. Right after we wrap up this case. And speaking of this case, how about you show me your cool computer room and let's pop in some attorney-client-privilege CDs and get back to work."

Will led her through several equally spacious and expertly decorated rooms, all done in a noticeably masculine style, but still the work of a talented interior designer. Lots of dark wood, leather, and glass. Masculine and modern, but that was okay with Julia. She was just tomboyish enough to like it that way. She supposed it beat the doilies, portraits of sullen-faced ancestors, and lace curtains of the boathouse, although she liked that, too.

"The master bedroom's upstairs. I'll show that to you later tonight, and every other night for the rest of the year."

"I'm going to hold you to that, Brannock."

"Promise?"

With Jasper padding beside her and Baby Cakes still yapping in their wake, Julia followed Will down an adjacent hallway that led to a large room with French doors that was obviously Will's home office. It overlooked the big, sparkling swimming pool. All four walls were lined with a variety of computers, printers, faxes, scanners, and some electronics that Julia didn't recognize. "Do you launch the space shuttle from in here, too?"

"No, but I probably could."

Julia didn't fall for that. "How long does

Baby Cakes bark before she collapses from exhaustion?"

"She just wants some attention," Will said, scooping up the tiny dog and cradling her against his chest. She lay like a baby in the palm of his hand, shut her eyes, and squirmed in delight when he scratched her belly. Julia knew how the tiny mutt felt. Chagrined, she squirmed, too, just remembering.

"Where do I go to work?" Her voice was curter than she intended. They would be working in close quarters together here at Will's house. Temptation was already rearing its sensual head. At least, for her it was.

"So, do you like my place?"

"What's not to like? It's beautiful."

"I love the water, and the way the trees reflect off of it."

"It's beautiful, Will. I love it out here."

Will grinned. He was pleased that she was pleased, she could tell. It was really easy to read his emotions, now that he didn't drop that sturdy steel curtain down to shield his every feeling, good or bad. He was really opening up.

"I need to make a couple of calls and feed the dogs. How about I take Jasper out to run with my dogs? The property's completely enclosed, so he can't get out."

"Sure. Looks like he's raring to go."

Will left her sitting in front of the HAL

supercomputer setup, with Jasper dogging his heels. Yes sir, Will was a techno-freak, all right. Waiting for all the bells and whistles to warm up for her pleasure, she gazed out the window at the water. It was funny that both of them liked the water so much. She stared at Will's race boat down at that honey of a double dock on the water and wondered if he water-skied. He was so athletic that she bet he did.

A few minutes later, she heard a sharp bark and saw Jasper and the beagles running down the backyard toward the lake, frolicking together like little puppies. Jasper wouldn't stray, but he might explore. She hoped Will didn't have land mines along the perimeter of his property. He was überserious about his security, and for good reason. Turning back to the computer, she slid in the CD and began the long and tedious ordeal of reading through all of Gloria Varranzo's cases and cross-referencing them with the ones in which Tam had found a connection between the judge and the shock jock. She was sure that when they found the right case, they'd find the Tongue Slasher. But, whoa, was she ever going to be computer blind by morning.

Chapter 22

Three hours later, Will and Julia sat outside on a white brick terrace and devoured fried bologna sandwiches loaded with sliced tomatoes, lettuce, and mayonnaise. The dogs sat in a semicircle in front of them, even Baby Cakes—three emitting low, imploring growls; one a periodic shrill yap of demand. Then they returned to their twin computers, silent, serious, both focused intently on their screens.

After about an hour, Will stopped for a moment and rubbed his temples with his thumbs. He was tired. His eyes ached inside the sockets and a headache was well on its way. He swiveled his chair around and stared at Julia's profile. She looked the same as always, pretty and damn provocative. No matter how many hours of sleep she got and how hard she worked, she still looked great. Since the first day they'd met, he had branded her as unintentionally sexy. She made no effort whatsoever to make herself so, but was still a woman most men tripped over their feet to stare at. Being with her so much, he'd noticed that reaction from other guys. He didn't blame them; he'd done the same thing the first time he'd seen her. He felt that sexual chemistry every time he laid eyes on her.

"What?" Julia inquired, swiveling in her desk chair and returning his stare.

"I was just admiring you. You look sexy in that baggy Tennessee T-shirt and those cutoff jeans."

"Yeah, right," she said, laughing as if that was ridiculous.

"I mean it. You got it, babe."

"So do you, babe. What I wish I had, however, is a connection that would solve this case and give us a Google road map to the perp's hidey hole."

"We'll get him."

"We need to get him yesterday. Because he's lurking around somewhere right now, casing out some poor victim."

"If he hasn't already finished the job."

"You think he's already struck?"

"He doesn't seem to waste much time between murders. It's like he's got an agenda and he's determined to carry it out before something goes wrong."

Julia inhaled deeply and ran slender fingers through her loosened hair. "I'm not stopping until we find the link, whatever it is. My gut tells me it's right here in Gloria Varranzo's caseload. I know it is."

"Most of the pictures of persons of interest are ready to e-mail. Varranzo's defense team always took pictures of the courtroom and the jury members for their files. I put them in, too. Who knows, maybe the killer liked to watch his victims' trials. Got himself all worked up that way." He leaned back in his chair, looked up at the ceiling, and huffed out his own tired breath. "I'm going to e-mail them to Archie York at LVPD. I hope to God Maria can identify somebody." He massaged the back of his neck. "Hey, want a beer? I've got some wine and hard stuff, too. Bottled water. Milk. V8 juice."

"Do you have sodas? I want to keep my mind clear. I like Pepsi better than Coke."

After he returned with an ice-cold Pepsi for her and his own bottle of water, they fell into a comfortable working silence again. Truth was, he was as eager as she to get this brutal bastard. Whatever drove the guy had to be something really bad. He'd not worked on that many mutilation murders, but this guy had a deep personal beef, all right. A big one. Revenge, hatred, anger—his gruesome acts dripped with all of that.

"Oh my God."

Will turned around to look at Julia, who was now leaning close to her monitor. Her voice sounded excited.

"What'd you find?"

"Pull up the State of Tennessee versus Folger Parmentier. June sixteenth, ten years ago."

Will did a quick search and watched the case flash up on his screen.

"Got it yet?"

"Gloria was defending Parmentier, who was eighteen at the time. He was accused of drunk driving and three counts of vehicular homicide."

"Judge Lucien Lockhart presided."

"Bingo," Will said. Skimming through Varranzo's notes and the transcript of the Parmentier trial, Will read aloud, " 'His passenger died in the crash, as well as two people in the other car.' "

Julia nodded. "Yeah, two of them were little kids: Abigail Cummings, two, and Thomas Cummings, four. Their mother was Victoria Cummings, a divorcée. The two children died at the crash site. The mother survived the crash with severe injuries. Oh, man, Will, this could be it. This could be the connection."

"This says Folger Parmentier's girlfriend, the girl who died in the crash, was Joanne Gentry. Says she's the daughter of Mack and Jennifer Gentry of Nashville."

That got Julia's attention. "Are you kidding me? She was Mack Gentry's daughter?" Julia asked him. "You've heard of him, haven't you, Will? He's a bigwig in Nashville, hobnobs with the governor and lots of other important politicos. Supposedly richer than Croesus. Always on the news, either charitable giving or hosting fund-raisers. But rumors abounded that a lot of his dealings were shady."

"Gloria won that case. Parmentier got off—not

even probation." Will scrolled down through the lengthy case history. "There were several appeals, but none of them worked. The boy walked every single time. Hung juries."

"Sounds like a good reason for revenge to me. The judge and his lawyer went down. Guess who's next?"

"Folger Parmentier."

"Dead right, Brannock."

Will reached for his cell phone. "We've got to warn him."

"Wait. Varranzo has news clips about the case attached to her file. Let's see if Roc VanVeter's involved. That would pretty much nail it shut."

Will clicked some buttons, and the first attached video appeared on a fifty-five-inch LCD screen attached to the wall across the room. The first one was from WDSI in Chattanooga. A pretty reporter with long brown hair and a Fox 61 black cap came on, her voice quick and breathless with excitement. "I'm reporting from the Hamilton County criminal court building in downtown Chattanooga at the Folger Parmentier trial. We have Gloria Varranzo here with us. As you know, she is the lead attorney for the accused driver of the vehicle, Folger Parmentier."

In her close-up shot, Gloria Varranzo looked like she'd stepped out of a *Vogue* photo spread. Ten years ago, she had been an attractive woman, oozing confidence and well-groomed elegance, never dreaming she would end up a mutilated corpse hanging off the bedroom balcony of her palatial house.

"My client is innocent of all charges. He wasn't driving the car. His girlfriend, Joanne Gentry, was not only behind the wheel but drinking and driving. Of course, we all mourn her passing, my client most of all, but he cannot be jailed for her wrongdoing. The driver of the other car, Victoria Cummings, has a DUI on her record. Unlike my client, she's also got a rap sheet for past criminal behavior. Folger's record is clean. He's innocent of any crime whatsoever, and I intend to prove that."

"What do you bet that Mack Gentry was furious over the remark about his dead daughter?" Will said. The second clip came on and was more of the same. Most of the contents smeared the deceased occupants of both vehicles: more allegations against Parmentier's girlfriend's history of drinking, rehab, and drugs; some against the Cummings woman, insinuating she was a prostitute, and worse. Another video clip revealed that Victoria Cummings had committed suicide, ostensibly because of the loss of her children. Several news cameras picked up Mack Gentry entering the courthouse, his face set in anger and anguish over the loss of his only daughter. He glared at the reporter who called out to him. Yeah, he had been enraged, all right.

Julia was watching as another TV station, this one the NBC affiliate, flashed up pictures of Victoria Cummings's two children. Both were beautiful, with blond hair and blue eyes, killed before they got a chance to live.

"This case is so sad, so many victims," he said to Julia.

"Yes, it is, and it's still going on."

They hit pay dirt with the next video. It was a clip from Roc VanVeter's televised radio show. He looked young and powerful and sure of himself, but his pompous attitude and the condescending vitriol that he sent out over the airwaves for anybody to hear, absolutely turned Will's stomach.

"Yeah, baby"—VanVeter was speaking with Gloria Varranzo, who was his solo guest—"it's probably a good thing both those bitches are dead. The Gentry dame is a cokehead and caused the whole damn accident. The world's better off without her. And that slut Victoria Cummings. What kind of mother was she? She's a drunk, too, and went driving around with her kids in the car. It's her fault they're dead, not anybody else's. She deserves to lose them with that kind of criminal background. They're better off dead, too, with a mother like her."

"Oh my God, Will, this is what they were saying about Victoria after she survived the crash. No wonder she killed herself."

"Did you notice Mack Gentry's face in those clips? He was out for blood."

"And didn't get it," Julia returned. "He was well-known in Nashville for getting even with his enemies."

"How?"

"Usually he just connived until he managed to bankrupt them. A few died under mysterious circumstances. He is not a nice man."

"But would he hunt down and mutilate this many people after so long?"

"I doubt it, but he's the kind of man who'd hire assassins to do his dirty work for him. Just like Oscar Kraft."

"I think we've heard enough to officially warn Folger Parmentier. Even if we're wrong. He needs to know he could be the next target."

"It won't hurt to interview him, either. He's obviously involved in this up to his eyeballs."

Will dialed up Quantico and asked for Folger Parmentier's current address and telephone number and then asked them to run a history on Joanne Gentry, Victoria Cummings, and Mack Gentry and e-mail it to his smart phone. He wanted to find out if anything Varranzo and VanVeter said about the victims was true. Somehow he doubted it. Roc VanVeter was known for smearing innocent people, and Gloria's firm had a built-in reputation for defending low-life types. He wanted to know where Gentry was and what he'd been up to since his daughter died. Parmentier's number came back to him after a couple of minutes.

"Yeah, and can you run a check on Victoria Cummings's husband? They had two children, Abigail and Thomas, both killed in a car crash on Signal Mountain around ten years ago." Will hung up and dialed Parmentier's number. No answer. No answering machine. "I say we go find him, interview him, and tell him to be on the lookout for any suspicious people around him."

Julia said, "I'm with you. Do you know how to locate his house?"

"Not exactly, but my GPS does. If my guess is correct, I'd say it'll take, maybe, fifteen, twenty minutes to get there, considering the mountain roads in that area."

"Let's go. You might have to hold me back, though. I'm beginning to understand the perpetrator's motives. I already loathe this creep."

"Not as much as someone else did. If the killer gets to him, he's never going to cast slurs on anyone again."

"Yeah, the fraudulent tongue shall be cut out."

Tam Lovelady left the medical examiner's office, a deep frown darkening her face. The test results she'd just gotten from Pete Tipton were not the ones they'd wanted. Julia Cass was not going to like it one bit. But she had to tell her. Julia and

Will were probably back from Las Vegas. She stopped at her car and punched in Julia's cell phone number. She waited.

Julia picked up on the first ring. "This is Detective Cass."

"Hey, Julia. It's me. Tam. Where are you?"

"We're on our way to a guy named Folger Parmentier's house. We think we've pinned down a case that's a good fit for a revenge killing and concerns all our victims. You need to take a look at it. I e-mailed the info to you about fifteen minutes ago. We didn't read it all the way through yet because we figured that Parmentier could be a target. We're getting close to his house now."

"I'll get right on it." Tam hesitated, not thrilled about telling Julia the bad news.

Julia noticed. "What's wrong? You okay, Tam?"

"Yeah, sure."

"Something going on with Marcus?"

Tam had to smile, just because things were going so well. "No, we're good."

"That's fantastic, Tam."

Tam was still putting off the reason for her call. "What about you and Will? You gettin' it on yet?" There was a short silence, and Tam could almost see Julia's face turning red on the other end. "Okay, I get it. That *what happens in Vegas* thing. That it?"

"On the nose."

432

"Okay, listen. I really hate to tell you this, but you know that dog hair you gave to Pete Tipton? He just got a report back from TBI forensics, and it's a match with the one found at the crime scene. Will should be getting the same report anytime now."

Silence at the other end. "Is he a hundred percent sure?"

" 'Fraid so. Sorry, Julia."

"Okay. I just don't see how that could've happened. I'm extra careful about any kind of trace evidence."

"I know, but transference happens. We've all done it at one time or another."

"Okay, thanks for letting me know. I'll see you tomorrow."

Tam clicked off her phone and turned the ignition key. Marcus was waiting for her at home. She couldn't wait to see him. He was back in her life, for good this time. Maybe they could start a family now; maybe they could be happy and not just content. She loved him. When she pulled up in front of the house they shared together, she felt an inner excitement that she hadn't felt in a very long time.

On their way to Folger Parmentier's house, Will glanced across the front seat as Julia hung up her phone.

She shook her head. "You know that hair they

found at the crime scene? It was Jasper's. I cross-contaminated."

"Don't worry about it. It didn't corrupt the crime scene."

"No, but it's careless on my part. I've never done it before, and I worked the K-9 unit for years."

"It happens."

"That's exactly what Tam said. I'm careful, Will."

"I noticed. Quit worrying, okay? Everybody makes mistakes." Will was watching the road as the GPS intoned the directions. "Parmentier's house should be right up there around this next curve. On the left."

Folger Parmentier's property was hard to miss. The house sat on the side of a mountain, forest above it, and the starry night sky was like a black velvet backdrop sparkling with silver glitter. The fields around the house were cleared of trees and underbrush—grassy and open.

"Looks like Parmentier prefers to see who's coming to visit," Will said as they turned off the road and found a white fence encircling the place, with a motorized gate and intercom box similar to Will's.

"This guy's as security conscious as you are, Will."

"Except that he left the gate wide open. Not exactly brilliant."

Will stopped the Hummer beside the intercom, rolled down the window, and pressed the button. He was polite that way. Julia would have just driven on through and forgotten formalities. Will pushed it again, and they waited again. There was not going to be a response.

"There aren't any lights on in the house," Julia pointed out. "But the dusk-to-dawns are on around the yard. Let's go on up. He didn't shut the gate—he can't get too ticked off."

"I can't figure him leaving in such a hurry that he doesn't take time to secure the outside gate. Why go to all this expense for security if you're so cavalier about using the precautions?"

"Good question," Julia said. "Except that this guy's a moron. And gets off every charge leveled against him. Let's go up and see if he's as arrogant and obnoxious as all his ex-girlfriends testified to on the witness stand."

Will drove up the narrow blacktop drive and rolled to a stop in front of the house. It was a big white Tudor, with lots of dark, heavy cross-beams. All was dark inside. All was quiet. Not a mouse was stirring, but maybe a rat was.

"I don't like this," Julia said, suddenly registering a very foreboding feeling. Her gut was screaming that something wicked this way came, had come, or was coming. When such instinctive and creepy sensations visited her inner psyche, she always paid heed.

Will's face was as wary as hers. "Maybe the killer's been here and gone."

"Yeah, or is here."

"Let's find out."

"Let's go."

Julia felt the familiar excitement roll up inside her chest, and her heart was pounding like some kind of crazy African bongo drum. That sixth sense of hers—she was going to listen to it. She would bet a week's salary that Folger Parmentier was the Tongue Slasher's next victim. Worse, he might be inside, already done for.

Weapons out and at the ready, they moved together toward the porch. Quiet, stealthy, keeping to the deep shadows. When they got to the front door, they stood one on each side, weapons down, fingers alongside the trigger. Julia tried not to think of Bobby.

"Ready, Cass?"

"You bet."

"Okay, stay behind me."

"Yeah, right, Brannock. I don't think so."

Brannock reached out and rapped on the door. "TBI, open up."

More silence. Heavy. Disconcerting. Nerve-wracking.

Julia reached out and tried the knob. It turned easily. She got the door open and pushed it back until it hit the inside wall. She reached inside and felt around for the light switch. When she found

436

it, the dark room blazed with light. It was empty, but they still went in low, guns out front, moving with their backs against the walls. They checked out the rest of the house and found nothing and no one, but they did find a locked door. The key was inserted in the lock, and Will turned it, revealing a stairway down to a lower level. They went down slowly and cleared the rooms, one by one. Extra bedroom, washroom, and storage room. Folger Parmentier was not home, but there was a second locked door with the key still in the lock. Julia turned the key and hit the inside wall switch.

Shocked, she could only stare at the terrible sight before them.

"Oh my God," Will said. "Parmentier's got a virtual torture dungeon down here."

"Yes, replete with blood. Look at that whipping post."

Sheathing his weapon, Will moved to it, side-stepping the bloody mess on the floor. "Somebody died in here."

"Yes, but there were no bloodstains upstairs. So where's the body?" Julia walked to another heavy metal door and turned that key. It opened to the outside and onto a sidewalk that led up the side of the house to the backyard. Julia flipped the light switch beside the door, and the outside path was illuminated by spot lighting all the way around to the back of the house.

"Looks like he brought a body out this way."

Careful to stay off the bloodstained sidewalk, Will and Julia followed the concrete path around to a waist-high retaining wall, where they could see the backyard pool, glowing like a blue topaz in the darkness. A man's body hung from a light pole near the deep end of the pool. They both pulled their weapons again and kept down low.

"That's got to be Folger Parmentier," Julia said, watching the wavering reflections from the pool's underwater lights create blurry patterns across the man's naked body, still dripping blood.

"He's still bleeding," she whispered to Will. "If he's still alive, the killer could be nearby."

Will nodded. "It's a fresh scene, all right. Go ahead, call for backup and get an ambulance out here. I'm going up to see if Parmentier's still breathing."

"Right."

Quickly, Julia phoned it in and requested the CSI team. She directed the ambulance as best she could, but she kept moving toward the pool, her eyes on Will making his way slowly and cautiously toward the body, his gun held with both hands out in front of him. She searched the surrounding darkness as she approached the low wall around the pool. Will had reached up and was taking the victim's pulse, after which he glanced back at her and shook his head. A movement out of the corner of her eye caught Julia's attention, halfway up the forested hill right behind Will.

"Will, get down!" she cried, going down on one knee behind the brick wall. But her warning was too late. The retort of a gun cracked and echoed through the quiet night, and though Will tried to lunge behind the wall, he was hit and dropped hard.

Julia stayed behind the barrier, rested her arm atop the wall, aimed, and opened fire on the spot where she'd seen the shooter. The echoes of her gunshots rolled through the stillness, but there was no return fire. He was probably on the run. Hunched over, she ran along the wall, keeping very low. By the time she reached Will, he was trying to roll over, groaning and clutching his right side.

"How bad is it?" She jerked a towel off a nearby lounge chair, wadded it up, and pressed it hard against his wound.

Will's chest was heaving, his words slurred. "I'm okay . . . he grazed me a little."

Now that she could see Will moving his limbs and speaking coherently, Julia felt better, confident he hadn't suffered a lethal chest or head wound. "It's no little graze, Brannock. Hang in there. The ambulance will be here any minute. Lie low. I'm going after him."

Groaning, Will managed to grab her wrist. "No, Julia, wait. Let the backup get here."

"And let him get away? Uh-uh. Don't move. I'll be right back."

"Julia . . . stop . . . he'll see you coming . . ."

Moving out very low, Julia ignored Will, anger pushing her along the wall toward the undergrowth below where she'd seen the shooter. She wasn't about to do anything stupid, but she wasn't going to let a killer get away, either, not after he put a slug in her partner. She kept down, listening for movement: bushes rustling, rocks falling down the hillside as the perp's shoes dislodged them, any sound to pinpoint his location. She heard nothing but her own labored breathing and the siren of a faraway ambulance. When she was about twenty yards up the hill behind the house, she heard a car start up somewhere in the distance. She searched the fields below for headlights, trying to spot a vehicle, but could see nothing. He was gone.

Sheathing her weapon, she ran back to Will. They had been so close to capturing the killer. So close, but now he was on the loose, to kill again. Their backup patrol cars arrived within ten minutes, but the ambulance beat them by three or four minutes. While the EMTs worked on Will, Julia stood back, jaw set, fighting rising emotions as she realized the medics were having trouble stopping the bleeding. The sight of Will lying there, so still now, his lifeblood pooling underneath his body, made her feel weak all over. She loved him. She really loved him, despite the short time she'd known him, despite any obstacles, despite everything. She hadn't realized just how much, but now, watching him fight for his life, she felt heartsick inside, sick that he was injured, that she was helpless, and most of all, that she hadn't had his back quick enough to warn him about the shooter.

As they worked on Will, Tam arrived, with the TBI forensic people close behind her. Julia helped the EMTs load Will on the gurney and watched them rush him off to the waiting ambulance. He was wounded, probably worse than he thought he was. They needed to get him to the ER quick enough to save him.

Fighting off her worry and guilt, she tried to fill in Tam on what had gone down, how they had found the body, the downstairs torture chamber, everything that had happened. Her voice finally broke, and her hands shook with delayed reaction —concern for Will, and fury that the perp had gotten away.

"He's going to make it, Julia." Tam's voice was low and comforting. She'd no doubt had lots of practice comforting victims in her tenure at CPD, and she was using it now. "Will's as tough as they come. Chances are he'll be fine."

"Yeah, I know. I know he will. He'll be fine. But the Slasher was here, Tam. Right here in this house. If we'd gotten here an hour earlier, Parmentier would probably still be alive."

"That also means the killer most likely left

more of himself behind. You surprised him—he had to run before he could clean up the crime scene. Don't blame yourself for him getting away. We're getting closer every day."

Julia knew all of that was true, but she still blamed herself. She tried to get Will's gunshot wound out of her mind and work the scene as if nothing had happened. She started more than once to call the hospital, but found herself afraid to, fearing what they would say. Oh God, what if he died, just now when they were finding each other? No, he couldn't. He wouldn't. He was talking. He was conscious at first. He was going to be fine.

After Peter Tipton arrived and examined, then released Folger Parmentier's body, they cut down the victim and laid him out flat on a forensic tarp. The word *FOUR* was written on the ground below him, in Parmentier's blood, next to a set of scales with part of his tongue on one side and the dimes on the other. But the Tongue Slasher had taken more than just the tongue this time. He had enjoyed cutting this victim up. As she and Will had surmised, the actual murder took place in the basement's Inquisition dungeon. The room was creepy and dark and full of cruel instruments and obscene objects. Folger had no doubt been into every perversion imaginable. The victim lived by the sword and whip and knife, and he had died the same way. For most of the night, Julia worked alongside Tam. About an hour before dawn, she left the crime scene investigation in Tam's capable hands, along with the other task force members, who were gradually showing up, one at a time.

"Go on, Julia. Go see if he's okay," Tam had kept insisting. "We've got plenty of people here. We can handle it. Come back later, if you want. Looks like we're going to be here well into the morning."

Julia finally agreed to leave, climbed into Will's truck, and drove down to the hospital on Hamill Road in Hixson. The ER was busy. One woman was screaming and fighting the nurses as she came out of a heroin-induced coma. An unconscious man was the victim of a motorcycle accident. An old woman had fallen in her front yard and broken a hip. Julia walked quickly through the crowded waiting room and sought out the nearest doctor.

The first physician she found was leaning against the nurses' station. She looked to be in her midforties, maybe. Her shiny chestnut hair was severely pulled back in a ponytail, her deep-set dark eyes looking out from behind large tortoiseshell glasses. She had on blue scrubs and a starched white coat. She was scribbling on a clipboard. There was a spot of blood on her coat, just above the pocket. Will's blood? The ID card hanging around her neck identified her as Retta Davis.

"Excuse me, Doctor. I'm looking for a law enforcement officer named Will Brannock. He was brought in here earlier tonight with a gunshot wound in the torso. Is he still here?"

"Yes, he's already up on the surgical floor."

Julia swallowed hard, nerves jumping. "Is he going to be all right?"

Retta turned then and looked Julia straight in the eyes. "We thought we were going to have to tie him down at first. Would your name be Julia, by any chance?"

"Yes. I'm his partner."

"He kept mumbling your name when he came out of sedation. We had to take out the bullet."

"Oh God, how bad is it?"

"It took out a good chunk of his side, but mostly muscle. Fortunately, it didn't hit any vital organs. He'll be all right. I stitched him up myself."

Relief hit Julia with a force she couldn't even explain. Her knees nearly buckled, and she had to brace one hand on the wall. The doctor nodded with understanding. "He's been grousing about getting back to work. You won't have to hold him down long—they'll be giving him an injection of morphine anytime now."

Relieved and able to summon up a smile now, Julia took a moment to pull herself together as she made her way to his room. Her emotions were still running pretty ragged. *Okay, Julia, Will is*

444

going to be fine, she thought. *Just suck it up and go see him.* She showed her badge at the nurses' station, and then found Will's room and opened the door. He was lying on his side, bare-chested, his lean torso wrapped in bandages. The IV taped to his left arm led to a rolling stand. A sheet covered the rest of him.

"I hear you're not exactly a model patient around here," she said, moving up next to the bed.

Will's eyes flew open and he grabbed the hand she held out to him. "Thank God, you're all right. You had me scared."

"I had *you* scared? You're the one who took the bullet."

"You took off after that guy alone. My God, Julia. Backup was on the way. You should've waited."

"I guess I did it for the same reason you would have if he'd just shot down your partner. Which would be me."

Frowning, Will said, "Damn straight."

"I couldn't catch him. I heard his car start up but couldn't see where it was. You were pretty out of it when I got back."

Twisting and trying to sit up, Will grimaced and held his bandaged side.

"So how do you feel?" Julia lowered her voice. "You ready to go home and show me that big bedroom of yours like you promised?"

"Ready and willing, maybe. But not able."

"Well, that's disappointing. I expect you to make this up to me." She smiled down at him, so relieved she couldn't see straight.

Will tried to smile but didn't appear to be in a particularly holly-jolly mood. "Did you work the scene?"

"Yeah, most of the night. Tam took over so I could come see you. She was an eager beaver about getting back to work, so I let her."

"I'm ready to get out of here. You got my truck?" When she nodded, he said, "Good. Let's go home. Hand me my clothes. They're in the top drawer over there."

"Sorry, Charlie, but the nurse says you've got to stay overnight. Maybe longer. So just relax and enjoy the time off."

"No way. Help me up. We've got to get back out to Parmentier's."

"We're handling it, Will. Calm down or you'll pop your stitches."

"I'm fine, damn it. I've gotta get out of here."

"Wait a couple of days till you're back on your feet and walking around. There's a whole task force working this case. Let us do our jobs. Besides, they're going to shoot you up with a painkiller any minute now."

"They already did."

"Then you aren't going to remember a thing a couple of minutes from now. Relax, rest, get a good night's sleep."

Will did not look pleased or appeased. "The victim was Folger Parmentier, right?"

"Yes, sans tongue and a few other things. The rest of the MO's the same as the other victims. Except he was flogged with one of his own ugly-looking whips. I'm going back to your place and read the rest of Varranzo's file on the Parmentier trial. So I'm going to have to get your card for the gate. Maybe I can figure out who's next on the killer's list."

"Call me before you do anything. Keep me informed. Promise me."

"Don't I always?"

Will took her hand, entwined their fingers, and squeezed tightly. "Will you stay awhile? Keep me company?"

"Sure. The doctor said that I might have to tie you down. Actually, I rather like that idea. Has an erotic ring to it."

"Now you're just being cruel."

"I can wait for the fun and games. We've got lots of time once you get out of here."

Will smiled at that and closed his eyes, but he didn't let go of her hand. She stood beside him and held it while he drifted off to sleep. Oh God, she was simply crazy about him. When did her feelings get this deep? After a while, when he was sleeping soundly, she covered him up with the sheet and blanket and retrieved the card to his gate and his house key from his possessions. She went back to the bed and gazed down at his handsome face, now quite relaxed and still. She kissed his cheek and smoothed back his hair, and then she left him in the care of the nursing staff at North Park, thinking he was no doubt having some very interesting pipe dreams. She just hoped she was in them.

Chapter 23

Around noon the next day, Julia finally made it back home to her boathouse. After leaving Will sleeping peacefully on the surgical floor of the hospital, she spent the rest of the night up at the crime scene. They had brought in floodlights and worked until after dawn. Tam had been great, taking over while Julia was with Will at the hospital, and she showed herself to be a good investigator, even though she'd only been at it for a year or so. They had collected some evidence, more at this scene than at the others, mainly because she and Will had surprised the killer.

Once daylight lightened the sky, she had found the spot where the Slasher had opened fire on Will. He had either not had the time to pick up the spent shell, or he couldn't find it in the dark. In any case, the TBI forensic team had it in their capable hands. They'd also found tire tracks in the small grove of pines where the killer had hidden his car. Maybe, just maybe, they'd get lucky this time.

Exhausted, she let Jasper out of the backseat. She'd gone to North Park again on the way home, just to make sure Will was still doing okay. He was sleeping, or maybe just drugged up on his own special drug cocktail, but Dr. Davis assured her that Will was going to be fine and up on his feet again in no time. All kinds of unfamiliar emotions had boiled up inside her as she stood looking down at him. She needed to sort them out, but one thing she did know. She was in love with Will Brannock. Whether that was good or bad remained to be seen.

Inside the boathouse, she fed Jasper, then took a long, hot shower, washed her hair, and felt much better. But she was dead on her feet. She sank down on the couch and turned on the television, hoping the press hadn't gotten hold of the details of Parmentier's ghastly murder. She tried to stay awake and watch the news but was gone to the world in two minutes flat.

When she woke up, it was late afternoon. She sat up and picked up her cell phone. Will had called. She hadn't even heard the phone ring. She needed some coffee, something to get her going, and then she'd give him a call back. She heaped in a couple of extra spoonfuls of Starbucks coffee and then added another teaspoon for good measure. She needed to be alert. She wanted to nail this guy. He had killed four people already. He had shot Will. She was going to get him for that alone.

Turning around, she leaned her back against the kitchen counter and looked out the window at the river. She could see a bass boat out on the water, moving upstream. It looked like Charlie Sinclair, but she couldn't tell for sure. It could be. It was Sunday; he always fished on Sunday. Sighing, still a bit groggy, she poured herself a cup of coffee and carried it into the living room. She sat down and sipped it, the warmth feeling good going down her throat. She dialed Will's cell number, but got his voice mail. He was probably talking to his mom, or to Phil. Or to a redheaded flight attendant flying high above the Atlantic Ocean. No, he wasn't like that. She knew that now. His feelings for her seemed sincere, and she believed him. He had been through a lot, lost his little brother. He had isolated himself for good reasons, and she knew that now, too.

Her gaze fell on the old photo album sitting on the coffee table, full of photographs of Lonnie's family. His mother had lovingly pasted in each photo held between those plastic pages. Julia wondered how long it had taken her to make such a beautiful book. Maybe someday she and Will would marry and have a family. She smiled at the thought of handsome little Wills running around the house. *Whoa, Julia, you're getting way ahead of yourself,* she thought.

Leaning forward, Julia turned the pages one at a time. She needed to make one for herself and J.D. Maybe that would make a great wedding present for Audrey and him: all the pictures from his childhood, his law enforcement career, and the more recent ones of Zoe and Audrey. When would she ever have enough time to do it? That was the pertinent question.

Mrs. Axelrod had started with pictures of her own wedding and moved on through the years: her children, their children, birthday parties, Christmases, Fourth of July celebrations. It was all there. Then Julia saw it. She stiffened and brought the picture up closer to her eyes. Two children were sitting on the boathouse dock, holding up double-dip chocolate ice-cream cones. Problem was, though, she'd seen those kids before. Last night. The same exact picture, cropped at the children's shoulders. In Gloria Varranzo's file on the Folger Parmentier vehicular homicide case.

The phone rang, and she grabbed it. It was Will.

"Will, you're not going to believe this," she began, trying not to panic. "You know those kids we saw in Varranzo's file yesterday?"

"Where have you been? I've been calling you all day."

"I've been asleep. Tam and I worked the crime scene all night."

"What about those kids?"

"Their pictures are here in Lonnie's family's photo album. You know, the big one that's sitting on my coffee table. You've seen it there, right?"

"Are you sure it's them?"

"I'm pretty sure they're the kids who died in that wreck."

"If they're involved somehow, Lonnie is, too."

"Oh my God," she murmured, half to herself. "If Lonnie's connected to these children, he could be connected to the murders."

"Are you saying he might be on the killer's list?"

"I don't know. Maybe not, but if they were his grandchildren, that means Victoria Cummings was his daughter. He could be on the Slasher's list. It's worth warning him about. Besides, maybe he can tell me something about the trial. He had to have been there. There might be someone he remembers who was spouting off or verbally abusive about Parmentier getting off. Maybe he knew the other victims' family members. The Gentrys. He might be able to give us a good feel for what went on at that trial."

"Yes, we need to talk to him. Wait for me. I'm coming over there right now."

"No, you're not. Don't be ridiculous. I can handle this. Stay put. Get well."

"I said I'll be right over. Wait for me."

"No way. I'll call you as soon as I talk to him. See you later."

Julia clicked off. She hoped he stayed right where he was and let that nasty wound in his side start healing. She dressed quickly in jeans and the pink T-shirt with a pink sequin bow that she purchased during breast cancer month, laced up her white Nikes, buckled on her Glock 17, and then clipped her badge on her belt. She intended to visit Will in the hospital, then revisit the Parmentier crime scene one more time. Ordering Jasper into the truck, she drove the short distance to Cathy's house. Cathy's car was gone, but Lonnie's Explorer sat in the carport. Jasper trailed her to the front door, where she knocked and waited. There was no answer. Lonnie was probably out back in his studio.

"Here, Jasper," she said, picking up an old gray sweatshirt of Lonnie's lying on the back of a rocker. "Go find Lonnie."

The bloodhound immediately bounded down the steps and headed around back. Julia followed. She had never been to Lonnie's private studio, didn't know exactly where it was, but Jasper would find it in nothing flat. He could find anything. She strolled after Jasper, who was sticking to the well-worn rocky path that wound its way out through the big trees and thick undergrowth, the cool darkness inviting and primeval.

She glanced around for Cathy's dogs but didn't see them. There was no distant barking as happened when they had squirrels treed and were jumping up at the trunk, trying to get to them. Cathy must have taken them out to Charlie's for shots or something. It was pretty quiet out in the deep woods, except for the slight rustling of leaves high in the treetops and the faraway buzz of a boat's motor on the river. Despite the heat of the sun, little of the warmth or bright light filtered its way through the heavy foliage in the canopy of trees stretching high above her. It was almost like trekking through a forest back in colonial days, shady and cool and silent.

After about a fifteen-minute walk on the meandering dirt path, she caught sight of the structure that Lonnie apparently used as his workshop. It was fairly large, and she had a feeling it had been the residence of an Axelrod relative at some time. It was certainly isolated enough for Lonnie to paint and sculpt and let his creativity blossom. Peace and quiet. Total peace and quiet. To an almost unnerving degree.

She made her way to the front door and knocked a couple of times but didn't get an answer. Jasper had followed Lonnie's scent directly to the door and now alerted her by sitting down beside her. She knelt and patted his head. "We aren't having much luck, are we, Jasper, boy?"

Standing, she tried the antiquated white knob. It

turned easily, so she pushed open the door and called out for Lonnie. All was quiet. Silent as a cemetery. She walked around inside the house, admiring the displayed paintings and worktables loaded with lots of paint tubes, sculpting tools, and blank white canvases. Surprised, she picked up a really exquisite metal sculpture of a woman sitting on a log. It looked a lot like Cathy. She smiled. Lonnie's retreat. All his favorite toys. Sort of like Will's fancy-as-Bill-Gates's computer room.

Suddenly she heard the low whir of some kind of machine. She crossed the kitchen to the back door. When she opened it, Jasper ran out the door and headed around the side of the house to explore. She saw Lonnie outside, working with a welder under a corrugated-metal lean-to, sparks flying. She called out his name, but he couldn't hear her over the sound of the welder. She descended the steps and headed out across the yard. When Lonnie abruptly stopped welding, he heard her behind him and whirled around to face her. Smiling, she started to apologize for scaring him, but then her gaze dropped down to the set of scales he was holding in one hand. Scales with a crossed-swords finial. The exact same scales that she'd seen at the Tongue Slasher crime scenes.

Stunned to a standstill, Julia couldn't move at first. Lonnie did. He came right at her, and Julia scrabbled for her weapon, got it out, and fired a round. He cried out as it winged him in his left arm. She fired again, but he was too fast and lunged to the right, out of range. He swung the heavy base of the scales hard at her head, so hard that it knocked her to her knees and made her vision go dark for a few seconds. Dizzy, eyes blurry, she felt him grab her weapon and wrest it out of her grip, just as Jasper shot around the side of the house and went after Lonnie, barking and snarling and tearing at his pants leg. Lonnie clubbed the dog and then hit Julia again, this time so hard on the temple that the world went dark. She sank into it and knew no more.

As soon as Julia hung up on him, Will lay back against the pillows, fuming mad. She could be so hardheaded at times, it was downright infuriating. On the other hand, she was a trained police officer. She knew what she was doing and how to do it safely. She was just going down the road to see her friend, Lonnie Axelrod.

Relax, Brannock, he told himself. He took a deep, cleansing breath, and then heard the low ding of his cell phone. He picked it up and looked at caller ID. Las Vegas PD. He pulled it up at once and found the picture Archie York had scanned in and e-mailed back. Maria Bota had drawn a circle around one of the men sitting in the courtroom gallery at the Parmentier trial. A seat right behind the prosecutor's table. He stared at it in disbelief. Their eyewitness had circled a picture of a younger Lonnie Axelrod. But it was him, no question about it. Oh God—Axelrod was the Tongue Slasher. And Julia was on her way to his house.

Will jerked out his IV needle and threw off the covers. Julia was walking straight into danger and had no idea that she was. It all made sense now. Axelrod had lost his daughter and two grand-children. The photos of the two kids were proof of that. Folger Parmentier was drunk when he hit them and had been living it up ever since. Varranzo was his attorney. Lockhart was the judge. Of course, of course, of course! Why hadn't they put it all together before?

Wincing with pain, he pulled on his jeans and T-shirt, dialing Julia's number with the other hand. She didn't pick up. He cursed to himself. When he headed out the door, a nurse showed up in the hall and gave him some trouble about leaving, but he brushed past her. Nobody was going to stop him. He could drive, and he'd steal a car if he had to. Then he remembered the security guard down in the emergency room. It wasn't far to Will's house. The guard could get Will to his boat. After that, Lonnie's place was less than ten minutes from there by water.

In the elevator to the lobby, he dialed J.D.'s number. If anybody could get to Lonnie Axelrod's place in record time, it was J.D. He put in another call to the CPD and Phil Hayes, just in case. Then he headed at a run for the ER.

Julia blinked her eyes, trying to think how long she'd been unconscious. All she knew was that her head felt like someone had taken a baseball bat to it. She tried to keep her eyes open but couldn't do it; it hurt too much. She could hear a dog hysterically barking somewhere far away. Jasper? She tried to garner her thoughts enough to remember what had happened. But her mind was immersed in a deep fog. She licked at dry lips and sank back into the hazy, strange dreamscape.

Later, when she came to again, she was shivering with cold. She was in a dark place, dank and damp. What—a cave? She tried to move, sit up, but couldn't seem to do that, either. Oh God, what? Were her arms and legs strapped down? Finally she got her eyes open enough to recognize that there were several electric lanterns hanging on some kind of line strung up above her. The light made her blink. Jasper was still baying, somewhere far away. He sounded scared. What happened to him? She struggled desperately for coherence, felt blood running down the side of her face, and slowly, agonizingly, finally regained her memory. When she did, she was sorry she had.

Fighting the straps holding her down, she turned

her head and tried to see where she was. On the table beside her, she could see the razor-edged fillet knife. A length of yellow ski rope was coiled neatly beside it, right next to the large pair of pliers. Lonnie Axelrod sat close by, in a rocking chair, calmly watching her. He had a clean white bandage wrapped around his arm where her slug hit him. Blood was seeping through the gauze. He said nothing and his face looked totally blank, his eyes on her face but completely unfocused. He looked like a different person, nothing at all like Cathy's quiet and agreeable and pleasant husband.

"Lonnie, Lonnie, look at me. Listen, please." Julia's throat felt dry, her words coming out so hoarse and scratchy that she barely recognized her own voice. She could taste blood inside her mouth. "Let me go. You don't want to do this. Cathy doesn't want you to do this. You know that. She's my friend. You'll break her heart."

Lonnie seemed to fight his way out of some kind of thick morass deep inside his mind. He stared at her, then shook his head. "Cathy will never know it was me. She's got no part in what I've done. She doesn't know I'm capable of these terrible things."

To Julia's shock, Lonnie began to cry—hard, wracking, self-pitying sobs. Tears ran down his pale cheeks, dripping onto the dark green welder's apron he wore over his street clothes. "You don't know what I've been through, Julia," he sobbed

459

out. "You've got no idea how they made me suffer."

Julia fought to remain calm. She swallowed down the cutting fear. "Yes, I do, Lonnie. I do, I swear. I understand all too well. I've read everything about the accident. About your daughter, Victoria. About her two beautiful little children. It's horrible what happened, a terrible thing. It's a miscarriage of justice. I don't know how you've stood it all this time."

"Because I thought that the truth would win out, that people would see the evil of Parmentier and the others. But they didn't. They were evil, too. They got him off." He began to weep louder, making his words halting and hard to understand. "I had to do it. I had to do it for Victoria, for Abby and Tommy . . . I couldn't live with myself anymore if I didn't get them justice . . . so I did it . . . before I breathed my last, I did it. I had to . . . and I'm not sorry, not at all . . . I'd do it again . . ."

Julia knew she had to make him see reason, but her heart was hammering so hard that she shook with it. "I know, I know you did. You got them all, all the ones who lied and bribed and said those awful things about your daughter. But now it's over. You've got to stop. Stop the killing. Do it for Cathy's sake. She loves you so much."

"Cathy doesn't need to know," Lonnie said again. Then suddenly his face changed entirely. He became angry, furiously lashing out at her. "Why did you have to come here? Go snooping around my house? Follow me back here? Everything was going along just fine until now. The media was beginning to find out the depths of their evil and depict them as the evildoers they were. I was going to stop the killing once I got Folger Parmentier. I was going to leave the jurors alive, the ones who were paid off to get those hung juries. Did you know there were four trials? All mistrials because of hung juries. All paid off by Parmentier's family."

"Untie me, Lonnie. This is wrong. You know it is. I had nothing to do with any of it. I'm innocent, just like Victoria was. You don't need to kill me."

Her last words seemed to make Lonnie stop and think. He sat back in his chair and slowly rocked back and forth as he pondered what she'd said. "I don't want to do this to you, Julia. I like you, I truly do like you. I was so pleased that Cathy had an old friend to spend time with. But then you had to get assigned to this case. You ruined everything when you came out here today."

"If you do this, Cathy will never forgive you. Never."

He rose and walked over to her. "They'll think you're just the next victim of the Tongue Slasher. That you got too close and he killed you. I'll take your body somewhere else after I'm done. She'll never know. But if I let you go, you'll turn me over to the police and I'll have to go to jail." He just stood there, staring down at her. Then another

461

voice came out of his mouth, a stranger's voice, and his eyes glazed over with some kind of dark, terrible intensity. Lonnie Axelrod was insane.

"Here, Julia, let me show you my collection." He moved across the room and out of her line of vision. He came back to her with a big scrapbook in his hands. He opened it so that she could see the photos of his victims. The first one was Lucien Lockhart. Julia felt bile rise up in the back of her throat when she saw that he'd glued part of the judge's tongue on the page. A souvenir for him to keep around and enjoy over and over again. He turned the pages, showing her the tongues of his other victims.

Julia squeezed her eyes closed and swallowed hard. Lonnie Axelrod was two different people, a split personality. The killer, a psychopath, completely crazy. Not the dutiful husband Cathy had thought him to be, not the mild persona that he showed to others most of the time. Right now, Lonnie was a killer who thought he had no choice but to murder her. She had to buy time. Will was on his way. He had to be.

"Lonnie, listen to me. You can't do this. Will Brannock knows where I am. I told him I was coming here to see you, that the pictures in your mother's album were the same kids who died in Parmentier's accident." And she had told Will not to come, not to worry about her. God, she hoped he hadn't listened to her.

Her words got Lonnie's attention. He smiled. "I don't believe you. You're just trying to change my mind. It's not going to work. Killing you is the only option I've got."

"Believe it, Axelrod! Get down on the floor, arms wide! Now!"

Julia's heart nearly stopped at the sound of Will's voice coming out of the darkness of the cave's tunnel. Will moved into sight, arms extended, gun aimed at Lonnie's chest. Lonnie grabbed Julia's Glock out of his waistband.

J.D. came out from behind Will, weapon on Lonnie as he moved along the opposite side of the cave. "It's over, Axelrod. We've got you covered. Put the gun down. Let her go. Don't make it worse for yourself."

Lonnie put the barrel of the gun against Julia's temple. "Back off, or I'll kill her. I swear I will."

"No, no, Lonnie, please don't! No!" That was Cathy's voice, crying out from somewhere in the dark—shrill, distraught, her words dissolving into loud groans of horror.

Julia tensed all over as Will inched closer, moving his aim to Lonnie's head. "Don't do it, Lonnie. Just put the gun down. Put it down, and nobody gets hurt."

"Cathy, Cathy, oh God," Lonnie cried out to his sobbing wife, who had come forward into the light and was begging him to stop. "I did it because Victoria didn't deserve what they did to

463

her. Neither did those sweet angel babies. They were so little, just toddlers. I loved them so much . . ."

Lonnie stifled his own sob, and then he suddenly stepped away from Julia and put the gun against his own temple. "I'm so sorry, Cathy, I'm so damn sorry. I love you. I love you more than anything in the world."

When he pulled the trigger, the noise was deafening in the underground cavern, and the caustic smell of cordite and the coppery odor of spilled blood filled the air. Cathy ran over and dropped to her knees beside her husband's lifeless body. She cradled him in her arms and wept. Will rushed over to Julia, slit the cords with the fillet knife, and frantically pulled her up against him.

"Thank God, we got here in time. Are you all right? You're bleeding."

"Yes, he hit me with the scales, I think. He was going to kill me, Will. He was going to cut out my tongue."

"C'mon, we've got to get you to a doctor. Next time, listen when I tell you to wait for me, damn it."

Will helped her sit up and held her tightly against him while he examined her head wound and tried to staunch the flow of blood. Weakly, Julia laid her head against his chest, trying desperately to calm the fear still surging through her bloodstream. She had almost died. She had been within minutes of being murdered and mutilated. If it hadn't been for Will and J.D., she would be dead. She would be Five.

"How did you find me?"

"You can thank Jasper. We heard him baying and found him lying outside the entrance to the cave. He'd collapsed there. Axelrod must have attacked him with something."

"Is he all right?"

"He will be, once we get him to the vet."

Then J.D. was there on the other side of her, brushing back her blood-soaked hair. "Oh God, are you okay, Sis?"

Julia nodded, but she was shivering all over, and she couldn't seem to make it stop.

"Man, you've got to stop doing this kind of thing. My heart won't take it."

None of them laughed at J.D.'s comment, but Julia thanked God that it was over, that the Tongue Slasher had found his last victim. And, by the grace of God, it wasn't her.

Epilogue

Almost four months had passed since Lonnie Axelrod had taken his own life. It had been a long, drawn-out inquiry, but the court had determined that Lonnie was the Tongue Slasher and had acted alone in perpetrating the murders. The case was officially closed, and Cathy had flown out of town to stay with her sister in Kansas City during the ensuing hearings and media blitz. She would be all right, in time, but it would be hard for her. But she would always be there for Cathy—always, no matter what, Julia thought. Jasper recovered from his head injury, and it was a very good thing that the howls of the poor, wounded bloodhound had led Will and J.D. straight to the brush-covered entrance of Lonnie Axelrod's underground lair, or she'd be dead herself. She still had nightmares about waking in that dark, cold, dreadful cave with Lonnie and his instruments of death.

Right now, however, as she stood waiting with Audrey and her bridal attendants in the back of the church, Julia had nothing but good, happy, lovely thoughts. All was right in her world. Zoe, of course, looked darling in her bridesmaid's gown, and very grown up, which had been quite an unwelcome revelation to poor J.D. Tam looked beautiful, too, as did all of Audrey Sherrod's other bridesmaids. Audrey had chosen the most beautiful shade of candy-apple red for her Christmas wedding. Red, black, and white for a beautiful and elegant December nuptial.

Julia felt a bit out of sorts in her strapless red silk gown and matching high heels, but Will had told her he really liked the way she looked in it—so much, in fact, he'd said, that he couldn't wait to tear it off her. She smiled to herself as she looked down at the red rosebuds tucked into a fragrant bouquet of evergreens and holly berries that she and the other girls would carry down the long center aisle. The sanctuary looked truly magical, like a scene from a fairy tale, with dozens of Christmas trees glowing with tiny white lights and red bows and silver globes. The smell of the holidays permeated the church, and Julia was reminded of Christmas mornings when she and J.D. were little kids and awoke at dawn to the smell of her daddy's secret recipe for hot cinnamon punch.

Down at the altar, the men of the wedding party moved into view from one side of the nave, dressed in elegant black tuxedos. Julia could not stop another contented smile at the sight of Will Brannock. It was embarrassing how her heart went wild now every single time she saw him. But things were going so well between them. During the last few months, now that they were no longer working together, their relationship had only deepened, both physically and emotionally. They fit together completely, in nearly every way. They thought alike, enjoyed the same things, and most of all, loved being with each other. He had proved over and over again that he loved her, not to mention the fact that he had saved her life in that dark, cold, horrible hole where Lonnie Axelrod planned his gruesome murders. He had already asked her to move into that lavish lake home of his, but she had been reluctant to take that next significant step. Tonight, however, she was going to tell him that she would. She loved him; it was as simple as that. She couldn't wait to tell him, to go home with him for good.

Mendelssohn's "Wedding March" began to play, soft and lovely and romantic, and Audrey's cousin, Bethany, was the first bridesmaid to walk slowly down the aisle. Tam was the maid of honor and would go last. Julia smiled at her CPD partner and was pleased that Tam was so happy, too, now that she'd reconciled with her husband, Marcus. Zoe walked the center aisle next, looking so grown up and lovely in her red gown, her lips glistening with red lip gloss. Wearing makeup at the wedding was a gift from her father that had pleased the fifteen-year-old immeasurably. Yes, J.D. was in danger of becoming a softy where his daughter was concerned.

Then it was Julia's turn, and she moved down the aisle with slow and solemn footsteps, her eyes lighting briefly on her older brother, recognizing the eager, excited look in his eyes. He was so content, now that he was with Audrey. They were both so ready to settle down in a life together, forsaking all others. Tonight they would do just that.

Then her eyes met Will's. She could not have looked away, even if she'd wanted to, and she didn't. She never wanted to look away from his handsome face again. He was smiling at her, his gaze hot and appreciative and conveying to her in no uncertain terms that he liked her in her long, red gown. Probably because he'd never seen her in any other evening gown, much less one that showed so much skin. She was not the strapless type, but maybe she should be, if it would engender that besotted look on Will's face. She took her spot before the altar and watched Tam move gracefully down the aisle to join the brides-maids.

The music stopped, and everyone rose as the organ began the traditional *here comes the bride* wedding song. Audrey appeared at the back of the church, looking magnificent in her sleek, white satin gown and fingertip-length lace veil, carrying white gardenias surrounded by Christmas evergreens. Julia had never seen her brother look so proud.

The ceremony proceeded, the familiar words warm and lovely and touching, but Julia was more pleased with Will's whispered words as he escorted her out of the church in Audrey and J.D.'s wake.

"We're next, Jules. Tomorrow, if not sooner. No argument, you hear me?"

Julia laughed at him. Will was teasing with that last part, but as she walked along, holding on to his arm, smiling up at him, she decided she liked his idea just fine. Yes, a wedding day was okay with her, any time, any place, just so she and Will ended up as husband and wife. That was what would make her happy. That was all she wanted. Big, handsome, sexy Will Brannock, all tied up in a big red Christmas bow.

About the Author

Beverly Barton is an award-winning, *New York Times* bestselling author of more than fifty novels, including *Silent Killer*, *Cold Hearted*, *The Murder Game* and *Close Enough to Kill*. Readers can visit her website at www.beverlybarton.com

The family of Beverly Barton would like
to thank Linda Ladd for her help
in the shaping and completion of
DON'T SAY A WORD.

Center Point Large Print
600 Brooks Road / PO Box 1
Thorndike ME 04986-0001 USA

(207) 568-3717

US & Canada:
1 800 929-9108
www.centerpointlargeprint.com